PRAISE FOR
HOW TO BE REMEMBERED

"*How to Be Remembered* is my favorite kind of book: a story with a 'wow' factor. Michael Thompson has taken a fun and intriguing idea—a *big* idea—and turned it into a wonderful, humorous, very human ride."

—Michael Poore, author of
Reincarnation Blues

"An engrossing story about keeping determination, hard work, and hope steady despite adversities. A coming of age with an intriguing supernatural twist, *How to Be Remembered* will inspire you to hang on tight to what you hold dear and will rekindle your appreciation for what it means to be human."

—Sarah Jost, author of
Five First Chances

"In Tommy Llewellyn, Michael Thompson has created a character you cannot help but root for, and built a plot as intricate as the workings of a clock. It is a brilliant exploration of what makes one's life indelible and is a story you won't soon forget."

—Ann Dávila Cardinal, author of
The Storyteller's Death

HOW
TO BE
REMEMBERED

a novel

MICHAEL THOMPSON

To Mum and Dad, for encouraging me to write, and to Sian, for making it possible.

Published by Sourcebooks Landmark, an imprint of Sourcebooks
P.O. Box 4410, Naperville, Illinois 60567-4410
(630) 961-3900
sourcebooks.com

Library of Congress Cataloging-in-Publication Data

Names: Thompson, Michael, author.
Title: How to be remembered : a novel / Michael Thompson.
Description: Naperville, Illinois : Sourcebooks Landmark, [2023]
Identifiers: LCCN 2022061839 (print) | LCCN 2022061840
   (ebook) | (trade paperback) | (epub)
Subjects: LCGFT: Bildungsromans. | Novels.
Classification: LCC PR9619.4.T478 H69 2023 (print) | LCC PR9619.4.T478
   (ebook) | DDC 823/.92--dc23/eng/20230106
LC record available at https://lccn.loc.gov/2022061839
LC ebook record available at https://lccn.loc.gov/2022061840

Printed and bound in the United States of America.
VP 10 9 8 7 6 5 4 3 2 1

PROLOGUE

Tommy had never intended to spend his last night at the old house sweating through three shirts and four pairs of underwear. But that was because he'd never really had a plan before. At least, not like this one.

He wished it included a way to keep cool. The sweat pooled in the small of his back, and he could feel the money already sticking to his skin. The rest of the notes bulged in wads stuffed in socks and pockets and between the layers of underpants. He laughed at the thought of how he must look: a wry, noiseless chuckle. He was alone in the small bedroom but the walls were thin, and the thick, soupy heat just seemed to make everything *louder*. He didn't need anybody knocking on his door because they'd heard him laughing in the dead of night. How would he explain that one?

So Tommy stayed silent and waited for sleep. If it worked, maybe he could keep what he'd earned, payment for his aching shoulders and calloused hands. And maybe—and this was the big one—he could find *her*. Tommy knew he hadn't entered her thoughts once since she'd left. That was hardly her fault, but it would make it infinitely harder to convince her that she used to love him.

Tommy peered around the darkened room. It had been his home for almost seventeen years, but he wouldn't miss it. Not if this worked. He'd be gone before the sun rose, leaving nothing behind. The others would eventually drag themselves out of bed and go about their day, not even remembering he'd been there.

Why would they?

They never had before.

1

Leo Palmer had a party trick, although even he knew it wasn't much of a showstopper. He could calculate on any given day exactly how long it would take the 457 bus to get from the city center to his stop at Ingleby—adjusting for traffic, weather, and an array of other complications. He could do it for other routes too, but that was barely of interest to him, let alone other people.

He'd demonstrated it once at his office Christmas party. He figured a bunch of accountants would appreciate something like that. His colleagues had been unenthusiastic, but that was a fairly natural state for accountants. Leo didn't mind. It was the numbers that he found fascinating. The people were a distant second.

Well, that wasn't entirely true. There were two people he cared about more than a balance sheet and more than the timetable of the 457. His wife and his young son sat at the top of this particular ledger, and as long as Leo Palmer had any say in it, that's where they'd stay.

All of this was somewhat standard fare, to be honest. An

accountant with a fondness for numbers was pretty normal; so too a family man who loved his wife and son. In fact, Leo's life was actually quite ordinary—which is, really, the point: Leo and Elise Palmer were *average*. They didn't do anything to be singled out for what was to come. They just were.

Of course, like any normal couple, they had their disagreements. They had one on the very day they signed the lease for their one-bedroom flat: ground floor, weathered bricks, and a cracked concrete path with dandelions that came up to their knees.

"Jesus Christ, you're a cheapskate, Leo," Elise had exclaimed as she gazed at their new home. She was only half joking, and her husband rolled his eyes.

"You knew that when you married me," he retorted, tugging at one of the weeds with both hands. At last it came free, and he threw it to the side with a satisfied grin. "It's not forever. Just stick with The Plan, and we'll be fine."

"The Plan," Elise repeated, and smiled despite herself. *The Plan* (it was always rendered with capital letters in Elise's mind, such was its importance to Leo) had been debated at length. Stage one of The Plan was five years in Ingleby, two promotions for Leo, three pay rises, and then they'd move on. Stage two was somewhere else entirely: a backyard, two bathrooms, two cars in the garage, three bedrooms, and a couple of kids to fill them.

The baby boy who arrived just over a year into their lease had never heard of The Plan, and had no regard for the fact that he'd disrupted stage one. But—and this was the biggest surprise of all to Elise, even greater than the pregnancy itself—Leonard Palmer welcomed the alteration. It turns out that some people are just born to be dads, and Leo was one of those. He gladly revised The Plan to include a round-cheeked, fair-haired boy in that one-bedroom flat in Ingleby. He also slashed two years off stage one—determined that the cot would soon move out of the living room, and the occupant would have his own bedroom. And the backyard, and all those other things that came with being a normal family. Because that's what they were: normal.

○

Elise knocked loudly on her neighbor's door—louder than would have been considered polite, but Mrs. Morrison was north of seventy and could barely hear her own TV. Elise could hear it, though, every night. She didn't mind; it reminded her of her grandma.

The door opened a crack, and a watery gray eye framed by wrinkles peered through the gap.

"Hi, Mrs. Morrison," Elise said cheerily, and the door opened the rest of the way.

"I'm sorry, love," Mrs. Morrison replied. "I didn't know it was you. Come in." She bolted the door behind them and shifted her gaze down to the boy nestled comfortably on Elise's hip.

"And you, you precious thing. You're getting so big!"

Elise grimaced. The dull ache in her lower back was proof of that.

Mrs. Morrison noticed. "Put him down, love. Still not walking?"

Elise lowered her son to the clean linoleum floor. "Not yet. Soon, I hope. He'll be the last in his playgroup to do it."

The old woman bent over in front of the little boy, and held out her hand like she was sprinkling invisible birdseed, trying to coax him to her. Unsurprisingly, he didn't move. If he hadn't got up on those stubby legs for his mummy and daddy, he was hardly going to do it for the lady next door.

Mrs. Morrison straightened, shaking her head. "Give him time. My Mark didn't walk 'til he was two. He's not even one yet, is he?"

"Nearly! It's tomorrow," Elise said. "That's why I'm here. If you're not busy, would you like to come over for cake in the afternoon? Maybe around three? Only if you're free, of course."

Mrs. Morrison smiled. She loved having a family next door, especially one that made an effort to include her. Until they moved in, she'd felt like the last of her kind—a stubborn reminder of the way things used to be. The smile faded as she remembered her own son. Mark had been a sweet boy too, and a lovely man, and it wasn't his fault how things ended up. It was those friends. And this neighborhood. Now, every time there was a knock on the door she was sure it was the police, delivering more bad news.

"You're still locking your doors at night, love?" she asked.

"Of course, Mrs. Morrison."

"I wish you could've seen it forty years ago," the old lady murmured, almost apologetically, and Elise needed no further explanation. Her neighbor had said this every time they'd spoken, and she knew what came next. She needed to change the subject before those faded gray eyes started to tear up.

"So three o'clock tomorrow. It'll just be you and the three of us. Leo's even calling in sick to work." This was a big deal and certainly wasn't in the original version of The Plan.

Mrs. Morrison came back to the present. "The cake," she said. "Is your oven still on the fritz? You can use mine if you want."

"It's alright, I've already made it," Elise told her. "It's just the thermostat that's busted. The edges are a bit burned, but there'll be plenty of icing. He won't notice."

The boy at her feet was playing with a doorstop as though it were a rocket ship. Elise scooped him up and he waved a fat little hand at the kindly lady next door. Mrs. Morrison waved back as they left, heart swelling with the pride of an adopted grandmother. She looked around the room, wondering what she could wrap up and give him for his birthday.

She needn't have bothered; Mrs. Morrison wouldn't be attending any afternoon tea. Nor would Leo or Elise Palmer, for that matter. Not that any of them knew it.

It was long after dark when Leo's return from work was announced by a key sliding into one lock, then another. He tiptoed inside and danced silently over the toys strewn in the entrance. He was sure kicking one—even the barest nudge with his toe—would mean waking the boy asleep in his cot against the living room wall. Leo looked in at his son, thumb tucked firmly in his mouth, a slight rise and fall of his chest as he dreamed. The metal bars of his cot gleamed dully in the light from the bedroom door beyond.

Elise lay on her side of the small double bed, propped up on pillows with a book in front of her. Of course she was reading; there was a mound of books on her bedside table.

"Sorry I'm late," Leo whispered. "Big day. Think I can feel a cold coming on. Don't reckon I'll make it in to work tomorrow." He winked, and his wife smiled. "I'll be back in a sec," he said. "Just want to check out the cake."

He tiptoed to the fridge. A beer bottle rattled as he pulled the door open, and he held his breath.

No noise came from the cot. A minor miracle.

Leo admired Elise's handiwork. Two plain butter cakes had been transformed into an impressive reproduction of Thomas the Tank Engine, the birthday boy's favorite TV show. The blue frosting looked thick and deliciously sweet, although Leo suspected it might be masking some burned edges beneath. He grinned. It'd be the thermostat's fault. It always was.

Next to a small vase on the living room table he spied the present he'd picked out. It had been carefully wrapped by Elise and now sat ready to be torn open by an excited child. He looked down into the cot, gazing fondly at his son's sandy-colored hair and soft, smooth skin.

"Night, buddy. See you when you're a one-year-old," he whispered, so quietly he could barely hear it himself.

Then he crept back into the bedroom and Elise switched out the light.

"Leo!"

He stirred.

Elise elbowed him in the chest. "Leo!" she hissed again.

"Mmm?" he mumbled sleepily.

"Wake up! There's someone out there!" Her voice cracked with panic.

Leo's eyes flicked open instantly and he felt a rush of adrenaline. He listened, barely moving, for whatever had distressed his wife so much.

There.

A small sound, almost like a snuffle.

Then silence.

Again, a noise. Rustling this time.

It was in their living room.

Leo had known this might happen since the day they'd moved in; an intruder wasn't part of The Plan but had always been a footnote, the implied risk of paying a pittance in rent. He'd sometimes wondered if he'd choose fight or flight, or even option three: cower.

But it wasn't a conscious choice at all. Without thought Leo sprang from his bed and stood at the doorway to the living room, listening hard.

He took a deep breath, reached around the corner for the light switch, and flicked it. Harsh yellow light flooded into the bedroom as he charged through the doorway, and then he stopped suddenly, blinking.

Silence.

"Leo?" Elise called shakily. "Are they still there?" Her heart was hammering so loudly she was sure Leo (and whoever was in the living room) would hear it.

Then, at last, her husband responded. His voice was strained. Confused, even.

"Come out here. Quick."

A lone police car arrived just eight minutes later, its lights strobing as the driver parked without haste or care at the front of the rundown block. Constable James Elliott had only been two streets over, but was more than happy to let them think he'd rushed here. *Good for the image*, he thought, looking up at the low-rise building.

He laughed humorlessly as he realized he'd been here before. Only once, though, about ten years ago, on his third day into what he was sure was going to be a stellar career of medals and honors and promotions (he'd been wrong, so far). His supervising officer had parked in pretty much the same spot, and sat in the car watching the young probationary constable shuffle nervously to the door of one of the ground-floor flats. Blooding the new recruit with his first death knock. Elliott grimaced, remembering the old lady's eyes filling with tears as he told her that her son had died in his sleep in a house nearby. He didn't tell her he'd choked on his own vomit, or that Elliott thought forty-four was too old to still be sharing a place with three other deadbeats.

He wondered for a moment if the old duck was still alive, and a moment later had his answer. Mrs. Morrison's door opened a few inches as he walked up the cracked, weedy path. She'd seen the flashing lights while making her way slowly to the toilet. (It was nearly two o'clock after all, and Mrs. Morrison had long ago surrendered any ambition of holding on all night.)

"What do you want?" she called defiantly through the gap, almost daring the officer to bring her bad news.

"Well, there you go," Constable Elliott muttered. "It's her."

"Did you call about the kid?" he asked her, voice echoing in the still night.

She looked at him blankly.

"Was there a kid here?" he asked.

The same confused stare.

"Go back inside," he ordered.

Mrs. Morrison did as she was told. She really needed the loo.

"Good start. Door number one, a geriatric," Elliott said to himself and checked his notepad. He knocked on the door next to Mrs. Morrison's, still shaking his head.

It was opened by a tall man with thick fair hair, who introduced himself as Leonard Palmer.

"You're the guy who called about a missing kid?" the constable asked.

"Well, yeah," Leo replied. "In a way."

"What's that mean?" Elliott snapped, his patience already gone. *Ten seconds*, he thought. *Might be a new record.*

"We haven't lost a kid," Leo said slowly. "We've…well, we've kind of found one."

○

Three times Leo and Elise told their story to the officer—once next to the cot, then twice more seated across from him at the dining table. Elliott pulled an assortment of faces and scribbled furiously on all three occasions.

"Right," Elliott said. "And whoever it was who left the baby…they set up the cot too?"

They nodded.

"While you were both asleep."

Nodded again.

"And what woke you up?"

"We heard him," Elise said, her face pale and drawn, still processing *why* they were being interviewed at the table where she usually ate breakfast.

"The person who left the cot?"

"No," she said. "Him." And she pointed to the small boy sitting up, sheet tangled around his legs. His eyes were darting curiously between the three people gathered near his bed, as if fascinated by the commotion.

"And then you called the police. Because your baby woke you up." Constable Elliott sighed. "Fuck *me*," he said, not quite under his breath.

Leo opened his mouth to respond, and Elise put a hand on his arm. Leo paused, composing himself.

"We've told you. It's not our baby. We…we don't have any kids. Yet." He wanted to add that it wasn't in this stage of The Plan, that babies were in stage two, but didn't think the cop would care.

He was right.

Elliott stared at them both again, then made an exaggerated display of looking around the room, as though inspecting for hidden cameras. Something didn't feel right here.

"This is a joke, right?" They shook their heads. "Okay. What have you taken?"

Elise and Leo looked at each other, confused.

"What. Are. You. On?" the officer asked, sounding each word out, not even attempting to hide his frustration. "Look, people don't break into apartments and leave behind a baby. So let me tell you what I think *actually* happened. You two had a big day on God knows what. Then you thought you'd waste my time with a call at two o'clock in the morning because you *forgot* you had a kid you're supposed to be looking after. Am I right?"

But even as he said it, he wasn't sure—not that he'd admit it to them. They didn't look like addicts. They looked more like teachers on a school trip, dragged out of bed in the middle of the night to tell the kids to go back to sleep. And the air in the living room didn't smell like stale pot. It smelled—well, it smelled like a baby. Like nappies and talcum powder. And milk.

A tiny hammer of a headache started to beat above his left eye. The flat looked rough from the outside, but in here it was neat as a pin: clean floor, nice furniture, shelves and shelves of books, pictures hung level on walls. (The presence of pictures in frames was actually pretty uncommon—in half the places he visited there'd only be a poster or two; David Bowie or Duran Duran, sometimes torn from a magazine, always covering a hole punched through the wall.) The table next to the cot was completely bare, save for a small vase with a posy of pink and white flowers.

"We're not *on* anything," Leo insisted. "We don't know what's happening. I know it sounds strange—"

"Oh really?" the cop interrupted. "You think so?"

The little boy started to cry. Leo and Elise looked at each other again, but didn't move.

The tiny hammer tapping inside the cop's skull grew slightly bigger.

"Aren't you gonna pick him up?" he asked as the child wailed. Elliott just wanted the noise to stop.

Elise got up and reached into the cot, lifting the boy out. She stood there, holding him uncomfortably under the arms.

That's weird, Elliott thought. *Even the fucked-up ones hold their babies on their hip.*

"Wait here," he instructed. "I need to call this in."

◖

Fifteen minutes later he returned, looking like he'd received bad news, or like he wanted to be somewhere else. Possibly both. The boy had stopped crying and was now sitting on Elise's knee on the couch, playing with her hair, twisting it around his pudgy fingers.

"You two have jobs?" Elliott asked, trying to sound casual but increasingly desperate to confirm his theory that they were everyday addicts.

"Of course we do," Elise replied. "Leo's an accountant, and I tutor English. High school. But I can do college level too," she added awkwardly, as though wanting to prove herself.

"Right," Constable Elliott said, waving her answer away. Something was off, something he couldn't quite identify, and he was counting down the minutes until it became somebody else's problem. "Here's what's going to happen," he said. "Child Services will be here soon. They're going to talk to you about your kid."

"He's not our—"

"Just stop. You're going to be drug tested. And they're gonna ask you why you never registered his birth."

"What do you mean?" Leo asked.

"There's no record of him living here." Leo and Elise both

started to protest, but Elliott held up his hands. "Hey, it happens. At least, it does round here."

Elise sprang to her feet, seemingly forgetting she was holding a child, and the boy playing in her lap slid to the ground. He screeched, a piercing noise that made Elise and Leo wince.

Elise picked him up again, almost holding him away from her, and Elliott exclaimed loudly over the boy's hoarse cries.

"What are you doing? Can't you, I dunno, give him milk or something?"

Leo opened the fridge. The beer bottle in the door rattled. They were out of milk; in fact, apart from the beer in the door, a packet of cheese, and three sausages on a plate, the fridge was completely empty.

"Forget it," the cop said. He'd heard a knock at the door. "I'm out of here."

Two officers from Child Services introduced themselves; the man and woman were both wearing suits, with rumpled shirts and no tie—the uniform of night shift workers who hadn't expected a call-out.

James Elliott briefed them quickly in the doorway, pointing back to where the couple sat on the couch. Leo now held the boy, the same dazed and confused look on his face that his wife had worn a few minutes earlier.

If I ever have kids, thought Elliott as he strode outside, *I hope I look like I know what I'm doing. More than Father of the Year there, at least. Give the kid a toy to play with, something to distract him.*

He was halfway back to his car, ache in his head pounding away, when it hit him. There *were* no toys. Not a car, not a building block, not even a teddy. Nothing in the living room. *Even junkies have toys*, he thought. Dirty ones, but still something for the kids to chew on while Mum and Dad sleep off a bender under the watchful eye of Ziggy Stardust, hiding those fist holes plowed through the wall.

But there were no posters in that house, just framed pictures hung neatly.

Pictures of Mum and Dad, together.

No baby.

2

Dust bunnies.

At least four of them; big fluffy balls of hair and dust and who knew what else. From where Michelle lay it was all she could see, these round clumps scattered in the shadowy gap beneath the bed, barely visible in the dim glow of the nightlight. She made a mental note to put it on the list of things to clean—not that it meant it would actually be done. She had more pressing matters than an infestation of dust bunnies; too many people needing her attention. But she was okay with that. It was why she was here.

Michelle's hip and shoulder ached, the blanket she'd spread on the floor of the bedroom offering no relief from the hard wood below. At forty-two—almost forty-three—she was too old to sleep on the floor anymore. Another mental note that would be ignored.

At least Maisie had stopped crying; the deep, heartbreaking sobs that had drawn Michelle to her room had gradually faded to a soft whimper, then finally silence as she fell into an exhausted sleep. Maisie was twelve and a newly minted resident, carrying more pain than a child should have to bear. Some nights she made it all the way through without waking; others, like this one, she wouldn't. Michelle wished there was something she could do to help, more than hugging her, or holding her hand, or lying next to her bed in the small room, waiting with her 'til sleep came. But Maisie had watched her mum, ravaged by breast cancer, make a slow, painful exit, and with nobody else to care for her, she'd wound up here. It would take time. Until then, Michelle Chaplin had vowed to fill the gap. She'd done it before, and suspected that the kids filled a gap in her own life too—a gap that, at forty-two years old, was unlikely to be filled in the conventional way.

The girl's eyes would be puffy and red in the morning, Michelle thought. She looked at her watch. *In a couple of hours*, she corrected herself.

She listened again—the raw, shuddering breaths were gone, and Maisie now breathed quietly—in, out, in, out. Definitely asleep.

Silently, Michelle got to her feet and crept out into the hall. Her own room was at the far end of the corridor, and she padded along past the rooms of her other charges, determined to snooze for an hour or two before the rest of them woke.

Her head hit the pillow and she was out instantly. If she'd stayed awake just a few minutes more, she might have heard the tires crunching on the Dairy's long gravel driveway.

The new arrival.

◑

The thing about the Dairy was that it wasn't a dairy at all; it never had been. In fact, there wasn't a cow within a dozen miles of the place. It was just a nickname for a house that had been given a much grander name by the man who owned it: *Milkwood House* was what it said on the sign at the front gate. Before that it had belonged to the Sisters of St. Therese, during its ninety or so years as a scenic rural outpost of the Catholic empire. The stone-and-wood structure had started as a convent, bedrooms lining the long corridors on both floors, with a communal dining room and a shared space where bookshelves braced the walls. But as demand had dwindled and the order came through from the archbishop to sell up, a For Sale sign was hammered into the hard earth at the end of the driveway. The notice in the real estate agent's window described it as a *Unique Rural Opportunity, just a stone's throw from the city. Inspect today!*

One inspection was all it took. Declan Driscoll was a wealthy man from an even wealthier family, and all four of his accountants were unanimous: a foster home was a great investment, and you couldn't go wrong with it being just a stone's throw from the city.

It would need to be a good throw. Leo Palmer—who was pretty handy with numbers—might have known it took one hour and twenty-two minutes by train, with exactly eleven stops between the city terminal and Upper Reach Station, if you caught an express. But Leo Palmer never took the express, never got off at Upper Reach Station, and certainly never visited Milkwood House, also known as the Dairy.

His son did, though.

Breakfast was in full swing when Michelle Chaplin woke. The sounds of children talking and bickering and laughing drifted up the stairs and through her closed door.

Her door. Someone was tapping on it, gently.

"Sorry to wake you—I know Maisie had another bad one," John Llewellyn started as soon as Michelle opened it. "But when you're ready, could you come to my office, please?"

Fifteen minutes later, Michelle sat opposite the director of Milkwood House in a small room that always reminded her of the aftermath of a storm. Paper was strewn across the desk and the floor, and spilled from the drawers of a filing cabinet. On top of the drawers, a small TV with rabbit ears droned quietly, the antenna still wrapped in Christmas tinsel, even though it was the first week of January. Bright morning light streamed in through the window behind John, silhouetting him against a wide expanse of grass dotted with trees and, beyond that, a fence line bounded by thick scrub.

Michelle looked curiously at John; she knew she wasn't in trouble but had no idea why he'd asked to meet her so early in the morning. The pair had a number of things in common. They were nearly the same age. (John had a few years on Michelle and, thanks to his lack of exercise since starting at the Dairy, was looking every one of them.) They were both teachers by trade, although the lessons they taught at Milkwood House were the ones that Mum and Dad would normally teach. Everything else was covered at Upper Reach Primary, and after that at the high school the next town over.

The third thing they had in common—and probably the most important—was that each was quietly in love with the other. It was a truth they'd never openly acknowledged, and instead they engaged in a type of middle-aged flirting that in a different setting might have been considered wooing. If any of the older kids had noticed, they would've been grossed out.

But this morning there was no flirting. John Llewellyn was a big Englishman who laughed easily and loudly. Not today. Today he seemed puzzled, worried.

"Got another one this morning," he said without any preamble.

"Another what?" asked Michelle. Her voice was soft, verging on a whisper—one of the reasons the kids all warmed to her so quickly.

"Another child," John replied, and Michelle Chaplin leaned forward, frowning.

"Unexpected?" she asked, and her boss nodded.

"Child Services arrived early, around five. They tried to get him into some of the foster families in the city, but they're full. I've set him up in room three. Reckon he could sleep most of the day, poor little guy."

"Little? How little are we talking?" Michelle was afraid of the answer.

John Llewellyn sighed. "I reckon he might be a year or so." He thought about it for a moment. "Yeah, probably about twelve months."

He wasn't to know he was right—almost to the minute.

Michelle closed her eyes. They didn't get many that young. "What's his story?" she asked.

A folder landed in her lap, and she opened her eyes and turned to the first page of the form from Child Services. It was a standard form, but she'd never seen one filled out like this before.

Name? Blank.

Date of birth? Blank.

Medical history? Blank.

Mother's name? Blank.

Father's name? Blank.

Scanning the pages, Michelle found a box that had some writing scrawled in it. Under the heading *Recent Circumstances*, one of the officers described how a young couple claimed to have found the boy in their apartment. Michelle saw the address of their flat, and grimaced.

"What's the bet they were on something?" she said.

"I thought the same thing. They're testing them. But Child Services said it was weird—there were no obvious signs of use. Maybe schizophrenia? I don't know…" His voice trailed off. "Biscuit?" he asked, producing a packet from his desk drawer. John's accent made the offer sound quite proper, as though the snack would be served with tea and cream and sugar. But he knew the chocolate would be soft and he'd likely make a completely improper mess. The summer heat just made everything a little bit difficult. He wondered if he'd ever get used to January being so hot; nobody warned him when he decided to move hemispheres all those years ago. Not that it would have stopped him.

Michelle shook her head at the sight of the cookies. *Not for breakfast*, she thought.

John took two, and Michelle smiled. She knew he couldn't help himself.

"And just like that," he said, through a mouthful of chocolate and crumbs, "Milkwood's full again."

John couldn't bring himself to call it the Dairy; never had. Even though one of his own staff had given it the nickname, declaring the owner to be milking the system.

"Jesus," the man had said, poring over the ledger and eyeing the flow of government funding. "Forget Milkwood—these kids are bloody cash cows. Driscoll should have called it the Dairy," he'd declared, unfortunately within earshot of not one but two of those cash cows. The staffer hadn't stuck around long after that. The nickname had.

"Twelve children," Michelle said, more to herself than John, but he nodded anyway. The crop now ranged from one year old right up to a couple on the cusp of becoming adults. When they turned eighteen their time at Milkwood would come to an end; the funding would dry up, and they would be required to leave and make their own way in the world.

Of course, some would take more work than others. Maisie's grief would eventually pass, there was plenty of time for that—she was only twelve. Then there was Aleks, who was nine but looked thirteen, and had finished the previous year with a flurry of letters home from Upper Reach Primary for hassling other kids to hand over their pocket money. A nine-year-old extortionist.

And Richie. She'd forgotten about Richie Sharpe. At three, almost four, he was the youngest resident (until the new arrival)—still too young for school, so he spent every day in Michelle's care.

"I think Glenda's going to have to take over with Richie." John almost read her mind.

"Oh, he's not going to like that."

"Neither of them are," he replied.

He was right again. Glenda Reilly was the third person employed at Milkwood House, and unfortunately had been born without compassion, a sense of humor, or a fondness for kids. How she'd fallen into social work and wound up at a home for parentless children was anybody's guess. All of the kids called Michelle "Miss Michelle"; they'd done it from the moment she'd started working there, and she loved it. Glenda Reilly was "Mrs. Reilly," although she preferred the children didn't speak to her at all.

"Where are the new boy's things?" Michelle asked.

John shrugged. "Everything that came with him is in the room. The cot, the pajamas he's wearing. That's about it, really."

"Right." Michelle stood. "I'd better get going," she said. She had work to do, and started making a list of everything she'd need to find. Clothes, some toys. Heck, even diapers. She shook her head, as the television flickered behind her.

"Getting your morning fix?" she asked John, gesturing with a smile to the cartoon playing on the screen.

"Sorry. I put it on to calm the little guy down before bed. He was a bit upset. But you should've seen him watching *Thomas the Tank Engine*. Don't reckon he blinked once."

Michelle laughed sadly, then paused in the doorway. "What do I call him? Does he have a name?"

John frowned. "He didn't come with one." He thought for a moment, and his eyes darted back up to the TV. "Let's call him

Thomas. No—Tommy. At least 'til his parents come to their senses and collect him."

Michelle didn't know how long he'd been standing there, watching as she dug through a bag of old clothes with her back to the door. There wasn't much for an infant. *Might need a trip into town*, she thought, and turned around.

"What are you doing, Miss Michelle?" Richie asked innocently, and Michelle jumped, startled.

There was something mildly odd about him. He was cute all right; a shock of dark brown hair, almost black, and deep blue eyes that seemed out of place on a child. She had to remind herself that his fourth birthday wasn't for another month or so. He looked and sounded older.

"I'm just looking for some clothes, Richie. A new boy has come to live with us."

A curious look passed over Richie's face, gone as quick as it'd come. He'd been abandoned too, not long after his last birthday. Another drop-off from Child Services, but at least this time they knew who his parents were—Dad had buggered off, and Mum was doing eighteen years for armed robbery. (Michelle thought that seemed a bit harsh, but she didn't know that dear old Mama had tried to cut the throat of the cashier when he refused to open the till. Only bad knife skills had seen her land eighteen years and not life.)

The thing about Richie was that he'd settled in unusually quickly, almost as if he knew this was a better place for him.

Michelle had found him to be mostly sweet, even if only to her. The rest of the kids avoided him, and he returned the favor. Michelle didn't know why. Maybe it was the eyes; she certainly found them unnerving. Richie just seemed to be watching, and taking everything in, and knowing. But then again, he was only a little boy, she thought. And he'd been through a lot.

"Look, Richie. Come here," she said, squatting and putting an arm out for him.

He went willingly.

"The new boy—Tommy—he's just a baby. He's going to need you to be a big brother for him. Can you do that?"

Richie didn't say anything.

"I'm going to have to spend a bit of time with him. I'm still here whenever you need me, but you'll get to have more fun now with Mrs. Reilly, too." Michelle knew it sounded like a lie; nobody had fun with Glenda Reilly.

Richie nodded silently.

She hugged him tight and then led him out of the storeroom and back up the main stairs to the common room, which was filled with kids of various ages. Michelle couldn't stay; she had to go to Upper Reach to get supplies for Tommy before he woke.

She paused at the bottom of the stairs, and looked at the closed door with a brass *3* tacked to it.

Inside, Tommy slept. In fact, he slept through much of his first birthday. He dreamed of his mum and his dad, who weren't dreaming of him. And when he woke, he cried out for them. But they didn't come.

3

Tommy took his first steps on the grass at the front of the Dairy. At nine o'clock every morning for the last two months, Michelle Chaplin had carried her new young ward outside and set up a play area in the dappled shade of a large tree. There was a swing set there, rust creeping into the metal legs from years of exposure to the elements. Next to the swings Michelle would spread out a checked picnic blanket and an array of soft toys and books. She was determined to do for Tommy what she would have done for her own child—or what the boy's own parents should have done for him. He followed her finger as she pointed out words on the page, and when he giggled as she made the toys talk in funny voices, Michelle realized that she was becoming increasingly fond of him. And so it was with an almost maternal pride that she watched Tommy let go of the mottled leg of the swing set and take one, two, then three wobbling steps across the grass.

"Well done, Tommy!" Michelle cried and scooped him up into

a bear hug. The little boy's pale face lit up with the praise. "Just wait 'til we tell Mr. Llewellyn. He's going to be so proud of you."

Two more attempts failed to replicate the same success, but Michelle knew it had been a milestone. The boy who had refused stubbornly to let go of the swings for two months had finally done so. Michelle wished his parents could have seen it.

Child Services had visited Milkwood House again a week after first delivering Tommy. It was the same pair, the man and the woman, but this time they were dressed more neatly. Day shift. They'd sat down with John Llewellyn in his office, surrounded by his scattered files, and later that afternoon John had relayed the information to Michelle.

"It's not good news," he said.

Michelle hadn't been expecting any. She'd never seen Child Services arrive bearing good news.

"The couple whose house Tommy was found in were both clean. No drugs. Seriously, nothing at all. And the psychologist who spoke to them reckoned they were of sound mind. Decent jobs, too."

"How's that not good news?" Michelle asked. "They can take Tommy home again."

John sighed. "That's the problem. There's no proof it *was* his home. The couple swear he's not theirs, and the psych says they're not lying. There's…well, there's no record of him living there." There was more he didn't go into: there'd been no record of Tommy's birth either. Not at any of the local hospitals. Not with any private midwives. No mention anywhere. That was strange—not unheard of, to live off the grid, but pretty unusual.

"What about—I don't know—DNA or something? Haven't they started doing tests for things like this?" Michelle asked, and John nodded.

"They have, and they said we have to take him into town at some point to have some blood taken. Poor kid—can't imagine he'll enjoy that too much. But they told me not to expect anything in a hurry. Samples have to be sent overseas, and even then cases like ours are a pretty low priority apparently." That wasn't exactly how Child Services had put it. They'd said there was a swimming pool of blood, semen, and saliva waiting to be tested, and Tommy would be somewhere behind murderers, rapists, and paternity tests with an inheritance at stake. It could be a year or two at least.

"I think we need to accept that he's not their kid, Michelle. He's been officially listed on the missing children register, but as one who's been found. It's his parents who are lost."

"What does that mean for Tommy?" Michelle asked.

"It means he's here for good. Unless his real parents claim him. And can explain why they broke into another house and left behind their little boy." It sounded ridiculous, and both John and Michelle knew it.

So Michelle understood, as she played with Tommy on the lawn at the front of the Dairy, that no matter how much she wished his parents could see him take his first steps, it wasn't going to happen.

But somebody else saw it instead. Inside the old two-story house, one of the other children was sitting on the edge of his bed, staring out the window with big blue eyes. Richie Sharpe, the now-four-year-old boy who still looked a year or two older, was nursing a sore, scratchy throat and an acute case of jealousy. He'd watched from his window as the other kids—except Tommy—trudged down the gravel driveway and boarded the bus that took them into town. The younger ones were dropped at the primary school, and the older children were delivered to the train station. With an official population of only 3,600 people, Upper Reach didn't qualify for its own secondary school, so the town's teens caught the train en masse to Mortlake, the next town along the line heading west. All the children who lived at the Dairy ended up going to Mortlake when they were old enough. It was just the way it worked. First Upper Reach Primary, then Mortlake High, then welcome to the rest of your lives, kids.

Once the other children had left, the door to Richie's room swung open and Mrs. Reilly charged through carrying a small tray. She was tall, thin, and mean. He didn't like her.

"I hear you're sick," she said flatly.

Richie didn't answer. He knew she didn't care.

"Open your mouth."

Richie obeyed, and a thermometer was thrust inside. Mrs. Reilly inspected the instrument, and frowned as she realized he was telling the truth. Richie wondered what would have happened if he'd been faking it. Probably a smack, he decided.

"Swallow these," she said, taking two tablets from the tray and holding them out.

Richie shook his head. Miss Michelle had never made him swallow pills; *she* always gave him something sweet and pink and sticky, measured out in a little cup.

"You know something?" Mrs. Reilly said. It wasn't a question.

"I don't actually care if you take them. Toss 'em out the window for all I care. Makes no difference to me. You'll be fine in a couple of days anyway; no pills today are gonna change that."

Mrs. Reilly left the room without another word, pulling the door closed behind her. Richie examined the tablets and touched one with the tip of his tongue. He gagged at the taste and turned back to the window, just in time to see Miss Michelle putting the new kid—the baby—on his feet by the swing set. He fell over straight away this time, and Richie smiled. It morphed into a scowl as Miss Michelle brushed off Tommy's knees and gave him a hug.

Richie didn't really remember his mum, so in his mind he pictured her as being just like Miss Michelle. She certainly wasn't (there was a video shop cashier who would gladly attest to that, and had done so at her trial), but that didn't matter to Richie. He knew he wouldn't be seeing his real mum again for a long time—they'd explained that to him (gently, of course) when he arrived. When he'd first been delivered to the Dairy it was Miss Michelle who'd met him at the door with the other man, Mr. Llewellyn. She'd taken him by the hand into a room with tables and chairs and given him ice cream. Lots of ice cream. She'd tucked him into bed that night, and kissed him on the forehead, and the next morning she was there when he woke up. She'd read him stories and played with him for months, and at around the same time the gavel came down in a courtroom fifty miles away, sentencing Richie's dear, sweet mother to eighteen years inside, Richie had entirely merged his memory of her with the caring, loving Miss Michelle.

Richie swallowed again. His throat really hurt, and he

wanted to go back to sleep. He put his head down on the pillow. Maybe when he woke up, the new kid would be gone.

He wasn't gone, but something else did happen while Richie slept. The resentment he'd felt watching *his* Miss Michelle playing with Tommy under *his* tree on *his* rug hardened, and when he woke it had grown into something new, the strongest word the four-year-old knew.

"Hate, hate, hate," he said quietly, testing it out. He liked the way it sounded, though he wasn't going to say it outside his room, and definitely not when Mrs. Reilly was around. They weren't allowed to say *hate*, or *stupid*, or *idiot*. But he was alone, and he was only saying it softly. Plus it was true.

Yes, Richie Sharpe decided he *hated* Tommy.

For a handful of months, life was calm for the residents and staff at Milkwood House. After three days in bed with his bout of tonsillitis, Richie had returned to the daily supervision of Mrs. Reilly, whom some of the older kids referred to as Smiley Reilly, for obvious reasons. Twelve-year-old Maisie turned thirteen, and was now sleeping through the night. Marcus, who at fourteen and a half held the dubious title of having been in more foster homes than any of the other kids, had gone a full six weeks without a single detention at Mortlake High. (Not that he hadn't done anything wrong during that time, but he had become infinitely better at concealing the evidence.) Kayla, who was the oldest resident, also had a birthday, with eighteen candles on the plain chocolate cake marking the end of her time at the Dairy. She'd scraped through her final exams the previous year and had been searching for a job ever since. Help came in the unlikely form of Mrs. Reilly, whose sister was leaving her job as a real estate agent's receptionist in Mortlake. Kayla was appointed as her replacement (the agent had liked the idea of an eighteen-year-old receptionist; his wife wouldn't be happy, but she didn't have to know) and moved in with one of her friends from school. The staff and kids of Milkwood House gathered on the front steps to see her off—a Dairy tradition. John Llewellyn drove Kayla to her new flat himself, all of her belongings in two bags in the back of the car. He left her there with a sense that this one could turn out all right.

Back at the Dairy, little Tommy could now walk unaided (albeit slowly, and with plenty of bruised knees). A couple of months shy of his second birthday, he'd also added to his vocabulary and could say his own name and a few different foods, in addition to already saying "up" when he wanted to be carried, as well as "mama" and "dadda." Both Michelle Chaplin and John Llewellyn thought this was a particularly cruel reminder of the young boy's circumstances. The pair—as well as being smitten with each other—were extremely taken with the little boy who'd landed on their doorstep with no parents, no possessions, and no name.

"Have you noticed," John said to Michelle and Glenda Reilly one evening, "how settled things have been lately? I don't think it hurts having a toddler in the house. The girls all love him." They were eating at a small table in the dining room. The children were at two large tables next to them; the raucous mix of cutlery and kids screeching made it difficult for the adults to hear each other.

Michelle nodded, and felt a swell of affection as she watched John gaze fondly at the children. On occasion, Michelle had found herself wondering if their friendship might someday evolve to something more, and she'd decided that it probably would. But it wouldn't be like in the movies: there'd be no sneaking around after dark, no grand gesture or declaration of love. They were both too…well, she supposed they were too *shy*, almost too respectful of their jobs for that. No, Michelle had a hunch that if it was meant to be—and she was a firm believer in fate—then they'd just grow closer and closer until they naturally arrived at the conclusion that they shouldn't be apart. Boring, perhaps, but the prospect filled her with a warmth that she found quite satisfying. She was in no rush.

"Yeah, I think you're right," Michelle responded, but Glenda Reilly just snorted dismissively. She treated her colleagues with as much regard as she treated their charges. To Glenda's mind these two were too earnest, and besides, she'd seen their coy looks and their quiet cups of tea. If she was honest (and Mrs. Reilly was nothing but honest), the thought of them together made her feel nauseous.

"Glenda, I'm serious," John insisted. "Look at them." He gestured across the room to where the little boy sat in his high chair. Maisie was supervising his dinner, wiping Tommy's mouth diligently and making sure he ate all his custard. A couple of the other kids were helping, leaning across the table when he dropped his spoon or providing Maisie with unsolicited advice, which she duly ignored.

Raised voices at the table closest to the adults broke through the usual dining room noise. Marcus, who'd been on such a good run at school lately, was yelling at Charlie, a boy two years his senior, over some perceived slight.

"Spoke too soon." John shook his head and heaved himself up from his chair to separate the two boys. He didn't notice Richie Sharpe sitting two seats down from Marcus. Despite the uproar, Richie had barely blinked. He continued to stare intently at the high chair across the room, and at the small crowd of children who were tending to its occupant.

Marcus and Charlie—the dining room brawlers—spent the rest of the evening on a timeout. Some of the others did homework in their rooms, while the rest gathered in the common room, reading or playing one of the old board games that were stacked on a bookshelf in one corner. Three kids, led by Maisie, were deeply engrossed in a round of Monopoly, on account of it being the only game that still had all of its pieces.

The younger children were bundled off to bed as soon as dinner had been cleared away. Miss Michelle took Tommy, bathing him before she dressed him in short-sleeved pajamas, glad for the longer spring days and warmer nights. While Tommy was tucked into his cot downstairs and kissed goodnight, upstairs Richie was escorted into his room by Mrs. Reilly, who was preoccupied by the fact that it was Thursday night, and only one more sleep until she had the weekend off. She gave Richie a cursory glance as he changed into his own pajamas before she turned out the light and left the room. The door was ajar, and a thin shaft of light from the hallway lanced into the darkness. Richie—who hadn't even made it into bed before Mrs. Reilly flicked the switch—perched on the edge of his mattress. He thought about how much he disliked the woman who'd just walked out the door. He gazed at his bed and matching wooden bedside table. He stared at the cupboard containing his few belongings—an assortment of picture books from the common room shelves, some colored pencils, and a drawer full of clothes that were almost entirely hand-me-downs from older residents. He looked again at the door and thought about the boy in the cot downstairs, the boy who had taken Miss Michelle for himself. The boy who'd stolen the one person who'd made this place home for Richie.

Hate, hate, hate.

Richie slid off the bed and walked to the door. There he paused, listening. He could hear voices drifting along the landing from the common room, a playful argument about money owed, and another voice telling the Monopoly players to shut up because she was trying to read. Richie crept along the hall, past the common room, to the stairs. He descended, stopping again at the bottom step to listen. All quiet. He peered around the edge of the door into the dining room—Miss Michelle was in there, sitting next to Mr. Llewellyn. Music floated softly from a radio on a side table, and they both had teacups in front of them and were deep in conversation. There was no sign of Mrs. Reilly. This made him happy. He tiptoed along the corridor and stopped outside a door. It had a small metal *3* on it.

Richie tried the handle, and it opened. The doors were never locked at the Dairy—in fact, only the adults had locks on their doors (nobody else had anything worth stealing). The room was the same layout as his own upstairs, but instead of a single bed, there was a cot with brass bars. Richie smiled thinly to himself. The inhabitant of the cot sat up as light from the corridor filled the room, and the little boy smiled at the intruder. Richie made his way to the cot and leaned against it, resting his chin on the top crossbar. He was face to face with Tommy.

He stood there, looking at the toddler, unsure what to do next. At not-quite-five years old, Richie Sharpe, the second youngest resident of Milkwood House, was practically a baby himself. He didn't have a plan; he'd just wanted to see his rival.

Richie put his hand on the corner post of the cot, and suddenly the crossbar he'd been leaning on dropped away. Without realizing, he'd bumped the release catch for the side of the cot, and the whole side slid down. Richie held his breath at the metallic clang. He knew he'd be in trouble, and only hoped it would be Miss Michelle who found him and not Mrs. Reilly. He froze, waiting for footsteps along the corridor and then a shadow at the door. But nobody came. He exhaled.

Tommy, who was still smiling at him, reached out with chubby fingers to touch Richie's face.

Richie pulled back. "Don't touch me," he hissed.

"Up," the little boy said.

That annoyed Richie even more. Before he knew what he was doing, he grabbed the toddler under the arms and pulled him down, straining under the weight as Tommy half slid, half fell from the cot. Taking him by the hand, Richie led Tommy from his room and along the hallway, the small child struggling to keep up on his short, unsteady legs. Richie held his finger to his lips—did the boy even know what that meant?—as they passed the dining room. The two grown-ups were still inside, absorbed in their conversation, and didn't look up.

The boys were in the entrance hall, then at the front door. It wasn't yet locked—it was the last thing John Llewellyn did each night before turning in—and the solid wooden door issued only a slight creak as it swung open on rusty hinges. Tommy looked up at the older boy as he was dragged, stumbling, down the front steps and onto the driveway. To their right was the large tree familiar to both boys from their time with Miss Michelle, and ahead of them the driveway ran down a slight slope before turning toward the road. Richie went left instead, and the two boys walked around the side of the house, past the old sheds where the staff left their cars, and into the backyard. A line of trees marked the boundary of the property, and a wire fence had been erected to prevent kids wandering into the dense scrub beyond.

Tommy stopped walking. He didn't like being outside without Miss Michelle, and he especially didn't like being outside at night. He tried to squirm out of Richie's grip, but the other boy's hand was almost twice the size of his.

Richie squatted down so he was at Tommy's eye level.

"What's wrong?" he asked.

Tommy didn't say anything, but a single fat tear appeared in the corner of his eye and rolled down his cheek.

"I just want to show you something," Richie told him.

Richie stood and, still holding Tommy's hand, continued walking toward the trees. The toddler allowed himself to be pulled along—he didn't want to be left alone. They reached the fence line, and the older boy with the dark hair and deep blue eyes stopped. Richie put his foot on the bottom wire and lifted the top strand up, the same way he'd seen some of the older kids do so they could slip through easily. He made the gap big enough for Tommy, but the little boy stood there, stubborn and afraid.

"Come on, Tommy," Richie coaxed him. "Miss Michelle said to."

At the mention of his favorite person, Tommy took a hesitant step forward. He was so short he didn't even need to duck to get through the gap. Richie bent down and climbed through after him, then he took Tommy's hand again and led him between the trees and into the scrub, twigs raking his bare arms as he pushed aside small branches.

After a couple of minutes he stopped. He still didn't have a plan; he was driven solely by a cold, cruel instinct. Looking around, he saw nothing but trees and a glimpse of the house in the distance behind him. The moon was approaching full, and now that they were away from the lights of the Dairy, Richie could see his own shadow cast in the moonlight that filtered down through the leaves. The shadows were much deeper ahead as the trees' thick canopy blocked any sign of the stars above. Richie didn't know what he was doing, but he knew one thing: he didn't want to go any further. He was still a little boy himself, and he had a healthy respect for the dark.

He turned again to Tommy and saw that tears were coursing down the toddler's face in a steady stream. His nose was all snotty, and Richie didn't like that.

"You stay here," he said to Tommy. "I'm gonna get Miss Michelle."

Tommy stared up at Richie through wet eyelashes. He didn't understand, but he again recognized Miss Michelle's name.

Richie dropped Tommy's hand and turned back toward the Dairy. In a flash he was gone, darting through the trees, under the wire fence, and running as fast as he could back to the safety of the lights at the house, terrified that *something* was going to grab him from the darkness before he could get there.

He slowed at the front steps. Was he actually going to get Miss Michelle? If he did, it would mean owning up to taking Tommy outside—and having to explain why he'd done it, which would be difficult when he didn't even know himself. And even worse was the thought of Miss Michelle rushing outside to look after the other boy, and Richie being left with Mrs. Reilly to take him back to bed.

Most of his decisions thus far had been made by instinct alone (an unpleasant instinct, one that came from an unnatural place for a not-quite-five-year-old boy), but this one was deliberate. Richie tiptoed up the front steps and slipped back inside unnoticed. Chancing a peek into the dining room, he could see Mr. Llewellyn still sitting in a chair with his back to the door. Miss Michelle was nowhere in sight. When he reached the top of the stairs, he could hear the Monopoly game still going at full volume; the argument about money owed had been resolved and Maisie was nearing victory. Richie had only been outside for a few minutes; it had felt to him like hours. He padded along the hall in his bare feet, sure that he would be caught at any moment.

But he wasn't, and soon Richie was inside his room, closing the door as quietly as he could behind him. Breathing hard, he lay down on his bed and waited. He didn't know what would come first—sleep, or the discovery of the problem he had created outside.

At the same time as Richie was climbing back into bed, little Tommy, not yet two years old, was gripped by the special type of terror that only toddlers know. One minute he'd been tucked up in his cot, and the next a boy had been in his room. Now he was outside, and he was alone. It was so dark, which was scary enough when the other boy was with him, but now he was on his own, it transformed into something truly frightening. Tommy stood completely still, surrounded by towering trees with branches that swayed slightly in the breeze. The shadows those branches cast on the ground looked like giant hands with angry, scraping claws.

Tommy screamed, a high-pitched wail of pure fear.

Inside the house, the three adults heard the cry. As one, they identified it as a scream fueled by horror, the kind experienced when a child wakes from a nightmare and can't separate dream from reality, but none could pick where it was coming from. Michelle, who'd finished a cup of tea with John and was now in the kitchen helping the cook to tidy up, made a beeline for the room where the youngest child slept. Throwing open the door, she saw with a jolt that Tommy was gone.

"Tommy's missing!" she called desperately and started searching the lower floor. Upstairs, Mrs. Reilly checked the common area. In the dining room, John Llewellyn jumped up from his seat, spilling the last of his tea, and ran straight for the front door. Opening a cupboard in the entrance hall, he grabbed a flashlight that he kept for emergencies and took the front steps in one leap.

He started down the driveway at a run, concerned Tommy might have wandered down to the road. It was hardly a main highway, but there were still plenty of cars using it (and at high speed, too). John was halfway along the driveway when he heard a second cry, similar to the last but not as loud. It was coming from behind him, on the other side of the house. John turned abruptly and started back the way he had come. He sucked in deep breaths, his chest heaving, and as he ran he regretted that he'd let himself go so badly, that he couldn't cover a hundred yards without grunting and groaning.

Skirting the house, he slowed as he reached the backyard, and listened. There—a sobbing, coming from well beyond the fence line. He flicked on the flashlight, and the beam played out across the grass and into the trees. John couldn't see anything except for the undergrowth. When he reached the fence with its two strands of wire, he put his foot on the bottom strand and pulled the top one up—he'd seen some of his older students do this when they thought he wasn't looking. Bending over, he squeezed his large frame through the gap, then stretched back up to his full height and rushed into the thick bushland, ignoring the pain in his chest as he picked his way between the tree trunks and the shrubs, following the noise of the child crying somewhere ahead of him.

"It's all right, Tommy, I'm coming," he called, although he still couldn't see the boy.

Rounding a tree, he nearly collided with the toddler, who was blinking in the bright light. Tommy was still standing in the spot where he'd been abandoned, as though rooted to the ground by fear. John scooped him up and held him tight.

Tommy nestled his head in the man's shoulder, and the whimpers turned to howls as relief washed over him. John rocked him back and forth, trying to catch his breath, until the little boy's cries gradually died away. As he carried Tommy back through the trees, he was reminded of the morning the boy had first arrived at Milkwood House; John had carried him into his office just like this. He'd grown so much in that short time.

Michelle, who'd spotted the glow of John's flashlight from one of the bedroom windows, was waiting for the pair by the fence. John passed Tommy to her over the wire before ducking down to step through himself. As he started to straighten up on the other side, he suddenly pitched forward. Michelle was already struggling under the weight of Tommy, but threw an arm out to catch John. She was a moment too late, and he hit the ground hard, his face grinding into the dry, uneven surface.

"John! Are you okay?" Michelle's voice, normally so soft and gentle, was high-pitched with concern.

He didn't answer.

He didn't move.

●

The funeral for John Llewellyn was held five days later; he was buried with three blocked arteries and a heart that had been unable to take the strain of his dash to find Tommy.

Miss Michelle left town before the wake had even begun. She'd been numb since the night it happened. The next morning, she'd stared at herself in the mirror, face pale and drawn, and resolved to stay and be strong. *For the kids*, she'd told herself.

But every time she looked at Tommy, or at Maisie or Marcus or any of the others, she felt herself starting to shake. And even though she tried to hide it, the emotion spread like a virus, with one child bursting into tears, then another, and Michelle knew she needed to get away. For the kids, and also for herself. Just for a little while.

"I'm going to visit my sister—I just need to clear my head," she told Mrs. Reilly, who didn't really care. She was focused instead on the impending arrival of Declan Driscoll, the owner of Milkwood House. Ostensibly there to shepherd the house through the chaos, Declan Driscoll was really there to protect his investment.

Six weeks passed with the Dairy enveloped in a fog of confusion and grief, and beset by a flurry of strangers. In the midst of all the fuss, nobody realized they were approaching the second birthday of little Tommy, which was also the first anniversary of his arrival at Milkwood House. Tommy didn't know either, of course, when he was put to bed on the night before his birthday by one of the temporary staffers filling in for Miss Michelle.

To view the old house from outside on the night that Tommy turned two, one would be forgiven for thinking that nothing particularly remarkable was happening. The house sat exactly as it had for many years, from its days as a convent to its second life as a foster home with a fancy name that only adults used, peeling paint just visible in the pale moonlight. It all looked so normal, and yet inside, when the clock ticked over to midnight, something completely abnormal occurred. As the residents slept, all knowledge, all memory, all awareness of one little boy was wiped from their minds, and all evidence of his very existence—from police files to DNA test forms—was scrubbed clean.

And so, on the morning of his second birthday, when most other kids would be showered with gifts and attention, Tommy was once again a stranger to all who had known him.

4

For a boy whose very existence was defined by the unusual, the years that immediately followed the death of John Llewellyn, the man who'd taken him in, were surprisingly straightforward. It turned out that Tommy's greatest ally was bureaucracy itself—a monstrous web of government departments and public servants that reduced children in the care of the state to names and numbers on a page. In Tommy's case, that page was erased as the calendar rolled from January 4 to January 5.

The scene the following morning played out the same way each year, and once he was a little older, Tommy found he could predict how it would unfold with startling accuracy. Tommy, first a toddler, then a boy, then a gangly adolescent, would wake in his room, a bare room now, that the previous night had contained a few possessions: a tattered picture book maybe or, as he grew, a notebook and pens in a hand-me-down backpack, a poster or two on the walls. The walls would be empty and those belongings gone—where, Tommy had no idea.

Then, when he stepped out of his room, whichever member of staff spotted him went through a process that never changed.

"Oh," they'd say. This was stage one, and it always started like this. But once the surprise wore off, they usually spoke in a soft tone, as if reluctant to startle him or send him scurrying out the door. (Only Glenda Reilly refused to lower her voice. She probably *wanted* him to flee.) "What's your name?" they'd invariably ask. At this point they'd be assuming (reasonably, considering the facility's purpose) that he'd been dropped off at the door overnight.

Second came anger—a call to Child Services, complaining about new arrivals being delivered unannounced, with no documentation or references.

Third—and this was where the bureaucracy helped out—was acceptance. Acceptance that, after half a dozen calls to various offices in the foster care network, nobody really knew anything. And despite case workers promising to look into it and find out where this boy had come from, Tommy knew he'd be staying.

The only exception to this routine had been the morning Tommy turned two. Nobody made any calls that day, because with John Llewellyn deceased and Michelle Chaplin away, the house was staffed largely by temps who had no idea who was supposed to be there and who wasn't. But order was restored when Michelle at last came back—she'd always planned to return once she'd come to terms with John's death. After all, Milkwood House was her home, and her charges were her children, even if the man she'd loved with all her heart was no longer there. She still spent too much time imagining what his final moments must have been like—keeling over on the driveway while closing the front gate. She wished she'd been with him when it happened, to help him or just to hold his hand, so he didn't die alone.

That was how Michelle remembered the evening, robbed of the too-awful memory of John Llewellyn facedown in the dust at the back fence, while Tommy howled in confusion in her arms. She *had* been there when John died, but any comfort she might have taken from that was collateral damage in the erasing of little Tommy.

Her homecoming was a source of great relief to both Tommy and Richie, not that they discussed it. Richie didn't discuss anything with anyone, and as for Tommy—well, he'd been so young that he soon forgot why he didn't like Richie. All that remained was an unpleasant sensation whenever he saw the other boy, the bitter aftertaste of a child's fear.

Miss Michelle gathered all the kids in the common room on her first day back with a solitary piece of very good news.

"Good morning, everyone," she said softly. Her eyes still looked a little glassy, although she hadn't cried for at least a day. "It's good to see you all again. Though I haven't met everyone yet," she added, smiling at Tommy, who had no idea what was going on. "Now that John—Mr. Llewellyn—isn't with us anymore, I'm going to be running Milkwood House."

Tommy didn't know it at the time, but this was the single greatest thing that could happen to a two-year-old boy whose parents had forgotten he existed. It meant Miss Michelle would be the one to make sure Tommy had everything he needed each year, when he started again with nothing. She'd rummage through boxes of left-behind clothes, cursing softly to herself, and would usually spend her own money to supplement whatever was missing.

It meant Michelle Chaplin was the one who accompanied Tommy on his first day at Upper Reach Primary, holding his small hand tight in her own as they walked through the gate, Tommy's stride getting slower and slower as they approached the classroom.

"It's all right, Tommy," she reassured him. "I'll be here to pick you up when the bell goes this afternoon. You'll have a wonderful time, I promise."

And it also meant Miss Michelle was the one the school called when they realized his enrollment form was incomplete.

"He can't come to school without a surname," the office lady told her, sounding almost panicked by the thought of a surname-less child loose in a classroom. "What are we supposed to file his forms under?"

Michelle Chaplin—who'd been eating a chocolate biscuit at her desk in the Dairy's office when the phone rang—hesitated. "Okay," she replied, looking at the crumbs on her plate and the tea leaves clumped in the bottom of her cup. Perhaps if the call had come at any other moment, she might have chosen differently. But at *that* moment, it seemed the right decision. Besides, although she'd only known Tommy for a couple of weeks, she could already tell he was a clever boy. If there was ever a five-year-old who'd be able to spell this name, it'd be him. "Llewellyn," she said, and felt a little shiver of sadness steal through her. But somehow she thought John would be okay with it. She suspected he would have liked young Tommy very much.

So in subsequent years, after emerging from his barren bed-room on the morning of his birthday, he introduced himself as Tommy Llewellyn to the friends who'd forgotten him over-night, never really noticing the flash of pain in Miss Michelle's eyes when she heard his name for the first time.

Tommy was a boy who made friends easily, which was lucky, as he had to remake them on January 5 every year. At first he tried to convince the other kids that they knew him—after all, he knew who *they* were, so why were they looking at him so strangely? But every year he was greeted by the same blank expressions, and by the time he was ten he realized he could avoid a couple of hours of funny looks and whispers about the weird new boy if he just introduced himself and did his best to slot back in. He still had questions—so many questions, mostly around *why*—but Miss Michelle hadn't been able to help him (in fact, she hadn't really understood what he was asking). So in spite of it all being rather strange, he just tried to get on with his life.

But then, when he turned fourteen, something exceedingly ordinary happened to Tommy. Of course, given his fairly unique circumstances, even the ordinary was going to be problematic.

Tommy Llewellyn fell in love.

●

He was the first to breakfast most mornings at the Dairy. It had been that way for almost as long as he could remember; he liked the quiet of the dining room before it was invaded by the small battalion of children he lived with. On this particular

Wednesday morning, Tommy sat at one of the dining tables, empty chairs on either side of him, with two pieces of toast and a book in front. There were bookcases in the common room upstairs that were full of picture books for the little kids and novels for those who could read on their own. Tommy had long ago graduated from the former to the latter and had soon read everything on offer. But every now and then Miss Michelle would bring in a new batch of secondhand books that she'd picked up from a shop in Mortlake. The one Tommy had propped up against the peanut butter jar was a new addition, and he was so engrossed in it that he didn't realize he had company. It wasn't until he heard a spoon drop and someone swear quietly that he looked up.

Carey Price was seventeen, and Tommy thought she was the most beautiful person he'd ever seen. He wasn't that much younger than her—just three years, not that he was counting—but compared to Carey, he felt like he should have still been reading the picture books. Carey Price was special. She had long honey-colored hair and the creamiest, softest-looking skin.

She sighed as she sat down opposite Tommy, and he noticed with a flutter that she was already dressed for school. (It was, he'd decided earlier in the year, the highlight of going to Mortlake High: the skirt of the school's uniform ended an inch and a half above the knee.) Tommy was disappointed to see she'd pulled on a cardigan over the school's white blouse, hiding the figure he'd spent way too much time picturing (he was fourteen, after all). But that wasn't his favorite thing about Carey, or not quite. No, Tommy liked the fact that she was *nice*.

"Hi, Carey," Tommy said shyly, his cheeks pinking a shade

or two. They'd done that almost every time he'd spoken to Carey in the six months she'd been at the Dairy, even after they'd become friends. Awe would do that to a boy. Tommy wished it wouldn't.

"Hi, Tommy," she replied, looking up from her bowl of cereal. The crispy pieces of rice popped softly in the quiet of the dining room. It sounded like a tiny crackling fireplace.

"You okay?" he asked. Her eyes were red-rimmed and puffy.

"I'm fine. Gonna be a hot one. Don't forget your water bottle." She was staring again at her cereal, as though fascinated by the sound.

"Are you sure?" Tommy persisted. "It looks like you've been crying."

Carey smiled at his lack of tact. "I'm fine," she repeated. "I just…" She looked around to see if they were alone. Through the door to the kitchen she could see Lee, a kind-faced man with shaved gray hair, bending over in front of the fridge, planning the day's meals. Lee fed every one of them, and had done for years, becoming as much a fixture of the Dairy as Miss Michelle. He was also deaf in one ear (a fact he was secretly thankful for at mealtimes). "Really, Tommy. I'm okay." She changed the subject. "Guess who I saw yesterday after school. Maxy!"

"No way!" replied Tommy. Max Cooper was one of the recent graduates of Milkwood House; he hadn't been back to visit since his eighteenth birthday a few months ago.

"Yeah. He's helping build houses, and he even bought a truck. Says he might swing by…" As Carey continued her update, Tommy found his mind wandering from what she was saying to what she was wearing, and then to whether she might ever be interested in someone like him. Maybe if she found him funny, or charming, or something like that. He wondered suddenly what it would be like to kiss Carey Price, and realized with horror that he was blushing again. Tommy hoped she wouldn't notice. At that moment, as he concentrated on his toast and tried to ignore the burning in his cheeks, it felt like *charming* might be beyond him. He'd even settle for mildly endearing, but still doubted it would be enough; Carey had boys falling over themselves to be near her at Mortlake High School. He'd seen them in between classes, sidling up to her in the hope of a conversation. All the seniors did it, except for one—Richie Sharpe. His dark hair was much thicker and curlier now, and in a strange way his features had changed to suit his eyes, which were still a deep blue but no longer looked too old for his face. He was broad across the shoulders, and tall, and girls were drawn to him as if he were a magnet. But Richie ignored the attention, choosing instead to spend most of his time in the library. At the Dairy, he barely left his room. Richie was clever—brilliant even—and seemed more at home among his books than with other kids. Tommy didn't mind; Richie had always made him uncomfortable.

But even without Richie as a contender, Tommy didn't rate his chances with Carey. Not yet, at least. He was tall himself, the result of a growth spurt, but was all out of proportion. It was a difficult stage; six months earlier he'd been a boy, and six months from now he'd be a man, but in the meantime, he was stuck in the middle, right where he didn't want to be.

Tommy knew it didn't really matter, though; there was no

point entertaining dreams of Carey Price, especially the ones that made his cheeks go red. For a start, the odds were stacked against someone like him—he was too young, too awkward. And even though his favorite books from the shelves in the common room were full of heroes beating the odds to rescue the girl—defeating dragons and bullies and all kinds of things—Tommy knew there was an obstacle he couldn't overcome: the extraordinary fact that everything in his life had an expiration date. The realization settled bitterly in his stomach, right there in the dining room alongside the very beautiful, very sweet Carey.

Come January 5, she'd have no idea who he was.

Carey tugged at the hem of her skirt as the bell rang, and wished for the hundredth time that day that it was just a little longer. An inch or two would do. A pair of pants would be better.

"Hey, Carey," said a voice behind her in the corridor, and she spun around. Students streamed by on either side.

"Oh. Hi, Cam," she said. Cameron Black was a nice kid. They had geography together, and maybe he was in her economics class too? She couldn't remember. Everything had just been so…confusing lately.

"How was your weekend?" Cam asked as he fell into step beside her. It was Wednesday, well past the point where you asked about the weekend.

Carey's heart sank. She'd heard this kind of small talk before. It was the prelude to another question, one that Carey didn't want him to ask.

"It was okay, thanks," she replied, trying to make her voice light and airy. *Keep it friendly*, she told herself. "How about yours?"

"What? Yeah, it was good. Hey, uh, Carey?" *Uh oh. Here it comes.* "Do you wanna eat lunch with me? Like, today?"

She was walking quickly now, just wanting to get into the classroom, where nobody was allowed to talk unless Mr. McGregor asked a question. Not that it stopped Rose and Amanda and Steph. Suddenly she slowed down. Better out here with Cam than in there with them. At least Cam was friendly. And he'd never moo at her.

"Um…" She hesitated, and Cam's eyes widened. He had a shiny forehead and his chin was covered in coarse, patchy hair that he was desperately trying to shape into a goatee. "Sorry, Cam, I can't today. Maybe another time, though. Come on, we'll be late."

Carey Price had no intention of eating lunch with Cameron Black or with any of the boys at Mortlake High. *Eating lunch* was exactly what it sounded like—sitting together while eating the sandwiches they'd brought from home. But at Mortlake High, it was the equivalent of hanging a gigantic neon sign above their heads declaring they were now going out. And Carey didn't want to go out with any of the boys. The other girls hated her enough already. She just wanted to go home, back to the Dairy, where people left her alone.

Out of all the boys, though, Cameron was probably the nicest, and if things had been different, maybe she could've gone out with him. *If things had been different*, she thought again, and her lips twitched anxiously. What things, exactly? If her mum—the strongest, most amazing, most beautiful woman who'd ever lived—hadn't died? People weren't supposed to *die* from the flu. Carey had said that to the doctor in the hospital and he'd *shrugged.* Shrugged! What the fuck? She'd wanted to slap him, punch his stupidly white teeth, but then her stepdad had put his arm around her and led her away, and then she cried for a week.

If things had been different. Maybe if her stepdad hadn't turned...well, weird after that. Right when she needed him, yeah? He was grieving too, obviously—the school counselor explained that to her, and she understood it, she wasn't an idiot. But he'd started to look at her strangely. He never touched her, of course. The change was all in his eyes. He'd looked at her like...like he hated her. Like he'd won second prize in a raffle having missed out on first prize—she'd died of the flu. And second prize was a girl who wasn't *his,* who reminded him of what he'd lost—a girl he was now kinda *stuck with.*

That look. It was like she disgusted him.

She hated the feeling of his eyes crawling over her when she walked into the living room, staring at her legs with...was that revulsion? He could go fuck himself. She started wearing pants and a cardigan and did it with great satisfaction, even when it was hot. Nothing to see here, fuckhead.

She still cried at night, though.

If things had been different. The one thing she wouldn't change would be the way he died, wedged under a forklift carrying a pallet of canned dog food at the warehouse. Seemed about right. The local paper did a story about the tragedy of Carey's mum and stepdad dying within a year of each other.

She told the reporter her mum was a saint and her stepdad was a piece of shit. They didn't use the quote.

She still had the newspaper article in her room at the Dairy, where she was one of the few official orphans. Most of the other kids had a parent in jail, or their mum had walked out, or their dad had just never bothered to show up, not even for birthdays or Christmas or anything. But her birth father had died just after she was born, so that was three from three: she was the real deal, a genuine orphan. What a ride.

Oh, and her stepdad's name was Cameron too. Another reason why she couldn't go out with the kid standing with her outside the classroom, staring at her with eyes containing nothing but hope. Hope and hormones.

"Okay," Cam said when she brushed him off. And he ducked into the classroom, where Mr. McGregor was already describing the features of a river delta. Carey followed and took the only seat left, in front of two girls whose eyes narrowed as she sat down.

"Hey, Carey?" one of them whispered softly, so softly that Mr. McGregor didn't even turn around.

Carey ignored the girl, but waited for what was to follow.

A noise so quiet it might have just been a breath. But it wasn't.

"*Mooooo.*"

●

"The worst part was I thought putting it under the bubbler might wash it out. Nope, apparently water doesn't get butter out. Who the fuck knew that? I had to go back to class with this yellowy kinda stain on my shorts. But wait for it—guess what Mrs. Cox said when she saw me?"

"What?" Tommy asked. His sides already hurt from laughing. It was a fairly regular side effect of being friends with Sean Barker.

"She told me it looked like I had an accident. Like I was a fucking baby and I'd pissed myself!" Sean slapped the table in the Dairy's dining room and howled with laughter. Tommy joined in, and even Carey smiled. Farther down the table, Richie Sharpe sat alone, frowning.

At sixteen, Sean was almost the same age as Carey, but had about as much hope as Tommy of being anything more than friends with her. Tommy liked him, and Carey did too. He'd arrived two years earlier, after his grandma died. She'd raised him from a baby (Sean never mentioned his parents, so Tommy never asked), and when her tar-filled lungs eventually gave out during a particularly frosty winter, he'd ended up at the Dairy. Tommy guessed that Sean's grandma had been a good cook, because two years after her passing, Sean was still carrying the evidence of having eaten very well. Add to that a moderate case of adolescent acne, and Tommy understood why Sean complained about not having any luck with the girls at school.

Carey stood up. She was still wearing the loose gray cardigan she'd had on that morning, and Tommy noticed she hadn't finished her dinner.

"I'd better get going," she said. "I've still gotta write a whole essay tonight."

"Bye, Carey," Tommy said, and Sean gave her an exaggerated salute.

"*Bye, Carey,*" Sean repeated in a falsetto voice when she'd gone, and Tommy punched him softly on the arm. "Jesus Christ, Tommy. Why don't you just ask her to marry you?" Tommy punched him again, slightly harder.

"It's not like that!" he insisted. His crimson cheeks suggested that it was.

Tommy wasn't far behind Carey in returning to his room; he had homework to do too. But he didn't mind sitting at his small wooden desk, textbooks open in front of him. He enjoyed math—there was something about it that made him feel calm. It all just made sense. And reading for school was hardly a chore given how much he loved books. He was, in fact, the perfect composite of his parents, who were blissfully unaware that their once-loved, now-forgotten son was only about sixty miles away in a foster home. Besides, Leo and Elise had two kids and lived in a very nice house (half of a duplex, actually, with a shared pool). Leo was now a senior auditor and Elise was tutoring at the university four days a week. Yes, the Palmers were sticking to Leo's Plan and had a very nice life indeed, and couldn't be blamed for Tommy's absence from it. It wasn't their fault.

Elsewhere in Milkwood House was a similar desk, also with study notes spread across it, but the air in this bedroom was thick with worry. A dull ache had started over Carey's right eyebrow. It was a hot night, just as it had been a hot day, and she'd sweated in the cardigan. It now lay discarded by the door, and she stared without focus at the blank pages before her. The essay she had to write was still unwritten. Instead, the breathy little noise the girls had made in class replayed itself again and again and again in her head.

The Dairy, she thought. *Why does it have to be called the Dairy?*

Carey Price was smart. She knew she was smart. But right now she felt like her dreams of college and law and a job that paid *real money* and would have made her mum proud were so far away. Impossibly distant and shrinking by the second, as though she were watching them pull away from her on a highway. Watching helplessly, stuck in a car spinning its tires, complete with a back seat full of sniggering, whispering girls who'd decided they hated her the moment she'd set foot on the school grounds.

Carey turned off her light and climbed into bed, pages still blank and that whispered lowing still echoing in her ears.

In his own room downstairs, Tommy was deep in a novel, squeezing in a few more pages before bed. The thought of Carey popped into his head every now and then, but he was oblivious to her anguish. He'd seen the gray cardigan that was too warm for a sunny spring day, and the plateful of food that had been poked at but not eaten. But she wore that cardigan every day, and maybe she just wasn't hungry. Why would it mean anything more to a fourteen-year-old boy?

Tommy was still a few months away from the clean slate he'd come to think of as his Reset (always with a capital R). But his life was about to change—and the impact would last well beyond his fifteenth birthday.

5

Tommy had known for a long time there was something different about him. It was pretty obvious, really—even when he was five or six. Those looks the other kids gave him when he insisted they were friends, well, they stung. Late one night, two days after his eighth birthday, he'd asked Miss Michelle about it. She'd been lost in her thoughts as she stared at a cup of tea, alone in the dining room, and jumped when Tommy appeared at her side. (She loved kids, but she would never get used to their ability to sneak up on adults.) Something was eating away at the new boy, so she put an arm around him and waited for him to speak.

"Why don't they remember me?" Tommy asked in a small voice.

"Who, sweetheart?" Michelle replied.

"The others," he said and burst into tears.

Michelle squeezed him tight, her heart breaking for him. His body shook as he allowed himself to be held, standing barefoot in an old, faded pair of summer pajamas. She hoped she was wrong, but Michelle was seeing a sea of red flags—neglect, abuse, mistreatment—that helped paint a picture of where Tommy had come from just two days earlier. (She *was* wrong—Tommy had never been abused or neglected or mistreated, and he hadn't arrived two days earlier, but how could she know that?)

Miss Michelle couldn't answer any of Tommy's tear-filled questions that night, but he felt better just being with her and letting it all out. He had so many questions—big ones—though even at eight he could see he wasn't going to get any answers at Milkwood House.

Those big questions returned to Tommy many times during his childhood at the Dairy, but he had a couple of things in his favor. He had no walls up, something the other children could sense, and so it didn't take long after each Reset for him to be accepted back into the fold. He also (perhaps a little uncommonly) enjoyed the challenges of his schoolwork, which meant he spent more time thinking about math and writing and geography and less time wallowing in the peculiarities of his own situation. And when he was fourteen, the year that everything changed, he had other important things on his mind too. Like Carey.

As the end of the year drew closer, Tommy finally started to worry about her.

Carey was twisting her hair around her fingers as she stood

at a bookshelf in the common room. She didn't know what she was looking for; she just couldn't look at her textbooks anymore. The dull pounding in her head hadn't eased for six weeks straight. Another second of those textbooks, those practice exams, the endless essays, and she might just go mad.

It was the greasy, knotted hair that did it for Tommy.

"Carey?" he began hesitantly. He'd looked up at her the second she'd walked into the common room. They were alone, which didn't seem to happen much anymore; Carey rarely ventured out of her room. "Are…are you okay?"

She nodded. "Yeah, I'm fine, Tommy." She forced a smile onto her face. It looked a little ghoulish against the gray tinge of her complexion.

"Are you sure?" Tommy hated how young he sounded. Like a kid seeking reassurance from a grown-up. Of course Carey was going to say she was fine. Grown-ups never bothered kids with their problems.

But to his surprise Carey flopped down on the couch next to him, the air escaping from her lungs with an audible huff. She was wearing her pajamas already: long sleeves, long pants. Tommy took in the limp hair and black smudges under her eyes and realized with a start that he couldn't remember the last time he'd seen her *laugh*.

She groaned. "I just want it to be over."

"Want what to be over?" asked Tommy. He'd only just noticed that Carey looked different; he was still playing catch-up on the cause.

"Everything! The exams, this whole year. School. All of it. This time next year, I'll be gone. Maybe I'll be studying law."

Unlikely, she thought. "Maybe I'll be in Paris or New York or, I dunno, Budapest or somewhere. Other side of the world. Somewhere a long way away."

She stared at a fleck of peeling paint on the wall as if peering through it, over the horizon, seeking out that place. A place far from school and those stupid, stupid girls. Far from her old house, forever tarnished in her memory by the cruelty of a man who was supposed to care for her. Then she started to cry silently, quivering.

Tommy looked at her in horror. Frozen. Then he did what Miss Michelle had done to him. He put an arm around her.

After a minute or two, Carey dried her eyes with the back of her hand and stood up abruptly. "Tommy, please don't tell anyone. Promise? I'm just stressed, that's all. It's the exams, they're doing my head in."

Tommy nodded, still dumbfounded. *He'd just sat on the couch with his arm around Carey Price.*

"Thanks, Tommy." She sighed, the kind of big rattly sigh that comes after a cry. Then she looked straight at him. "You're a good friend." She bent down and hugged him, and then she was gone. Back to her room and the books and the preparation for exams that were only a week away and getting so, so close.

Tommy replayed their conversation in his mind, the book in his lap forgotten. He wanted to tell Sean that Carey had hugged him, that he'd spent a couple of minutes with his arm around her. He wanted to tell Miss Michelle that Carey wasn't okay, that she was struggling and the pressure was making that honey-colored hair all stringy and turning her smooth, even skin sallow.

But he'd promised Carey he wouldn't tell.

It was a promise he should have broken.

Carey Price went missing two days before her first exam. It wasn't really missing in the conventional sense. She didn't pack a bag, leave a note, hitch a ride somewhere or get lost in the thick scrub that bordered the Dairy on three sides. She just wasn't where she was supposed to be—and Tommy was the only one who noticed.

Where she was supposed to be was on the train after school, heading from Mortlake to Upper Reach, then onto the bus back to the Dairy. Tommy and Sean usually sat together, but Carey always found a seat nearby, using the time for extra studying but within the safe orbit of her friends.

Her usual seat was empty.

"Carey's not here," Tommy observed.

Sean shrugged. "She's stressed, mate. Give her some space. She's probably sitting with friends from school."

But Tommy shook his head. He and Sean *were* her friends. She didn't have anyone else. Something was wrong.

"I'm gonna look for her," he declared.

Sean grinned. "Mate, she's probably with another guy. What's-his-name—Jay or something. Pretty sure he catches the train too. But suit yourself."

Tommy took off, racing through the carriages, the knot of anxiety in his guts doubling in size with every step. Some instinct told him Carey wasn't just traveling back to Upper Reach with the latest bloke to have a crush on her.

He reached the last carriage on the train.

No Carey.

Tommy turned to the nearest person for help, and nearly turned away again. It was Richie Sharpe. He decided to ask him anyway; it was for Carey.

"Richie," he said, "have you seen Carey?"

Richie stared back at Tommy, unblinking. He shrugged. The expression on his face was one of almost feline disinterest.

Two seats behind Richie was another Dairy resident: Nicole Pratt, a thirteen-year-old with thick mousy brown hair and a voice that was always a few decibels too loud. Tommy addressed her instead. "Nicole, I can't find Carey. Have you seen her?"

"Nah," replied Nicole, at a volume she considered acceptable for a train carriage. It was still too loud. "Not since lunch. I saw her talking to some girls. Why you wanna know?" Nicole raised an eyebrow suggestively.

Tommy ignored her, desperately trying to figure out where Carey could be. Maybe she'd left school early and made her way home; it was the only answer that made sense.

At last the train pulled in to Upper Reach, and the Dairy kids transferred onto the bus. Still no Carey, and as the old bus roared its way out of town, dropping other kids along the way, Tommy could almost feel time slowing. He needed to get home. He needed to check Carey's room and make sure she was okay. He needed to tell Miss Michelle. She'd know what to do.

When the bus pulled up in front of the metal sign that said *Milkwood House*, Tommy was already at the door like a sprinter waiting for the starter's pistol. His feet barely made a sound as he flew up the gravel driveway, the others watching with amusement from far behind. Tommy only slowed as he approached the front steps to the house.

Then he stopped.

Something was different, something he'd barely noticed in his mad dash up the drive—but now it pulled him up like a billboard screaming at him to stop and look.

Off to the side of the big old house, partway around the back, was a set of sheds—one large and open, for parking machinery out of the weather, and two more small tin structures with doors closed to the elements. The machinery shed wasn't used anymore (and hadn't been for many years), so the staff parked their cars there instead. In the two smaller sheds were tools for taming the grounds: rakes, shovels, sprays for the weeds—though the only thing that ever saw daylight was the lawn mower, used by an unlucky kid every few weeks, and always under duress.

Every day when Tommy arrived home, the scene was the same. The sheds sat squat and silent, off limits to everyone but the staff on account of snakes and spiders and poisons and sharp tools. It was a rule that everyone respected—they had no reason not to—and, as a result, the sheds were largely ignored.

But today, something had changed. Tommy had almost missed it, but now he backtracked to stare at the structures. The cars were all there—Miss Michelle's dusty white Camry, Mrs. Reilly's hatchback, a little SUV for the newest staffer Miss Ellmore, who didn't seem much older than a few of the senior kids at the Dairy. An old Yamaha motorbike ridden on weekends by Lee the cook rounded out the collection. All present and accounted for.

No, there was something different about one of the other sheds. The door to the larger of the two, normally shut tight, was slightly ajar. And protruding from the darkness within was a tiny fragment of electric blue, bright and unnatural against the muted tones of the yard.

It was the same electric blue as the bag Carey carried her schoolbooks in.

Tommy tore across the brown, crunchy grass and charged through the door, almost tripping over Carey's bag abandoned in the doorway. He blinked, eyes adjusting to the dim light after the glare of the afternoon sun outside. Along one wall of the long, windowless shed ran a workbench, old tools rising from the dust like islands. To Tommy's right was a ride-on lawn mower—mature enough to be classed as vintage—and next to it lay bags of fertilizer, many well past their use-by date. On the walls hung hoses and spools of wire of various lengths and thicknesses, and on a shelf up high was an array of plastic bottles with childproof lids—pesticides and herbicides and the like. But Tommy ignored all of this, because at the far side of the shed, with her back to him, stood Carey.

"Carey!" he blurted out.

Startled, she turned. "Tommy? What are you doing here?" Her voice sounded strained.

"I was looking for you," he replied.

The shed smelled strange, he noticed. There was an unpleasant mix of chemicals, oil, and something else.

"It's lucky I found you," he added. "I was about to tell Miss Michelle to ring the police. How'd you get home?"

She didn't answer.

"Carey?"

"Go inside, Tommy," Carey said. "Please—just go."

Suddenly Tommy realized she was crying. Through the darkness of the shed he could see tears trickling down her cheeks.

"What's wrong?" Again, he winced at how young he sounded. How naive. In that instant he longed to be older.

"Tommy, please," Carey repeated, her voice catching. "You need to go."

"Why?" Tommy asked, confused. He took a step toward Carey and she shifted slightly, as though to hide something on the bench behind her.

"Carey, what's going on?"

She didn't answer, and instead gave a tiny shake of her head, warning him not to come any closer.

The relief Tommy felt when he'd found her drained away. In its place, a sick feeling took up residence in the pit of his stomach, a sense that he was in over his head. He reached for Carey's hand but she pulled back.

"Please, Tommy. Leave me alone."

Her words were whispered but her tone—the sad, almost tired determination in her voice—chilled Tommy, and he knew in a heartbeat that Carey was in danger. Something was wrong; something awful and serious and *oh shit shit shit shit shit.* Tommy lunged forward and grabbed Carey by the wrist, pulling her toward him. She offered little resistance, and he stared in horror at the bench behind her, at what she'd tried to hide.

A dirty cup, the kind used to scoop and measure all manner of things, sat on the workbench next to a hard plastic bottle. The label on the bottle was thick with grime, and Tommy could only just make out the name of the weed killer. But even in the shed's gloom the yellow warning labels were clear, almost as though someone had wiped that part clean. Just to be sure.

The bottle's lid was missing.

"I can't do it. The exams. And the…fuck, I hate them so much." Carey stared past Tommy at nothing in particular. The shed was silent, but before Tommy had burst through the door, the thick, dusty air had been filled with the specter of a dozen stupid girls, moos echoing off the tin walls and bouncing back and forth, up and down, 'til it felt like there were hundreds, thousands of fat, panicking cows crammed into a space far too small to hold them all. Carey pulled at her skirt again without thinking. All she could hear was the mooing. All she could *feel* was a dead man's gaze fixed on her thighs. The disgust.

"Fuck *them*."

Tommy continued to stare at the bench. The cup was half empty and he could see some of the chemical had spilled, pooling on the dusty timber. The fumes invaded his nostrils, worming down into his mouth. He wanted to vomit.

"Carey?" he asked, hesitating despite the dread that rose within him. "What have you done?"

He wished Miss Michelle were there. She'd know what to say.

Carey ignored him. She was mumbling to herself as she wiped her nose on her sleeve, and her eyes were distant.

"Carey!" he repeated, almost yelling, trying to break through her daze. But his voice cracked, and suddenly he was furious. Angry with himself for being too young, angry with Carey for doing this—whatever *this* was.

"What have you done?" he demanded shrilly.

Carey looked him straight in the eye. The distant look was gone. "I threw up. All of it. I think I got scared."

And Tommy realized what the other smell was, the odor that had mixed with the chemicals and the oil and the stuffiness of the closed-up shed. Vomit. He looked down; Carey's shoes were splattered with drops.

"Scared it'll hurt, you know?"

Tommy didn't know.

"I don't want it to hurt. But I've just had enough." There was that tone of weary resignation again.

Tommy swallowed hard. "Can we go inside, please? Miss Michelle will know what to do, or..."

Tommy had started walking backward, not to get away from Carey but to run for help. Or maybe to stand in the doorway and yell as loud as he could so that somebody *older* would come and take Carey out of this shed. Out of this place where she was trying to...Tommy didn't even like to think it. Trying to hurt herself.

Carey was looking at the ground. Mumbling.

"Or I can go and get her," Tommy said, "and you just stay here and wait until I get back, and then..."

He'd reached the open door where the dust floated gently in a shaft of sunlight, settling now after Tommy had charged through. He had one hand already touching the rough tin wall, warmed from the outside by the baking sun.

Then it happened.

Thinking he'd gone, Carey turned back to the workbench and grabbed the plastic cup, filthy from years of hands measuring out herbicides and other poisons; all those hands careful not to spill a drop. Carey raised it to her lips.

The next instant it was cartwheeling through the air. Tommy had covered the ground between them faster than he imagined possible, and taken a wild, desperate swing at the cup. The contents sprayed over them both and the cup bounced on the ground, hitting once, twice, then coming to rest on its side. A trickle of weed killer dribbled out onto the dusty floor, but Carey made no move to save it. Instead they both stood there, covered in the dripping, stinking chemical. Tommy shook as adrenaline surged through him, then Carey's arms were around him and her head was on his shoulder, body heaving with great, racking sobs. Tommy didn't know what to do, so he just held her.

Three years earlier a kid called Nick—who had an encyclopedic knowledge of most vehicles, and specialized in emergency services—had told Tommy something about ambulances. Nick said you could judge the urgency of a medical crisis not just by the speed at which the ambulance transported the patient to the hospital but by the combination of lights and sirens. If the ambulance took off with lights flashing and everything blaring, then you knew the patient was in serious trouble. Nick had shared this gem with Tommy as they watched an ambulance tearing along the road outside the Dairy: high speed, lights, sirens—the full package. "Definitely gonna die," Nick had declared confidently.

Tommy supposed it was a good sign that the ambulance carrying Carey pulled out of the driveway sedately, and never even looked like turning on the lights and siren. *No siren, no rush*, Tommy thought, as he stood on the steps of the Dairy with Sean, a couple of other children, and Mrs. Reilly.

Miss Michelle traveled with Carey to the hospital—she hadn't vomited up everything, it turned out, and the remnants needed some mopping up—and the next morning the pair spoke at length about what had happened in the shed. Carey knew with absolute certainty that Tommy Llewellyn—gangly, awkward, fourteen-year-old Tommy—had saved her life.

Miss Michelle gazed sadly at the emaciated wreck in the hospital bed. Her job was to keep her children safe, and she'd let this poor girl down. She'd seen the skinny wrists and sunken cheeks but assumed it was the pressure of her final-year exams. Exams that the rest of her classmates would now be taking while Carey lay in the hospital.

"What am I supposed to do now?" Carey was saying. It was a familiar refrain; she'd asked the same question several times an hour in the hospital, and twice in the back of the ambulance.

"Maybe you can do your senior year again?" Michelle suggested gently. "You'd probably get credit for—"

Carey was already shaking her head. She wasn't going back to Mortlake High. The next year would be exactly the same; nicknames and cruel words had a way of surviving long after those who'd started them had moved on. She felt the familiar despair wash over her again, and looked out the window to stop herself crying. If she'd been looking at Miss Michelle, she might have noticed a flicker of an idea in the older woman's eyes.

Four days later, Carey Price returned to the Dairy. Tommy was sitting on his bed with a book in his hands, and when Carey knocked on his wide-open door he said "hi" a little too quickly to be cool. He cursed himself, but then Carey sat down on the end of his mattress, and his heart began to beat a little faster. Tommy knew it had only been a few days, but he could have sworn the life had returned to her hair, and her eyes were no longer ringed by the black shadows of insomnia.

She stared at the floor as she spoke. "Thanks, Tommy," she said to the ground. Then she looked up at him. "For what you did."

Tommy searched desperately for something to say that was sensitive, funny, and about three years older than he was. He failed, and had to make do with a nod.

Carey went on. "I've got some news. Good news," she added quickly, as though Tommy might think she was announcing something dire. "Miss Michelle might have found me a job. It's in the city—nothing fancy or anything, but it's a job. If I get it, I'll start after Christmas sometime."

She explained that she'd be working as an office assistant at an insurance company (as long as the interview went okay, obviously), and while it wasn't exactly what she'd wanted to do, she was pretty sure she'd get to see the legal department in action and maybe, just maybe, she'd find a way to get to college. The words came out in a rush, and then she was on her feet again.

Carey kissed Tommy on the cheek, and left the room.

Tommy gazed at her departing figure, gaunt and wasted but

still so lovely, then fell back onto his bed with a broad smile. He was in love.

Maybe it was because Carey had only been at the Dairy for less than a year. If she'd arrived earlier, Tommy would've still been a kid, and she might've become more of an older sister. But by the time Carey was orphaned, Tommy had started shaving, his voice had changed, and when he saw her for the first time, not even his flushed cheeks could make him look away.

Maybe it was something more serious: maybe it was the trauma of what happened in the shed, forging a bond between them (albeit a bond that would soon be one-way).

Or maybe, in the end, it was just because she was *nice*.

Whatever the reason, Tommy Llewellyn was completely, irrevocably, eternally in love with Carey Price. Five weeks later she would forget him, as would everybody else, but he would go on loving her.

Life had plenty of cruelty in store for Tommy. But surely nothing could be crueler than that.

6

The instant he woke it hit him with a force that took his breath away.

It was January 5. The Reset.

The night before he'd lingered in Carey's doorway, listening to her as she chatted excitedly about her new job and her new home. It had been a frequent topic of conversation between them over the past five weeks.

"Miss Michelle says they're lovely. I've never met them, but if she says they're lovely then I'm sure they are. But Christ, Tommy, I'm a bit nervous about starting work. What am I supposed to wear?"

Tommy had just been enjoying the sound of her voice, happy and optimistic; he hadn't been expecting her to ask a question that required an answer.

"Uh…" He frowned. "Maybe a…a skirt and…"

Carey laughed. "I'm kidding! I'll figure it out. Hey, are you gonna come visit me? You could catch the train down; I'm sure Miss Michelle wouldn't mind."

Maybe she would have been okay with it, if she remembered who he was beyond that night. And that was why Tommy was lingering in Carey's doorway. He was trying to remember exactly how it sounded when she spoke to him as a friend. When she looked at him as someone she knew, someone she trusted, someone with whom she'd gone through a *thing* that neither of them discussed.

He wanted to remember it all, because in just a few hours the slate would be wiped clean. The next time Carey spoke to Tommy it would be as a stranger, and he just didn't know if he could take it.

Tommy lay in bed, unwilling to open his eyes. To do so would mean it was real, that it had happened again. He wanted to hold on to hope for as long as he could, like trying to keep alive the dying memory of a happy dream.

At last he rose and opened his cupboard to get dressed. Empty, as it was every year. His books were gone, and his schoolbag was missing. All he had were the pajamas he was wearing. As always.

It meant, of course, that Carey would have forgotten him.

Frustrated, he wrenched open the door and charged straight into Miss Michelle. She stepped back, startled.

"Who are you?" Her voice was soft but edged with suspicion. "That room's empty."

"I...I'm sorry. I didn't mean to scare you," Tommy said. This wasn't how it usually went. He was usually calmer. More ready. "My name's Tommy Llewellyn. I was dropped off overnight," (now it was coming back to him) "and Child Services said to let myself in, that they'd sort it all out today." (Back on script, word-perfect.)

Michelle stared at him skeptically, not quite knowing what to make of this strange skinny boy with sandy-colored hair, still disheveled from sleep.

"Right," she said. "I'll need to make some calls." She seemed to hesitate, and Tommy thought he saw her repeat his name to herself. *Llewellyn.* She shook her head. "Why don't you go through there, into the dining room and have some breakfast, and I'll be in shortly."

Tommy nodded. He knew how this would play out now. Miss Michelle was about to get entangled in a web of phone calls and government departments and unanswered messages.

Tommy went into the dining room, ready to reintroduce himself, but at the same time hoping that Carey wouldn't be there. He wasn't prepared for that encounter, not yet—because he so desperately wanted it to be different. After everything they'd shared that afternoon in the shed, the air thick with fumes, mightn't there be a chance that she would remember him? Tommy was still clinging to that glimmer of hope like a drowning man to a life raft, but the glimmer wasn't real.

Sean, another boy named Phil, and one of the newer kids—Chelsea, who was eleven or twelve—were in the dining room, and Tommy stuck out his hand.

"Hi, guys. I'm Tommy."

Sean was the first to respond. "Good to meet you, Tommy. This is Phil and Chelsea. They're not important, but I'm kind of a big deal around here."

"Yeah, you got the big part right," interjected Phil, slapping Sean's stomach with the back of his hand.

"Fuck off, Phil," said Sean, laughing. "Anyway, Tommy, I'm here to help. If you want tips on chicks or who to avoid or anything like that, I'm your guy."

Tommy smiled. He'd been through this process twice already with Sean, and each time could see why it was so easy to strike up a friendship. Tommy sat down with them and poured himself a bowl of cereal while Sean filled him in on everybody else in the house. Tommy knew it all already, but he let Sean go on.

"The first thing you'll notice about Nicole is her voice. It's also the last thing you'll notice, 'cos it drills right through your fucking ear and into your brain, and then you're dead." They all laughed at Sean's description; it was alarmingly accurate.

"Then there's Carey," Sean continued. "She's just about to turn eighteen. Stunner, but she's taken."

Tommy dropped his spoon midway to his mouth. Cereal and milk splashed down his pajama shirt, and Sean looked at him quizzically.

"Sorry," Tommy spluttered. "My hand slipped."

"Careful, sunshine," said Sean. "Don't want to mess up your best PJs. Anyway, just wait 'til you see Carey." He pretended to bite down on his knuckle, only stopping when Chelsea kicked him under the table.

"Don't be gross, Sean," she said. "And she doesn't have a boyfriend. It's not allowed."

Sean held up his hands apologetically.

"Yeah, fine. She's not technically taken, I suppose, but everyone knows she's got it pretty bad for someone. Not me, in case you're wondering. Yeah, I'm surprised too. But you won't get much time with her—she's leaving us this afternoon. Got herself a job. She'll be bringing in the big bucks soon."

Tommy had been written out of Carey's life; he'd been expecting that. But he hadn't been expecting somebody else to be written *in*.

He was just finishing his breakfast when Miss Michelle came looking for him. She'd been on the phone to Child Services, and they didn't have any information about who dropped Tommy off overnight, so she'd left messages at all the regional offices. (So far, Tommy thought, they were sticking to the script without the slightest variation.) In the meantime, he was welcome to stay on—she wouldn't turn him away when he had no other home to go to.

Tommy murmured his thanks.

"And Tommy," Miss Michelle called after him as he left the dining room, "I've put some clothes and a few bits and pieces in your room. There're some books there too. You might as well think of this as your home—until we know where your real home is, at least."

And that was why he'd loved Miss Michelle after every single Reset.

Tommy didn't technically meet Carey until two minutes before she left the Dairy, and it was every bit as painful as he'd expected it to be. All the residents gathered at the front steps to see her off, forming a semicircle next to Miss Michelle's car. (The old white Camry was Carey's ride to the station, from where she'd take the 2:20 p.m. express into the city.) Carey made her way around the group, giving the younger boys high fives, while Nicole, Sean, and even Lee the cook received a hug. When it was Tommy's turn, Carey hesitated, then extended a hand.

As he took it—the same hand that had trembled while holding a plastic cup of glyphosate—Tommy looked into her eyes, searching for some flicker of recognition. Instead, he saw a sweet, kind, beautiful girl who had no idea who he was, and he wanted to cry.

"Hi and bye, I suppose!" she said cheerfully. "I'm Carey. I think you'll like it here."

"Thanks. I'm Tommy," he said softly, but she was gone, moving on to the next kid.

Sean whispered loudly in Tommy's ear, "Hey, mate, see what I mean? Stunner." He winked at Tommy, who just looked back at him, dazed.

At last Carey made it around to the final person in the group. Richie Sharpe squinted in the afternoon sun, looking like he'd rather be somewhere else. Tommy felt Sean's elbow in his ribs, then heard the whisper again. "Check this one out. Awkward they're doing it in front of everyone, hey?"

Tommy was confused. He watched as Carey hugged Richie tight; Richie barely seemed to reciprocate. But then, as Carey pulled back, she turned and gently kissed Richie's cheek, exactly as she'd done to Tommy on his bed, back when she remembered him. The kiss lingered, just a second or so, but enough to make the point.

Now it was Tommy who did the whispering. "What's that about?" he asked Sean, trying to sound nonchalant.

"That's Richie. Doesn't come out of his room much, but Carey's had the hots for him for a while now. Something happened in the shed out the back a few weeks ago, I don't know exactly what. Heard she tried to top herself. She was in the hospital for a few days, but when she got back all she talked about was Richie and how he'd saved her life." Sean shook his head. "Richie's a weird one. All the girls at school love him, but he couldn't give a fuck. Carey's wasting her time with him if you ask me. She needs someone who knows what he's doing. Give my left nut to swap places with him. Wouldn't you?" He grinned, but Tommy didn't see it. He'd stopped listening when Sean had mentioned the shed.

At the same time that Carey climbed into the passenger seat of the Camry, waving out the window like she was on a royal tour, Tommy climbed the steps back into the old house. He went to his bedroom, closed the door, slumped on the bed, and cried. Not just because Carey had forgotten him, or because she loved somebody else, or because that somebody else was Richie—who couldn't have cared less about what happened to Carey the day she tried to hurt herself. He was crying because it was just…unfair. It was worse than that, but he couldn't put it into words. That was *his* life, *his* relationship, *his* experiences— and he'd never get to claim them, good or bad.

When Michelle Chaplin got back from the station, she went in search of her new arrival. She didn't have much to tell him— just that a couple of the regional offices had returned her calls, and no, they hadn't heard of Tommy Llewellyn, and no, they hadn't dropped anybody off unannounced, but yeah, sometimes it happened and hey, at least he had a roof over his head, right? In the meantime, she had a few questions, but when she saw him sitting with his head in his hands, the timing didn't seem right for an interrogation. Instead, she sat by his side and put an arm around him. He didn't even flinch.

Miss Michelle, who was now in her midfifties but clung to her forties with the help of L'Oréal hair color, had seen a lot of things in her time at Milkwood House. Add in her years in the public school system, and not much surprised her anymore. (She'd once seen a girl stab her own friend in the cheek with a colored pencil in the middle of a busy classroom. She couldn't remember what the fight was over, but could remember that the colored pencil was baby blue. Strange.) She supposed this boy was like so many others she'd dealt with; brittle and at risk of snapping clean in two, almost without warning. Yes, the questions could wait. For now, this boy just needed a hug.

They sat together for almost half an hour, not saying a word. Then, all of a sudden, Tommy stood.

"I'm sorry," he said. "It's just…a lot has happened in the last little while. I think it kinda caught up with me."

"That's all right," Miss Michelle replied, her voice soft. "Tommy, there are a few things we need to talk about, but you look exhausted. Why don't you have a nap, and we can talk later."

Tommy nodded meekly as she left the room. But he didn't lie down. Instead, he stood at the window and stared out at the driveway, at the place he had last seen Carey before she drove off to start a new life. A life where her only memory of Tommy Llewellyn was of a strange, lanky teen who'd met her for the first time just as she was leaving the Dairy forever. And even that memory would disappear in the next Reset.

A mass of rage and self-pity started to tumble and swirl inside his head.

He knew there was something different about him, something uniquely…wrong. Normal kids don't wake up each year as a stranger in their own lives, their entire existence wiped clean from the planet, the same way he arrived at class each morning to find the previous day's lessons scrubbed from the chalkboard. But it wasn't entirely like that, he thought—at least the students remembered what had been on the chalkboard the day before. When he went through the Reset, it was as though he'd never existed and the holes that he'd left in others' lives were either wallpapered over or neatly filled in by other people.

Of course it'd be Richie who filled the gap, he thought resentfully. *Use the loner with no friends. No strings attached, fewer loose ends.*

Tommy collapsed onto his bed, and the last thing he saw before he closed his eyes was the blank wall of his room—the same room he'd occupied since he was one year old. It was as bare and sterile as the day he'd arrived.

7

If somebody—perhaps looking down from above, because nobody on earth could do it—was to compare fourteen-year-old Tommy Llewellyn with the new fifteen-year-old version, they would have noticed a few differences. It was more than just the physical changes, like his skinny frame filling out (at last). No, there was something else. The earnest boy seemed a little bit less earnest. The boy who'd always done his homework on time now didn't bother to do it at all. He just didn't seem to care.

Tommy started the new school year as a different person. His shoulders were slumped and there was a listlessness to him that, had anyone remembered him from the previous year, would have seen him called before the principal to find out what had changed. Drugs? Unlikely; he was a Milkwood kid, and they were kept on a tight leash. Girls? Possibly. Or maybe it was just the last hurrah of puberty, rendering him irritable and moody. But nobody noticed, so nobody asked, and Tommy started to drift.

The one bright spot for Tommy was the departure of Richie Sharpe. Richie wasn't quite eighteen (his birthday had always been observed in mid-February—Richie didn't do celebrations), but he'd moved out early, and without warning. In fact, Tommy didn't even realize he'd left until a fortnight afterward. Curious, he asked Nicole (with the drill-like voice) if she knew where he'd gone. Nicole's bedroom had been next to Richie's, so she was the closest thing the Dairy had to an expert on him.

"He's gone to college 'cos he's a massive nerd," explained Nicole helpfully. "Not that he said anything to me about it. I lived next to him for, I dunno, eight years or something, and I reckon he said a total of ten words to me. Some of the girls at school thought he was hot." She pulled a face that left Tommy in no doubt of her own opinion.

All of this had been projected at Nicole's regular volume, but then suddenly—and unusually—she lowered her voice. She beckoned Tommy to lean in closer.

"I heard he left in a huff. Cracked it with Miss Michelle because she wouldn't let him come back to stay next Christmas or anything."

Tommy smiled, a little too indulgently.

"No, I'm serious," Nicole insisted. "I heard it myself. He was so shitty. Said he just wanted somewhere quiet to study, but I reckon he's in love with her. What a creep." She let out a short cackle, and Tommy smirked. If Nicole was right (a fifty-fifty chance at best), then Richie would have been crushed by the rejection. No wonder he left in a hurry. *Good*, he thought, which was most unlike the old Tommy. But the old Tommy had lost Carey in the Reset, and Richie had stepped in to fill the Tommy-sized gap. Richie might have been an unwitting stand-in, but at least his was a face Tommy could hate.

There were moments when the old Tommy made an appearance. One morning in the middle of the year, an English teacher named Julie Lewis walked into the staff room at Mortlake High before the school bell rang, carrying four sheets of paper. The story had been the last thing she'd read before she switched out the light the night before, and then she'd stared at the ceiling for a good hour or two. She put the typed pages down in front of another teacher.

"Larry, read this one for me, please. Tell me what you think."

Larry did what he was told.

"This is really good. Great, actually. Who wrote it?" he asked, looking for a name on the paper but not finding one.

Julie told him.

"Tommy Llewellyn," Larry repeated, trying to place the name, even though he'd taught Tommy the year before. "Can't picture him. New kid?"

"Yeah," replied Julie. "The kid can write. He's far and away the best I've seen for a while. Probably since...what was her name? Lauren something. Taylor? What's she doing now, d'ya reckon?"

Larry shrugged.

"Still," Julie went on, "he's getting a C."

"Jesus, Julie, that's harsh!" Larry exclaimed. "What's he done?"

"He only handed in the assignment yesterday. It was due three weeks ago."

But after lunch Larry noticed four sheets of photocopied paper pinned to the faculty noticeboard, with a pink Post-it Note saying *READ THIS!!!!* stuck to the front. The pages had half a dozen pinholes—clearly his colleagues had done as the Post-it instructed.

At the same time as the copy of his assignment was being passed around the staff room, Tommy received the original back with a big red C on it and flicked to the last page. In neat red writing, the teacher had printed: *Great idea, wonderful writing, but LATE LATE LATE.* He tossed it to one side. It was just some bullshit story he'd made up about a girl who may have borne some resemblance to Carey. What did it matter if he got a C, or an A, or even an F? It'd all be wiped clean come January 5 anyway.

The change in Tommy's demeanor might not have been noticed at Milkwood House either (since no one knew what his demeanor had been before), but his generally poor academic performance landed him on the radar of Miss Michelle. She was still trying to figure out what to make of the boy who'd arrived so mysteriously in their midst, and she wished—as she did more often than she'd admit—that she could sit down with John Llewellyn, a packet of chocolate biscuits open between them, and together work out what to do with the distant young man who just happened to share John's surname. Instead, she stared alone at Tommy's midyear report card. It would have been a case study in the decline of a model student to compare that report with the one from the year before, but of course when

Michelle Chaplin saw the list of Tommy's marks (English: B−; Math: C; History: C; Physical Education: F), she had no way of knowing just how unlike him they were—and how much he needed her help.

Tommy knocked on Miss Michelle's door, unsure of why he'd been summoned, but not particularly concerned.

"Come in, Tommy."

He saw she had his report card open on the desk. *Ah*, he thought. *That'll do it.* It was the only paper in sight—everything else was in its place, either filed in the cabinets to one side or tidied away into the desk drawers. Michelle pulled one of these drawers open.

"Biscuit?" she offered, showing Tommy the corner of a packet like she was offering him contraband. John Llewellyn might have been dead (and the cookies might have contributed to that), but in some ways he lived on.

Tommy shook his head, and Michelle closed the drawer.

"Tommy, are you all right?" She waited for a response but didn't get one. "You came here, what—five, six months ago now. I barely see you outside your room, you don't hang out with the other kids, you *still* haven't told me where you lived before you arrived at Milkwood. I...I..." She was casting around, looking for the right thing to say. Something that might break through to the quiet, sullen boy sitting opposite her.

She closed the report card and slid it to one side of the desk. "Forget about that. Tommy, what's wrong?"

An almost overwhelming urge bubbled up inside Tommy, and for a moment he wanted to tell her *everything*. That she'd known him last year, and the year before that, and the year before that. He wanted to tell her about Carey, about how he loved her, even though he was just a kid and she was off working somewhere, being an adult and living an adult life. He wanted to tell her that it wasn't Richie who saved Carey. He wanted to ask her *why*. Why did it happen to him? But she hadn't been able to answer that last time; she hadn't even understood the question. So he didn't say anything.

Later, in the dining room, Tommy asked Sean if he'd ever been called into Miss Michelle's office.

The older boy snorted. "Every time I get a report card. And a few other times too." He smiled at the memory. "How many'd you get through?"

Tommy looked at Sean blankly.

"Biscuits. Did she bring out the chocolate ones?"

Tommy nodded.

"The trick is to ask her about career pathways. That'll get her going for a while. The more obscure job you ask about, the longer you have. One time I asked her about being a whale researcher. Got through the whole fuckin' packet."

Now it was Tommy's turn to snort, then Sean started to chuckle, which turned into a loud, honking laugh, and soon they both had tears rolling down their cheeks.

Tommy thought how much he'd miss Sean when the older boy moved out the next year. They'd managed to become friends after each Reset, and Tommy would miss Sean's ability to find the joke in, well, pretty much everything.

Sean, on the other hand, wouldn't remember Tommy at all.

○

Like Michelle, Julie Lewis at Mortlake High was intrigued by Tommy Llewellyn. It was now September, and she'd already given him detention on four separate occasions for a range of offenses: twice for failing to submit homework on time, once for being disruptive in class, and once—the most serious infringement—for truancy. To be fair, Tommy had *intended* to go to his English class, but had found himself catching the train back to Upper Reach instead with a mate called Caleb, a new arrival at the school that year who'd ended up his friend by default, since everyone else was taken.

Most of the other teachers had written Tommy off as a lost cause ("one of the *troubled* kids from Milkwood" was how the principal had put it), but Mrs. Lewis didn't think that was quite right. He could write, and he was no slouch at math, but he was just so unfocused that it made her angry to see his talent wasted. A discussion in the staff room one day turned toward whether he'd benefit from suspension; a two-week break from school so he could learn some discipline, perhaps. Mrs. Lewis had argued loudly against it, pointing to the sheets of paper still pinned to the corkboard. In the end, she'd won, but she hadn't been rewarded by any change in Tommy's behavior. Finally, she asked him to stay back when the bell rang for lunch.

"Tommy," she said, once the rest of the class had cleared, "what's going on with you?"

"Nothing, Mrs. Lewis," Tommy replied. "I'm fine."

"Bullshit," the teacher said, and Tommy recoiled. *Good*, she thought. *Gotcha*. "You're better than this. I've seen what you've written, I know what you can do. So why won't you do it?"

"I just…I just can't be bothered, Miss," Tommy replied. It was the truth, and they both knew it.

"Well, Tommy, let me give you one piece of advice." Mrs. Lewis's voice was tight with frustration. "The decisions you make today can affect the rest of your life. If you choose to make no effort and coast through just because you *can't be bothered*, well, that's up to you. But I think it's stupid. You're capable of more, Tommy. Don't waste it. You…well, you don't get a lot of second chances in life."

You're wrong, he thought. *All I ever get is second chances.*

After the lecture from Mrs. Lewis, Tommy found Caleb outside the library eating a peanut butter sandwich. Caleb had brought the same thing for lunch every day since they'd met— he'd once confessed it was because he had to make his own sandwich each morning, and he was just too lazy to change it up. Caleb wasn't exactly what Mrs. Lewis would have called a good influence, but he wasn't the opposite either—he was actually quite happy to let his friend call the shots and had followed willingly when they'd ditched their class a few weeks earlier. As long as his dad didn't catch him, of course—his papa was a little old-fashioned, right down to the big-buckled leather belt he used for discipline if he thought the crime warranted it. Caleb wanted to remind his dad that it wasn't the fifties anymore, but he wasn't that dumb. He said it in his head instead while he gritted his teeth.

"What was that about?" Caleb asked as Tommy sat down next to him and opened his own lunch, a sandwich produced by Lee that morning.

"The usual," Tommy replied. "Thinks I'm slacking off."

"And are you?"

"Yeah, probably." Tommy laughed. "I can't cut class again for a bit. She reckons the school wanted to suspend me last time, and if we ditch again I'll be home for two weeks."

Tommy wasn't going to admit it to Caleb—or to anyone else—but he was secretly happy to comply with Mortlake High's ultimatum. Somewhere deep inside, the old Tommy was lying dormant. And if he'd been sent home for a fortnight, the disappointment on Miss Michelle's face might well have crushed what was left of him.

But by the time the new year rolled around, the change in Tommy's attitude was pretty much cemented in place. The aimlessness was now accompanied by a solid bitter streak. For weeks he'd been dwelling on the questions of *why me* and *how*— questions that seemed to get bigger and darker the longer he spent in his room on his own.

He was lying on his bed, looking at a book but not really reading it, when a kernel of an idea took hold. The Tommy Llewellyn of twelve months earlier would never have thought of it. But the Tommy Llewellyn who had the shits with the world did. If his slate was wiped clean on January 5, then who cared what he did on January 4—or January 3, for that matter? A giddy thrill raced through him as he realized what that meant.

A knock broke the silence.

"Come on, mate." It was Sean. "We're going out."

Tommy sat up.

"What do you mean, going out? I'm not going outside—it's

too hot." And it was—the afternoon sun was beating down, and not even the giant old tree in the middle of the front lawn offered any relief.

"Nah, mate, not here. We're going to the pool." There was a public pool in Upper Reach. "Grab your swimmers."

Tommy slid off the bed and rummaged through his drawer. He didn't actually own any swimwear, but a pair of pre-loved shorts would do. *I'm what, the fifth kid to wear these? Sixth? Aleks, Maxy, Phil. Who else?* Tommy continued the roll call as he pulled the shorts on and joined Sean in the corridor.

"Where'd you get the money for the pool?"

Sean didn't answer Tommy but winked at him instead. Tommy guessed he'd either pinched it or won it in a bet; either way, he knew to leave it alone.

The pair walked outside.

"Anyone else coming?" Tommy asked.

Sean shook his head. "Nah. Only got five bucks—that's just enough to cover you and me."

Tommy set off down the driveway, already feeling the sun bouncing off his neck, and he wondered if the visit to the pool was worth the hike into town in this heat. He turned to ask Sean, but his friend was no longer beside him.

Sean was still standing at the foot of the stairs from the house, dangling something in one hand. It was a set of car keys for a dusty white Toyota Camry parked in the machinery shed at the side of the old house.

Tommy climbed into the passenger seat; Sean settled in behind the steering wheel. There was still a bit of a stomach there, and the seat took some adjustments before Sean declared himself comfortable and ready to drive. He backed out, and the Camry crept down the gravel driveway.

"How on earth did you convince Miss Michelle to lend you her car?" Tommy asked.

"Ah, well," Sean replied. "I reckon if I asked her, she would've been okay with it. The important thing is she doesn't need it right now, and we'll be back before she notices it's gone."

"You're stealing her car?"

"Come on, Tommy. Don't be like that, mate. It's hot, and we need to cool down. Besides, I did a bit of recon, and everyone's having a lie-down. It'll be fine."

They drove in silence for a minute, and it occurred to Tommy that Sean didn't have a license. Nobody had driving lessons at the Dairy.

Christ, he thought. *We're stealing a car. And Sean's never driven one before.*

"Sean?"

"Yeah, mate?"

"Are you up to something?" He looked at Sean, who stared straight out the windshield at the road in front of them.

"I, uh, it's just, well, it's bloody hot," Sean replied. Tommy noticed his cheeks—which were now entirely clear of acne, but still bore the faint scars—turn slightly pink.

"You're meeting someone, aren't you?" Tommy exclaimed.

"Fine!" Sean said, a grin spreading across his face. "Yeah, I'm meeting someone. Her name's Hannah. Reckon I might get a BJ."

Tommy laughed and shook his head. Sean's expectations and reality were often vastly different.

They parked outside the public pool and paid their money at the small kiosk next to the entry turnstile. Sean scanned the crowd. The pool was full of kids from all around town, jumping, splashing, pushing each other underwater and having a good time. The smell of sunscreen and chlorine hung heavily in the air, and Tommy could see some of the swimmers blinking furiously from the chemicals. Sean continued his search, focusing on the patch of grass that ran from the cement surrounding the pool right out to the perimeter fence. Trees were dotted around the grass, and every inch of available shade was filled with teens in swimwear lying on towels.

"There she is," said Sean, and he turned to Tommy. "Meet me back here. Say two hours, yeah? Wish me luck." He jogged off, his large frame bouncing a little with each step. Tommy watched in disbelief as he approached a pretty girl in a bikini who was propped up on her elbows on a towel. She smiled at Sean, and he flopped down on the grass next to her.

Tommy took off his T-shirt and slipped into the pool. He breathed a sigh of relief as he bobbed in the cool water, wondering what he was supposed to do for the next two hours while Sean tried his best with Hannah. Then somebody surfaced next to him and gave a loud *moo*.

"I didn't think they let you out of the Dairy," Caleb said, and Tommy rolled his eyes. The pair splashed about for a bit, before—inspired by Sean—they climbed out of the pool and approached a group of girls chatting in a tight circle nearby. It was a swift and brutal dismissal.

"Want to get out of here?" Tommy asked Caleb, the sting of rejection smarting.

Caleb shrugged. He wasn't expected home until dark. The pair pushed back through the turnstile and headed up the street. It was late afternoon, and most of the shops had closed for the day. The small supermarket (which was really more of a large convenience store) was still open, but the pharmacy was shut, as was the hardware store, which doubled as the Upper Reach post office (an odd combination but the owners had to make a buck somehow). Apart from the occasional car on its way to pick up kids from the pool, the streets were deserted, and the two boys walked without purpose.

They came to the Royal Hotel, the sole pub in town: a rambling building with dark, narrow windows and a large wraparound veranda. It was to the adults of Upper Reach what the pool was to the kids—the only place to be on a day when the mercury was nudging the upper end of the thermometer, on account of the cold beer on tap and industrial-strength ceiling fans that had just one speed: fast. The veranda itself was propped up by half a dozen drinkers, pickled men who'd been there most of the day and had a line of empty glasses as proof. They ignored Tommy and Caleb as the boys walked past.

"Ever been in there?" Tommy asked Caleb.

"Nope. You?"

"Nope. Wanna give it a go?"

Caleb didn't want to; his dad and the leather belt flashed through his mind. But Tommy was already walking up the steps.

The men leaning against a high table on the veranda watched them. One of them put down his glass. "Fuck off," he called, and the others laughed. The words came out of one side of his mouth. The old bloke had put away a lot of beer, and talking took more effort than he really had to spare, but he was a bit of a showman. "Fuck off," he drawled again as he picked up his drink. "Ya little cunts."

More laughter, and Tommy blushed.

He retreated down the steps, Caleb close behind, all hopes of seeing the inside of the Royal Hotel dashed. They hurried around the corner, out of sight of the drinkers.

"Yeah, that was a bad call," Caleb said.

Tommy didn't reply.

Attached to this side of the Royal was a drive-through bottle shop, the kind where people too busy to get out of their car could pull into the driveway, order their six-pack of beer, and have it brought to them. Tommy was wondering how many people in Upper Reach were really too busy to get out of their cars when a sudden impulse grabbed him. The attendant for the bottle shop had ducked back into the pub, and Tommy raced up the driveway and into the small alcove where the cash register stood. The shelves there were lined with wine and spirits. Without thinking, Tommy snatched the nearest bottle, then bolted back to where Caleb watched with his mouth hanging open.

"Go!" Tommy hissed, and the pair sprinted along the street, away from the pub and the bottle shop, further away from the pool and the rest of the shops, and around a corner into a lane.

They stopped, almost bent over double as they caught their breath in the dry, baking heat.

"Drink?" asked Tommy, holding up the bottle he'd grabbed.

"What the hell, Tommy?" exclaimed Caleb. "What if my dad finds out?"

"Come on, let's just try it," coaxed Tommy. "I've never done it before either." And that was the truth. Until that afternoon, he'd also never stolen before. Didn't matter—in a couple of days, all his sins would be forgotten.

The boys came to a small playground. Tommy sat on the bottom of the slide, but sprang up when the metal singed his thighs. Instead, he sat in the thin strip of shade under the slide, with Caleb squatting beside him, and together they examined the bottle closely.

"Johnnie Walker Red Label Blended Scotch Whisky," Tommy read aloud. The liquor inside was a syrupy brown. He twisted the lid and the seal gave way with a crack.

Tommy lifted the bottle to his lips and took a swig. If he thought the slide had burned his legs, it was nothing compared to the fire in his throat. Coughing, he held the bottle out to Caleb.

"Your turn," he gasped. "Easy as pie." Recovering, he smiled.

Caleb took the bottle reluctantly and sipped. He started to cough too, before the cough turned into laughter. He handed the bottle back to Tommy. The sun dipped lower, and soon half the bottle was gone as the two boys passed it back and forth, each time coughing less and less until they were drinking like they'd been doing it for years.

"Christ!" Tommy jumped up suddenly. His head cracked painfully into the underside of the metal slide, but he hardly registered it. "I'm supposed to meet Sean." He took off out of the park at full speed, leaving Caleb behind with the bottle. Caleb turned it on its side, watching the rest of the liquor glug into the dry earth.

Tommy sprinted down the lane. His head was spinning and his stomach turned over with every step.

Sean's gonna be so pissed off, he thought. *Hey, I wonder if he got his BJ?*

His mind lurched from one thought to the next.

Christ it's hot.

He could almost hear the whisky sloshing in his stomach.

Hope Miss Michelle can't tell.

Slosh, slosh, slosh.

Better not go near the Royal.

Slosh, slosh, slosh.

Should cross here.

The car hit him right in the center of the road; right where neither of them should have been.

Tommy bounced off the rust-colored station wagon and lay flat on the scorching asphalt.

The driver squinted out the windshield.

"The fuck was that?" he asked out the side of his mouth, then shrugged. This was why he'd called time on the session at the Royal. Starting to imagine things. Hallucidating, or whatever the fuck it was called.

He barely felt the second bump as he drove slowly away, and certainly didn't hear the crack of splintering ribs. Instead, he carefully followed the line in the middle of the road, the line he thought would lead him home.

He'd wake the next morning with a monstrous stinking hangover and the cops at his door, asking about a boy hit by a car. The day after that, both the pickled drunk and the cops would only remember the rust-colored station wagon colliding with a fence post.

8

While Sean Barker considered himself an expert in many things, much of the information he traded in was actually gossip, nearly all of it unsubstantiated. Like the time he reported breathlessly that Paige Ellmore, the youngest of the staffers at the Dairy, was having an affair with the girl who worked at the pharmacy in Upper Reach. He offered no supporting evidence, but declared it with such conviction that the rumor was accepted as fact. It wasn't true (Paige Ellmore was in fact sleeping with the *owner* of the pharmacy, who'd assured her that his marriage was all but over) but Sean had a way of presenting rumor as rolled-gold news.

It stood to reason, then, that Michelle Chaplin wasn't quite sure which parts of Sean's panicked phone call to believe.

"Calm down, Sean," she said patiently. "Where are you?"

A couple of children near her office door fell silent. This sounded interesting.

"At the Royal. They said I could call you. You need to come."

The kids outside her door drew closer as Michelle's normally hushed tones raised a few decibels. "What are you doing at the—"

"Tommy's been hit. By a car. On the road." Sean was breathing quickly; he'd been standing at the pool turnstile, watching, waiting. He was so late and was busted *for sure*. Then Tommy had come barreling around the corner and, well, Sean was pretty sure he'd just seen his mate die.

The rest of the events of that night seemed to pass in a blur for Michelle. First she reached for her car keys, which at that moment were in Sean's pocket as he paced anxiously between the Royal Hotel and Tommy Llewellyn, lying in the dead center of Upper Reach's main street. Then she borrowed Miss Ellmore's car, and drove into town much faster than she'd ever driven before.

The ambulance took almost another hour to arrive; an excruciating fifty-seven minutes in which Michelle sat by Tommy and waited, never taking her eyes off the steady rise and fall of his chest. The paramedics were apologetic but explained there was only one vehicle to service Upper Reach, Mortlake, and two other nearby towns that afternoon, and they'd been stuck at the hospital dropping off an old lady who'd had a heart attack in the heat. "Didn't make it," they told Michelle. It was information she didn't need to know.

Michelle traveled with Tommy in the ambulance to Mortlake Hospital, the nearest with an emergency department. There he was stabilized and his injuries assessed. There were the obvious ones that anybody could see, like the broken nose and bruising to half his body. But then there were the others—eight cracked ribs, a damaged spleen, a perforated eardrum. The registrar explained the spleen would probably require surgery.

"The rest'll heal on their own. The nose might not be straight, but it'll make him look tough, hey."

Michelle didn't smile.

"We'll keep an eye on him tonight, but he'll have to go to a bigger hospital for the operation tomorrow," the registrar continued. "We can't do that kind of thing here."

So that was how Tommy ended up being wheeled into surgery on the afternoon of January 4, the eve of his sixteenth birthday, in the same city where he'd spent the first year of his life. As the crow flies, he was only a dozen or so miles from where his parents were going about their day, completely unaware their son was about to be cut open.

Anesthetic coursed through the veins where Johnnie Walker had been just twenty-four hours earlier. The only benefit of the induced coma he was kept in during the ambulance transfer and then the operation was that he never felt his first hangover. Michelle couldn't go with him—she had to manage the fallout at Milkwood House—but she'd held an unconscious Tommy's hand and promised that she'd drive up to visit him the next day, and would bring Sean, and maybe his friend Caleb from school.

Sadly for Tommy, by 12:01 a.m. Miss Michelle had forgotten her solemn vow.

Nobody from the Dairy was by his bedside when he woke the following morning.

"Who's the kid in bed 14C?" asked one of the nurses on the pediatric ward. "I think he's coming round, but I can't find any of his documentation."

The shift supervisor checked her notes and swore under her breath.

"Christ almighty, how many times have I gone through this? Resuscitate. Medicate. Notate. In that order. Two out of three isn't good enough." But even she had to admit the reams of documentation were a bit overwhelming. "Come on, Amy. Have you checked his wrist tag?"

The nurse went back to the patient's bed and lifted his wrist, turning the tag around to read his name.

"Llewellyn, Thomas. Age fifteen."

The supervisor returned to the nurses' station and flicked through the records, before typing the boy's name into the computer. She wasn't expecting to see anything come up—the computer was only new, and transferring their records onto the system was just one task on a painfully long list—but she was surprised not to find anything in the hard copy notes either. She scribbled a reminder to call the night supervisor later in the day once he woke up.

Tommy blinked and groaned. The nurse, a blond woman in her late twenties, looked down at him. She lowered his hand onto the bed.

"Easy there. Don't move too much." She spoke with a soft Irish lilt.

"Where am I?" Tommy asked. Both eyes were ringed by deep purple bruising, and his nose was stuffed with gauze.

The nurse smiled reassuringly. Disorientation wasn't unusual in post-op patients. "You're in the hospital."

"Where's Sean?" Tommy mumbled.

"I'm sorry—who?"

"Sean. S'posed to meet him."

"I'm sorry, I don't know who that is. But I'm sure you'll have some visitors soon."

Amy didn't actually know that for sure, but kids always had visitors sooner or later. She wasn't to know Tommy wasn't like most kids.

Tommy closed his eyes and lay perfectly still, assessing where the pain was coming from. Everything hurt, from his head (why was his ear ringing?) to his ribs and stomach. Even breathing burned his chest, like he was buried in hot coals. He groaned again. Then a thought: How long had he been out? Without opening his eyes again, he spoke to the nurse, hoping she was still there.

"What day is it?"

"It's Tuesday," came the reply in that accent, gentle and soothing. "Now, just lie still."

"No, I mean the date. What's the date?"

"It's"—Amy paused as she checked her watch—"the fifth of January."

Tommy sunk deeper into his pillow. The Reset must have already happened. But surely the medical staff would know why he was there.

They didn't.

"This is a bit embarrassing—for us, not you—but I can't find your file right at the moment, so I'm not a hundred per cent sure what you've had done. I know it's abdomen—your tummy—and a bit of other stuff too, by the looks of it." Amy gestured to his face, even though he had his eyes closed.

She was expecting the boy to look surprised on learning that his details had gone missing, or perhaps angry. Instead, he just exhaled. Exhausted, probably.

"I'm sorry, Thomas. It'll turn up. And when it does, I'll talk you through your recovery and we'll have you home again in no time."

Tommy's eyes snapped open.

"How'd you know my name?" A monitor beeped as his pulse quickened. He felt groggy, like his mind had been shaken to mush, but the nurse calling him Thomas had sliced straight through. It was January 5, his Reset—and yet she knew who he was. Maybe he'd outgrown his curse. Or something had broken it. He had a vague recollection of a car, and then pain: a squashing, squeezing sensation. Maybe that had done it.

But if there was a way to ensure he was remembered, being flattened by a foul-mouthed old man who'd had fourteen beers wasn't it.

"It's on your wrist tag," said the pretty young nurse. "You got it when you were admitted."

In that moment, the sheer logic of it—the disappointment—nearly crushed Tommy Llewellyn. The wrist tag was on him at the time of his Reset, so it was unaffected, like the pajamas he usually slept in. But everything else—everything back at the Dairy—would be gone.

He would have cried, but he was too tired for tears. Instead, he fell into a deep sleep and dreamed he was being chased by something he couldn't see, something dark and unpleasant and unrelenting. Every time he found somewhere he thought was safe to hide, it caught up with him and he had to run again, searching for somewhere warm and calm and light. He ran and ran and ran, until at last he gave up and it took him. Then his sleep was dreamless.

When Tommy woke again the sun was still streaming through the gaps in the blinds. There were three other beds in his ward, but he'd got lucky and scored the window. He blinked in the bright light and grimaced as he waited for the pain to come rushing at him. His chest still hurt with every breath but he noted with some relief that his ear and nose had settled to a dull ache.

"Good morning, Thomas." The blond nurse stepped out from behind a curtained-off section, where Tommy assumed another patient lay. "How are you feeling?"

He tried to answer, but all that came out was a dry rasping noise.

"You've been asleep for nearly twenty-four hours!" Amy put a straw in a cup of water and held it up to Tommy's mouth. "We increased your morphine while you were out. It should've helped with the pain. Your ribs'll still be sore though."

Tommy felt the water soften the arid desert of his mouth and throat. "Thanks," he whispered. "And it's Tommy, not Thomas."

"Ah, okay," Amy replied. She hesitated, as though she had something else to say but couldn't quite bring herself to do it.

"What is it?" Tommy asked. His voice sounded small.

"You're our mystery man, Tommy Llewellyn. You've got

my supervisor pulling her hair out, because she can't find your admission papers or surgical report anywhere. We had to do new scans, and I had to start a new chart for you." She pointed to a clipboard at the end of his bed. "It'd be funny if it wasn't serious—the night team thought you came in during our shift, when you *obviously* came in during theirs. The worst part is, they think it's our fault—but I'm pretty sure I'd remember if you'd been brought in while I was on!"

Tommy smiled inwardly. *No, you wouldn't*, he thought.

"Anyway," Amy continued, "I reckon you'll be here for another few weeks while everything heals. Then it'll be off home for you. Which is…?"

"Upper Reach," replied Tommy. His voice was starting to come back.

"Upper Reach," Amy repeated. "Never been there. Sounds lovely." She smiled at Tommy. "Is there anything else I can get for you?"

He nodded. There was, but he wasn't quite sure how to put his request. He wanted to know how he could get back to the Dairy, how he could get Miss Michelle to pick him up and take him home to room number three in that creaky old house. But Miss Michelle didn't even know he existed.

"What is it, Tommy?" asked Amy. There were nearly a dozen other patients to look after across three wards, and she had to keep moving. But she had a bit of a soft spot for this boy, and if she could get him some chocolate or some books or something to make his recovery a bit easier, well, she'd see what she could do.

"Nothing," Tommy said, and closed his eyes.

The next morning, Tommy was unpleasantly surprised to find the nurse was now a matronly woman in her fifties, with a stern, pinched face and no sense of fun. She reminded Tommy of Mrs. Reilly. He shuddered at the thought of a world with two Smiley Reillys; one was more than enough. As the older nurse changed the dressing on Tommy's surgical scar, he asked her where Amy was.

She rolled her eyes. Amy was popular with the young male patients. "Day off today," was the abrupt reply. "You're stuck with me."

There was no Amy again the next day, and this time Tommy didn't ask after her. The older nurse—Janette, according to the name badge pinned to her shirt pocket—was in no mood for conversation as she maneuvered Tommy into a sitting position in his bed. Neither was Tommy, for that matter—as his broken ribs pressed together, he tried not to cry out in pain. But sitting up did give him a better vantage point, and he could see the rest of the ward more clearly now. Of the three other beds, one had the curtains drawn, and the other two were occupied by children quite a bit younger than he was. Those kids weren't like him: they had family members sitting by their beds, chatting quietly. Tommy was alone, with only the TV screwed into the ceiling for company.

He was trying to find something to watch early the following morning—he'd almost memorized the TV guide and knew he was in a bit of a dead zone before the good stuff started at 7:00 a.m.—when Amy appeared by his bed.

"Morning, Tommy," she said cheerfully.

Tommy sighed with relief.

"What's that about?" she asked, smiling.

"Two days with Janette," he replied. "She's a bit…rough."

Amy laughed as she checked Tommy's stitches. "You're healing nicely," she said. "I reckon we'll have you back at Upper Reach in no time." She started to walk away, then spun back. "Oh yeah—you've got a visitor." She waved to somebody out in the hall and gave them a thumbs-up.

Tommy's heart soared. A visitor. Miss Michelle!

It wasn't.

"Sorry, I didn't mean to startle you," said the woman who approached his bed. She was in her forties with dark-brown hair gathered in a messy bun. "My name's Sonia. Sonia Williams. I'm a social worker with the hospital. You must be"—she consulted her folder—"Tommy."

Tommy nodded.

"Do you mind if we have a quick chat? There are a couple of questions I need to ask you. Nothing to worry about; all fairly standard really when we have someone here in your circumstances."

Whatever that means, Tommy thought. He gestured to the chair next to the bed, and Sonia flipped open the folder containing a notepad and some hospital records.

"If you're in too much pain at any time, just let me know and we can finish this later," she said.

"Nah. I'm all right. Fire away." Tommy was keen to get it over with.

"Okay. First, the obvious, yes? What happened to you, Tommy?"

"What do you mean, what happened to me?" He knew exactly what she meant, but he needed a moment to collect his thoughts. He'd been hit by a car, but there wasn't a person in the world who could support his story. Not even the driver, whose conscience had been wiped clean.

"Why are you in here? You've had surgery, broken bones, significant injuries to your face. How'd you do it?"

"I don't know. I think I had a fall," he lied.

Self-harm, Sonia scribbled on her notepad.

"Look, Tommy, it's not uncommon for people who suffer severe trauma to have no recollection of the incident that caused it. But is there anything you can tell me about how you felt leading up to it?" She paused. "Were you depressed?"

"What? No!" replied Tommy. *Far from it*, he thought—he'd been pretty well buzzed on Johnnie Walker. "I didn't hurt myself, if that's what you think. I reckon I must have tripped on something."

Sonia wrote some more, nodding slightly. "And who was there when it happened? Mum? Dad?"

Tommy laughed, and Sonia looked puzzled. "I wouldn't know my mum and dad if they were sitting right beside you."

The concern in Sonia's eyes deepened, and Tommy realized too late that he'd dug himself into a hole. It was gonna take a hell of a lot more information for the social worker to leave him alone. He sighed dramatically—just for effect—then began to concoct a story.

"I never knew my mum; she died when I was a baby. Last I heard, my dad's still alive, but he left me with his sister when I was three. Things were okay there, until she got cancer and died too. How unlucky's that, yeah?"

Sonia nodded, but didn't say anything.

"I was in a foster home with my cousin for a year or two, but that wasn't for me, you know what I mean? I've been on the street since then, probably three years now." Tommy thought it sounded pretty good. Sonia wouldn't know Tommy had just embellished the life story of Phil, one of the boys from the Dairy.

Sonia had a strange look on her face, a mixture of disbelief and sympathy, as she scribbled quickly, trying to keep up.

"Thanks, Tommy. What street were you sleeping on when you were hurt?"

Ah, shit, thought Tommy. He didn't know the name of any streets in the city. "Couldn't tell you, sorry." He shrugged. "I've moved around a lot."

Sonia's expression shifted in favor of disbelief. "Okay, here's my problem," she said. "I can't approve your discharge if you're going back onto the street; the state won't allow it. And when you're only fifteen—"

"I'm sixteen now," Tommy interrupted.

"Sorry, sixteen—you need to have a guardian. So unless you have another family member whose care we can discharge you into, then I think you'll have to go into a foster home. Not for long," she added hurriedly. "Just until you're eighteen."

Tommy saw an opportunity open up before him, wide and inviting. It was worth a shot.

"Well…there's a place I know that a couple of mates have gone to in the past. I think it's like a foster home, a bit out of the city. Maybe I could go there?" He hoped he sounded casual as he gave her the name, which she wrote down.

Sonia stood, urging Tommy to get some rest and promising to look into Milkwood House.

Tommy nodded off, and when he woke again a lunch tray—with something he couldn't quite identify nestled in a bed of starchy clumped rice—sat on a table to one side. Tommy decided it was safest left where it was.

"How much of that was bullshit?"

Tommy looked up. The curtains around the bed opposite him, which so far had been drawn the entire time Tommy had been on the ward, were now pulled back. A boy about his own age was staring straight at him.

Tommy knew he wasn't much to look at himself, but he thought the other boy was worse. Much worse. His skin was a sickly yellow color, and even the whites of his eyes looked like faded egg yolks.

"Hi," said Tommy, and introduced himself.

"I'm Josh," the other boy said.

"What are you in for?" asked Tommy.

"Liver's stuffed," Josh replied. "Hoping I might get a new one, but it's not looking great. Someone's gotta croak before I get it." He looked Tommy over. "How's *your* liver? Anyone got dibs on it?"

They both laughed. It felt good: relaxed and easy. Josh shifted on his pillows, propping himself up a little higher. He lowered his voice conspiratorially, enough that the other two inhabitants of the room couldn't hear.

"How much of that was bullshit?" he asked again. "The stuff with the social worker?"

The smile faded from Tommy's face. He started to deny that he'd lied, then stopped. Something told him he could trust this kid. Maybe not with everything—nobody would believe him about the Reset, and he didn't want to end up locked in a secure ward for another eleven months until they forgot why he was there—but surely confiding in Josh a little would be okay. *Kids don't rat on other kids*, he thought. *Especially when they look like they're about to die.*

"Most of it," he admitted.

Josh snorted. "Thought so. Did you really fall over? Must have been some fall."

"Nah," Tommy said. "Got hit by a car. I was…I was kinda drunk, though."

"What about that stuff you told her about living on the street? And I wanna get this right—your mum died and your dad took off and your aunt died too. Any of that true?"

Tommy smiled at him. "Nope."

Josh burst out laughing and clapped his hands. "Bloody brilliant! It's all in the detail. You're a full-on bullshit artist. Where do you actually live?"

"It's a bit complicated," Tommy said. "But what I told her about the foster home is the honest truth. I've had a few friends go there and I want in."

"Fair enough," said Josh. "Fuck, mate, my story's pretty— oops, sorry." One of the parents further down the room was glaring at them both. "My story's boring compared to yours."

"Yeah?"

"There's really not much to it. A few years ago I started getting sick and was in and out of the hospital a lot. They thought I had cancer or something, but turns out it's my liver."

"What's wrong with it?" Tommy asked.

"It just doesn't work properly. Anyway, I've been on a stack of medications but it's not getting any better, so now I have to stay here until I get a transplant. It'll be five weeks this Friday. Mum and Dad come to visit a bit, though not at the same time—Dad in the morning and Mum in the afternoon. You'd think having a kid in the hospital would be enough to bring you back together, but apparently nothing'll make those two play nice." He stopped and sipped the water by his bedside.

"Why's the curtain always closed?"

"Trust me, Tommy—some of the stuff they have to do in here, you don't want to see it. You can thank me later. Plus, it means I get some extra alone time with the hot nurse."

"Janette? She's all yours," said Tommy.

Josh laughed again and closed his eyes. He looked tired. Tommy felt a stab of guilt. He'd been swimming neck-deep in pity since he woke after surgery, but at least he'd be leaving soon. Josh's stay sounded open-ended. Tommy wanted to know more about him, about his school, and his friends. He opened his mouth to ask when he heard a faint snoring and realized the questions would have to wait.

"It's part of the recovery process, you have to do it," Amy insisted, positioning the wheelchair in front of an easel.

"Josh doesn't have to," Tommy argued.

"Well…" The nurse hesitated. "Josh's situation is a bit different. He's—"

"Refusing to do it," Tommy finished. "He told me."

Josh had tried to warn him. "It's a kids' ward," he'd said.

"They're gonna make you do stuff with the others as soon as you're well enough."

"Okay," replied Tommy. That didn't sound so bad. "What kind of stuff?"

Josh shrugged. "Dunno. I've never done it. Not really a little kid, you know? I just stay here and sleep. Or read." He patted a stack of magazines by his bed; Tommy could see the cover of one, a muddy blue trail bike sending up sprays of dirt and stones. "I'm not even into motorbikes. Dad just keeps bringing them. Sometimes he brings these too, though." Josh looked around. When he was satisfied none of the parents at the other end of the room were paying attention, he pulled a magazine from the bottom of the pile and held it up. A woman with wet hair pouted at Tommy from a swimming pool, her hands covering her naked chest. "I'm pretty sure he reads them before he gives them to me, but I try not to think about that." Josh grinned.

It was only Amy's persistence—and the pleading look she gave him—that persuaded Tommy to get out of bed and into the wheelchair.

"Where are we going?" he'd asked her.

"The playroom," she replied, and Tommy heard a snort from behind Josh's curtain.

And so he found himself propped up in front of an easel in the playroom with a tray of watery-looking paints and a thick paintbrush. A bright mural stretched all the way around the four walls—jungle became a beach which became a mountain top and then another beach.

Tommy glanced at the kid next to him. "What are we supposed to paint?" he asked.

"Whatever we want," the girl said and slopped a dollop of red onto the middle of her paper. "What's your name?" she asked. She looked about twelve or thirteen; Tommy wasn't sure because she didn't have a hair on her head. No eyebrows, no eyelashes, nothing. Just smooth, white skin where her hair should've been.

"Tommy," he told her.

Her name was June, and Tommy was right—she was twelve.

"Painting day's pretty good," she said. "But we do a heap of other things too. A lady comes in with a stack of instruments and we get to play them. If it's sunny we do some stuff with water in the courtyard." A splotch of green joined the red, then some blue.

Tommy's painting was hung next to June's to dry, one in a row of half a dozen pictures. June's was by far the best.

Amy came to collect Tommy, and another nurse took June back to her room, but not before the girl extracted a promise from Tommy that she'd see him tomorrow.

"Music day!" she declared loudly, and a couple of the other kids clapped.

"All right, music day," Tommy agreed.

And so Tommy returned to the playroom the next day—more willingly this time—and waited while the other kids were brought in. There was a young boy who looked perfectly healthy, except for the drip attached to his arm. Another girl a few years younger than June had both arms and one leg wrapped in a suit that seemed so tight it was like she was being squeezed. Three or four others arrived, then Amy returned with another wheelchair.

"I *can* walk," Josh said, arms folded.

"I know, I know. But I didn't think you'd actually get here unless I brought you myself." She parked him next to Tommy.

"Ran out of magazines," Josh said.

It was a lie, but Tommy just nodded. He introduced his friend to June, and June told them who everyone else was, and nothing more was said about Josh's sudden appearance in the playroom. Even the fact that Tommy and Josh were older than the rest seemed to be ignored. Outside of the playroom, outside of the hospital, a gap that big for kids that age would have seemed like a lifetime. But not here.

Both Tommy and Josh ended up with tambourines, and within minutes they were hammering them on the arms of their wheelchairs, the pure aggression of it helping Josh to hide the fact he was actually having fun. This egged on the boy with the triangle, and the girl with a drum, and then the entire playroom erupted in a deafening blast. The volunteer who'd handed out the instruments stood by helplessly, wondering exactly how she'd lost control of a room full of sick, sad kids, all of whom were now grinning and laughing like they'd forgotten where they were.

○

"How are you feeling today, Tommy?" Sonia Williams asked him. The social worker took a seat by his bedside and opened her folder again. "Tell me, have you had any revelations about what happened to you?"

Tommy shook his head. "I still think it was a fall. Makes

sense. I might have had a drink or two." At least that part was true.

Sonia scribbled something in her case notes then said, "I've got some good news. I had a phone call yesterday afternoon with the head of the foster home you mentioned to me. She said they've got a spare room at the moment, and they're prepared to take you once you've recovered."

Tommy's spirits lifted instantly. If his ribs weren't still knitting together, and his ear still leaking some fluid, he would have hugged Sonia.

"You're doing your rehab? Good. Well, keep it up and with a bit of luck we'll have you in Upper Reach before you miss too much school."

No sooner had Sonia left than Amy arrived.

"Why do you look so happy?" she asked. "Did I miss something?" Her eyes darted suspiciously between Tommy and Josh, like she'd walked in on the punchline of a joke.

"Just had some good news," Tommy told her. "Got a home to go to."

In the bed across from him, he could see Josh gesturing not particularly subtly at Amy. Tommy smothered a laugh.

"I'm very happy for you Tommy," Amy said as she tested his blood pressure. "I'll miss you when you leave."

Tommy flushed, and Josh exploded in laughter. He made no attempt to stifle it, and Amy looked up quizzically.

"Ignore him," said Tommy. "He's just an idiot." But he started laughing too.

Amy took his temperature and checked his pulse, then left the room, shaking her head at teenage boys and their stupid sense of humor. She didn't want to admit she was a little bit flattered.

●

Tommy woke the next morning to see a man ducking behind Josh's curtain, a magazine tucked under his arm. Then the curtain was flung back, and Tommy saw an adult version of Josh. He had the same dark brown hair, cut kind of spiky, and the same long nose. But his skin was a more natural color (which wasn't surprising), and he had a short, neat beard.

"Dad, this is my mate Tommy," Josh said.

"G'day, Tommy. Call me Dave," said Josh's dad. "I'd shake your hand but I'm not sure what's broken there." He grinned then turned back to his son. "Sorry, but I can't stay long. Got a few more errands to run before work."

"So I'm just one of your errands. Cheers, Dad," Josh said indignantly. Tommy couldn't tell if he was joking. He didn't think so.

Dave sighed. "You know what I mean. I can't just sit here all day."

"Dad runs a bar," Josh explained to Tommy. "It's open from lunchtime 'til late, so he only comes in the morning. That's why Mum does the afternoon. Couldn't possibly get you two in the room at the same time, could we, Dad? Might kill me off entirely." He stuck his tongue out and pretended to die.

Dave ignored the performance and started flicking through the magazine he'd brought for Josh.

Amy appeared at the far end of the ward, where she stopped

to speak quietly to the mother of one of the other patients. She leaned over the little boy's bed to change the dressing on his leg, and Tommy heard them both giggle at something he said. Next she came to Tommy, still smiling.

"He's a funny kid, that one," she said. "How are you feeling today, Tommy?"

Tommy answered honestly—his chest was hurting more than normal, and he was kind of hoping he might get some extra painkillers. As Amy bent over to check his stitches, he saw Dave lower the magazine slightly to watch her.

"Your dad's got a cool job," Tommy said to Josh when his father had left.

"Yeah, he does," replied Josh. "You should see the bar. It's awesome. Really dark, they play good music, and it's even got some old-school pinball machines. It's not far actually—just over on Hunt Street. We should stage a breakout. Take everyone on a field trip."

Tommy laughed. "Eight kids walk into a bar." Then he paused. "Hey, why doesn't your dad stay here with you? Or your mum?" The parents of the other kids in the ward seemed to be there all the time.

Josh made a face. "They used to stay a bit. Well, Mum did. But I think they just assume I'm here for the long haul, so they better keep working and all that. Plus, I'm old enough to fend for myself. Mum spends as much time here as she can, but with Dad it's different, yeah? In and out in a few minutes. Used to be every day, now it's a couple of times a week. I reckon he'd skip it altogether if Amy wasn't on."

Noticing Tommy's reaction, Josh chuckled. "You saw it,

didn't you? Yeah, he's a perv. Reckon that's why he and Mum broke up. She probably found his stash of these," he said, pointing to the magazines by his bed. Tommy knew he wasn't talking about the dirt bikes.

Over the next week a couple of the kids went home, a couple of new ones came in, and Tommy inched closer and closer to going back to Upper Reach and the Dairy. The ringing in his ear had stopped, and he no longer feared sneezing and the violent spasm of pain it would bring from his ribs and broken nose. Apparently his spleen was healing too, though he had to take the doctor's word for that. But probably the most profound change was that he no longer had to be wheeled to the day's activities by Amy, Janette, or one of the other nurses. He could walk. It felt good.

"I reckon you'll be out of here soon, Tommy," Josh said to him. "Which one are you gonna pick?"

They were in the courtyard off the children's ward, a drab concrete space with a plain gray sail stretched overhead for shade. Someone had decided that planting a garden would be a good group activity *and* help to brighten up the place. Planter boxes had been set up along one wall, and now sat full of dirt, waiting.

Tommy pointed at a small pot in a tray.

"The cactus," he said.

June frowned. "Why?" she asked. "It's not very pretty."

Tommy shrugged. "I don't know. I just like it."

"'Cos you're a bit of a prick?" Josh whispered.

Tommy laughed. "Probably."

One by one each of the kids chose a plant; some chose two. Little white seaside daisies, a fuchsia whose label promised would stand out in any garden, some cheerful orange impatiens. Tommy helped one of the younger boys dig a hole, then held a plant in place while the child sprinkled soil on top, most of it missing the mark. Finally Tommy pressed the dirt down around his own cactus, tucked away in the corner. When they were done, they all stood back for a moment to admire the haphazard arrangement.

"Looks fantastic, guys!" Amy declared and started shepherding them back to their beds.

Sonia Williams was waiting in the ward for Tommy.

"Tomorrow's the day, Tommy," she said. "The head of Milkwood House—what is she, the director? She'll pick you up at eight."

"She's coming here herself?" Tommy felt a warm glow at the prospect of seeing her again. He was a stranger to Miss Michelle, but she was still going out of her way for him.

Sonia nodded. "She didn't want you traveling on the train. Not with your injuries."

That night, Tommy's mood seesawed between excitement about going home with Miss Michelle and sadness at leaving Josh. Not that he confessed it to his friend. Instead they talked about what came *after* the hospital, each struck by the realization that adulthood was almost upon them. Soon they might have to make decisions.

"I haven't been giving it a lot of thought lately," said Tommy.

He'd been too busy drifting to think of the future. "When I was a kid I wanted to write. Maybe I could be a reporter or something. What do you reckon—can you see me on telly?" He grinned at Josh, nose crooked from the break and the faint bruising around his eyes still giving him a slightly demonic look. "What about you?"

Josh grimaced. "I'd just like to get out of here and not come back." He swallowed, and when he next spoke his voice was different. "You know I might die here, yeah?"

This was new ground for the pair. They'd discussed all kinds of things—Josh's school, his friends, why he'd decided to live with his mum, even how she'd threatened to give his dog away because it kept taking a leak under the kitchen table. But Josh had never spoken about dying.

"I figured that," Tommy replied uncomfortably. "But…it's not gonna happen, right?"

"It might. If I don't get a liver, I'm pretty well fucked. How's this, though—the doctor's never actually told me that herself. I just heard her say it to Mum one day. I mean, come on. I'm not a kid. If I'm gonna die, at least tell me. I've got things I want to do first."

"Like what?"

"Mate, I'm sixteen. What do *you* think? Mum says there's no need to rush into things, but that's easy for her to say."

Tommy didn't know how to respond; he was shaken from hearing Josh admit he might actually die. (In weeks? Months? How much time did he have left? Tommy didn't know and wasn't sure if he should ask.) But alongside the shock was something else, something unexpected: something that felt a little like shame. Shame that he'd let the old Tommy lie dormant for so long, and allowed the new Tommy to drift.

Josh was still talking. "Yeah, there's some other stuff too, apart from getting a girlfriend. Dad says I can work with him for a bit once I'm eighteen, so I'll definitely do that. Learn the ropes. But if I could do anything? I'd have my own place. Kinda like Dad's, but better. My own bar, make my own money. And not be a dick about it." He paused. "Hey, we should do it together—from hospital beds to business partners. What a story."

Tommy liked that. Nobody had ever included him in plans for the future before, except for Carey that one time, inviting him to visit her once she moved out. For the next few minutes they threw back and forth ever more outlandish ideas for their bar, from a roped-off VIP section for all their friends to a separate menu for dogs—because who wanted to go drinking without their dog?

"Seriously though, Tommy, we should do it. God, we'd have some fun, wouldn't we? Running a bar with your best mate. When you get out on parole from that place you're going to, come and find me."

Come and find me.

It was a throwaway line, sure. But at that instant, Tommy was going through a reset of a different type. The aimless, drifting Tommy was gone, banished to wherever his belongings went on January 5 each year. And the boy in his place—the original Tommy—latched on to that line and tucked it away.

"Parole? I'm not going to jail, you idiot," Tommy replied, and they both laughed hard until a parent of one of the other children on the ward shushed them.

Josh winced. "First I'd better fix this liver, though. I've given up on getting yours, by the way. Unless I smother you tonight. Don't go to sleep, Tommy."

Tommy snorted, earning himself another shush.

"Sorry," Tommy whispered. But he could still hear Josh across the darkened room, giggling into his pillow like a little kid.

At 7:55 a.m., Tommy was standing beside his bed waiting for Miss Michelle, wearing a shirt, pants, and shoes Amy had scavenged from the hospital's charity bin.

Josh hadn't stirred yet, and his curtain had been drawn during the night. Tommy didn't want to wake his friend, but equally didn't want to leave without saying goodbye. Finally, he stuck his head between the curtains tentatively.

Josh was gone. His entire bed was gone.

"He's in surgery," a voice behind him said.

Tommy spun around.

"A liver came in," Amy told him. "It all happened in a hurry; it always does. There was a car accident not far from here and the man was a perfect match for Josh. He's been in the operating theater for a few hours already. Then he'll go to intensive care for recovery."

Tommy stood there beaming at her. Josh was getting his liver. He had so many questions for Amy, but instead of asking them, he just grinned. Then he heard footsteps approaching along the ward.

It felt strange to shake Miss Michelle's hand and introduce himself. He'd done it so many times before, but this time felt different. As Tommy climbed into the old Camry, he glanced back at the great gray monolith that had been his home for weeks. He tried to picture where in the labyrinth of wards, corridors, and theaters his friend lay.

Somehow, he knew Josh Saunders would be okay.

What were the words he'd used last night?

Come and find me, Josh had said.

All right then, Tommy decided. *I will.*

9

Tommy flicked between radio stations, waiting for a nod from Miss Michelle each time before pressing the button. Finally she smiled at a song—something old; something Tommy thought he might've heard before but couldn't quite place— and he leaned back in his seat. Two and a bit hours in the car with someone he knew and loved but who didn't know or love him back—it was awkward in a nice way. Until he turned the radio on, much of the trip had been spent in what Tommy had heard described as a "comfortable silence."

As they got closer to the Dairy, Miss Michelle started telling Tommy about the other residents, the kids she hoped he'd get to know and maybe even think of as his family. She got to the end of the list and he realized she hadn't mentioned Sean.

Sean Barker had left, having turned eighteen while Tommy was lying in a hospital bed, and the impact on the house was almost tangible. The Dairy seemed a little quieter, a little less fun. But Tommy had to wait until one of the other kids brought up Sean before he could casually ask where he'd gone.

"Yeah, he got a job—selling cars in Mortlake."

"He's not *selling* cars. He's a trainee. They wouldn't let *Sean* actually talk to customers. No way." That was Nicole, who was now fifteen and a bit less dumpy, but possibly louder than before. Bigger lungs, Tommy supposed.

"I'm still amazed that Miss Michelle didn't kick him out." Nicole paused to build suspense. "He stole her car," she told Tommy dramatically.

"Seriously?" he replied, hoping she'd go on.

"Yeah. Buggered off to the pool a few weeks back. I heard he went to see a *girl*."

Yep, thought Tommy. *He did.*

"He was gone for, like, three hours. Problem is, when Sean's not here you kinda notice it. He's pretty loud." She seemed to completely miss the irony of this observation. "Miss Michelle was waiting for him when he got back. *Busted!*"

As Tommy sat listening to Nicole, he marveled at the simplicity of it. There'd been two people in the Camry when it drove into Upper Reach on January 3, but in the telling of the story now, there'd only been one. Just like that, the universe had written him out of the narrative in the Reset two days later. Nothing too complicated, no elaborate backstory—just enough to wipe him out.

It would have bothered him a few months earlier. In fact,

it would have more than bothered him—it would have fueled Tommy Llewellyn's tailspin, spiraling and crashing over the unanswerable question: *Why me?* And sure, the question still lurked, but he kept pushing it down. It was easy enough to do.

Come and find me.

●

Tommy returned to Mortlake High with two years left to serve. Again, had anybody remembered him, the change *back* to the old Tommy would have been noticeable. But nobody remembered the sullen, aimless boy from the previous year, or the sweet, kind boy from the year before that. He was just the new kid from the Dairy.

The difference certainly wasn't noticed by Mrs. Julie Lewis, the teacher who'd tried so hard to straighten Tommy out. But she also had other things on her mind. On her lunch break she'd reread a story pinned to the corkboard in the English faculty staff room, and couldn't stop thinking about it. In fact, she'd had to duck to the ladies' room for a few minutes, hoping that none of her colleagues would notice the slight smudge of her mascara on her return. It got her every time. She made twenty-five copies of the story and handed them out to her English class after lunch.

"This was written by an old student," she told them. It was a tiny fib. Nobody in the English faculty was quite sure *who'd* written it (there was no name on the assignment, and Julie thought it had probably been there for years, before the current crop of teachers had started), but they all agreed that it was a great story.

"Read it, and then we can discuss it as a class."

Tommy looked at the first line and recognized it in an instant. His mouth fell open.

Mrs. Lewis called on him for his thoughts on the story's true meaning. Tommy fumbled his way through an answer; he knew exactly what it was about. It was about him and Carey and love and angst and all that stuff—but all he could think was: *HOW?* How had his story survived when all other traces of his existence were wiped out?

Then he realized that Mrs. Lewis was talking about the story's author and he tuned back in.

"So if you're referring to it in your essay, you'll have to use *Anonymous* as the author," she was saying.

He hadn't put his name on it. And he'd printed the pages on the Dairy's scratchy old printer that was always low on ink— *yeah*, he thought, *it looks like it could have been printed ages ago*— so there was no handwriting to link it back to him. It had meant so little to Tommy, and this photocopy was so far removed from him, so distant from the original with its C grade marked in red, and so completely *anonymous*, that the Reset must have missed it.

The lesson finished, but Tommy kept staring at the pages. He wasn't quite sure what he was staring at, but he suspected it was a loophole.

A way to trick the Reset.

Over the coming weeks, Tommy focused on little else. Each night he lay in bed, thinking about things he could leave behind, hidden away; things so obscure that they might slip through the crack he'd discovered. But it was harder than he first thought. All the objects he came up with were either linked directly to him—like his schoolbooks, with *Tommy Llewellyn* printed neatly on the inside cover—or meant too much to him. This almost guaranteed they'd be erased.

As Tommy got closer to his seventeenth birthday, he felt the frustration rising. Here was an opportunity to test a theory—to trick the Reset into letting him keep something—but every time he thought he'd found it, he realized it wouldn't work.

Pencil case from school? Name was on it. Letter to himself? Too meaningful. Report card? No way—not with sentences like *Tommy's got a natural ability with numbers.* That thing had a one-way ticket on the Reset express.

On the eve of his birthday he was sifting through his belongings, steeling himself for the vanishing act they'd perform later that night. Schoolbooks, a baseball cap, the clothes he'd accumulated since returning to the Dairy.

A hospital bracelet.

Miss Michelle had snipped it off his wrist when she showed him to his room, and Tommy had dropped it in his drawer. Now, as he turned it over in his hands, he remembered Amy calling him Thomas, and how it had crushed him when he learned she'd read it off the bracelet. But something about that little strip of plastic and the tiny letters printed on it made him wonder.

He tore a page from one of his textbooks—the act felt so wrong, so violent, but the book would be gone in a few hours anyway—and scribbled a couple of words on it. Then he tucked it into the pocket of his pajamas, climbed into bed, and closed his eyes.

●

It was still there the next morning.

Tommy pulled the page from his pocket and smoothed it on his sheets. There, in between the equations of the textbook, were the words he'd scrawled:

Hope this makes it through.

It had. He'd started out with one loophole, now he had two.

And this one was big.

Just like his pajamas, just like the hospital bracelet, that little scrap of paper had stayed on him through the Reset. An idea planted itself in Tommy's brain. It was going to take some work—a lot of work—but he had a year before it would be tested.

A year. The clock was ticking on both his time at Mortlake High, and his days at the Dairy.

Josh was out there. Carey was out there too, somewhere. He wondered how Josh had recovered after his surgery and if he was back at school, and if he still planned to learn the ropes at the bar with his dad. He wondered if Carey had found a way to get to college. He wondered—of course—if she had a boyfriend.

They were both out there, and he was going to join them.

Come and find me.

The thought sustained him as the year galloped by, and the seed of his idea germinated and grew some more. He added detail, and did research, and pretty soon it had bloomed into a fully-fledged plan. Then, seemingly without warning, his final exams at Mortlake High were on him. They were now more of a formality—almost a distraction from what he was going to do afterward—but he threw himself at the challenge, partly to prove to himself that he could succeed. He'd inherited the abilities of both his parents, and while he'd toyed once with the idea of university—journalism, or finance, or even both—he knew any offer of a place would be erased on January 5, handed to some other kid who probably didn't deserve it quite as much. He squashed the bitterness down.

Stick to the plan.

With his exams done, it was time for the real work to begin. He was suddenly on a deadline—six weeks until his Reset, which would have been fine if he just intended to walk away and start afresh *out there.*

But this time, when the Reset stripped him of everything, he'd be ready for it.

Tommy knocked on the office door just as the sun appeared in the bottom corner of the window.

"Good morning, Tommy. You're up early," said Michelle from behind her desk. She liked this time of day; it was her chance to keep the paperwork for Milkwood House in order. There was just so much admin. So many forms. She shook her head in disbelief. "What can I do for you?"

"I need to earn some money," he said bluntly as he sat down.

"I've got six weeks until I turn eighteen, and I need cash so I can move to the city. So I can eat," he added unnecessarily.

Michelle Chaplin leaned back in her chair and looked at the young man across from her. Tommy Llewellyn was a good kid. *Llewellyn*, she repeated to herself, almost absent-mindedly, and for the briefest of moments she thought she could feel *him* here. In *his* office. *John would have liked Tommy*, she decided, unaware that she'd reached the same conclusion so many times before.

"You don't have to go straight away once you turn eighteen, Tommy," she said. "Legally you're not supposed to stay"—*because there's no funding*, she thought—"but you could certainly spend a few weeks as a guest. Even a month or two." It was a courtesy she hadn't extended to Richie Sharpe.

Tommy grinned; he'd kind of expected that. "Thanks very much, but either way I'm not going to be here much longer, and I really need to make some money to get myself set up." He paused. "I've got a proposal for you."

He outlined his plan, and Michelle listened, nodding slightly and asking the occasional question. She smiled as she realized how much research Tommy had done, but even she had no idea how many library books and magazines he'd stashed under his bed. At the end of the conversation they shook hands on the deal.

Tommy started work that same day, following a trip into town for supplies with Miss Ellmore. After lugging a ladder from the old shed (that place made him shudder; it was a constant reminder of the day he'd found Carey inside), his first task was to sand back the exterior walls of Milkwood House. Tommy's arms and shoulders ached as he stripped the paint that had already been peeling when he arrived as a baby.

When he woke the following morning he felt a stiffness in his shoulders; the books hadn't warned him about this. But by 7:00 a.m. he was back up the ladder, scraping and sanding.

He kept this up day after day, and a week later the huge old house stood nude in the middle of the lawn. Tommy stepped back to admire his handiwork, but not for long—soon he was carrying two large cans of paint toward the eastern wall. The clock was ticking loudly in Tommy's ear; he had to keep moving. There was so much to do and the deadline was set in stone.

Within another week the house had two undercoats of paint, and a week after that it shone with creamy white walls and a green trim. Tommy had transformed it from a last-stop facility for optionless kids into…well, into a home they could love.

Tommy turned his attention to the garden, and burst out laughing as he remembered the chaotic plantings in the hospital courtyard almost two years earlier. But after half a dozen trips with Miss Ellmore to a nursery at Mortlake, he'd created garden beds where once the weeds had grown tall and lush.

"Come next spring," he told Miss Michelle, "everything should flower at once, and you'll have a heap of color right around the house. Well, that's what the lady at the nursery told me. If she's wrong, take it up with her, 'cos I won't be here to fix it!"

Miss Michelle had smiled, then her brow furrowed as she spotted a tiny cactus, wedged in between the peonies.

Next, Tommy attacked the trees along the back boundary with shears and a saw, tidying up branches that threatened to fall and crush the thin wire fence. There was no shudder here, not like in the old storage shed. Of course, he'd been too young to remember Richie leading him through the thick undergrowth; too young to remember that climbing through this fence to rescue Tommy from the dark had been the very last act of John Llewellyn, who'd died in the dust right next to it.

Finally, in the days between Christmas and New Year, he moved his efforts inside, sanding doors and furniture and repainting chairs.

By January 2, he was finished. He'd done the work, and he knew that Miss Michelle would uphold her end of the bargain. He only hoped his plan would succeed.

The following day, January 3, was payday. At noon, as the sun was dead overhead and doing its best to scorch the new paint off the Dairy's walls, Tommy knocked again on Miss Michelle's office door. The woman who'd spent so many forgotten mornings with Tommy on a rug out under the tree in the yard gestured for the young man to take a seat. He looked at her and noticed for the first time how much she'd changed over the years. She was on the cusp of sixty, and now wore her experience proudly. Her dyed blond hair was conceding victory to the gray, and she had more wrinkles fanning out from the corners of her eyes. They didn't age her so much as enhance her kindness, her softness.

"You've done a wonderful job, Tommy," said Miss Michelle, breaking into his thoughts. "When I step outside now it looks like I'm in a different place."

"Yeah, well, it was long overdue." Tommy smiled. "From what I've been told," he added.

Miss Michelle reached into a drawer of her desk and pulled out a compact, black metal box. She took her keyring from her pocket and inserted the smallest key.

"We agreed on a hundred dollars a day, am I right?" she asked.

Tommy nodded.

"And Christmas Day was your only day off?"

He nodded again.

She pulled out a wad of fifty-dollar notes from the box and started counting, peeling off more money than Tommy had ever seen in one place.

Finally she stopped, and wrapped a rubber band around the pile of notes before putting the wad in a thick white envelope.

"There's three and a half thousand dollars in there, Tommy," she said, but she didn't pass the envelope to him. "Are you sure about this? Please let me write you a check instead. I don't like the thought of you carrying so much cash."

"No, thanks," he replied. "Strange as it sounds, it'll be safer if I take it in cash."

Miss Michelle looked at him curiously. "Well, look after it. Now tell me: you're eighteen in, what, two days? Are you sure I can't convince you to stick around for a little while? At least stay until you've got something lined up."

Tommy shook his head. "Thank you, but no. I'll head off on my birthday, otherwise it's just kind of delaying the inevitable. I don't have all the details yet, but I've got a fair idea where I'm going."

"Can I at least drive you to the station then? We'll make sure everyone's out the front to give you a big send-off."

"That'd be nice—thanks, Miss M," he said. *Yes, that certainly would be nice,* he thought, *but I won't hold you to it.* Come January 5, nobody would be farewelling him out the front—they wouldn't even know who he was.

◑

Tommy was so nervous he barely touched his breakfast. He'd developed a monstrous appetite from all his labors, so the sight of a bowl of cereal growing soggier as he poked at it raised eyebrows.

"What's up, Tommy?" asked a girl sitting further down the table. "Worried about getting old tomorrow?"

Tommy laughed tightly and shook his head. "Nah, just got a few things on my mind," he said and returned to his room. From under his mattress he pulled out the white envelope Miss Michelle had given him the previous day. He'd already checked it was there a dozen times. He hoped it might just be the start of something—money begets money and all that. But first he had to keep it through the night.

He ran through his plan again, but he could only go over the steps so many times before his mind started to wander. How would he say goodbye to the people he'd miss, who'd been there for him for so many years now, when they'd only known him for the last twelve months? The smell of paint still hung in the air, and it occurred to him that maybe his work would be his way of saying goodbye, his thank you to Miss Michelle and the kids he'd been living with. Perhaps even something for the kids who'd come after him, each of them at a difficult, lonely time. He imagined Child Services pulling up to a house that looked proud to be standing: bright, fresh bedrooms, and gardens overflowing with flowers. *Yes*, he thought. He'd be all right with that as his parting gift, even if nobody knew it was him who'd given it. Maybe it would be like the story he wrote at school; he hadn't signed his name or anything on the freshly painted walls. It was just paint and soil and flowers— nothing to really link it back to him. Maybe the Reset would choose the path of least resistance and just wipe the memory of Tommy doing it, and *not* replace him with someone else. He'd like that. A blurry little legacy, slipping through the loophole.

As the shadows lengthened and the halls of the Dairy became dark, he finally felt himself relaxing. He'd been through it so many times now, and there was nothing more he could do. At dinner he sat quietly, enjoying the laughter of friends, having what was for him his last supper at his childhood home. Then, as the other children went back to their rooms or drifted upstairs to the common room, he found himself alone with Miss Michelle.

"All set for tomorrow, Tommy?" she asked, scraping some of the plates left behind.

"I think so," he replied. *I'd certainly want to be by now.*

"I thought we could leave at nine; there's a train at nine thirty which will get you into the city with plenty of time to get to your friend's place."

Tommy had told her he was staying with a mate, which wasn't true, because no one who knew him today would still know him tomorrow. He couldn't say with certainty where he'd be sleeping—but he did have an idea.

"Sounds good to me," Tommy said.

"We're going to miss you around here, Tommy," Miss Michelle said. "I think you've been good for this place. And not just for the work you've done." She gestured vaguely at the walls around her. "Some of the little kids look up to you, you know. I know it sounds a bit strange, but I kind of wish we'd found you earlier. I would have liked a few more years of Tommy Llewellyn here."

Tommy didn't say anything. Instead, he took a step toward Miss Michelle and hugged her.

She was surprised at first, then hugged him back.

"Are you okay, Tommy?" she asked, concerned.

"I'm fine. It's just…it'll be sad to leave, you know?"

Tommy wished he could tell Miss Michelle everything: remind her of how they had read books and played games on the front lawn when he was too young for school; of how she'd slept in his room when he had night terrors as a four-year-old. He wanted to thank her for scooping him up when he fell down the steps two days after he turned seven, and for being there when Carey was carried off in the ambulance. Tommy wanted to ask the name of the song that was playing on the radio the day she picked him up from the hospital, taking him in yet again as the new kid. But he couldn't do it. She wouldn't believe him, and it would have ruined his final moments with her. So with that hug, and a reassuring pat on the arm from Miss Michelle, Tommy turned away.

He needed to get this next part right, or it would all be for nothing.

From his closet he pulled an armful of clothing—all his best hand-me-downs from the last year: a blue long-sleeved shirt that had been donated back to the Dairy by a former student; a good pair of jeans; a polo; a light gray T-shirt (his only one without holes); four pairs of underwear; two pairs of socks; and his most comfortable shoes (an easy choice, as he only had two pairs). Tommy put everything on, then looked at himself reflected in his bedroom window. He was surprised at what he saw: lit by the lamp on his desk, he looked older. He was ready to leave.

A drop of sweat ran down the small of his back.

He pulled the envelope from its hiding place and after a quick count (it was all still there) started stuffing notes into his clothes. He folded wads into the pockets of his jeans, slipped some between the layered underwear, and then tucked a few notes into his socks. It was nearing 9:00 p.m.; not long until lights out. The final step was to grab his backpack, the one he'd used through his last year of school. He hooked an arm firmly through the strap and lay down on his bed, with the bag to one side. Tommy chuckled softly to himself. If anyone saw him now, well, good luck explaining that one.

His thoughts flitted back to that hospital bracelet, and to the scrap of paper he'd torn from his textbook. It made sense—every year, when he woke up on January 5, the only things he still possessed were the clothes he was wearing and the sheets he slept on. Everything else had vanished, and his achievements or failures were assigned to other people by some unexplained power in the universe. It stood to reason—or at least Tommy hoped it did—that if he slept in more than his pajamas, and held tight to everything he wanted to keep, they'd still be there in the morning. As for the cash, well, it had worked for a page from a schoolbook. It was a gamble, he knew, but he'd been dealt a losing hand every year since he was born. It was time for the cards to fall his way for once.

The air in his room felt thick and heavy, and the sweat on his back glued the layers of clothing to his skin. Tommy lay still, eyes adjusting to the dim glow from the moon outside as he peered around the room. He wouldn't miss it, he thought. It was plain and simple and too easily wiped of all traces of him.

Then he closed his eyes, and sleep took him.

When Tommy woke it was still early. The eastern sky was just starting to lighten, the inky black of night softening into the predawn gray. He lay there for a moment, briefly unaware of the significance of the morning. Then it hit him, and a sharp spike of adrenaline rushed through his body, instantly waking him fully and sending his heart racing. Within seconds he was almost overwhelmed by the heat; the drops of sweat that had stuck his shirt to his back the night before had been joined by many more, and his clothes were drenched. *His clothes!*

Tommy felt his arm: a cotton sleeve and, under that, more material. He struggled to sit upright, hampered by the layers.

His pulse quickened again as he remembered the money. The clothes were useful, but if the cash hadn't come through with him, then his new life would be infinitely tougher. He thrust his hand into his pocket and felt a wad of notes. Tommy collapsed back onto the bed, elated.

He hadn't just confirmed the second loophole, he'd driven a bloody truck straight through it.

I can do this, he thought.

Five minutes later, all of the money was spread across the mattress—$3,500 exactly. He piled it up again and stood in his underwear, enjoying the relief of air on his skin. He couldn't stay for long, he knew; through his window the sky was getting lighter, and sunrise wasn't far away. Tommy dressed in a single layer of clothes, marveling at his range of options, choices he'd never had before on the morning after his Reset, then reached for his backpack.

It was gone.

He ripped back the sheet, then dropped to his knees and peered beneath the bed frame. Nothing. Tommy thought hard. The bag must have come off his arm sometime while he slept, and if he had no contact with it when the Reset struck, then it would have disappeared with the rest of his belongings— vanished, wiped, reallocated, whatever. It didn't matter where it was now; Tommy didn't have it. It was a setback, but a minor one, and he stuffed the rest of his clothes inside a shirt and tied it all up in a ball. He laughed softly. All he needed was a stick to attach it to, and he'd really look the part.

With his cash wrapped in a sock, tucked deep inside his pocket, Tommy took one last look at his room—a barer version of the room he'd gone to sleep in. The halls were silent as he crept out, carrying his shirt full of clothes in one hand and his shoes in the other. Tommy knelt under the big tree on the front lawn to put the shoes on, and when he stood again he looked back at the huge old house where he'd spent the last seventeen years. All the windows were dark, and the Dairy was quiet and peaceful. As the first glow of the sun started to light the walls and gardens, he admired the work he'd done. Part of him was curious to know how the building's refurbishment would be explained now that he'd been forgotten—or whether there would even be an explanation. (As it happens, Miss Michelle assumed the work had been arranged by Milkwood's owner, Declan Driscoll, while she was on a break. Declan Driscoll knew nothing about it, and didn't really care. As for the kids, well, they thought it had been done before they arrived at the Dairy, or while they were at school, or just when they weren't paying attention. Funny that the smell of paint was still so fresh, though.)

Tommy trudged down the driveway. He needed to leave before somebody spotted him. A strange man standing in the grounds of a children's home with three and a half grand in his pocket? He'd surely be arrested for trespassing, and that certainly wasn't in his plan for January 5. There was still so much to do.

10

The train pulled into the city terminal at nine sharp, bursting with commuters and one nervous, wide-eyed young man. Tommy felt as if everybody was looking at him, carrying a bundle of clothes wrapped in a shirt, so he hung back until the platform was clear. Then he took a deep breath and followed the signs to the exit, emerging onto a city street, right into the middle of a surging wave of workers late for the office. His senses were overloaded: the constant roar of engines and the hum of conversation, punctuated by car horns and the urgent, insistent tone of traffic lights announcing it was safe to cross. The breeze carried a potent mix of exhaust fumes and frying bacon; a handful of men and women waited impatiently at a café window, then, as they were handed their coffee, joined the throng of people on the footpath. The smell from the small kiosk made Tommy think of the Dairy. The dining room would be empty by now; his friends would've eaten their breakfast a couple of hours ago, paying no attention to the empty chair where Tommy usually sat. Why would they? As far as they were concerned, the chair had been empty yesterday too.

Tommy joined the queue at the coffee shop counter and copied the man in front of him, handing over his money for a bacon and egg roll. He wondered how long the wad of cash in his pocket would last him.

The crush of commuters eased while he ate (he imagined them arriving breathlessly at work, apologizing for their lateness and blaming the train or an accident or the kids) and soon he was able to walk without being jostled. The first thing he needed was somewhere to stay. Sticking to his plan was going to mean putting his hand in his pocket again.

The only time he'd been into the city since he was a baby was when he was fifteen, and he'd turned sixteen while unconscious in a hospital ward. He remembered staring up at the skyscrapers as Miss Michelle drove through the morning traffic and picturing what was inside. Now he read the signs printed on front windows or embossed on plates next to revolving glass doors: law firm, bank, another bank, insurance company. He stood outside that last building and gazed up. Carey Price had left the Dairy to work for an insurance company, and for a moment he wondered if she was up there somewhere, sitting at a desk, typing away, taking phone calls, doing something *important*. At that very second she could be looking out over the city, not knowing that Tommy stood on the street below. Not knowing who Tommy was.

Somehow, he was going to change that.

Scattered amid the steel-and-glass towers were smaller, shabbier buildings, with shops on the ground floor and only half a dozen stories above. The shops had signs hanging over the footpath, suspended from the awnings, and Tommy was mesmerized. He counted eleven clothing stores on one block, and three shops selling discount souvenirs, with windows full of T-shirts and soft toys and jewelry that twinkled behind glass.

Then he found the sign he'd been looking for, and a young couple on their way out held the door for him. A woman in her early thirties sat on a stool behind a counter.

"Morning," she said to Tommy.

He didn't answer straight away. Every inch of the wall behind her was covered in notices, plastered over the top of each other so that only the outer layer could be seen. The most prominent one read *NO SMOKING*, although someone had used a Sharpie to add the word *INSIDE*. Others were a mix of handwritten and printed:

Guests responsible for own valuables.

Payment upfront. No refunds.

Guys—be considerate! Quiet after midnight! (That one was handwritten.)

Hairdryers were also available for a small fee, and discount tickets to local attractions. Tommy stared, reading sign after sign, before he realized the woman was still looking at him, waiting.

"Oh. Sorry," he said. "I'd like a room, please."

She smiled indulgently. "We don't do rooms, just beds."

"Oh," Tommy said again, flushing. "I'll have a bed, thanks."

The woman flipped open a folder in front of her and picked up a pen. She wore beaded bracelets that rattled as she moved, and her nose was pierced with a single gold ring.

"How long you looking to stay?" she asked, pen poised.

Tommy considered this. He didn't really know. "Let's say six weeks to start with," he decided, "and I'll extend if I need to."

The woman behind the counter scribbled in the folder. "What's your name?"

As he spelled out *Llewellyn*—"Two L's and then two more"—a thought occurred to him. He was starting over. He could be Elvis Presley or Donald Duck—or pretty much anyone. He could have told her anything, but he didn't. He *was* Tommy. He wasn't trying to run, or hide. Quite the opposite, in fact. He wasn't hiding; he was finding.

"Got your passport there?" she asked.

Tommy shook his head.

"Driver's license?"

Still no.

"Any ID at all?"

Tommy shrugged. "Sorry," he said. "Don't have a passport yet and I can't drive. I've got cash, though," he added hopefully.

The woman raised an eyebrow, and Tommy thought he was about to be sent packing. But then he saw her write a number in the "passport" column of her sheet and close the folder.

"Fifteen bucks a night, and you'll have to pay the first month now. There's an extra twenty for the…uh, identification waiver." She grinned at him.

Tommy handed over the cash, mentally tallying how much he had left, and watched the extra twenty disappear into the pocket of her tight jeans.

"Welcome to Sunrise Backpackers," she said, smiling broadly and pointing through the door on her right. "Head up the stairs, grab any empty bed in the first room on the left. Bathroom is further down the hall on the right. Have a great stay, Tommy."

Tommy picked up his bundle and followed her directions to the room she'd indicated, his home for at least the next six weeks.

The smell momentarily took his breath away. The air was stale and soupy with the aroma of unwashed clothes and feet, mixed with bodies sweating out countless beers through sticky summer nights. There were four sets of bunk beds, with two lined up end to end against each of the longer walls. At the far end of the dorm, a security grille screened the only window, which was—for some inexplicable reason—closed tight. Overhead, a single ceiling fan spun lazily, as if it knew any attempt to push the air around the room was pointless.

Tommy counted one, two, three, four of the mattresses covered in clothes and bags. A bottom bunk closest to the window looked clear, and Tommy started unpacking his makeshift backpack.

"Christ, mate. You on a budget or what?" a voice behind him exclaimed.

A young man, perhaps a few years older than Tommy, was lying on the top bunk across from him; Tommy had mistaken his motionless form for a pile of clothes. He was wearing a scruffy old T-shirt, his straw-colored hair was sticking out at all angles, and he looked like he hadn't had a shave in a few weeks at least.

"I thought *I* was cheap. At least I've got a bag to put my stuff in."

Tommy smiled as the young man climbed down from the bunk and extended his hand.

"I'm Stuart. But call me Stu," he said. He spoke with a British accent, but something about it seemed vaguely familiar.

"Tommy," he said. "Where are you from, Stu?"

"Liverpool," he replied, and Tommy realized: he'd heard the same accent blaring from the tinny speaker of the old television in the Dairy's common room. Every afternoon until he was five he'd watched *Thomas the Tank Engine* on the flickering screen, and just a few words from Stu had taken him straight back there.

Stu was up for a chat.

"Five nights a week I stacked shelves to save for the trip. Soup's the worst. Dropped a can on my toe—check it out." He pointed at his left foot. "I reckon I broke it. Doesn't look right, does it?"

Tommy pulled a face.

"Come on, it's not that bad!" Stu said in mock offense. "Just a bit crooked."

"No!" replied Tommy, his cheeks reddening slightly. "I just...I don't know how you sleep in here. The smell—it's like..." He tried to place it. "Sean, one of my mates, *never* opened his bedroom window. His room smelled like feet for three years straight. Does this open?" He gestured to the grimy window next to the bunks.

Stu shook his head. "Locked. Maybe jammed? I dunno. But everyone tries it on their first night. If you want my advice, the trick is to have enough beers that you don't notice the smell."

Tommy peered closely at the lock while Stu continued talking. He'd moved beyond his work in a Liverpool supermarket and was now describing his economy-class flight in glorious high-definition.

"And she just kept bringing me beers! I was like, am I supposed to tip you or something?"

"Got it!" Tommy exclaimed and reefed something out of the window lock. He showed it to Stu. "The bolt snapped," he said and slid the window up smoothly. Warm air rushed in; it wasn't much cooler than the room itself, but it didn't smell like sweaty shirts and jocks.

"Hey, Tommy—you know what this means? We need to celebrate," said Stu. "How old are you?"

"Eighteen." Tommy hesitated. "Today, actually."

"Seriously? How about that! You got the window open *and* it's your birthday! Guess we're getting on it tonight."

Tommy laughed a little uneasily and agreed to meet Stu back at the hostel later. But first, he had a few things to do.

After piling his clothes on the end of his bed, Tommy hit the streets again. This time, he walked with purpose, clutching a map of the city that he'd grabbed from a display rack in the hostel's foyer. He knew he looked like a tourist, and even a casual observer would have noticed his free hand going to his pocket regularly, as though he was checking to make sure something was still there. That pocket contained $3,500, minus the cost of his train ticket, breakfast, and accommodation. He was worried about carrying so much money around, but he figured it was safer in his pocket than hidden under his mattress. Stu was hardly going to keep an eye on it for him; he'd fallen asleep just as Tommy left the hostel, having declared his intention to spend the day sleeping off the previous night's beers before starting again with Tommy that night.

Tommy ticked off the street signs on his map as he got closer and closer to his destination. Finally, he saw it—Hunt Street. It was quieter than the main thoroughfares. The buildings themselves were more modest, topping out at four or five stories, and the ground floors seemed to be mostly given over to restaurants and cafés, with tables and chairs spilling outside. There was little traffic, but the footpaths were already packed with noisy diners—a mix of tourists and office workers—squeezed around small tables.

The smell of food made Tommy's stomach groan, and he eyed the plates hungrily. *Later*, he told himself.

Hunt Street was a long one, and he walked nine city blocks, losing hope the further he went, before he spied something promising. While most of the other places he'd passed had large windows to let the sun in, this establishment was built for gloom, with thick panels on either side of the doors to keep out the light. Tommy tried to peer inside. He couldn't see much past the entrance—but somehow he knew this was the place. He straightened up, steeled himself, and walked in, trying to look more confident than he felt. But all confidence evaporated as he tripped, falling victim to the dim lighting and a half step up to the bar's interior.

"You all right, mate?" A man was suddenly at his side, having darted from behind the counter to help Tommy up.

"Yeah, I'm fine," said Tommy.

The man held out his hand anyway and Tommy took it. He recognized the bartender instantly with his spiky brown hair, long nose, and neatly trimmed beard. The last time Tommy had seen him, Dave had been visiting his son in the hospital.

"Are you sure you're okay?" Dave asked.

Tommy nodded. "Just didn't see that step."

"Catches a few people out. That's why I put up the sign."
Dave pointed to the wall. A piece of paper the size of a Post-it
Note was stuck there, and written on it in tiny block letters was:
BEWARE OF STEP.

Tommy laughed. He looked around the bar Josh had
described so clearly, taking in the details as his eyes adjusted. It
was long, burrowing deep into the building. A wooden counter
ran along half of one wall, and the rest of the space was occupied
by a row of leather booths on the opposite wall and a scattering
of small wooden tables in between. It was softly lit—Tommy
had learned that the hard way—with old-fashioned lamps in
the booths giving it a speakeasy feel, like the kind he'd seen in
movies. Clashing with the old-world vibe was a trio of arcade
games at the back of the bar—two pinball machines and a vintage Pac-Man unit complete with joystick, and all with flashing lights and tinny music. But there was also a faint aroma of
spilled cocktails and mid-range whisky, the kind of smell that
encouraged drinkers to stick around, because things could get
a bit loose.

"Come and sit for a sec, make sure you're okay." Dave led
Tommy to a stool at the bar. "You here to meet someone?"

"Well, actually," Tommy said (acutely aware of everything
hinging on this moment), "I'm here to see you, I think."

"Me?" Josh's dad looked surprised.

"You're the manager, right?" Suddenly Tommy felt unsure of
himself.

"Yeah, mate, that's me. Dave. Dave Saunders."

"Tommy Llewellyn."

"Good to meet you, Tommy Llewellyn," said Dave. "Now, what can I do for you?"

"I'd like a job. Any job, really. I haven't had much experience making drinks but I'm keen to learn. And I'm happy to do anything. Wash glasses, mop the floor, whatever." Tommy was talking quickly; far too quickly, he realized, to appear cool and confident. Too late now.

Dave smiled. He liked this boy. Besides, kids with no experience were cheap. "Why here?" he asked. "There are plenty of other places on the strip where you'd see a lot more action. You just hitting up every business with your CV?"

Tommy shook his head emphatically. "No way. This is the only place I've been to. And I haven't got a CV. A mate told me about it a few years ago. He wanted to work here. Guess it kind of stuck with me too."

For a moment Dave looked curious, and Tommy waited for him to ask who'd praised the bar so highly. But Dave was actually doing sums in his head, wondering what he could get away with paying him.

"How old are you, Tommy?"

"Eighteen. Well, only just. Today, actually, Mr. Saunders," Tommy added deferentially.

"Well, happy birthday. But don't try that 'mister' shit. I'm too young for that. Everyone calls me Dave." He stroked his beard as he thought. "Tell you what, Tommy. Why don't you come back tomorrow afternoon, say five o'clock. Friday's our busiest day, and I could use an extra set of hands. I'll give you a trial at half-pay. Do a good job, and I'll roster you on."

Tommy felt the grin spreading across his face.

"You won't be behind the bar, though," Dave said. "You'll be picking up glasses and washing 'em. If you're okay with that, then I'll see you tomorrow."

"More than okay. That's brilliant. Thanks, Dave."

Tommy was stepping carefully over the trip hazard in the doorway when he heard Dave call out.

"Hey, Tommy. Who was it?"

"Who was what?" asked Tommy.

"Who was it that told you about The Hole? The one who wanted to work here?"

Tommy stopped. "Just a kid I met a few years ago. Can't remember his name." Tommy remembered his name just fine, but Josh wasn't going to remember *his*. No, if Tommy was to stand any chance of restoring a friendship with Josh, then he had to play it cool. For now.

Dave shrugged. "Never mind. All right, see you at five tomorrow. Don't be late."

Tommy smiled. "I won't let you down," he promised.

Tommy made a couple of other stops on his way home. The first was a small shop whose name was advertised in scratched paint on the front window. Inside, clothes were displayed not on racks but in large wire bins, with the price scrawled on a sign on the side. An elderly man with thick, bushy eyebrows and a money belt nodded at Tommy as he entered. Tommy picked out half a dozen shirts—trying to get as close as he could to the tight shirt Dave had been wearing in the bar—then some pants to match.

With his savings further depleted, his second stop was a supermarket, where he picked up a toothbrush, toothpaste, and a razor. As he did, he heard his stomach squeal in protest. Surrounded by cans of soup and packs of dry pasta, it hit Tommy that feeding himself wasn't as simple as visiting the dining room to see what had been prepared. He was going to need groceries, and he was going to need to do something with them. For the first time, Tommy wondered if he'd bitten off more than he could chew. He'd taught himself to sand and paint an entire house, to fix furniture and plant a garden, but the thought of a kitchen full of raw ingredients waiting to be turned into something edible was almost too much. *That'd be right*, Tommy thought—he could find loopholes in something extraordinary like the Reset, only to be brought undone by everyday things his mum and dad could've taught him.

Fifteen minutes later Tommy shuffled along the street, weighed down by plastic shopping bags. By the time he reached Sunrise Backpackers, the handles had formed deep red crevices in his fingers, and his arms were burning. He carried his groceries to the kitchen and made himself two large sandwiches before depositing the bags on a vacant corner of a shelf. Almost as an afterthought, he tied the bags' handles in a knot—a woefully inadequate deterrent to other guests.

Tommy returned to his room with his plate, hoping to find Stu or someone else to talk to, but the dorm was deserted. He sat alone on his bunk and ate, the thin plastic mattress squeaking under the threadbare sheet. As he looked around at his new home, he thought about how much his life had changed in only a matter of hours and a wave of exhaustion washed over him.

Alone, and with his stomach now full, there was nothing to stop him from nodding off as the afternoon sun streamed through the small window.

Excited voices echoed around the dorm and Tommy sat up with a start, nearly hitting his head on the bunk above. The narrow slice of sky visible through the window was almost completely dark, and the overhead lights—two fluorescent tubes, one at each end of the room—flickered on as Stu led a group inside.

"Birthday boy! You're up!" Stu cried. He already held a beer.

"Yeah, sorry if you needed the room," Tommy replied sheepishly.

"Didn't bother me, mate. Just figured you were charging up for tonight." He grinned, and Tommy felt a faint flutter of alarm about what was in store. "Have you met anyone else yet?"

Tommy shook his head. Looking past Stu he could see another guy about the same age, and two girls.

"This is Pete. Yes, we're both from England, no, we didn't travel together, and yes, he disappears when it's his turn to buy a round."

Pete rolled his eyes and told Stu to fuck off.

Stu shrugged. "Just telling the truth, Petey," he said, and turned to the two girls behind him. "This is Katerina, and this is Alex. Unlike me and Pete, they *are* traveling together."

Tommy shook hands with Alex first, then Katerina. They were wearing near-identical clothes—singlet tops and shorts that showed off their long, smooth legs—but that was where the similarities ended. Alex's dark brown hair was cut short, and her skin had a reddish tone to it that suggested the sun had not been her friend in recent days. Katerina's hair was lighter and pulled back in a long ponytail. She'd managed to pick up a golden tan, and when she smiled at Tommy, her teeth were a brilliant white.

"Hi," said Tommy a little shyly. "Where are you from?"

"Germany. From Munich," Katerina said. Her accent was strong but she spoke clearly and confidently. "Are you the one who fixed the window?"

He nodded, and she raised an eyebrow at him, impressed.

"Your first day, and you've already saved our lives," she said dramatically.

Tommy blushed, and searched for something to say. Anything to take the attention off his red cheeks.

"Stu, guess what? I got a job today."

"So hang on," Stu said. "You got a job, it's your birthday, *and* you got the window open. Get dressed. We're celebrating. We'll wait for you outside."

Tommy quickly pulled on a new shirt, one of his bargain-bin purchases, and checked his reflection. (It was, in fact, the first time in his life that he'd actually cared how his hair looked.) His hand went to his pocket again. Reassured that his money was safe, Tommy went to join his new roommates.

The floor of the pub was sticky, and if the room had been quiet, Tommy would have been able to hear his shoes release from the carpet with a soft *thhhk* on every step. But the room was not quiet, with revelers crammed shoulder to shoulder and a steady bass pounding from hidden speakers overhead. And Tommy probably wouldn't have noticed anyway—he was well on his way to a state he'd only experienced once before, under the slide in the playground at Upper Reach. He was older now, though, with more body weight to absorb the booze as it seeped into his bloodstream. Six or seven beers in—plus two shots of something he couldn't pronounce—and he was in a good mood. He actually found himself disappointed when Pete leaned across the small table they were clustered around and suggested it was time to head back.

"Come on, guys! It's still early!" Tommy shouted to Pete over the music.

"Nah, Tommy," Pete replied. "Eight nights straight and I'm beat. We'll go again tomorrow, though. Friday night's always bigger."

"I'll have one more with you, Tommy," said Katerina, winking at Pete. "You guys go on back, we'll see you there in a bit." She put her mouth to Alex's ear and spoke to her. Alex looked confused at first, then shrugged and got up off her stool. Alex, Pete, and Stu pushed their way through the crowd.

"Stay here," Katerina said. "I'm getting you something special for your birthday."

She returned a few minutes later with two glasses of a brownish liqueur, topped with a thin creamy layer.

"Espresso martinis, they're my favorite," Katerina said with a smile. "Happy birthday, Tommy."

They clinked their glasses. Tommy's drink sloshed down the side and pooled on the table.

Tommy asked Katerina about her trip and about her life at home. Her accent combined with the loud music to make the responses almost indecipherable, but he smiled and nodded as she spoke. He liked the way her hair bounced in its pony-tail as she talked, and she gestured wildly to make her points clear. She sipped between each question, and soon their glasses were empty.

"Come on, Tommy, it's time to go," Katerina decided, and Tommy followed her obediently out of the pub and onto the street. The quiet of the night air outside rang in his ears; he suddenly felt light-headed, and pictured himself sprinting along the road in Upper Reach, full of stolen liquor, dashing across the street and then—well, nothing after that. Just pain.

But the memory faded as they walked along the footpath, the city calmer at night but with enough traffic and pedestrians to give it a lively feel. Tommy couldn't help but compare this to nights at the Dairy, where the only noise was the occasional blast of a shotgun as the owners of a nearby farm picked off rabbits. He wanted to share the observation with Katerina, but even with his inhibitions dulled he worried that she'd think of him as a timid country boy, loose in the big city.

Tommy and Katerina walked side by side, occasionally paus-ing to let others pass.

"What's with Alex?" Tommy blurted out. "I get the feeling she doesn't like me much."

"No, no, it's not that." Katerina laughed. "She doesn't speak much English, so I think she just doesn't know what to say."

"Well, *your* English is perfect," Tommy said.

Katerina reached over and took his hand, and a thrill ran

up his arm. They continued along the footpath, and when they arrived at the hostel, he opened the door for her.

Their dorm was already dark, and they could hear the rhythmic breathing of all three roommates sound asleep. Pete was snoring softly, and Tommy and Katerina stifled a laugh when his nose whistled. Katerina threw her handbag on her bed near the door, but didn't stop. Instead, she led Tommy to his own bunk at the far end of the room.

"Sit down, Tommy," she commanded in a whisper. "You're drunk."

"So are you," Tommy replied, but he did what he was told. As he lowered himself onto the mattress, the back of his head collided solidly with the frame of the bed above.

"Are you all right?" Katerina asked, voice concerned.

Tommy nodded. He actually felt a little dazed, but he wasn't sure if that was the knock on the head, the drinks, or the fact that a beautiful girl was helping him to bed.

Katerina sat down beside him. "Are you sure?" she whispered, her face close to his.

He nodded dumbly again, and then Katerina's lips were on his. She kissed him, biting his lip gently, and he pressed against her.

Jesus Christ, he thought. *What am I supposed to do now?*

"Lie down," she said softly, as if reading his mind. "I'll be back in a minute."

Tommy meekly followed her instructions and lay back on his pillow as he watched Katerina's silhouette tiptoe toward the door. He closed his eyes and found himself wishing he hadn't had so much to drink, so that he might remember this more clearly tomorrow.

Katerina stood impatiently in the corridor outside, waiting for her turn in the shared bathroom. Finally the occupant—a tall blond man—unlocked the door and stepped out, giving a half smile of apology as he slipped past Katerina. She was enveloped in the stench of stomach acid, and pulled a face; Tommy wasn't the only person in the hostel who'd had a bit too much to drink that night.

Soon she was walking back to her dorm, wondering what state Tommy would be in when she arrived. She closed the door behind her and listened carefully; there was no noise apart from Pete's soft nose whistle, so she padded along past her own bed to where Tommy lay on his bunk. She sat on the edge of the mattress and bent to kiss him again, expecting an enthusiastic reaction.

Instead, there was no response.

Tommy was fast asleep.

Tommy stared up at the underside of the bunk above him and strained to remember where he was. His tongue felt thick and dry, and he tried without success to swallow, wanting to get rid of the sour milk taste in his mouth. He lay still, trying to recall the events of the previous night. He remembered Katerina taking his hand as they walked home, and smiled when he thought of her kissing him: his first proper kiss. But he wasn't sure what had happened after that. Surely something had happened—the kiss had certainly been full of promise—but he drew a blank. He'd have to ask her.

Tommy sat up and whacked his head again. The previous
night the same impact had barely bothered him; now it felt
like he'd turned the handle on a vice squeezing his temples.
He winced.

"Morning," said Stu from the bunk across the way. He was
sitting cross-legged, reading a book. He grinned mischievously
at Tommy. "What'd you two get up to last night?"

Tommy smiled modestly—partly because he didn't know the
answer—and peered along the room to see if Katerina was still in
bed. She wasn't in her bunk, and Alex wasn't in hers above. In fact,
the girls' clothes and bags were gone, and the beds had been stripped
of their sheets too—he could see the brown vinyl of the mattresses.

"Where are the girls?" Tommy asked Stu.

"They cleared out early, probably six-ish," he said.

"What?" exclaimed Tommy. "Katerina told me they had
another few weeks here. Why'd they leave?"

Stu shrugged. "No idea, mate. They didn't say anything to
me, I just saw 'em go. Figured they must've got a better offer.
Maybe a ride somewhere. It happens." Tommy must have looked
crestfallen because Stu added, "Chin up, mate. She didn't break
your heart—you only knew her for a few hours."

"Yeah, I suppose so." Tommy agreed. "A good few hours."

"Yeah, it was a fun night," Stu said, closing his book. "How's
the head this morning?"

"It's been better," admitted Tommy.

"Go and have some toast," Stu advised. "And water. Coffee if
you drink it. You'll feel heaps better, trust me. I've had a bit of
experience. And get changed too. Looks like you wore some of
your drink last night."

Tommy looked down; he was still in the clothes he'd been in at the pub.

He slipped on a clean shirt. As he struggled out of his pants, he remembered his wad of cash—he'd need to transfer it to his shorts.

He fished around in his pocket. Empty. He tried the other one, but there was nothing in it except for a torn cardboard coaster from the pub.

After two minutes of frantic searching, in which time he turned his mattress over and picked through every item of clothing in his possession, Tommy came to the same conclusion he'd leaped to at the start. His money—every last dollar—was gone. And he suspected it had left at around six o'clock that morning.

11

Tommy waited for a gap in the traffic and darted across the intersection. It was a long walk to The Hole, and there was no way he was going to be late for his first day.

He looked good, he thought. Better than he felt. Definitely employable. He was wearing a shirt almost identical to the one he'd seen Dave in the previous day (it was more suited to someone Tommy's age than Dave's), and he'd combed his hair neatly and had a shave. It was the best he could look with a crooked nose and the shadow of a hangover.

On the outside, Tommy might have looked calm, if a touch jittery ahead of his first shift, but inside he was seething—not just at Katerina, but at himself. He was the one who'd had too much to drink. He was the one who'd thought Katerina had been interested in him, and not just the wad of cash he'd peeled notes from when it was his turn to buy. And he was the one who'd been naive enough to keep it in his pocket in the first place, and lose the lot on the first day of his adult life. He'd told the woman on the front desk—Bridget—who had called the police for Tommy, and he'd filed a report, but even he realized how stupid he sounded once all the excuses were stripped away.

"I went to the pub with three grand in my pocket, got drunk, came home with a girl, and passed out."

The police officer hadn't been particularly sympathetic. "Right. You're in a dorm. There's no lock on the door. How do you know she's the one who took it?"

"Well…I don't know for sure. But it's definitely gone."

Tommy suspected the report didn't make it past the cop's notebook. Especially when the officer asked him for ID and he couldn't supply anything, not even a library card. He'd have to do something about that.

His headache had cleared several hours earlier, chased away by a painkiller from Pete, but the pill did nothing to ease his nerves the closer he got to The Hole. As he entered (mindful of the step), he saw there were probably a dozen or more customers already there—mostly after-work types, and at least one table of three he suspected had come for a drink after lunch and failed to leave.

Dave was behind the bar and he nodded when he saw Tommy. "You're early. Good start," he said. "I'll give you the tour, but it'll have to be quick. Rush won't be far off now."

The tour was brief indeed, and consisted of Dave pointing out the counter area, with bottles of spirits lined up against the mirror at the back of the bar like an alcoholic cityscape, the arcade games ("*Twilight Zone*'s playing up again. I've got a tech coming Monday to fix it, but the customers won't mind. They expect them to break down. Part of the experience."), and finally the kitchen. This was where Tommy was going to spend most of his time, he was told.

"Every fifteen minutes do a lap around the bar, from back to front, and collect the glasses. Careful not to drop them. One or two's okay, accidents happen, but any more and you'll be paying for it. Once you bring them back to the kitchen you can chuck the beer glasses—these ones—in the washer, but only set it off when it's full. Anything that's not a beer glass—that means cocktail glasses, plates, whatever—you wash by hand. Got it?"

Tommy nodded.

"Good. Any questions?"

Yes, thought Tommy. *Where's Josh?*

"No," he said.

"All right. Now, you might've seen Renee out there wiping the tables…" Tommy certainly had seen Renee, a slender blond woman in her late thirties. "She'll be serving as well, and anything she says goes. Jamie's on food." Dave pointed to a girl on the other side of the kitchen, who looked up at the mention of her name and waved to Tommy. "We just do cheese and olives and stuff. Cocktails get hit hard from eight, so there's another bartender in then. Good luck."

He hurried back to the bar, and Tommy stood alone in front of a commercial dishwasher and two empty sinks.

Two hours later his fingertips were wrinkled from the soapy water and his legs ached from standing in one place. But Tommy was enjoying himself. He particularly enjoyed knowing that he was slowly earning money; there was a hole in his pocket he needed to fill. He and Jamie had spoken only a handful of times, with the friendly young woman sending out plate after plate of snacks, but she seemed nice, and she hadn't pushed Tommy for more information about where he'd come from. (She was, in fact, just pleased Tommy hadn't attempted to hit on her. The last glassie had only waited thirty minutes before asking whether she had a rule about sleeping with colleagues. She'd complained to Dave, but he'd just smiled and told her she should be flattered.)

Tommy leaned past a customer to collect glasses from a table, adding them to the stack in his hand. He didn't mind being in the kitchen, but he already preferred his laps around the main floor. He could see the customers, even have a laugh with them, and listen to them talk about work and money and sex and all kinds of things he'd never really encountered at Upper Reach.

He was shifting the weight of the glasses slightly, a precarious tower of glassware snaking all the way from his left hand to his shoulder, when laughter exploded at the table behind him. Startled, Tommy spun around and watched as the top two glasses sailed off the stack. They soared in a neat arc, and smashed one after the other on the polished concrete floor, the noise shearing through the hum of the bar like a gunshot. There was a moment of silence, then all around the darkened room conversations picked up where they'd left off. Tommy carried the rest of the tower to the counter, where Dave passed him a broom.

"That's your limit, mate," he said.

Tommy felt his face burn a deep crimson, right to the tips of his ears. Crouched down next to the shattered glasses, he surveyed the damage—shards spread around on all sides like shrapnel from a blast. Tommy started sweeping, the light tinkling of the broken glass barely audible over the chatter. He was secretly relieved to be squatting—at least nobody could see him here. But then a pair of shoes appeared beside him.

"You must be the new guy," a voice said. "Don't worry about Dave. It happens to all of us."

Tommy looked up to see a younger, clean-shaven version of the bar manager standing over him.

Josh.

Tommy sprang to his feet and shook Josh's hand way too enthusiastically, the way old friends would greet each other.

Josh looked amused. "What's your name, new guy?" he asked.

"I'm Tommy." Tommy reminded himself that as far as Josh knew, they were meeting for the first time. Their encounter in the hospital had been two Resets ago; he wasn't even a distant memory to Josh. He was a stranger.

"Good to meet you, Tommy. I'm Josh. And yes, before you ask, Dave's my dad. Nepotism at its finest." Josh grinned.

Tommy looked closely at his friend. Gone was the sickly yellow tone, replaced by a normal healthy complexion.

"You'd better get that swept up before someone steps in it," Josh said, pointing to the pile of broken glass. "If you get us sued on your first day, he'll *really* have the shits."

Tommy crouched down again, but his mind wasn't on the mess. *Come and find me,* Josh had said. Well, Tommy had found him, and now they were working together at the very place they'd discussed so many times in the hospital. Sure, Josh didn't really know who he was right now, but as far as Tommy was concerned, that was a minor detail. He suspected some people were just meant to be friends.

Tommy worked the next night too, and the following week his shifts increased to three. By the end of the month, Dave had put him on full time, due in no small part to the fact that Tommy's broken glass tally had stalled at two.

"He's quick, he's careful, he's friendly with the customers," Dave said to his son as they cleaned up the bar at closing time. "As far as I'm concerned, he can have all the shifts he wants."

"He could even replace Renee, I reckon," replied Josh, elbowing his dad in the ribs. The relationship between Dave and the blond waitress was the worst-kept secret on the street. Josh didn't mind, except when he caught Dave watching Renee leaning over to wipe a table. *No son should have to watch his dad ogling like that in public*, he thought. Still, at least it meant he focused his attention on just one person, instead of hitting on every girl who walked into the place. Josh only wished his dad had been that focused on his mum.

"Hurry up and clean the benches so we can close. You might be family but I'll still fire you," Dave replied as he counted notes, sliding cash into envelopes. "And I'll keep this too."

"Dad, please! This isn't the eighties. You know you can pay us straight into our accounts."

Dave decided Josh was starting to sound like Renee, who insisted that getting cash in an envelope from the man she was sleeping with made her feel dirty. But this was how he'd always done it. Plus, he kept some of the wages off the books, which made the owners happy, and in turn kept Dave—and the rest of them—employed.

The last customers had left ten minutes earlier—a group of six or so heavy drinkers, celebrating so hard that they'd forgotten what they were celebrating.

"Still on for tomorrow, mate?" Josh called as Tommy emerged from the kitchen.

"Yeah, absolutely," Tommy replied. The pair were meeting up for a drink on their day off. It had been Josh's suggestion, and Tommy had cheered silently.

With his week's pay tucked into his pocket, Tommy turned for home, where the smell of unwashed travelers no longer bothered him, and he was just one of the gang. The week after he'd started at The Hole had been a hungry one for him, caught between the theft of his savings and his first wages. He'd gone through his supplies in the hostel kitchen by day four, and over the next couple of days lost a few pounds through sheer starvation. Stu had helped him out, sharing a bit of food, and the two had become good friends. But eventually he too packed up his gear and headed off, snaring himself a discount ticket and a window seat on a Greyhound bus heading a long way north. *At least he didn't leave without saying goodbye*, thought Tommy, *and didn't leave with anything that wasn't his.*

Once he'd received his first envelope from Dave, Tommy had sat down with a scrap of paper and a pencil he'd pinched from the bar. He could get a loaf of bread for a buck and a half at the hot bread shop two blocks over, and it'd last him two days. The hostel kitchen had little packets of biscuits—so dry Tommy could almost feel them sucking the moisture from his tongue—as well as teabags and sachets of bitter instant coffee.

It was less than a pauper's lifestyle, but he needed to save some cash. He hadn't come to the city just to live in a hostel. It was a means to an end for Tommy.

He had plans.

He'd already discovered one, then two loopholes in the Reset, and found Josh. Now all he had to do was track down Carey, and find a way to be remembered.

Easy.

12

Sunrise Backpackers had more than a few similarities to the Dairy. Tommy had to share a bathroom, for one thing, and everyone dined together at long tables. There was a common room, too, which was home to some squishy threadbare couches (although these couches smelled a lot worse than the Dairy's, and Tommy preferred not to dwell on why) and a small TV that was rarely switched on. The room also featured a row of blue vinyl-covered chairs lined up against one wall, and despite being supremely uncomfortable, Tommy found that more often than not there'd be a handful of the hostel's guests lounging around on them.

It was strange being the only local in an international mix, with the room a confusing combination of conversations in halting, accented English or rapid-fire Italian, German, French, or who knew what else. With the exception of the couches, the stale cloud that settled in the dorm rooms was less over-whelming here, thanks to the bigger windows and the fact that sleeping in the common room wasn't allowed. It was, by far, Tommy's favorite room in the building. He'd met some fascinating travelers—one guy claimed to be a golf pro booted from the European circuit for cheating. Tommy assumed he was full of it, but a whisper of shame in the man's voice suggested otherwise. But this wasn't why he loved it.

No, Tommy was drawn to the common room at Sunrise Backpackers because of the two computers, a pair of chunky Hewlett-Packards. Pinned to the wall above them was a sign detailing the booking system and cost ($1.50 an hour). He'd scrawled his name on the booking sheet next to an 11:00 a.m. slot. He could sleep off the late-night shift, and—perhaps most significantly—he'd have some privacy. If they weren't recovering from a hangover, the rest of the hostel's guests usually took advantage of the slightest glimpse of sun to head to the beach, coming home late in the day with a pinkish glow to their unseasoned skin.

At 11:00, Tommy sat down and stared at the screen. The night before, he'd lain in his bed and pictured how this might work. He imagined researching his—what? Affliction? Curse?—and finding an expert somewhere, with a PhD in the kind of bizarre stuff that Tommy had inherited when he was born. He dreamed of a long-distance phone call with an academic who was delighted to find another case to support his research, and who could explain why, how, and what to do to stop it. But that was just a dream. The reality was a blank screen on a computer.

Tommy pulled up a search engine. His fingers hovered over the keyboard, unsure what to type. He'd always thought of it as his Reset, but that was just a nickname for something he couldn't explain. He supposed plenty of other people had sat at this very machine and searched symptoms that they couldn't explain either. But most of those could probably be attributed to a combination of drink, drugs, and sex.

Betcha nobody's searched for this before, Tommy thought, and he typed: *Why do people keep forgetting me?*

The computer whirred as the internet connection strained. Finally he scrolled down through the search results, his heart sinking. Every page promised assistance, but none offered what he needed: *First impressions count! How to make yourself more interesting*, or, *Sales pitches to stand out from the crowd*. Even a dating website that *guaranteed* memorable encounters.

He shook his head, and typed: *Memory loss every year*.

The search results came back faster, as though his first attempt had primed the connection. As Tommy read through the page, he knew he was on the wrong track. He was quite certain he didn't have dementia or Alzheimer's, although he now knew the symptoms to look out for. He tried one more time, frustration building. The first result was an online gaming site featuring the card game Memory, and he exited the browser, abandoning the common room just twelve minutes into his hour-long booking. Tommy knew he was wasting his time. What he was looking for was just not there. He didn't have a problem standing out in a crowd or remembering where he worked. No, his issue was that once a year, the entire world forgot who he was. And clearly WebMD and self-help sites weren't going to fix it.

He had one more idea, but first there was a small hurdle to overcome.

◯

On Wednesday nights the bar closed at 10:00 p.m., unless there was a large group wanting to carry on. Dave described that one as a no-brainer. If a posse of suits on a junket asked to see the whisky list, none of the staff went home 'til they'd tried everything The Hole had to offer.

"Just keep pouring until the Amex comes out," Dave had told his team one night, and some three hours later a shaky hand was signing a bill for almost one and a half grand of Scotch and Japanese whiskies. But that had been a few years ago, long before Tommy, and on this particular Wednesday night there was no such group. Just two tables were occupied—a young couple on a date, sipping martinis (they both hated the taste but didn't want to admit it), and three friends who'd had three gin and tonics and two bowls of olives, and had run out of things to talk about after the first round. On quiet nights like this, Tommy was promoted to serving—a fancy name for wiping down tables—while Josh took over the main bartender duties from his dad, who considered himself more of a supervisor anyway.

"Hey, Josh," Tommy said, his voice soft and conspiratorial. "Can you help me with something?"

"Sure, mate. What's up?"

"I need to get some ID."

"What, a fake?" Josh looked at Tommy curiously. "Aren't you already eighteen?"

"Yeah, I am, but I don't have any proof. Long story."

Josh wasn't really surprised. Tommy had told him he'd come from a foster home and didn't know his parents. "No birth certificate, no driver's license, nothing. Haven't even got a bank account," Tommy said.

"Who doesn't have a bank account?" asked Josh incredulously. "I've had one since I was five—we had to get them in kindergarten."

"Seriously. Never had one." This was a half-truth—he'd had one started for him when he was in primary school, just like Josh. But unlike Josh, Tommy's account had vanished into thin air. "I just need someone who can supply me with a license, or a passport or something. It's not really illegal if I'm over eighteen, is it?"

"Can't you get an official one? I'm sure they'd have requests from people all the time who haven't got a birth certificate—street kids and that kind of thing."

"Already tried. Can't do it." He needed someone who'd known him for a decade to vouch for his identity. He could also have a signed letter from his school, but considering he'd ceased to exist in the eyes of Mrs. Lewis and everyone at Mortlake High, that was a dead end.

"So what do you need it for?" Josh asked. "Surely not to get into places like this. I wouldn't ID you if I was working the door." He gazed at Tommy, assessing him, and decided he would have picked him as twenty-two. Something about the sandy hair and crooked nose made him look older. He would have been popular in high school, Josh thought—you need someone who looked old enough to buy beer and smokes.

"Well, don't laugh." Tommy hesitated. "I want to borrow some library books, and I can't do it without ID."

Josh did laugh. He clutched his stomach and threw his head

back, cackling. It was the same laugh Tommy had heard him smother with a pillow in his hospital bed.

"You serious?" Josh asked after he'd caught his breath.

Tommy nodded as Dave appeared from the kitchen, drawn by the commotion.

"What's going on?" Dave asked. "You're not paid to chat. Tommy, go and replace Jamie if you're finished out here. She can leave early; she costs more than you."

Tommy turned toward the kitchen, and Dave disappeared into the back storeroom.

"Tommy?" Josh said in a low voice.

Tommy turned around.

"I know someone who can help. It'll cost you, though. Two hundred. That cool?"

He nodded.

"Sweet. Bring it tomorrow, yeah? And a passport photo of yourself."

"Thanks, Josh," whispered Tommy.

He arrived the next afternoon with four fifty-dollar notes folded in his pocket, alongside two passport-sized photos of himself. He'd paid for the photos at a camera store, and tried not to think about how expensive the whole exercise was becoming. Tommy loitered near the counter, waiting for a chance to pass the money and photos to Josh, but the opportunity didn't arise; Dave was hovering, it was student night, and The Hole was busy. Nobody drank like college students getting a two-for-one.

On these nights, Tommy preferred being out on the floor around people his own age. He couldn't help but think that if the circumstances had been different, he might have been one of them, living in a student dorm instead of a backpacker dorm, and going for cheap drinks at The Hole instead of wiping up the cheap drinks after they were knocked over. There was also a small part of him that wondered what he'd do if he spied Carey Price in the crowd, just one of the many pretty girls in short dresses with straightened hair, dressed up for a night out.

He kept looking, but there was no Carey Price.

When the last of the student crowd cleared out at around midnight in search of a dance floor, Tommy was finally able to give Josh the money and photos. Josh pocketed the cash but paused to chuckle at the pictures.

"What?" asked Tommy.

"You look like you've got the shits!" replied Josh. "Perfect for an ID." He told Tommy he'd pass them along to his friend, and with a bit of luck, he should have a driver's license in Tommy's name within a week. "And he'll put a nice long expiration date on it too. Should be good for the next five years at least. Just do me a favor, and don't actually use it to drive a car."

The week passed slowly for Tommy; each evening he'd look at Josh hopefully, and each evening Josh would shake his head.

"I've never seen someone so impatient to get to the library," he said to Tommy. "What's got you so worked up? A librarian?" He winked.

Tommy shook his head. "Nah," he said. "Just doing a bit of research." He hoped Josh would leave it at that.

Josh didn't. "Research? Into what?"

If he'd been asked in the future about that moment—which turned out to be far more significant than either Tommy or Josh realized at the time—Tommy might have wondered if there was something bigger guiding his response. Perhaps the legacy of a man named Leonard Palmer (the father who could remember huge sums and the metro bus timetable but forgot his own son). Or perhaps it was Tommy thinking under pressure, joining the dots: from the conversation in their hospital beds about starting their own bar, to the pile of money he was trying to amass for just that reason. Maybe he saw the opportunity to plant a seed and seized it.

Or maybe he just said the first thing that came into his head.

"Really, it's nothing," he said finally. "Just some business stuff."

Josh looked thoughtful. "I didn't know you were into business," he replied. "How come we've never talked about it before?"

We have—in the hospital. And I found you, and here we are, Tommy wanted to say. But instead he shrugged.

"Can I run some ideas past you sometime?" Josh asked. "I've got plans, you know. Wouldn't mind a bit of input from someone who's got his nose in books."

Tommy wasn't sure if Josh was making fun of him. He looked at his friend; there was no trace of a smile on Josh's face.

"Sure," said Tommy. *Christ,* he thought. *How the hell did that happen?*

Almost like it was meant to be.

◐

The next evening, Josh crept up behind Tommy, who was elbow-deep in the oversized sink, and slipped something into his pocket.

"Looks good," Josh whispered, "but don't check it out 'til you get home."

So it wasn't until Tommy was approaching the door to Sunrise Backpackers that he took a peek at what was his first-ever official identification (not including the birth certificate his parents had received in the first year of his life, which had vanished when their tiny flat was cleansed of his existence). Far from the scrap of cardboard he'd feared it might be, it looked like the real deal— when he held it up to the glint of a streetlight, he could even see watermarks that might get it past a discerning eye.

Josh would never reveal that his supplier in fact spent his days issuing legitimate licenses to kids who'd passed their driving test. He'd never reveal that this humble public servant supplemented his $40,000 per annum desk job with an occasional cash-in-hand favor. And he'd certainly never reveal that this friend was actually his dad's friend first, and that he'd been helping out Dave for years—so long, in fact, that the Harley-Davidson in his garage had been paid for in cash, courtesy of the manager of The Hole. So when Tommy looked at the driver's license under the sterile white hum of the streetlight and saw fake watermarks that might fool a critical eye, he was actually seeing genuine watermarks that would convince the cops in a heartbeat. Tommy hadn't blown his money at all.

Tommy Llewellyn: one. Universe: zero.

Tommy supposed Josh had been right to laugh at him for buying an ID to borrow library books. Most teenagers would use it as a way into pubs and clubs, or even a way out of the country—instead, Tommy was standing outside the city library. With its monstrous sandstone blocks and huge arched windows, it would have been impressive a century and a half earlier. But now, surrounded by towers that soared into the sky, it seemed sadly out of place, like an old man in the corner of a nightclub.

Inside, it resembled a library from the movies—walls of books, tables with lamps, and a small battalion of librarians who looked like they'd shush their own mothers if they breathed too loudly. The only thing missing were tall ladders on wheels leaning against the shelves. Tommy supposed there may have been some artistic license taken by Hollywood producers—the library at his school in Mortlake hadn't had them either, nor had the Upper Reach town library, and so, counting the building he was currently standing in, that was none out of three.

On the third floor he found himself in front of a row of medical texts and reference books. The first one was coated in a thin layer of dust, and he sneezed. Dusty or not, the book was no help, and it was the same story for the next half dozen. Before long, Tommy felt the same creeping despair he'd had sitting in front of the computer in the common room at Sunrise Backpackers. He consulted the list of options he'd printed from the library catalogue. There was just one title remaining—a hefty volume on the shelf right in front of him. He pulled it down, turned to the table of contents, and started reading.

Two hours later, Tommy looked up with a start. If he didn't leave immediately, he'd be late for work. He scooped up the book and was rushing to the loans desk near the front door when he remembered Josh.

Shit. Tommy doubled back to the nonfiction section and grabbed the first book he saw about business, an introduction to the concepts of marketing. That'd have to do.

When he handed over his new identification at the front desk and asked them to sign him up, he was struck by an unfamiliar feeling. Here was a librarian—tight bun, glasses, and almost impossibly quiet taps on the computer keyboard straight out of a film, even if they didn't have any of those ladders to reach the top shelves—entering his information from his official-looking ID. His file on the computer would disappear again on his birthday, but it was nice to know that, for now at least, he actually existed.

Tommy thanked the librarian (who broke with the stereotype to give him a smile that bordered on flirtatious) and galloped out the door with the two books under his arm.

A young woman sharing his dorm at the hostel watched curiously as Tommy dumped the books on his bed, dressed for work, and disappeared again before she'd even had a chance to say hello. As he jogged toward The Hole, his mind raced. He'd been completely absorbed in the textbook, and even now in the bright afternoon sunlight he was chilled by what he'd found.

At first Tommy had felt a thrill as he'd read about dead men being condemned and all traces of their lives removed. Never mind that it happened on the orders of ancient Roman emperors when somebody had annoyed them; the idea that all mention of a person could be scrubbed from the history books was the closest thing he'd ever found to describing his own situation. But as he'd read on, he couldn't quite make the piece of the jigsaw fit. He doubted his legacy had been condemned—for one thing, he wasn't dead yet, and for another, the worst crime he'd ever committed was stealing a bottle of whisky from the drive-through bottle shop in Upper Reach and getting drunk under a scorching playground slide. Hardly the kind of thing he'd be wiped out of history for.

And besides, it had happened to him every year since he was a kid. What horrific sins could he possibly have committed as a newborn that would warrant this kind of retribution? No matter how he turned the puzzle piece around in his mind, it wouldn't drop into place.

As he waited impatiently at a set of traffic lights on Hunt Street, he decided that it must be something else. And by the time he'd reached The Hole (two minutes early, thank you very much), Tommy had concluded that the answer to his predicament didn't reside in the textbook he'd borrowed from the city library and left in the dorm at the hostel.

He squirted detergent into the sink and stared as the bubbles grew on the surface of the steaming, swirling water. He jabbed at them, watching them pop, and it occurred to him that there might not be an answer at all. Though something still bothered him from the chapter he'd read: the part that had chilled him. It just seemed so *unfair*. The dead victim had no way of retaliating, of preserving their legacy. But, Tommy thought as he turned off the taps, this was where he had an advantage.

Every year on January 5, the memory of him was erased.

He knew how it would happen to him, he knew when it would happen, and he knew he'd still be around afterward. He may not know *why*, but maybe he didn't need to.

He'd already found a couple of loopholes. He could find another.

Tommy Llewellyn, washer of dishes, was going to be remembered.

13

The weighty book on memory that Tommy had lugged home from the city library remained on the end of the bed for two weeks, unopened by Tommy and unappealing to book thieves. Instead, he started to read the other book he'd borrowed, the one he'd grabbed on the way out for a crash course on the principles of business. By chapter four he was hooked. At the end of the fortnight he returned the two books to the library: one unopened and one read from cover to cover—twice. He borrowed four more.

Tommy Llewellyn was now officially the longest tenant of Sunrise Backpackers Hostel; he'd also gained a reputation for being the most boring. When the other residents laughed and talked and hooked up at meet-and-greet barbecues (unlimited sausages and wine from a cask for just five bucks a person), Tommy was either on the common room couch (the peculiar aroma of the cushions no longer bothered him) or lying on his bed, reading. The more he read, the more he was drawn into a world of sales and advertising, of long hours and hard work, of staff and spreadsheets. (Leo Palmer, had he remembered his son, would have been so proud.) The books were filled with examples of small enterprises that had morphed into empires.

Tommy was working five evenings a week at The Hole. The bar was closed on Sundays and Mondays, giving all staff a delayed weekend, and on these nights Tommy—who was now accustomed to going to bed in the early hours of the morning—would stay up, his nose buried in a book, studying like a student cramming for an exam the following day. Indeed, on Tuesday mornings, Tommy felt like he'd soaked up so much information that he could've passed any test put in front of him. It was lucky, then, that it was on a Tuesday—some time after Tommy's first visit to the library—that Josh arranged to meet for lunch.

"How was your weekend?" Josh asked as they sat outside a café a block down from The Hole. A couple of other tables were occupied, the nearest one by a man sitting alone with a cigarette butt dangling from the corner of his mouth. He used it to light another, inhaling deeply before letting the smoke waft gently over Tommy and Josh.

"Quiet," replied Tommy, his face screwed up at the smell. "I spent most of it reading."

"God, you're boring," Josh said, laughing. "Why the hell haven't they kicked you out yet? Bad for the vibe of the place, you know."

Tommy shook his head. "I thought they would have by now"—one of the many signs at check-in warned of a three-month limit on stays, though Tommy figured it was just decorative, much like the sign about security cameras—"but I keep paying, and they don't say anything. Money's money, I suppose.

Plus, I don't cause much trouble." He thought back to his first night, and his encounter with a German backpacker named Katerina. There was always an exception to the rule.

"Seriously, though, what are you doing there? Is it just 'cos it's cheap? Or is it because you want first crack at the new arrivals who are looking for someone to show them around?" Josh put on a deep voice. "'I work at a bar—I'll get you girls cheap drinks.' Fuck, they'd be throwing themselves at you. 'Til they find out the only thing you do is wash the glasses."

Tommy laughed. "Not me," he said. "I made that mistake on my first night. Cost me a lot of money. Besides, there's someone…" He trailed off, considering for a moment telling Josh a little bit about Carey but dismissing it just as quickly. Too many questions would follow. Plus he'd sound like a bit of a creep, searching for a girl he'd lived with once. A girl who didn't know he was looking for her. "Never mind. What about you? Anyone on the scene?"

Josh shook his head. "Nothing serious. It's kinda hard having a proper girlfriend with these hours."

Tommy wondered what constituted a *proper* girlfriend in Josh's mind. He thought back to their conversation in the hospital, and Josh's short list of things he had to do before he died.

"Mind you, plenty of opportunities," Josh added. "You've got no idea how many times chicks have asked what time I finish up."

"And yet you don't take advantage of it. What a gentleman," teased Tommy.

"Are you kidding? Of course I do. But not when I'm still at work; if Dad caught me with a customer, he'd sack me for sure. Bit rich considering half the shit he's done." Josh sighed.

"Having said that, he's probably gonna punt me anyway. Kinda get the feeling he's had enough of having his kid around. 'Specially when I've got ideas, you know?"

Tommy leaned in, desperate for detail, but had to wait as a young waitress came over with a notepad to take down their lunch order.

When she was gone, Tommy cut to the chase. "Go on," he prompted. "You said you had ideas. Spill."

Josh smiled. He liked getting Tommy worked up. He was too placid sometimes.

"All right. You know I love working at the bar, right?"

Tommy nodded.

"School kinda sucked. I spent a lot of time in the hospital— have I ever told you that? I used to have a dodgy liver. It's why I hardly drink. Anyway, the thought of working at The Hole helped get me through. There's something about it, you know? The pinball machines, I dunno. The way the place smells, how dark it is. I guess it's to do with the way everybody who's there actually *wants* to be there. It's not like working in a supermarket or something. Nobody ever *wants* to sell groceries, and the person who's buying the toilet paper and bananas and shit doesn't want to be there either. It's different at the bar. People only come in because they wanna be there and they wanna have a good time. Good for the soul, I guess."

This was unusually profound for Josh. Tommy was enthralled.

"I've been watching the way my dad does things. He's good behind the bar. Like, seriously good. You name a drink, he can make it. From memory—no instructions or anything. Anyway, he told me that once I left the hospital he'd show me what he does, and for once he actually did what he said: taught me how to mix drinks, and let me practice on customers. I was still a kid, so it was illegal, but he did it anyway. Probably the first decent thing he's done since he bought me a bike and showed me how to ride it. Yeah. When I was six. Long time ago."

He paused, as if wrestling with whether to go on. "But I tell you what—he's fucking awful at running the business."

Tommy raised his eyebrows, a little surprised at the frank assessment.

"Come on, Tommy, don't be like that," Josh said. "No judgment, okay? It's not disloyal to say the bar could be doing better. Think about a Friday night. How busy would you say it is?"

Tommy pictured his regular runs out onto the floor to collect glasses amid the heavy after-work crowd.

"Packed. Probably only a couple of stools left at the bar, and one, maybe two tables available. The small ones."

"Yeah, that's not packed," said Josh. "Packed is standing room only. Packed is a line out the door waiting to get in. Packed is people talking about leaving work early to make sure they can get a table. The Hole is *not* packed on a Friday night, but it should be—and I think it's Dad's fault it's not doing better."

Josh stopped talking again as their burgers were delivered to the table. Looking at his friend, Tommy saw the stress of the conversation pinching at his face. Josh picked at a string of melted cheddar running down the side of his burger.

"The hard part is that I've tried to talk to Dad about it. How cool would that be—father and son, running a bar together?"

Yeah, thought Tommy, recalling their conversation in the hospital. *Like running a bar with your best mate.*

"I've got some ideas—good ones, I know they are—but he doesn't want to hear them. Well, that's not true. He heard them—he just doesn't want to do anything about them. He told me so, straight up. Some stupid line about not fixing something that's not broken. I don't know whether it's because he thinks I'm just a kid, or because I'm *his* kid and he doesn't want to be shown up by me. Whatever it is, it's bullshit." He stopped talking as he plucked the cheese strand off the bun and put it in his mouth.

"What are they?" Tommy asked, curious. He had his own suggestions to make. He picked up his burger and took a bite, then another as he waited for Josh to start talking again. It took a minute or two—Josh was focused, ordering his thoughts. But when he started speaking, he didn't stop for a long time.

About twenty minutes later, Tommy's burger was gone and his plate had been wiped clean with the fat, greasy fries that had accompanied his meal. On the other side of the table, Josh's burger sat uneaten, although the top of the bun had been knocked off the patty—a casualty of Josh's exuberance. But he wasn't the only one excited; Tommy had been swept up in the plans for The Hole, and had contributed his own ideas. Between the two of them, they covered everything from simple menu changes to a marketing strategy that'd make The Hole seem the place to be, even if it wasn't. Yet.

"So what are we going to do?" asked Tommy. He didn't realize he'd said *we*. Josh noticed though. "It all makes sense to me."

"Yeah, this is the worst bit. Every way I look at it, I keep coming back to the same answer. Dad's got his head in the sand, thinking he can keep doing the things he did twenty years ago and everything'll be okay. Tommy, I've seen the books. The place is barely breaking even. I think…" Josh fell silent. Tommy waited. "I think maybe it might be better if I was looking after the business side of things."

"How?" Tommy asked. "If you took over as manager, then your dad'd be out of a job."

"I know that," snapped Josh, then immediately looked sheepish. "Sorry. It all just feels a bit shitty, you know? If Dad got the sack because of me, I'm pretty sure he'd never talk to me again. And what kind of a prick does that to his own dad? Even a pretty crappy one, like Dave?"

It was a question that didn't need an answer, but when Tommy looked up, Josh was waiting for one.

"Uh, well…have you thought about talking to him again, this time showing him how much more money the bar could be making?"

"Tried that. Same result. If anything, it was worse. He accused me of trying to undermine him."

Tommy was surprised to see tears of frustration in his friend's eyes. Josh wiped them away with his palm.

"Well, I don't know then," Tommy said, raising his hands. "How would you even go about taking over?"

"I'd have to talk to the owners. There's three of them; they put up the cash for the bar twenty years ago and hired Dad to run it. They come in occasionally; I'll point them out next time. Though you'll probably be able to pick 'em. Three old dudes that carry on like they own the place." Josh chuckled at his own joke. "I reckon I could convince them my ideas are good. They're in business for the money. Might have been something else when they started it, but now it's just a retirement fund for them. I don't know how they'd feel about moving on from Dad, though. Loyalty and all that. Not that I'm one to talk."

They both fell silent, and Josh finally picked up his burger. Stone cold. He put it back down.

"There's another option, you know," Tommy said. *One we talked about a few years ago.*

"Yeah? What's that?" asked Josh. Tommy had his full attention.

"You could start your own place. Go out on your own, do everything you think you should be doing at The Hole, but be your own boss. It might even keep you on speaking terms with Dave."

Josh shook his head. "Mate, I'm eighteen. Maybe I'd be able to convince the owners of The Hole to put me on as manager. They know me, and they know Dad. But starting a new place would cost a bomb, and no bank will back a teenager to start their own bar. They'd probably assume I'd drink the profits."

"Well…" said Tommy slowly. Here was his chance. "What if you had a business partner?"

"Who? You?"

Tommy nodded, and Josh smiled. There was no cruelty in the smile. If anything, there was a hint of sadness.

"Thanks, Tommy. That'd be fun. But in case you hadn't noticed, mate, you're the same age as me, and what's worse than one eighteen-year-old asking a bank for a loan? Two of us. Don't forget, I know what you get paid, and I know you sleep in a hostel. I don't think you've got a little trust fund tucked away there that we could use—correct me if I'm wrong. Please. I hope I am, but I don't think so."

"I wish," Tommy replied, and they laughed. It was an easy, happy laugh—the sound of two mates who'd known each other for years, not months. Tommy looked at Josh and marveled at how quickly they'd rediscovered their friendship. Like it was something left behind, just waiting to be picked up again.

Suddenly he saw in his mind a story he'd written as an angry, aimless fifteen-year-old boy—a story about a girl like Carey. He saw the pages being handed out in class. The story was nameless, its author was unknown—but it was *his*. He frowned, puzzled. Why had he thought of that now, all this time later and miles from Mortlake High? Back when he'd been asked to study it in class, it'd given him so much hope—that a piece of him could exist somewhere else in the world, and survive the Reset. While he'd been wiped, his work had remained and he hadn't been replaced. That piece of him had made it through. The changes to the Dairy—the fresh paint, the gardens—were another. Nobody knew it was him, but what he'd done had lived on after the Reset.

After the Reset.

That was it.

Josh was going to forget him again come January 5. But maybe Tommy could work through his friend to leave something behind. Some changes, some *ideas*, that were pure Tommy. Ideas that Josh would carry through the Reset. Ideas that would escape the cleanse, just like the story did, sufficiently removed from Tommy so that, when everything else was scrubbed clean, a little bit of him was missed. And then they could pick up where they left off.

Tommy sat up a little straighter. "Yeah," he said, "but we won't be forever. Eighteen, that is. Let's keep working on your dad. Make small changes where we can—things he might not notice or, even if he does, can't object to. And in the meantime, push him on the bigger ones. That way, if in a few years' time nothing has changed, we'll know we did everything possible before we try to take over. And at the same time, we both save every cent we can. If you can't convince the owners to back you as the boss—or you don't want to—then we go out on our own with our savings, plus whatever the bank will give a couple of guys in their twenties. Either way, we'll do this. It'll just take time. And maybe a bit of patience."

When Tommy was finished speaking, Josh closed his eyes. He sat motionless for so long that Tommy wondered if he'd dozed off. Then Josh's eyes sprang open. He got to his feet and extended a hand.

"You've got a deal," Josh said. "Either we take over The Hole, or we go it alone. Together, I mean."

Tommy and Josh shook hands as the waitress reappeared and deposited the bill on their table.

"We're supposed to be saving cash—should we do a runner?" Josh laughed as they pulled their wallets out, aware it would be the last time he'd be spending money on a café lunch for a while.

Tommy laughed too, but it wouldn't require many changes to *his* lifestyle.

They walked the block back to The Hole for their shifts—both of them way too early to clock on—and Tommy thought about the deal he'd made with his friend. The Hole would be the challenge they undertook together; the Reset would be his own.

◑

As summer arrived, The Hole started to pick up in trade. But even at its busiest—Friday and Saturday nights—Tommy noticed Josh had been right. There was always a scattering of empty seats, and even though the bar buzzed with the sound of people enjoying themselves, there was never a queue at the door waiting to get in. But Tommy and Josh had made a deal—they would bide their time, work hard, and save their money. Their weekly pay was still hand-delivered by Dave in a white envelope; this was one of the many changes Josh wanted to make to bring the bar into the twenty-first century, but for now it suited Tommy just fine. He saved almost every dollar, tucking his cash away in a metal box in his locker at the hostel—and he was going to need it in cash if he was to keep it through his Reset.

As the first strands of Christmas tinsel were hung in the corridors of Sunrise Backpackers, Tommy started using the computers in the common room again. At 11:00 a.m. on Sundays, he could be found perched in front of an aging Hewlett-Packard, peering at the screen. He was doing research. Sometimes it was for his job (he searched for *screwdriver* + *drink*, *Tom Collins* + *drink*, and eight or nine other things he'd been too embarrassed to admit he'd never heard of), but mostly it was decidedly unrelated to work.

Each time he sat at the computer, Tommy entered the name Carey Price, occasionally tweaking the search terms, hoping something different might come up. He wasn't looking for much—just some reference to her on a website that would tell him where in the city she was living, and if she was working, studying, or just getting by. But the results were always the same—the top one was a page promising the *Best Price on Drew Carey Show DVDs!*—and he wondered two things: first, what was he doing wrong, and second (and far more significant), what if she'd moved away? Even the thought of it made him feel uneasy; if he couldn't track her down in the same city, what hope did he have if she'd left altogether? Tommy dreamed about bumping into her on the street, but really, what would he do if he did? Relationships were not exactly his specialty, let alone a relationship with the girl he'd loved for years and who no longer knew he existed.

Fortunately for Tommy, 11:00 a.m. on Sundays were prime hangover time, and most travelers didn't surface until midday at the earliest. It meant few people were around to see his blank stare as he gazed at a spot about an inch above the computer monitor, playing out a scenario in which he encountered Carey on the street or at The Hole. It also meant that he was caught completely off guard when a girl suddenly sat at the computer next to him. Instead of switching on the machine, she turned to Tommy.

"What are you doing?" she asked in heavily accented English.

Tommy hid his browser with a panicked click. The girl was very pretty, in her midtwenties with thick brown hair and full lips, but Tommy was wary of all travelers after Katerina. Especially the pretty ones.

"Nothing special—just something for work," he lied, hoping she'd be bored by the response. He wondered why this girl wasn't asleep in the stuffy dorms like everyone else, sweating vodka out through their pores.

"Oh, you have a job here?" she asked, and Tommy cursed to himself. "What do you do?"

"I work in a bar," he said as he turned back to his screen.

"Which one? Would I know it?" The girl was persistent. "I've been to a few here. Not last night, though. I wanted to see the sunrise this morning. It was spectacular."

Despite himself, Tommy liked the way she said "spectacular," her thick accent rounding out the syllables. There was something enticing about the way the girl spoke, and he wanted to listen to her do more of it. He turned slightly toward her, and it was all the invitation she needed to unload more questions.

"What's your name?" she asked.

"Tommy."

"And I'm Clem," she said. "Tell me, Tommy, what are you really doing? You hid it very quickly! Are you writing to someone? A girlfriend, perhaps?"

"No, I don't have a girlfriend," Tommy replied. He felt his heart rate increase ever so slightly.

"How interesting," she said. "Then if you're not writing to your girlfriend, what are you doing inside on a morning like this?"

Tommy didn't know what to say.

"We should go and eat. You eat breakfast, don't you, Tommy?"

"Well, yeah," he said, willing at that moment to trade almost anything for some of Josh's charm.

"Then turn that computer off and come with me."

Tommy turned back to close the browser window. But as he did,

he reread the latest combination of search terms he'd devised—
Carey Price + lawyer + Upper Reach—and felt a pang of guilt. It was
misplaced, he reminded himself. Carey would hardly be waiting
for him; she didn't even know who he was anymore. Still, he shook
his head. "I'm sorry," he said. "I've really got to finish this."

"Oh, come on," Clem replied, leaning over him, reaching for
the mouse.

Tommy swatted her arm away. "I said no, okay?"

Clem's face clouded over. Her full lips set in a firm line as
she stood.

"Well, fuck you, Tommy," she said, at pains to enunciate each
word perfectly (though he understood her meaning just fine),
then she stormed out.

Tommy slumped in his chair. He hoped he'd made the right
choice, even if he'd probably question it for some time.

Outside of Katerina the thief, who was back home in Germany
and had almost forgotten her encounter with the rich boy she'd
robbed one night in a hostel, the somewhat frosty exchange with
Clem was the closest Tommy Llewellyn got to romance that
year. He found himself living vicariously through Josh and his
tales of the various women who'd passed their numbers across
the bar at The Hole. Tommy's turn would come, though. There
would be several brief dalliances with travelers who chose their
moment better than Clem, but nothing would last more than a
night or two of awkward fumbles in dorm rooms while others
snored nearby. Without exception, they were halfhearted affairs,
with Tommy a somewhat reluctant participant at the time, and
a regretful one afterwards. But although he didn't know it as he
watched a furious, embarrassed French girl stalking from the

common room at Sunrise Backpackers, his searching for Carey Price wasn't necessarily in vain.

He wasn't going to find Carey on a computer.

But he *was* going to find her.

Before Carey could come crashing back into his life, Tommy had a more pressing problem to deal with. It was rapidly approaching January 5, and he wanted to keep his job on the other side of the Reset.

The benefit of living a half-hour walk from The Hole meant he had plenty of time to think, and as he strolled home in the early hours of January 2, he paused outside a thrift shop. It was closed, obviously, a security screen lowered over its glass front doors, but the mannequins still pointed silently from the window, elegant in secondhand dresses. Tommy had passed the same shop many times during daylight hours, when it was bustling with people; it was a favorite with the destitute and the unemployed, doing their best to dress themselves with whatever cash they had. He'd wondered a couple of times whether he might end up there too, if he couldn't find a way to keep washing glasses at The Hole. But on this night he spied his reflection in the window, illuminated by the white glow of the streetlight above. He could see himself inside, digging through the racks of donations, and it suddenly struck him. It seemed counterintuitive, but in order to keep his job, he might first have to lose it.

Everything he'd learned, everything he'd figured out about the Reset, was about to be tested.

14

On the night Tommy turned thirteen, he'd set a trap. It wasn't a trap in the traditional sense—he thought of it more as an experiment. On his desk in his room at the Dairy, he'd made a little pile of the belongings he'd accumulated in the last year. It was a slightly sad collection: a pair of shoes, two schoolbooks, three pairs of underwear, and, balanced on top, half a dozen scraps of paper. On the paper he'd drawn some pictures, written a few words, even labeled it with his name—something to mark it as his own.

Then he got into bed, and watched.

The closer it got to midnight, the more Tommy convinced himself the mound was just going to vanish before his eyes. Maybe there'd be a *pop*, like Cinderella's carriage turning back into a pumpkin. Maybe it would be silent. Maybe he'd blink and it would be gone.

But when the clock in the Dairy's entrance hall chimed twelve, the shoes didn't move. The books, the jocks, the paper—all still there.

Tommy climbed out of bed and prodded them, half expecting his finger to go straight through, as if poking a shadow. The books slid to the floor with a bang like a cannon in the night, and he held his breath. Nobody stirred.

An hour later Tommy finally nodded off, feeling a curious mix of disappointment (he'd wanted to see something magical occur) and hope. Hope that, for some reason, the Reset wasn't happening. That after a dozen years it'd just worn off or something.

Of course, the pile was gone when he woke.

Tommy hadn't been entirely wrong in his assumption that it was supposed to happen at midnight. It usually did; there was a certain neatness to it. Simplicity. But then again, it was hardly going to happen when he was awake, moving around, talking to people, creating waves. On those occasions, the universe—or whatever it was—had to improvise. Wait for the moving parts to be still.

To be asleep.

Tommy's plan to keep his job at The Hole was going to come down to careful timing. Timing, and a few other things going his way.

Now, while Tommy was largely a creature of habit—he'd followed the same path to and from work for nearly twelve months, yet another trait unknowingly inherited from his father—he did break his routine on January 4. First, he went to his locker at the end of his bed and took out the small metal box inside. It was heavy in his hands, crammed with every dollar he'd saved from a year of hard work and frugal living. (Tommy might have been a creature of habit, but he'd come to loathe his diet of cheap bread, free biscuits, and whatever fruit was on sale at the grocer he passed each day.) There was far more money in front of him now than he'd brought to the city a year ago.

"Holy shit!" a voice behind him exclaimed. "Where'd you find *that*?"

A guy about Tommy's age was staring wide-eyed at the cash.

"I didn't find it," Tommy replied, snapping the lid shut. "It's mine."

"Hey, Amelia. Come and look at this! It's like a fucking treasure chest."

The guy's girlfriend appeared at his side. "What is it?" she asked. "What's in the box?"

"Money. Lots of it. Thousands, I reckon. He found it."

"I didn't find it!" Tommy repeated. *Jesus*, he thought. *I haven't even left yet and I've already messed up.* He shoved past the couple and locked himself in the bathroom.

Two minutes later he waddled out, underwear stuffed with wads of cash and his ID. The tin lay empty on the tiles next to the toilet.

He was uncomfortable: it felt like wearing a swimsuit full of sand, and Tommy was going to be working until 2:00 a.m. He knew the Reset would wait until he was asleep, but he wasn't going to take any chances—especially not now that some greasy-haired kid and his girlfriend knew about the stash.

Next stop was the common room. With a glance up at yet another sign sticky-taped to the wall (*BLACK-AND-WHITE PRINTING, TEN CENTS A PAGE, PAY AT RECEPTION*), he printed a single page featuring just a handful of words in a bland, generic font.

"Owe you ten cents," he said to nobody in particular, and left the hostel.

Tommy's shift at The Hole didn't start until 4:00 p.m., but he needed to speak with Dave first. As he walked, repeating his lines and rehearsing the conversation that was to come, he realized that at that exact moment twelve months earlier, he had still been preparing for his grand escape from the Dairy. Back then, he was a child. Now he was an adult, with money in his pocket (or, rather, chafing his groin), a job, a best mate, and plans for the future. And if all went as he hoped tonight, he'd still have most of them tomorrow.

"You're early, Tommy," Dave called from behind the bar as he entered.

Tommy approached and leaned against the counter; the stained wood gleamed from Dave's daily polishing.

"Have you got a moment, Dave?" he asked. Suddenly he was nervous.

"Uh, sure. What's up?"

Dave walked around the bar to sit beside Tommy. They were on the same stools as when Dave had offered him the job. *Funny the way these things work*, thought Tommy.

"I'm really sorry, Dave, but I have to quit," he said.

The manager looked at him in surprise. "What? Why? I thought you liked your job."

"I do, believe me," Tommy said. "But I'm moving interstate. Had another offer. It's a lot of money."

"I dunno, Tommy." Dave rubbed his beard, and his eyes

narrowed. "Seems kind of…what's the word? Ungrateful. You didn't know a thing about working in a bar, and I trained you up. At my own expense too," he added.

Dave had never taught Tommy anything beyond how to pick up glasses and wash them.

"I'm really sorry, Dave. And believe me, I'm grateful for everything you've done," Tommy said. "I'll be around for a few more weeks, though, and I'll help you find a replacement too; I made a sign to stick up out the front after my shift tonight."

Dave just nodded, snatched the piece of paper Tommy had printed in the hostel common room, and turned away.

But if Tommy thought that lying to Dave had been tough, the hardest part was still to come.

"What the fuck, Tommy?" It was Josh, standing red-faced in the kitchen doorway a few hours later. He looked angry, and he looked hurt. "Dad just told me. When were you going to mention it to me? We've got plans, remember? We shook on them."

"I know, I know," Tommy replied, trying to calm his friend down. "Let me explain."

"Nah, fuck your explanation. I know you've got another gig. Dad's happy for you to work for the next couple of weeks, but I told him you should go tonight. First time he's actually followed my advice."

"What do you mean?" Tommy asked, confused.

"There's no point to an *employee* staying here if they wanna go somewhere else." His emphasis on *employee* signaled the change in their relationship loud and clear. They weren't partners anymore. "When your shift finishes tonight, you're gone." And with that, Josh walked out.

Tommy had expected it might go badly, but this was much, much worse than he'd imagined. For the first time, he actually longed for the Reset, wanting to undo some of the damage he'd inflicted.

The rest of the shift was painful for Tommy. Every time he was out on the floor, reaching around customers to retrieve empty glasses, he looked across at the bar to see if Josh's mood had improved. The vein in his forehead finally stopped pulsing, and the violent *clunk* of bottles being slammed down on the counter eased. But he still looked hurt.

At 2:00 a.m. Tommy dried his hands and put away the final glass. On the main floor of the bar, one last group of drinkers was yodeling something unrecognizable with gusto.

Dave beckoned Tommy over and handed him a white envelope. "Your last pay," he said sullenly and went back to wiping down the bar. Tommy waved to Renee at the back of the room, and walked past Josh, who ignored him.

He was almost out the door when he heard his friend call to him. "Oi, Tommy." The corners of Josh's mouth were twitching up slightly. "Happy birthday. Even if you *are* a prick."

Tommy returned the smile then stepped outside. As he did, he looked back at The Hole, and saw his sign taped next to the door: *HELP WANTED. APPLY WITHIN.* Dave must have stuck it up during the evening. The pieces were almost all in place.

In less than an hour, Tommy was back at his dorm and dressed in several layers of clothes, looking like a badly wrapped present. He opened the window next to his bunk, praying some fresh air would find its way in.

It was hot, he was sticky, but he didn't care. Tommy would get to keep his clothes, and the cash stowed in his pants, and even the driver's license he'd now tucked into his pocket. As he fell asleep, he realized he was getting good at this.

○

He woke to a warm, gentle breeze on his face: the window was still open. His handiwork in fixing it a year earlier had made it through the night; the Reset hadn't decided to snap the bolt, jam it shut, and erase all trace of his efforts. Tommy understood why: it wasn't tied to him, nobody would know he had been the one to fix it, and the Reset had much bigger fish to fry, like the mess he'd left at The Hole. End result? There was a little piece of Tommy Llewellyn for the future residents of Sunrise Backpackers. *You're welcome*, he thought, and smiled.

The young man in the bunk opposite woke up while Tommy was removing his fourth shirt, and watched silently as Tommy pulled off three pairs of pants. Deciding he was still drunk (which he probably was), he rubbed his eyes, rolled over and went back to sleep. Tommy noticed the movement, and tiptoed to the bathroom to remove the cash from his underpants.

Downstairs at the check-in desk, everything looked the same as it had the previous day; in fact, everything looked the same as it had when he'd first walked in off the street with a pocketful of money and his clothes wrapped in a shirt. Bridget with the bracelets was still behind the desk; Tommy had actually gotten to know her quite well over the past year. Maybe she just appreciated a constant face amid the steady stream of travelers, but she'd always been up for a chat whenever Tommy paid for his lodging. Her grandfather owned the hostel, and she'd been in charge since the previous manager handed in his notice and took off an hour later ("some notice," Bridget had remarked bitterly to Tommy). She hated changing sheets and *loathed* cleaning up vomit, but she'd had an office job once before, and this was still better.

Bridget usually gave him a friendly greeting, but as he walked down the stairs that morning her customary smile had been replaced by a scowl.

"No unpaid visitors allowed. Who were you here with?" she asked immediately.

Tommy had been expecting this, being no stranger to the signs on the wall behind her.

"Sorry. I met some of the guys at the pub last night, and they said you had some vacancies. They let me in; it was really late."

Bridget's suspicious expression didn't change. She'd heard that line before from other travelers hoping to get a night's accommodation for free.

"I'm here to pay for last night," Tommy offered. "And another month, if I can, please."

Instantly Bridget's pursed lips softened, and she gestured him over to the counter. This time, when she asked for identification, he produced his driver's license instead of forking out twenty bucks for her to overlook it again. *This thing's already paying off,* thought Tommy.

He rented a locker, cursing as he remembered the metal box he'd left on the bathroom floor. It'd be gone now. But if that was the worst thing that happened, he could live with that.

◗

Tommy had often found it ironic that The Hole opened for lunch at midday, considering they barely served any food (item number eight on his and Josh's list of improvements) and the heartiest thing on the menu was an English stout. Tommy was standing on the footpath at 11:59 a.m., and he saw Dave's shadow getting closer and more distinct behind the dark glass of the door. As the lock clicked back, Tommy stepped forward.

"Excuse me," he said. "Can I speak with you for a minute?"

Dave looked Tommy up and down, taken aback at being accosted so early in the day.

"You're not selling anything are you?" came the reply.

"Only myself," Tommy said with a smile. Then, realizing how that sounded, he flushed. *Great start*, he thought. "I'd like to talk to you about that," he said, pointing to the *HELP WANTED* sign next to the door.

Dave took Tommy inside.

Seven minutes later, Tommy walked out of The Hole, thinking about his first shift later that night and whether he'd just succeeded in influencing what happened to him by handing the sign to Dave when he quit. He wished he'd asked why they were looking for staff. He was more than a little intrigued by the narrative that had replaced the memory of him overnight.

Dave Saunders watched the new guy leave. He was lucky to find someone so quickly, just a day after printing and sticking up the sign. They were getting busier, he thought, despite what his son reckoned. Hiring a new glassie might remind Josh who was actually in charge. Also, it'd make Renee happy to be out in the front more and not stuck in the kitchen, and it would make Dave happy not to have her constantly nagging him. Yes, by 12:07 p.m. Dave Saunders was very pleased with himself. He'd quashed two rebellions—Josh and Renee—and never suspected for a second that he'd been played by both the universe and Tommy Llewellyn.

Tommy was banking on his theory that some people were always meant to be friends. Josh Saunders met Tommy for the first time that night in the kitchen at The Hole, just twenty-four hours after he'd stood in the same spot, fuming at Tommy's treachery. Tommy had worried a great deal about how to navigate this with Josh. He hoped—no, he believed— that their friendship was a little like a gold nugget buried deep underground, a solid mass unchanging while the earth moved around it, just waiting to be discovered. The bond between them had started in the hospital, had reignited when they worked together at The Hole, and it was strong. Strong enough to convince Tommy they could rebuild their friendship within a month or two.

But even Tommy was amazed at how quickly Josh dug up the nugget; in less than a fortnight, the two were sitting at a pub on their day off, perched on bar stools at a tall table. Josh hadn't said much. Instead, he'd spent most of the time listening to Tommy talk, biting on the inside of his cheek as he appeared to wrestle with something. As if deciding whether he could trust his new friend.

"Can I tell you something?" he said at last. "And this has to stay in the vault."

Tommy nodded.

"I think I might have to quit The Hole."

"What?" exclaimed Tommy.

"I know, and you've only just started. It's not you, I promise." Josh grinned briefly then sobered. "It's my dad. You know Dave's my dad, right?"

Tommy nodded again.

"Right. Well, I shouldn't be telling you this, but…he's kinda running the place into the ground. It's not making any money, and he just won't *listen*. I've got ideas, you know? Ones that could keep us all in a job. Including him."

Tommy acted surprised, but the only real surprise was that Josh was being so open with him after just a couple of weeks. Gold nugget indeed.

"Don't you reckon if we started serving lunch—like, proper meals—we'd lock people in for the full day? They'd roll out at midnight. We'd make a mint. And I had a few other thoughts, too…" Tommy smiled as Josh then proceeded to list the ideas that Tommy himself had outlined to Josh before the Reset.

Two hours passed in what seemed like minutes, and Tommy had to keep reminding himself that as far as Josh was aware, they'd only just met. It didn't feel like that. To either of them, really. Finally, he proposed the same deal they'd already shaken on once before. "We save our money, and either take over The Hole or go out on our own."

Josh agreed, and Tommy was struck by a sense of déjà vu. A small part of him doubted it could be considered déjà vu when he'd deliberately recreated the moment from the past, planting the seeds to make it happen. But it didn't really matter. All that mattered was that he'd done it—he'd managed to get his job back, his best friend back, and now they were planning again for the future.

It spurred Tommy on, and later that year, when others might have started looking for an apartment—a small one-bedder in a walk-up building, or a shared flat with a pair of college students complete with split bills and two shelves each in the fridge—Tommy chose to stay on at Sunrise Backpackers. He'd grown up sharing facilities with a bunch of people, and he quite enjoyed meeting new arrivals from around the world. Besides, he had a routine there and knew exactly what time he had to leave in all weather conditions to arrive precisely ten minutes before his shift. Above all, though, he couldn't argue with the cost, and his priority was growing that pile of cash in the bottom of his locker.

But soon the mound had become so large that Tommy ticked off another first, one that somebody living an ordinary life wouldn't have thought twice about. But Tommy's life was far from ordinary, so as he stood at the bank counter, he felt his palms get clammy. The teller—a woman in her thirties wearing horn-rimmed spectacles that aged her prematurely—was staring intently at his driver's license. Tommy held his breath as she turned to make a copy of his ID, and then it was done and she was sliding the license back across the counter to him. He handed over three envelopes of cash—she barely raised an eyebrow at this—and next thing he knew, he'd been issued a bank card (another form of identification; Tommy felt almost ordinary, and it thrilled him) and a receipt for the deposit.

His account balance continued to grow, with Tommy making a weekly visit to deposit the wages Dave stubbornly insisted on paying in cash. Tommy knew it was safer in his account than at Sunrise Backpackers for most of the year, but come January 4, he was waiting impatiently outside the bank when it opened. The teller (a different one this time, whose glasses matched her age) glared down her nose at Tommy.

"All of it?" she repeated.

"All of it. In hundreds please. Or fifties." Anything smaller and there'd be too many notes to fit in his underwear. She continued to stare and Tommy refused to blink, as if by breaking contact for even the briefest of moments he would forfeit his own money, and it would stay deep within the bowels of the bank forever (or at least until it disappeared or was reassigned that night). Finally, she looked away and Tommy silently declared victory.

The rest of the day followed the script he'd written the previous year. Act One was high drama: his resignation from The Hole and the full force of Josh's hurt. Act Two saw him cocooned in layers of clothes with money stuffed in every pocket, before Act Three brought redemption of a sort: his return to the bar, albeit as a stranger, begging for a job that was already his. All the actors performed their roles perfectly.

A week later, Tommy Llewellyn was once again working at The Hole, and Josh was once again his best friend and business partner—and with Tommy's hoard of cash, they almost had the money they needed to make a move. As they raised their glasses, toasting their future, neither of them had even the slightest suspicion the move would be made for them.

15

Two hundred and fifty bucks seemed like a lot of money to Tommy. And it *was* a lot of money; even more than he'd spent on his driver's license. But Josh had given him a list of reasons why he needed to buy a phone.

"You don't want a girl calling you at that place." *That place* was Sunrise Backpackers. "You give them a landline and they'll think your mum's gonna answer."

Tommy didn't find this reason particularly compelling. He'd never given his number to anybody at the bar; he didn't actually meet that many girls while washing glasses.

Josh tried again. "You could use it to text your friends, like your mates from school. What do they do now, write you letters?"

Tommy hadn't answered that one. Josh probably wouldn't have believed him. *Nobody from school writes me letters because they don't remember me.*

"Well, what if your shift is canceled? Or you need to come

in early?" Josh's eyes had lit up. He knew he'd found it. "Extra work, mate—it'll pay for itself."

And with that, Tommy's arm was twisted into handing over an obscene amount of cash for something he hardly used. The only person who ever messaged him on it was Josh.

Beer tonight?

Sure.

You cool to stay back 'til close?

Of course.

Lunch?

Long as it's cheap.

The phone was, he decided, a waste of money, and he vowed never to let Josh persuade him to buy anything ever again. But then, out of the blue, came a message that made the phone worth every cent he'd spent on it.

Tommy was lying on his bed reading; a girl on the bunk above had left a novel behind, so he pinched an extra pillow and settled in for the afternoon. He wasn't due at work for another few hours.

At first, he ignored the vibration from his pocket. Josh could wait until the end of the chapter.

Another vibration.

Tommy sighed and fished out his phone.

Josh's first message was cryptic. *Doppelgänger much?*

The second didn't help. *Seriously. This is weird.*

Tommy started to tap out a response. *What are you talking about? I'm—*

A photo appeared on the screen. It was grainy, taken in the half-light of The Hole. It showed a cluster of men with a couple of women sitting around a table, some with mouths open, some blinking, all midconversation. The photo had been snapped from across the room and was slightly blurred, as though the photographer had been trying to hide what he was doing.

Another message. *So???? What do you reckon???*

Tommy zoomed in on the picture, trying to see what Josh was talking about. He squinted, moving from one shadowy face to the next.

Then he saw him.

Even through the fuzzy pixels, it was like looking in a mirror—but a mirror that added decades to the reflection. The man in a white business shirt and dark blue tie blended in perfectly with everyone else at the table. But this man's hair was the same tousled, sandy mop that Tommy ran his hands through every morning. The man almost had the same nose as Tommy, although his was a lot straighter on account of it *not* having been broken when hit by a car. He had, Tommy thought, the same mouth. And if he could have zoomed in even further, Tommy would have bet everything he owned that the middle-aged man in the photo shared his eyes too.

Tommy stopped breathing.

The photo was blurred, distant, dark.

But he knew, without a single sliver of doubt, that he was looking at his father.

●

"They were only here for a drink," Josh said and shrugged. "Looked like they were gonna stick around, but they all left about two minutes after I messaged you. This is what I was telling you about! If we were serving lunch, they would've stayed."

Tommy was breathing hard; he'd sprinted the distance between the Sunrise Backpackers and The Hole at speeds he hadn't reached since he was fifteen, racing back toward the pool at Upper Reach with a bellyful of Johnnie Walker. "Did they make a booking?" he managed.

Josh shook his head. "Nah, mate. They just turned up, about eight or nine of them. If we had a proper lunch menu, we would have made a coupla hundred bucks, easy. Instead, what was it?" He pulled a receipt out of the cash register. "Sixty-nine dollars, plus a tip."

Tommy pointed at the receipt. "They paid by credit card?"

Josh looked at him, curious. "'Course they did. Business expense, yeah?"

Tommy snatched the slip of paper and examined it closely.

"See what I mean? It's the company paying for it. So if we were dishing out something other than bloody olives—hey, where are you going?"

Tommy Llewellyn was already out the door, still clutching the receipt.

●

Tommy's phone received messages, made calls, and that was about it. For anything else he needed the computer in the common room. For once, though, luck was on his side and the room was empty, both computers available.

His heart was pounding a furious rhythm, fueled in equal

parts by the run and anticipation. He typed the company's name into the search engine, and it brought up a sleek, professional-looking home page for an accounting firm. *Meet Our Team!* the menu offered, and Tommy clicked on the tab, wondering if the team included the man he'd seen in the grainy picture. He didn't know what he'd do if it didn't.

Photo after photo after photo, all shot in stylish black and white. He scrolled down through the faces, ignoring the names.

There. His hair had grown since the photo was taken, but it was definitely him. Head of Audits, Internal and Commercial: Leonard Palmer.

Leonard Palmer.

Jesus Christ, thought Tommy. *My dad's name is Leonard Palmer. I should be Tommy Palmer.*

It sounded foreign to him, the name of a stranger.

All of a sudden he wanted somebody to walk into the room, sit on the couch, and ask him what he was doing. He wanted to tell someone: *I found my dad!* He wanted to ring Josh and tell him. Run to Miss Michelle, to Carey. Share the moment with somebody, anybody—Tommy Llewellyn, the boy everybody forgot, had found his father. Surely they'd be excited for him.

But the couch was empty, and nobody walked through the door. Miss Michelle was at the Dairy, unaware of Tommy's existence. Carey didn't know him, and he didn't know where she was. He could pick up the phone and call Josh, but what would he say? "My dad forgot me, but it's okay, because I found him, and now I'm gonna make him remember me"?

No. Josh wouldn't understand. But maybe he was looking at the person who would. A black-and-white image of the man who must've been there when all of it started. Somebody had to be the first to forget Tommy, and now he was going to have a chance to ask why.

An elegant lady with gray hair and diamond earrings that caught the sun narrowed her eyes suspiciously at Tommy as she drove past. She'd first spotted him almost an hour earlier from her upstairs window, loitering on the street below, watching the houses. Waiting for something.

If he's still there when I get back from the shops, I'm calling the police, she decided, and fixed him with her most intimidating glare.

Tommy didn't see her. But then again, he hadn't been looking at her car or even *her* house. He'd been standing outside the property belonging to a Mr. L. Palmer, an address he'd found in the White Pages. There had been fourteen L. Palmers, but after calling Luke Palmer, Lincoln Palmer, and Lou Palmer, he'd struck it lucky.

"Leo speaking."

Tommy froze.

"Hello?" the man said. "Anyone there?"

Tommy started to say something—he still wasn't sure what—but it came out as a strangled, gurgling sound.

"Hello?" Leo said again, then he hung up.

Tommy only hoped that when he actually met Leonard (or Leo, as he now thought of him), he'd be a little more eloquent. Or just say real words, at least.

But first he needed to summon the courage to cross the road and approach the house: half of a duplex, with a paved driveway and a smooth path to the front door, bordered on each side by a miniature hedge that was trimmed to a sharp edge. The grass was neat and even, glistening with remnants of the morning dew, and the front windows (both upstairs and downstairs) were wide open, framed by shutters painted a clean, crisp white. Tommy could describe every feature of the pristine house and garden; he'd been staring at it for long enough, willing himself to just walk up and knock on the door.

But he couldn't. He was, quite simply, terrified of what Leo might say. After all, Tommy was just *assuming* that Leonard Palmer had forgotten him at some point, before Tommy could even remember. But what if he was wrong? What if Leo knew exactly who he was, and they'd abandoned him as a baby? What if they'd given him away because they couldn't afford to keep him? Or worse, because there was something *wrong* with him? Because they couldn't love him?

Suddenly Tommy found himself moving up the path, drawn forward as if his own body had grown tired of waiting and had to find out.

The doorbell's chime echoed through the house, and Tommy thought he might just be sick into the hydrangeas next to the door. He wanted to turn and run, but his legs held him there.

Then footsteps, and a rustling noise, and the door was flung open.

A tall man stood in the doorway, with thick, gray-flecked sandy hair and kind, hazel-colored eyes. It was Leonard Palmer—the man from The Hole, the man from the website.

Leo looked at Tommy, and in that instant Tommy knew his instincts had been right. This was his dad.

Leo's eyes widened, and for one brief, remarkable moment, hope soared in Tommy. His knees felt on the verge of buckling, and he put a hand on the doorframe to steady himself.

"Do I...do I know you?" Leo asked. He sounded unsure. Shaken.

"I, um... I think you..." Tommy stammered, and trailed off. The words he'd hoped would come when he needed them were nowhere to be found.

Leo's brow furrowed. "Is this a joke?" His eyes darted past Tommy, up and down the street, as though looking for a camera crew or a surprise party, somebody to burst out and say *gotcha!*

Tommy shook his head. "No, I..." *Come on, Tommy!* he scolded himself. *Get it together!*

"If it's not a joke, then..." The confused frown was replaced by a small smile as Leo's shock subsided. "This is bizarre. You look like me. Or me about thirty years ago." He shook his head in disbelief. "Anyway, what can I do for you?"

His tone was friendly, but businesslike. The way a well-mannered man would speak to a salesman on his doorstep.

The way he'd speak to a stranger.

The hope leaked from Tommy like a deflating balloon. Leo didn't know him after all.

"Are you all right?" Leo asked.

Tommy nodded sadly. "I'm sorry to bother you. I think...I think I made a mistake. Wrong house." There was nothing to be gained from talking to a man who didn't remember him. He wasn't going to know *why* he'd forgotten Tommy if he didn't even know that he had.

No answers, just more hurt.

"Okay," replied Leo, bewildered. "Have a nice weekend."

Tommy's shoulders slumped as he trudged back down the path.

Leo watched him leave, but he didn't close the door. Something was stopping him. It wasn't a sense of recognition, some kind of unspoken bond, or anything like that. He had no idea who this young man was; the knowledge had been erased two decades ago.

No, it was something else that made Leo Palmer wait in the open doorway. There was something so defeated, so sorrowful about the boy's walk.

"Hey," he called.

Tommy turned.

"I was just about to make a cup of tea. Want to join me?"

It was the smell that hit Tommy first. It was fresh and clean, and at the same time strangely familiar. It was as though the lived-in, warm feel of the lounge room, with its book-heavy shelves and two soft, well-worn couches, tapped into a subconscious memory of how Tommy's family home had smelled in his first year of life. Leo and Elise Palmer might have upgraded to a bigger, better house, but some things stayed the same. The smell of that front room might as well have been bottled and brought with them from the living room at Ingleby.

"What's your name, mate?" Leo asked.

"Tommy."

"I'm Leo." Tommy's father stuck out his hand, and Tommy felt a shiver as he shook it. This was *his* dad, shaking *his* hand.

"Come through to the kitchen," he said, leading Tommy down a hallway. Through an open door Tommy caught a glimpse of a bedroom: a single unmade bed, clothes strewn about the floor, and a dresser crammed with model planes—at least a dozen of them—gathered in a protective semicircle around a Lego *Millennium Falcon*. A boy's room. Tommy peered through the next door, open just a few inches. The bed in there was made. A woven dream catcher dangled from the ceiling above, and in the corner was a desk stacked high with textbooks. A gold trophy sat triumphantly on top; Tommy couldn't see what it was for. Three pairs of shoes were lined up next to the desk. School shoes: shiny Mary Janes, next to two pairs of sneakers.

Two kids, Tommy thought. A girl and a boy.

Jesus, I have a brother and sister.

"What do you do, Tommy?" Leo asked, as he boiled the kettle. They were in the kitchen now; a bright, open space with a wide bench and a large dining table with four chairs spaced evenly around it. It looked like a scene from a magazine: a vase of bright pink and cream flowers stood beside an overflowing fruit bowl. But the room was comfortable, too. The chairs were scuffed, and a lopsided pile of books leaned against the wall near the table, as though whoever was reading just tossed their book on top the moment they finished it and started on the next one. Next to the pile (and at risk of being crushed should it topple over) was a large, mottled cat, asleep in the patch of sunlight coming through the door, with just the occasional twitch of an ear confirming that it was, in fact, still alive.

"I work in a bar in the city," Tommy replied.

"Oh really?" Leo said. His interest seemed genuine. "I work in the city too. Which bar? It's not really my scene—I'm a bit old for all that—but maybe I've walked past it."

"The Hole," Tommy said. "On Hunt Street."

Leo's face lit up. "I was there yesterday!" Then he fell silent, and Tommy wondered if he was making a connection between his visit to the bar, and Tommy's arrival at his house. But if he was, he didn't say anything. The only noise was the kettle bubbling lazily and a splash that seemed to float in from outside.

Leo gestured to the yard visible through an open door (more neat grass) and grinned. "That'd be Ethan. I don't know what you were like as a kid, Tommy, but he practically lives in the pool. Sugar?"

Tommy nodded. "How old's Ethan?" he asked.

"Twelve," replied Leo. "And Katie's fourteen. My wife's taken her to her hockey game today. Katie's in the regional team," he added proudly.

That explains the trophy, Tommy thought.

"Do you play any sport, Tommy?"

Tommy shook his head.

"Yeah, me neither. I don't know where Katie got it from. It didn't come from her mother, either. Elise—my wife—would pick a book over a run any day. Sorry you won't get a chance to meet her."

That was a lie. Leo loved Elise dearly, and she loved him back with everything she had. He had no idea what she'd say, though, if she walked in to see a young man the spitting image of her husband sitting with a cup of tea at their dining table.

Leo had nothing to hide: he hadn't so much as flirted with another woman since the day Elise first kissed him. But surely his fidelity would be called into question by the evidence before them. Even *he'd* questioned it for a moment when he saw the boy standing at his door.

He stirred sugar into the two cups of tea, then handed one to Tommy.

The tea was sweet and milky; it reminded Tommy of Miss Michelle.

The pair sat opposite each other at the table, and while Leo examined the young man, Tommy's eyes moved around the room, stopping at a framed photograph on the wall. It was the kind of family portrait you paid a photographer for in a studio, but the picture looked like it had been snapped a few seconds after the formal shot—there were no forced smiles, no stiff backs. Instead, Leo and Elise and Katie were all looking at Ethan and laughing, mouths open wide, eyes gleaming. Clearly Ethan had said something or done something, and this instant of sheer delight was the picture that made the cut. Tommy couldn't stop staring at it. He blinked, part of him hoping that when he opened his eyes the four people in the portrait would have become five.

Leo took a mouthful of tea, and watched as Tommy stared at the family photo. He sighed. "Tommy, why did you come here today?"

Tommy dragged his gaze back from the photo, eyes wide, struggling to respond. He couldn't think of anything that would sound believable. With nothing else to draw on, Tommy chose something close to the truth.

"I saw a picture of you at The Hole."

Leo waited for more.

"And I thought you might be my dad."

Leo Palmer smiled, a kind, gentle smile completely devoid of derision.

"Yeah. I can see why." He put his tea down on the table, just as Tommy picked his up. Tommy needed something to focus on, something to hold, to look at. Something to hide behind.

"I'm sorry, mate, but I don't really know what to tell you. It's not me."

"Are you...are you sure? Couldn't there have been, I dunno, *something*? Twenty years ago?" Tommy asked desperately. He didn't know what he was hoping Leo would say—that he'd confess to an affair, or that he and Elise gave up a baby they couldn't afford, or that he'd suddenly slap his knee and go, *Oh, yeah. We did have another son. I completely forgot. Wonder what happened to him?*

Leo gazed at Tommy. The young man was looking for something he couldn't give him.

"I'm sure," he said softly. He wanted to add that it was impossible; he'd only ever slept with his wife and the first baby they'd conceived was Katie. They'd stuck to The Plan. But a look at Tommy told him silence was the better option.

A minute passed, then two. Tommy stared again at the picture on the wall, at the cheeky grin on Ethan's face and the joy in the eyes of the others.

"Tommy, can I tell you something?" Leo didn't wait for an answer. "When I was a kid we were in a car accident, a bad one, me and my mum and dad. A truck ran into our car. Dad was okay, I broke my arm—but mum died."

"Oh," Tommy said simply. "I…I'm sorry."

Leo waved this away. "It was a long time ago. I had my arm in a cast for what felt like months. But I got it into my head that when my cast finally came off, my arm would be fine and everything would go back to normal. For some reason, I thought Mum would be back too." He shook his head, as if he couldn't believe he'd been so stupid.

Another splash from outside.

"So when they cut off the cast, not only did my arm not quite heal right—this finger still doesn't straighten properly, see?—but Mum, well, she was still dead. Obviously. God, I was so pissed off. At the doctor, at the bloke driving the truck—it wasn't his fault, really; the traffic lights had malfunctioned and everyone had a green light. I was even angry at Dad. I missed Mum like you wouldn't believe. It never occurred to me that Dad missed her too. Stupid, yeah?"

Leo's eyes had taken on a slightly distant look. They were dry—he didn't cry for his mum anymore—but it was as though he wasn't really in the room. He exhaled.

Suddenly there was a boy at the back door. His hair was plastered to his head, and the drips from his board shorts were pooling around his feet.

"Hey, Dad, you promised you'd swim with me," Ethan said.

Leo smiled apologetically at Tommy. "Ethan, mate. Manners. This is Tommy. Tommy, this is Ethan."

"Hi, Ethan," Tommy said. *I'm your big brother*, he added silently.

"Hey," Ethan said, barely glancing at Tommy. "Dad, you promised!"

Leo smiled ruefully. "So I did. Give me five minutes."

"Okay. Do you reckon Katie'll swim too when she gets back?" Ethan asked.

"I don't know, mate. Maybe." Katie had become *very* self-conscious lately. They'd gone to the beach over summer, and she'd dashed into the water with one arm braced protectively across her chest. Leo had wanted to tell her she was perfect and didn't need to hide, but he knew she'd be embarrassed. At least she still swam in the pool a bit. Maybe she felt safer here. "Either way, five minutes and I'll be with you."

Ethan disappeared and a few seconds later they heard a giant splash.

"Sorry about that," Leo said. "It looks like I have a prior engagement. But anyway, Tommy, I *was* going somewhere with that story, I promise. The thing is, I spent a lot of time wishing for something that I just wasn't going to get back. I think Dad tried to tell me that, but you try telling a kid who misses his mum that he needs to move on. And I think he was just trying so hard to keep everything together that he—"

"Daaaa-aaaad," Ethan called from the backyard.

"That definitely wasn't five minutes," Leo muttered. "Sorry, Tommy, but I might have to get out there."

Tommy stood. "Thanks for your time, Leo," he said. It felt strange calling him that.

"Sorry if I went on a bit," Leo said, the slightest flush of color coming into his cheeks. "And I didn't mean to lecture you."

Tommy shook his head. "You didn't. Not at all."

"Good. Come on, I'll walk you out."

Tommy and Leo left the kitchen, that wide, bright open

space, filled with glimpses into a life that could have been Tommy's. They walked back past the kids' bedrooms, each one an image of a childhood he didn't have.

But as Tommy turned to shake Leo's hand again, on the threshold of the living room filled with books, with a smell that made him feel like he was home, he realized that he wasn't actually jealous of Ethan or Katie. He wasn't jealous of their bedrooms filled with toys and clothes that didn't disappear on their birthday; he wasn't a kid anymore, and this was *their* home, *their* life. Now that he'd found it, he couldn't just slip back in. Come January 5, Leo Palmer would forget all about the visitor he'd had, and Ethan would have no recollection of the stranger he'd ignored, sitting at the table drinking tea.

No, he decided—if anything, he was jealous of *Leo*, of what he'd built. The sanctuary he'd made in which the outside world seemed a little less important and a little further away. Maybe Leo had done it because of his mum, because it's what he longed for as a kid. It didn't matter, really. This place—this life—was closed to Tommy.

But he could make his own.

Perhaps he'd been wrong to come to Leo's house looking for answers; there was no all-knowing guide to help him, just a dad who'd forgotten his son. But what he'd found instead was an idea—a feeling, really—that he could build the same kind of sanctuary, a cocoon, for himself. And maybe inside that cocoon things might be different.

Maybe he could be remembered.

Leo watched as Tommy stepped off the path between the

hedges and started walking down the street. He could have sworn the young man looked a little taller than when he'd arrived.

"Hey Tommy," he called. "Are you catching the bus?" Tommy nodded. "Get the 415 from East Road. This time of day, it'll be a quarter of an hour faster."

"Thanks," Tommy said.

"But you better run," added Leo. "It leaves in two minutes." The young man waved and broke into a jog.

As Tommy disappeared around the corner, Leo had a curious sense that he'd just met somebody special.

In a different life, he wouldn't mind at all having a son like Tommy.

16

Business was always slowest at the tail end of the winter months. The Hole was hardly unique in that regard—right up and down Hunt Street, coffee shops and restaurants couldn't muster up enough customers to fill the seats inside, cozy and safe from the elements, let alone the outdoor tables that were assaulted every afternoon by a bitter wind whistling along the road. It was around this time each year that tempers at The Hole seemed to fray, perhaps fueled by the weather, more likely by concern about the till being a little too empty. It didn't help that each year it seemed to be a little emptier.

Tommy had taken all of these factors into consideration when he thought about the events of August 18, and he decided they'd probably contributed. But then again, sometimes relationships just end. Unfortunately, sometimes it happens publicly, and sometimes violently. In this case, it was both.

The Hole was manned by a three-person skeleton staff—Dave had dusted and re-dusted every bottle on the shelves,

Renee was cleaning tables that weren't even dirty, and Tommy was confined to the kitchen. But there was a sense of unease in the air. Even Tommy—who was infinitely more worldly than when he'd first tripped up the step into the bar, but still naive compared to other guys his age—could see Renee was upset. Her eyeliner and mascara were smudged, and her eyes were glassy.

"Are you okay?" Tommy had questioned her when he'd arrived, and almost involuntarily the glassy eyes flicked toward the bar. Tommy looked in the same direction, to where Dave had just bent below the counter.

"Oh. Did you guys have a fight?" he asked without much tact.

Renee's lips tightened. "This morning," she said. "A big one. I don't really want to be here right now, but I could hardly call in sick, could I?"

Dave stood up and looked at them both. Renee fell silent; Tommy took the hint and retreated to the kitchen. As the afternoon passed with nobody but a sink full of water to talk to, he found himself wondering what Dave and Renee had been arguing about. In fact, he didn't really know what anybody in a relationship argued about. Money? Sex? Kids? Tommy was reminded yet again of just how inexperienced he was with women. He dropped a glass into the sink with a plop and watched it disappear under the greasy surface. So much for his idea of creating his own cocoon.

His regular online search for Carey Price had failed so far to bear fruit. She might as well have vanished, for she was invisible on the internet and certainly wasn't listed in the phone book kept under the counter at The Hole. She could be anywhere in the world, he thought glumly, and he had no idea how to find her. (The truth was that at that very minute, Carey was sitting at a desk about half a mile away from him. But Tommy wasn't to know that. Yet.)

Alone in the kitchen, his job was offering no distraction. The after-work rush had barely been worthy of the description. At its peak, he'd counted just twelve people spread across three tables. By 6:30 p.m. there was just one table remaining: two men in their late thirties nursing a glass of whisky apiece.

Almost at the stroke of 7:00 p.m., Tommy heard a glass smash out the front. He grabbed the broom, pushed through the kitchen door, and stopped dead.

The bar was completely silent.

The two whisky drinkers were still sitting at their table halfway between the kitchen and the exit. Both were staring at the counter, eyes wide.

Dave was in his usual spot behind the bar, his face crimson with rage. Leaning against the other side of the counter, between stools normally occupied by customers, was Renee. Her long blond hair had fallen forward to cover her face, but Tommy could see her hand on the polished wood, blood pooling out from her fist where she still clutched the jagged remains of a shattered whisky tumbler.

"Jesus! Renee! Are you all right?" Tommy cried. She didn't answer. Neither did Dave. They just stood there, Renee's eyes fixed on the counter between them, and Dave breathing heavily.

Panic bloomed in Tommy as he pictured the shards of glass being jabbed into someone's face or slashing at some other exposed skin. He raced to Renee's side and put an arm around her; at the same time he grabbed a cloth normally used for spilled beer and melted ice. He gently lifted Renee's hand off the bar, and felt his stomach heave as half of the whisky glass, deeply embedded in the soft flesh of her palm, rose with it.

"Go back to the kitchen, Tommy," Dave said quietly. "We're fine."

Tommy looked at Dave. He was shocked by the cold intensity of the other man's stare. "She's gonna need an ambulance, I reckon."

"She's fine," Dave replied, still frighteningly quiet. "Just an accident."

"Bullshit," said a voice behind Tommy. It was one of the drinkers. "You said something that upset her. I saw you." He pulled a mobile phone from his jeans pocket. "I'll call the ambulance if you won't."

Now Dave turned his stare on the customer, who ignored him and held the phone to his ear. As Tommy led a shaky Renee to a table at the gloomy rear of The Hole, something changed in Dave's demeanor. Every muscle that had been tensed suddenly relaxed, and for a moment Tommy thought Dave was going to collapse. But he didn't, and he didn't attempt to follow Tommy and Renee either. Instead he started to rearrange one of the fridges below the counter as though everything was completely normal, and Renee's blood wasn't congealing on the benchtop.

"Are you okay, Renee? What happened?" Tommy asked as he pressed the towel to her bleeding hand, avoiding the wedge of glass that still protruded from her palm.

"Nothing," she replied in a sad, almost weary voice. All the fight had left her too. "I just lost it. I wanted to hit his stupid face with the glass, but I just slammed it down instead. I didn't mean for *this* to happen." She raised her injured hand slightly and winced.

Tommy felt a hand on his shoulder. It was the whisky drinker, reporting that an ambulance was on its way and that he and his mate were going to take off because this was all a bit intense. Tommy looked over at Dave, who was still busying himself behind the bar, and nodded.

Renee was now crying quietly. "He found some texts on my phone. It was nothing, I swear—it was just a friend. We went to school together. Then this morning we were getting ready for work and out of nowhere Dave says I cheated on him. And I *didn't.*"

She picked up a napkin from the table with her good hand and wiped her eyes. The smudged mascara became a smear.

"He's been stewing all afternoon. Then just now he said he wants to break up with me. Said I was a liar and a bunch of other things. Really horrible things." She paused. "Fuck, I could've killed him." It sounded like a realization, and the tears came again.

Tommy sat with Renee until the paramedics arrived, and after a quick inspection of her injury—"Yeah, that's a deep one. Maybe got the tendon. You'll need surgery"—they helped her outside to the waiting ambulance. Tommy could hear Renee describing how she'd tripped while carrying a tray of glasses. Then she was gone, and Tommy was alone with Dave.

The bar was spotless, except for the sticky red pool where Renee had slammed the glass down. Tommy grabbed a rag.

"We all right, Tommy?" Dave asked casually from the other end of the bar.

"What do you mean?" Tommy replied.

"I know it didn't look good, but all couples have their fights. I'm just sorry you had to see it."

Tommy scrubbed hard; some of the blood had already dried onto the wooden bench. He'd just heard Renee with the paramedics, covering up what had happened; maybe she didn't want anyone knowing. He swallowed loudly. He didn't want to make it worse for her, but he couldn't let Dave carry on like it was okay. It wasn't.

"Didn't look like a normal fight to me, Dave. Normal fights don't end with your girlfriend going to the hospital."

"What the hell would you know?" Dave snapped. "Have you ever even *had* a girlfriend?"

Tommy stayed silent.

"Look, let's just leave it. Renee and I are through anyway." Dave was counting the money in the till, each coin making a sharp *chink* as he dropped it into a bag. "She was seeing someone else," he added, almost by way of explanation.

Chink, chink, chink.

"Are you sure?" Tommy asked.

"Oh yeah. No doubt about it. I saw the texts; some guy she went to school with."

Chink, chink, chink.

"I don't know, Dave," Tommy said. "She seemed pretty upset. Her hand was seriously messed up."

Silence.

Tommy looked up. Dave was staring at him.

"Listen, Tommy, she did it to herself. Everyone saw it. It's not my fault if she loses her shit and cuts her bloody hand."

Tommy returned his gaze, unblinking.

"I'm closing up early," Dave said. "Get out of here."

Tommy left without another word.

On his walk home he called Josh and told him everything.

"Fucking hell. It's Mum all over again. Shit. Poor Renee."

"What do you mean?" asked Tommy.

"Yeah, Dad's got some jealousy issues. He was like this with Mum before they split up, even though *he* was the one playing around." He sighed. "I'll check in on Renee now. Thanks for letting me know, mate. I'm sorry you had to deal with it. With *him*, I mean."

Renee didn't return to work at The Hole after that. After four hours of microsurgery to repair nerves in her hand (and about the same time for Josh on the phone with the insurance company), the wound was stitched and the medical bills covered. She never saw Dave again, though she did see his son, who introduced her to a friend who just happened to be looking for a waitress. It was, Josh thought, the very least he could do.

When winter finally dragged itself to a long-overdue end, the liquid lunchers and after-work drinkers started to return. But there was still a frostiness in The Hole, emanating entirely from the manager. Dave Saunders hadn't said more than a dozen words to Tommy since the incident, and Tommy half expected each shift to be his last. Josh had tried to talk to his dad about what happened, but Dave had shut down the conversation. He thought about sacking his son on the spot, but realized that if he punted Josh and the nosy little shit who washed the glasses, he'd be pretty much on his own. *Fuck 'em both*, he thought. But he still needed them.

"Have you ever seen him this bad?" asked Tommy one Monday afternoon; the bar was closed and he was sitting with Josh at a pub. Dave, now single, had been hitting on the customers—very few of whom had any interest in a sleazy barman who appeared to think he was twenty-five years younger than his actual age.

"Nope," Josh admitted, sipping his beer. "He's always been a bit of a perv but seriously, this is next level." He drained his glass and sat back. Josh had a one-drink limit, and even then it was light beer—after all, he was using somebody else's liver, and had been given pages and pages of notes on how to look after it. "Did you see him with that chick on Saturday?"

Tommy shook his head.

"Stared at her tits the whole time he served her. Then comped her the drink. Jesus, it's just embarrassing. And you could tell she hated it too."

"What can we do?" Tommy asked.

"Mate, I don't know. I'll try to talk to him again, tell him to pull his head in. What's the bet he tries to sack me?"

"Yeah, you're gone for sure," agreed Tommy. "Hey, Josh…is it time to talk to the owners?"

Josh sighed. "Maybe. Tell you what: I'll go visit Dad at home this weekend, see if he listens. If he refuses, or if he punts me, then we go to the owners. And if *that* goes south too, well, looks like we're doing it ourselves."

Tommy knew exactly how much was now in his bank

account—his cheap diet (he kept expecting Bridget to stop stocking the hostel kitchen with biscuits, on account of him ignoring the sign imposing a two-per-day limit) might have been boring as hell, but it was a good financial plan. Between him and Josh, they *could* almost afford to go out on their own.

Not that it was going to get that far. Dave was on a downward spiral, and he hit the ground hard before Josh even had a chance to speak with him. Thursday was student night, which had become Dave Saunders's favorite evening, and the least favorite of the staff who had to witness his behavior. Tommy shuddered as he saw Dave sticking a sign by the front door of The Hole advertising ten-buck margaritas. It was like a predator luring prey.

"I'll keep an eye on him," Josh said, and Tommy—who was spending more time on the main bar floor now, in the absence of Renee—offered to help.

Afterward, both of them could pinpoint the exact moment it came undone. Despite the pulsing music and hubbub of dozens of conversations, a shrill voice cut through.

"Yes you fucking *did*," a woman cried. "I saw it!"

Josh's head snapped toward the voice, and Tommy froze with an armful of glasses near the arcade games. Both hoped the source of the trouble wouldn't be Dave. The same sick, ominous feeling told them it would be.

Two girls—both just a touch older than Tommy—stood at the counter. One of them was pointing at Dave, eyes blazing.

The bar manager was in the final stages of preparing margaritas. Two frosty glasses sat side by side on the sticky bench, but only one was full.

"You put something in my glass. What the *fuck*?" the girl exclaimed.

The music still played, but the crowd was now silent.

"No, no, you're wrong," Dave said. He looked flustered.

"I saw you put something in there," the girl insisted. "Someone look in the glass," she said, not taking her eyes off the man behind the bar. "It was a fucking pill or something. Someone look!"

Even from the back of the room, Tommy could see beads of sweat on Dave's forehead.

"Yeah, love," he said, trying to sound casual. "It was salt."

"Bullshit," the girl said.

"Listen, I'll make you a fresh one, and it's on the house." Dave quickly tipped the glass into the sink behind him.

"Fuck that," she said. "I'm calling the cops."

Josh appeared beside her. "Ladies, can I speak with you outside for a moment?" he asked in a voice just audible over the music. "It's too loud in here."

"This guy tried to spike our drinks! I fucking *saw* it!" the girl said fiercely.

"Okay, okay," Josh said, holding up his hands. "Let's talk about it outside."

"No way—you're just gonna take his side. I'd rather let the cops deal with it."

Behind the bar, Dave rolled his eyes. "Calm down, sweetheart. I didn't do anything." His bravado was returning.

"Dave, shut up," Josh ordered.

Dave recoiled like he'd been slapped by his son. There was something about the way Josh had said his name: he was in charge now.

"Go and wait in the kitchen."

Without another word, Dave skulked through the kitchen door.

"Tommy, watch the bar," Josh commanded, and he led the two girls outside.

Within moments, the volume inside returned to normal as groups of drinkers excitedly discussed what they'd seen before promptly moving on to other things, the alcohol already dulling their recollections.

Through the doorway, Tommy could see an animated conversation on the footpath outside. The girl who'd accused Dave was waving her arms around, her mobile phone in one hand. Her friend had joined the discussion, bolder now they were no longer in the spotlight. Tommy marveled at Josh's approach to the angry duo—everything about his stance, his body language, even the expression on his face was disarming, nonthreatening. Five minutes later, the girls disappeared down the street, and Josh returned.

"Christ, that was close," he whispered to Tommy. "They're not calling the police, but Dad's gotta go."

"When?"

"Right now."

Good, thought Tommy. If the girl was right—and he didn't doubt that she was—Dave had crossed a line from stupid, leering, ugly behavior to something much, much worse. But any evidence had gone down the sink, which seemed mighty suspicious to Tommy. He shuddered to think what might have happened if the two girls hadn't been watching closely. They were right to demand that Dave lose his job. Dave Saunders was lucky he wasn't in the back of a police car, bound for a jail cell.

Josh ended up meeting with the owners of The Hole two days later. All three men were in their late sixties, but their wardrobes had been frozen in time from the day they opened the bar more than two decades earlier. One wore a Guns N' Roses T-shirt under a suit jacket, another sported an open-necked polo with a tuft of gray chest hair peeking out the top, and the third had squeezed into a black button-up shirt that was probably already tight when he'd bought it twenty-five pounds ago. The trio sat at one of the booths along the wall, looking like an old band plotting a reunion tour.

Josh joined them, and Tommy watched from his new position behind the bar, knowing his friend would recount the conversation verbatim later but still wishing he could lip-read.

"He's gone, right? We all agree on that?" asked one, and the other two nodded.

"I like Dave," another said, "but he's a bit of a liability."

"Yeah, good word—liability," the third man repeated, and they all murmured solemnly.

Together, they anointed Josh as Dave's successor.

"Don't know how you kept this place out of the papers," the first guy said. "Would've been a bloody disaster. When I was your age, I wouldn't have known how to…hey, how old are you?" He shook his head. "Actually, I don't care. Just keep the place running, okay?"

"Thanks," Josh replied. "I've got some ideas about improvements we could make. Me and Tommy have a bit of a list." He gestured toward the bar.

The man in the tight black shirt said, "Mate, do what you need to. Think we've done enough business today, yeah, boys? How about a few beers?"

It was, after all, the reason they'd opened a bar in the first place.

Tommy was elated. With Josh now running the show, Tommy was promoted to barman. He certainly didn't mind when one of Josh's first acts as manager was to ban any kind of fraternizing between staff and customers. ("It's all about reputation, Tommy," Josh explained. "Sorry Dad's stuffed it up for everyone.")

No, Tommy wasn't concerned at all.

Of course, he might have protested a little more if he knew that Carey Price was just a handful of blocks away. Although at that moment, visiting bars was the last thing on Carey's mind.

17

Tommy tried to find Carey; he really did. Countless online searches had seen him come up empty-handed time after time, and he could hardly stick an ad in a newspaper or a poster on a wall. (*Has anyone seen this girl? She doesn't know me but I'd like to find her.*) It didn't help that he knew precisely nothing about her life in the years after the Dairy, and with a jolt one day it dawned on him: maybe her name wasn't Carey Price anymore.

Maybe she'd married.

He hated the idea, and almost preferred the thought that she'd moved away. But he kept looking, and every day as he walked to and from work, he dreamed of seeing her golden hair swishing along the footpath in front of him, even if he didn't know what he'd say.

It wasn't as though Carey didn't want to be found. She just didn't know anybody was looking. And while Tommy's search might have been fruitless, at least his gut was accurate. Carey

Price wasn't Carey Price anymore because she had indeed taken her husband's name.

On the very same morning that Tommy realized he might have lost Carey to someone else, Carey Gallagher was staring at herself in the mirror, wondering if frauds ever got caught out. *Fake it 'til you make it*, her best friend Rachael had advised her—but what if she was busted before she made it? It was easy enough for Rachael to be glib like that. She'd never had to fake it; she was one of those girls for whom opportunities seem to be created without any effort on her part. Not exactly silver spoon, but pretty close. Was there such a thing as a semi-precious spoon, like brass or something? Carey shook her head. *Focus*, she told herself. *Get out the door. Don't be late.*

She crept back into her bedroom. Her side of the bed was barely disturbed; Aaron's was a different story. He was still in there somewhere, buried under a mountain of sheets and blankets. Carey peeled back the layers until she found him, still fast asleep, a strand of saliva linking his mouth to the pillow. She shook him gently by the shoulder, and his eyes blinked open, bleary and unfocused.

"I'm off. Love you," she said softly.

He grunted and rolled over, pulling the quilt back over his head.

"Aren't you going to wish me luck?" she asked, her voice louder.

"With what?" came the muffled reply.

"My first day?"

"Ermf," Aaron grunted again. "Good luck."

Carey waited a moment longer, thinking he might sit up

and kiss her goodbye. But there was nothing, just the steady, rhythmic breathing that declared Aaron was asleep once more.

As Carey hurried down the steps from their little apartment on the third floor, she could feel the hurt simmering away like a pot on a stove; sometimes it bubbled right up to the rim and threatened to boil over. Today's effort (or lack of it) could be put down to the fogginess of sleep. But she knew it wasn't that. As the person who knew Aaron best, she'd come to the unfortunate realization that he wasn't actually a very nice person.

Carey might have been late, but the bus was too, and she reached the shelter just as the doors hissed open. She breathed a sigh of relief. She couldn't afford to be late—not today, of all days—but equally couldn't afford the taxi fare if she missed the bus. One of the downsides of living so far out of the city center was sometimes it felt like she was halfway back to Upper Reach.

Shit, she thought. *Upper Reach. Miss Michelle's birthday. Is it today?* Carey fished around in her bag for her diary. *Shit. Last week. Shit.* She made a mental note to buy a card on her way home that night, a mental note that was promptly forgotten as the bus took a corner at speed.

Carey knew she owed Miss Michelle a hell of a lot more than a card each year on her birthday. Without her, she never would have met Mr. and Mrs. Henderson, never would have got a job or a degree, and never would have made it here: locking the door to her *own* apartment, barreling toward her first day at what—without wanting to be cliché about it—could well be the role she'd always dreamed of.

Eli and Olive Henderson had been kind to Carey, opening their door to her after just one call from Michelle Chaplin.

They had two spare bedrooms in their old terrace house, a narrow two-story home sandwiched between more of the same. One bedroom was a time capsule, ready for when their daughter came home. But Angie had followed an urge to travel abroad, a trip that began as one year, which became two, then three, then Eli and Olive started to suspect she wasn't coming back. That had been twenty years ago, and as Olive sometimes lamented, they'd seen Angie just three times since—a punishment for a crime they didn't even know they'd committed.

How they knew Miss Michelle was never made clear to Carey, but in the end it didn't matter. They charged her a pittance for board and food, as long as she helped with the washing and folding and cleaning the bathroom. The arrangement suited Carey just fine. Carey filled a gap in the Hendersons' home and they provided her with everything she needed to find her way in life. In fact, it had been Eli Henderson who'd sat with Carey and planned how she might leap from lily pad to lily pad, all the way to law school.

Lily pad one: Work hard at the job Miss Michelle had lined up.

"*I* started out as an office assistant, you know," Eli told her, grinning. "Trust me: office assistants know where all the bodies are buried."

Lily pad two: Study at night to graduate high school. This part was relatively easy. Carey had always been smart—very smart—and without the girls at school tormenting her, she breezed through the work.

Lily pad three: Get into law school. This part seemed harder because it *was* harder. But for weeks on end, Eli and Carey had sat up late, the front room of the terrace blazing with light into the small hours of the morning. He quizzed her on contracts and torts and sentencing, far more than she ever needed to get *into* law. She passed the entry exam easily. Hell, she could have graduated right then and there.

She'd been in her final year of law when she noticed something changing; something subtle that—if she hadn't been living with Eli and Olive for so long—might have passed undetected. Eli Henderson, who by now was in his midseventies, spent the best part of thirty minutes each morning on his daily grooming—an elaborate ritual of shaving, then combing Californian Poppy hair oil through his hair, trimming his fingernails, then shaving again. ("Hair's a peculiar thing," he'd explained to Carey. "It can hide from the razor blade once, twice, even three times. But if you return a few minutes later, you can take it by surprise." Carey didn't think that was actually true, but she was hardly going to question it.) Olive had endured this routine with good grace every day since they were first married, and confided to Carey that she'd never even seen her husband with a five o'clock shadow.

"Beards are for people with something to hide," she explained in a hoarse, smiling imitation of Eli.

The day things changed, Carey and Olive were in the kitchen when the scent of Californian Poppy announced Eli's imminent arrival. As he sat down at the table, Olive rose to fetch her husband his breakfast.

"Morning, Eli," Carey said. She had started off calling him Mr. Henderson, but he'd said it was too formal. Carey thought it was wrong to call a gentleman fifty years her senior by his given name, but he'd insisted.

"Morning, love," Eli replied cheerfully, as he always did. He turned to his wife, and as he spoke, Carey watched him closely. Something didn't seem right, but she couldn't quite identify what. It wasn't until Eli leaned back to chuckle at something Olive said that Carey realized. Eli's chin was struck by a beam of sunlight lancing through the kitchen window, illuminating a fine speckling of snowy-white prickles.

"Eli! You haven't shaved!" Carey cried in mock outrage.

Eli looked at Carey, then at his wife, and the grin melted from his face, replaced by a brief flash of confusion. His hand rose to his chin, and Carey could hear the rasping of papery skin against the stubble.

"Oh," he said. "Apologies, ladies. I'll be back in a few minutes."

Carey left for a lecture and promptly forgot all about Eli Henderson's shaving oversight. But when she returned home late that afternoon, it was clear Olive Henderson had not forgotten. She'd asked her husband about it at lunchtime, and he'd dismissed it with a wave. It worried her.

"Fifty-three years in May, and he's never forgotten before," Olive said quietly as Carey helped peel carrots, the long orange strands curling into the kitchen sink. And when she put it like that, Carey agreed—it was most unusual.

What they'd both witnessed, of course, was the first outward sign of dementia. But now that they were alert, more red flags appeared almost immediately.

Eli never forgot to shave again—having had his attention drawn to it, it was foremost in his mind every morning—but the following week, when he and Olive set off to walk to the shops, Eli turned left; the shops were, and always had been, to the right.

"This way, Eli," Olive said.

"I know, love," he replied. "I was just..." He searched for some excuse, but came up blank.

It was three months before Olive was able to coax her husband, the impeccably dressed, well-mannered Eli Henderson, to go to the doctor, who confirmed what Olive and Carey had feared.

It was another six months before that same elegant, polite gentleman paused near Carey in the hallway outside the kitchen, and she saw his eyes wander down to where her skirt ended slightly north of her knee. Then he shuffled past her and never said another word about it, as though he'd forgotten it had happened at all.

It had been a brief, lusting glance, completely unlike the strange hate-filled glare of her stepfather, but for a moment Carey was sixteen again. This time, though, instead of mourning the loss of her mum, she was grieving for the man who'd taken her in and been so, so kind. Mourning the loss of the real Eli.

The same week, Carey asked Rachael if she'd like to share an apartment. She withheld the true reason for the suggestion; it somehow seemed disrespectful to Eli Henderson to paint him as a lecher when a disease was stealing its way through his mind, robbing him of the sweet and gentle nature that had defined every other minute of his life. After a difficult conversation with Olive Henderson (who felt like she was losing another daughter), Carey moved into a small rental in an inner-city suburb with her best friend from law school.

The bus took another corner too fast, and Carey grabbed the seat in front to keep herself from sliding into the aisle.

Jesus Christ, she thought. *Remind me again why I moved to Ingleby.*

She'd moved to Ingleby because Rachael got a boyfriend. Both girls were working—Rachael at a small law firm, Carey in the legal department of the same insurance company where she'd been an office assistant (Eli was right—she *did* know where the bodies were buried)—and over time, a string of boyfriends had passed through their tiny flat. Then one stayed.

"Daniel's gonna move in," Rachael announced. "Don't worry, we'll split the rent three ways. You'll actually be *saving* money." She'd presented it as a good deal for Carey, but both of them knew it was a bit of a dud. After several months of being the third wheel in her own living room, Carey decided it was time to buy her own place. Gazing at a map, each inch away from the city center was a step closer to being affordable, until finally she settled on a suburb she'd never heard of.

Ingleby wasn't much to look at, but it was a start. The one-bedroom flat came with a strong deadlock on the door, and even though the apartment was on the third floor, the windows had security screens that'd need an angle grinder to cut through. She felt safe—and safer still when she met Aaron.

Aaron was a friend of Rachael's partner, Daniel, and because a relationship is almost contagious, as soon as Rachael was in one she felt Carey needed to be too.

"You two would make seriously beautiful babies," Rachael said, nudging Carey with an elbow that said, *Go on, what have you got to lose?* And it was more than just the strong jaw and broad shoulders—Aaron had a cheeky sense of humor and a magnetism that drew people to him. Carey found herself falling for him: first on their evenings out with Rachael and Daniel, and then on the nights he stayed over at her little flat in grungy Ingleby.

It wasn't until he moved in that he stopped making an effort, as though the work it took to charm strangers outside was all too much when it was just the two of them, day after day. But still, Carey felt *safe* when he was there. Never mind that he didn't show her much affection. Or that he'd smirk when he disagreed with her in a way that was both dismissive and belittling. Deep inside she still felt *safe*, which was a shocking betrayal of Carey by her own instincts.

The first time he hit her was without warning.

"I thought we could leave at six and meet the others at the restaurant at seven," she told him. "You're still coming, right?"

"Nah, not tonight," he said, and turned back to the fridge, rummaging about for something. A beer, most likely.

"Oh, come on. It'll be fun. It's that place I showed you the other week." Carey grabbed his arm and tried to turn him around to face her. "The restaurant's attached to a distillery, so they make their own—"

It was probably an accident rather than an *actual* hit, Carey told herself later. Aaron shrugged her off, his elbow driving sharply into the side of her head, just above her left ear. Plenty of hair to cover the bruise. Carey didn't go to dinner that night either.

Perhaps the most sinister aspect of the whole episode was that Aaron didn't mention it afterward. There was no apology, no declaration of love, not even an attempt to blame Carey for what she'd made him do. If it hadn't been for the throbbing pain in her head, she might have questioned whether it had even happened. But it had. And it happened again.

Carey would have left Aaron if she hadn't missed her period. The idea that she, Carey Price, was going to have a baby terrified her for three reasons: she had no idea what to do with a child; she didn't *want* a child with a man who was a lot less perfect than advertised; and, finally, her career was just rumbling into gear.

"You know, you've got other options," Rachael said delicately, when Carey asked her what she should do. (Of course, Rachael didn't know about the violent side of Aaron Gallagher, and Carey didn't tell her.) "I'd come with you to the appointment. Just think about it, yeah?"

But the option Carey chose was not the one Rachael had been suggesting, and suddenly Rachael and Daniel were witnessing the registry office nuptials of Aaron and Carey, who became Carey Gallagher, wife to a reluctant and decidedly awful husband.

Two weeks later Aaron shook Carey awake.

"What the fuck, Carey. Did you piss yourself?" Aaron was always more unpleasant when his sleep was interrupted.

In the dark, Carey felt the sheets: they were soaked.

"I...I think so," she said, appalled. "I must have. Sorry, Aaron."

But the damp on her fingers had a coppery smell—the scent of blood. She cried to Rachael for hours that day; not just at the loss (which she felt more keenly than she would have expected), but at the ring she now wore on her finger like a manacle.

The ring, and her new name. (Hiding her from Tommy, who was searching but never finding.)

Carey's nerves tightened as the bus slowed, the traffic growing heavier around it. They were getting closer to the city now, and God she was nervous. Starting a new job was scary enough, but starting one she felt completely unqualified for? Well, that was something else altogether. Never mind the fact that she'd aced a two-day interview process. Aaron had laughed at her when she went for it, but the recruiters had seen that Carey Price, now Carey Gallagher, was infinitely more capable than her husband's smirk would have her believe.

Carey waited in reception on the eighteenth floor for her new boss, fighting an almost overwhelming urge to get back into the elevator, onto an outbound bus and home to her little flat, where Aaron was probably still asleep. But as the minutes ticked past, she became less enthusiastic about that idea, and not just because of the lackluster farewell she'd received that morning. In fact, she almost found herself hoping that Aaron wouldn't be there when she got back, that his on-again, off-again work as a contractor was on again and had taken him far away. The thought eased her nerves, and when Carey's supervisor materialized in front of her, she still had a half smile on her face.

"Carey, good morning," Rose said. "It's great to see you again—welcome to Kirk & Singh."

Of the three lawyers who'd sat on the interview panel, Carey had liked Rose the best. She had an air of authority and confidence that was softened (but in no way weakened) by something slightly maternal. She reminded Carey a little of Miss Michelle.

Carey stood and straightened her skirt.

"Hello, Rose," she said, hoping she sounded less shaky than she felt.

Rose took Carey on a whirlwind tour of the eighteenth and nineteenth floors, during which she was told many names but remembered very few. On the other hand, she was remembered by almost all who met her, including a number of men who nudged their colleagues and muttered to each other. (One of them was given a two-week suspension by Human Resources. Fortunately, Carey was none the wiser.)

Carey's first week passed remarkably quickly, and it turned into a month, and then two. Then another junior associate started at the firm, and suddenly Carey was no longer the new girl, but just Carey. The hours were long, and Carey had lost count of the number of times she'd been one of only a handful of people on the late-night bus, front door key gripped tightly between white knuckles.

"What are you gonna do with that, love?" an older woman asked her one evening from across the aisle.

Carey shrugged. "I don't know," she admitted. She wasn't sure if she had the stomach to drive it into an attacker's eye, or cheek, or wherever, but holding it gave her some comfort. She tried not to read too much into the fact that when she pictured herself using it, the bad guy always had Aaron's jaw and short blond hair.

But in the end the key was never used for self-defense. In fact, the only time Carey ever thought she might need it was the night she came home to find her apartment empty. The moment she turned the door handle, she sensed that something was different. *Shit*, she thought, *I've been robbed*, and she whipped the key out of the lock and clenched it between her fingers. But as she looked around the living room, reality set in. Burglars don't usually have a key that they slide back under the door when they leave.

Carey pulled out her mobile phone and dialed her best friend.

"He's gone, Rach," Carey said.

"What do you mean, gone?" Rachael asked.

"He's left me. Sometime today, it must've been—he was here this morning."

"Oh." Rachael was silent for a moment. "Are you sure? Maybe he's been called away for work."

"He took the TV. And"—Carey paused, spotting something on the kitchen bench—"he left his wedding ring."

"Oh," Rachael said again. "Well, that's pretty clear, isn't it? How are you feeling?"

Carey considered the question. She thought about Aaron, and the way he'd looked at her hungrily when they first got together. She thought about what it was like to live with him. To be bruised by him.

"Good, I think. I'm sorry, Rach, I know he's a mate of Daniel's, but it's…um…it's good."

Aaron had actually left just minutes after Carey headed off to work that morning. He'd been lying in bed, waiting to hear the door close, and as soon as it did he was up and dressed. His car already had most of his clothes in it, and he'd looked around the flat, seeing what else he could lay claim to.

"Fuck it," he said to himself and unplugged the television.

"I'm the only one who watches it." And he lugged it down to his car. He returned only to remove his ring and put it on the bench, then lock the door and slide the key back underneath. It was a half-hour drive to his new apartment and the girl he'd started seeing six weeks earlier.

If Rachael had been worried that Carey would grieve the end of her marriage, she was quickly proven wrong—as far as Carey was concerned, the marriage had been sick from the start, and clinically dead for some time. Aaron's departure from the flat was just the cremation of the body. Her grieving was done, and the divorce would be a simple formality. If anything, she was more upset about the TV.

But still, Rachael felt like she should step up, because that's what best friends did, right? The following Friday afternoon, right at 5:30 p.m., Carey's phone rang. She was still at work (naturally), and the ringtone echoed loudly in the large room, bouncing around the cubicles set aside for associates. She saw a couple of other heads bob up at the interruption. Carey wasn't the only one staying back.

"Hello?"

"How long are you going to be at work?" It was Rachael.

"Not long—maybe another an hour or two. There are a couple of things I want to finish before the weekend."

"Right. I'll be outside your building in fifteen minutes. Be downstairs, or I'm going out without you." Rachael hung up, and Carey smiled.

Fifteen minutes later Carey stood outside the office tower. It was a warm late-January evening, and the pavement had retained the heat of the day.

"Lucky. I really would've left without you," Rachael said from behind her.

Carey hugged her friend tight. They set off down the street, without any particular destination in mind but moving toward the hub of the city's nightlife. As they walked, they chatted, and Carey had the feeling that she was being assessed for damage, to see how much emotional first aid was needed in the wake of the breakup.

"Really, Rach, I'm fine," she insisted. "I'd tell you if I wasn't. The truth is, Aaron wasn't…well, he wasn't a particularly nice person. And now he can be somebody else's problem. The main thing is I've still got my apartment. It was mine before I met him, and if he tries to make a claim, then good luck to him."

Rachael smiled at this. She wouldn't want to take on her friend in a legal battle.

"It's a clean break. No more Aaron. No more guys at all, actually, for a while," Carey added.

They turned a corner and wandered up a street dotted with cafés and restaurants.

"Let's have a drink before dinner, yeah?" Rachael suggested, pointing to a place across the road.

Carey nodded, and they crossed over to join the end of a queue. The line moved quickly, and as they shuffled forward Carey and Rachael caught up on each other's news.

"Daniel's up for a promotion. But how about this—he has to do three rounds of interviews first. Three! For an internal promotion!" Rachael was saying as they reached the front of the line and stepped inside.

The place was packed, and Carey scanned the dimly lit room for somewhere to sit.

"You say you've given up on guys?" Rachael asked as they weaved their way through the crowd, her lips close to Carey's ear to be heard over the music and chatter.

Carey nodded vehemently.

"Shame," Rachael said, "because that one's been staring at you since we walked in."

Carey turned to where Rachael was gesturing, and saw the barman, a tall, fit-looking man in his late twenties, standing motionless behind the bar. He had thick, sandy-colored hair and a crooked nose, and his mouth hung slightly open as Carey looked him up and down.

Tommy hadn't found Carey. She'd found him.

18

Before Carey walked into The Hole on that summer night, it had been an evening notable only for its sameness. Tommy Llewellyn and Josh Saunders had become a well-oiled machine, albeit one where the parts had to be reintroduced on January 5 each year. But having perfected his routine of applying for a job that he created himself (he no longer thought of it as *tricking* the Reset; more a case of working *through* it), Tommy found he was able to slot neatly back into his role as head bartender, and he and Josh resumed their friendship almost where they'd left off. Josh never felt a sense of déjà vu, never had a feeling that he knew Tommy from somewhere, but he did wonder how he got so lucky as to find someone who complemented his own skills and personality so well. In the years since Dave's departure, the pair had worked and worked and worked, implementing the changes they had been intent on for so long. (Sometimes Dave regretted not listening to his son. That was usually at about 3:00 a.m., halfway through his shift pulling beers for red-eyed travelers in an airport bar.) The result was the queue that Rachael and Carey had joined.

Tommy, who'd taught himself to fix furniture and paint a house from books, had transformed much of the seating in the bar, somehow improving its capacity without losing its charm. Josh had redesigned the wine list and cocktail menu, and persuaded a chef from a nearby restaurant to jump ship and reinvent the kitchen. That chef brought her best waitress, a homecoming of sorts for Renee.

And yes, they started serving lunch.

The three old guys who owned The Hole were thrilled—a line out the door every Friday and Saturday night, and filled to bursting every other day. With new management, The Hole had become one of the city's hottest venues. It certainly had a buzz about it.

And it was into this buzz that Carey and Rachael strolled, completely unaware that Tommy's world had changed in a heartbeat. As luck would have it, they pushed through the crowd and a young couple jumped up from a small table at the back of the room, realizing (too late) that the movie they were going to see had started five minutes earlier. Rachael spotted the table and raced over, waving to get Carey's attention. Carey was still looking at the man behind the bar.

"Carey!" Rachael called. "Over here!"

Carey turned to see her friend waving at her, and she joined Rachael at the table.

"What do you reckon?" Rachael asked.

"About the table? Love it."

Rachael rolled her eyes. "You know what I mean. What do you think of him?" She nodded toward Tommy.

Carey glanced over again, just in time to see Tommy finally look away, his focus reluctantly pulled back to the customers waiting three deep at the bar.

"Rach, I'm serious—I'm taking a break for a while. Hey, I forgot to tell you: Aaron tried to call me during the week."

And, distracted, Rachael leaned in to hear the rest of the story.

Behind the bar, Tommy's heart pounded as though he'd just run a sprint. He'd done a double take, then a triple, as disbelief set in. It was a face he'd pictured hundreds of times, *thousands* of times, imagining again and again what would happen if she walked through the door. And now she had.

Christ. She's here.

Everything else—the customers, the laughter, the music, the puddle of beer he was standing in—had vanished.

She's actually here.

Then she'd walked past him and sat down at a table with her friend. He stared at her, unwilling even to blink. The last time he'd seen Carey, she'd been sick: bony wrists, stick-thin legs, jutting collarbones. Now, Tommy thought, she looked…*healthier*. He hoped that wasn't offensive.

"Excuse me?" said a man, tapping his credit card impatiently on the bar. "I know it's busy, but I've been waiting for ages, and I—"

"Oh. Right. Sorry," said Tommy, shaking his head as if rousing himself from sleep. He set about making the man's drinks, an uncomplicated order that he somehow managed to mess up twice. It set the scene for the next half hour, as he considered what to say to Carey, whether he should say anything at all, and what he would do if she walked back out of the bar and out of his life before he made a decision.

Josh appeared by his side. "Mate, are you all right?" Josh asked. "Just saw you serve a gin and tonic with lemonade. I'd rather not comp too many more drinks."

"Yeah, sorry. Won't happen again," said Tommy.

"Something's up. What is it? Bad news?"

"Not exactly," Tommy replied, and his eyes darted toward the table where Carey and Rachael were deep in conversation.

Josh grinned. "The chick in the corner?" he asked.

Tommy nodded dumbly.

"Hey, isn't it time for your break?" Josh added. Tommy looked at him in confusion. He was supposed to work straight through to the end of his shift. "Why don't I take over for a minute and you have a quick breather?" Josh winked at Tommy.

The ban on fraternization had clearly been lifted.

Tommy wiped his hands and squeezed past Josh and the other two bartenders. If his heart was racing before, now it boomed in his chest as he approached the table where his first (and only) crush sat, still with no idea what to say when he got there. Rachael saw him coming, elbowed Carey, and disappeared to the ladies' room.

Suddenly the crowd parted and Tommy was there, standing in front of Carey's table. He felt like he'd walked on stage, thousands of eyes fixed on him under a hot, bright spotlight.

"Hi," he said, and groaned inwardly. All this time, and the best he could come up with was *Hi*.

"Hi," Carey replied. Then she smiled. It was, without a doubt, the most beautiful thing Tommy had seen in his life.

"Can I sit down for a moment?" he asked.

Carey nodded.

As he sat, he looked her in the eye. There was no recognition there, of course, but what he did see encouraged him—a slightly indulgent, bemused expression that suggested she might just hear him out.

"Look, I don't normally do this," Tommy started, and Carey let out a snort. "No, really, I don't! It's not allowed," he insisted, his voice going higher with indignation. He cleared his throat and continued. "My name's Tommy. Tommy Llewellyn. I was wondering if I could buy you a drink?"

So far that night, Carey had twice declared that she was finished with men. But there was something disarming about Tommy, something a little…helpless. So instead of dismissing him, as she'd intended to do, Carey found herself weakening.

"Okay," she said, and Tommy gestured to Josh (who'd been watching with all the subtlety he could muster, which was none).

"Carey Gallagher," she said, putting out her hand, and Tommy's breath caught. *She's married*, he realized, and he felt his elation start to splinter. But then Carey made a snap decision. "Actually, Carey Price. Long story." It was a story Tommy wanted to hear, but the message was a simple one. He glanced at her hand. There was no ring.

Josh took Carey's empty glass and replaced it with a full one. "I know you've only just met him, but this one's a keeper," he said.

Carey rolled her eyes, but chuckled.

"So, what do you do, Carey?" Tommy asked. There was so much he wanted to know.

"I'm a lawyer. Just an associate, really. At Kirk & Singh."

Tommy had no idea what Kirk & Singh was, or what an associate did, but he didn't care. She was a lawyer. *She'd done it.* It was hard to refrain from telling her how proud he was. Not only would it have sounded odd, but it would've raised a whole lot of difficult questions that he didn't know how to answer. Instead, Tommy looked at his watch. "I've got to get back to work. I don't know what your plans are, but if you guys are sticking around, I finish at eleven. Otherwise…" He hesitated. "Maybe I could give you my number and we could see each other again sometime." He held his breath as he waited for her response.

"We'll see," she said airily, and he exhaled, deflated.

"It was nice to meet you, Tommy," Carey said, and Tommy returned to the bar as Rachael slid back into her seat. Tommy had sensed them both watching him as he walked away, and the color rose into his cheeks—the old familiar flush he hadn't felt for a few years.

Barely a minute went by without Tommy checking the table in the back corner by the pinball machines. *The Twilight Zone* was long gone (the flippers had fallen off, and the tech had quoted a grand to fix it), but *Indiana Jones* had taken its place, and the sound of a whip cracking and a few notes of the theme song occasionally blared out from the tinny speaker. As the night rolled on, Tommy felt his hopes rise that Carey and her friend would still be there when his shift finished, and he could pick up where he'd left off, trying to connect with a girl he'd loved in absentia since he was a kid.

Fifteen minutes before he was due to clock off, Tommy heard

Indy's whip crack and glanced up. His heart sank. Rachael had put away a bottle of champagne almost on her own and took a moment to steady herself as the pair stood. Then, with bags over their shoulders, the two women picked their way through the crowd to the exit. Tommy lost sight of them at the door, and he felt like he could cry. Not just because they'd left—he was sure he could find her again, now that he knew her married name and where she worked—but because she'd left without saying anything to him. If it was Carey's way of sending a signal that she didn't want to be pursued, then Tommy had received and understood it all too clearly.

But the rejection seemed so unfair. For Carey, it was merely knocking back the advances of one awkward bartender, a man she'd never met before and would likely never see again. For Tommy, it was the summary execution of a hope he'd kept alive for half his life.

Tommy went blindly through the motions of finishing his shift. The rush was over, the two other staff behind the bar were more than capable of handling what was left, and Tommy found himself longing to be out of The Hole. At precisely 11:00 p.m. (Tommy had never been a clock-watcher, but that night he just didn't care), he poured his last drink and wiped his hands on the front of his black button-up shirt, the uniform he and Josh had introduced four or five Resets earlier. He waved goodbye to Josh, who looked at him quizzically then beckoned him over.

"You know I finish at eleven, right?" Tommy said.

"Yeah, of course," Josh replied. "I just don't know why you're heading home. Missed opportunity if you ask me; she seemed pretty keen."

"Josh, she left fifteen minutes ago," Tommy explained. "I didn't miss the opportunity. She didn't want it."

"Oh," said Josh with a smile. He was enjoying himself. "Must be her twin then."

"What do you mean?" asked Tommy.

Josh pointed to the table where Carey and Rachael had been sitting together. Carey now sat alone, legs crossed, idly flicking through photos on her phone as she waited.

Waited for Tommy.

Three hours later, Tommy and Carey were still at the small table at the back of The Hole, the flickering lights and distorted music from the pinball machines barely a distraction as they talked and laughed. Carey had explained how she'd put her friend in a cab and sent her home, having spent most of the evening weighing up the pros and cons of staying behind for an impromptu date. The pros had won out, and here she was.

"I'm glad you stayed," said Tommy shyly, and Carey smiled. She told him about her life, about the part he already knew and the part he didn't. He heard about the sweet old couple who'd taken her in, and her heartbreak at the recent death of Eli Henderson. She dispensed with her soon-to-be ex-husband in a couple of sentences, but spent more time on her joy at working in law, laughing as she described her inexplicable love of contracts.

"I don't know what it is. Maybe I just like finding loopholes and closing them. Does that make me weird?"

Tommy skipped over some parts too, starting his story on the day he arrived in the city and then implying he'd worked at a variety of bars before finally landing a job with Josh. Carey found it hard to believe he was still living in a hostel for backpackers, and when he tried to justify it by explaining he was saving for something, he knew what the next question would be. Carey watched as Tommy started to talk about the business; hesitantly at first, but once that trickle breached the dam wall, he could hold nothing back. He pointed out the changes he'd contributed: the things she could see around the room, and the things she couldn't. If Carey had been completely sober, she might have realized that Tommy was describing improvements made over years, and not just the month that he'd officially been working at The Hole.

He concluded with a conspiratorial whisper about his ultimate plan to buy The Hole with Josh, the first step in making their fortune.

They talked and drank and ate, and time seemed to pass for Tommy in a series of snapshot images. There he was, sitting with Carey in the darkest corner of the bar, then Josh was at their table, reminding them that the last customers had left some twenty minutes earlier. The next snapshot was the pair in a westbound taxi, and then Tommy taking Carey's hand as they walked up the stairs to her flat.

For the first time since he moved to the city a decade ago, Tommy didn't return to his bunk at Sunrise Backpackers.

◐

Tommy and Carey spent much of the following day together; his shift at The Hole didn't start until the late afternoon, so he had no excuse to rush away. Not that he wanted one. He'd woken up in bed beside the woman he'd dreamed of for so many years; Tommy couldn't remember a time in his life when he'd been more blissfully happy. But as content as he was, something pinged gently in the back of his mind. Every time Carey smiled at him, or let out a soft, sweet laugh, he heard it. Tommy did his best to ignore it, pushing it aside as they showered and dressed. He dismissed it again as they ate a late breakfast, side by side at the kitchen bench in Carey's apartment. He flatly rejected it as they returned to bed in the early afternoon, and it wasn't until Tommy had kissed Carey goodbye and was sitting in a taxi, returning to the city to go to work, that he afforded that ping some space in his head.

It was a sense of foreboding more than a fully formed thought, but by the time the cab pulled up outside the hostel, it had hardened into a very real, tangible threat to the happiness he'd just found. Although January 5 was almost a year away, the Reset hung over him like a guillotine blade, glinting dully as a constant reminder that everything in his life was temporary. And he now had so much more to lose.

When he arrived at The Hole just a few minutes before five, Josh was already there. He looked at Tommy expectantly, waiting for something—confirmation, denial, details.

Tommy grinned at him, and Josh clapped his mate on the back. "Well done, Tommy," he said. "But please tell me you didn't take her back to the hostel; she deserves better than that shithole!"

Tommy told Josh they'd gone to Carey's place, and that they'd spent the day together. He left out the details (though he knew Josh was fishing for them) but added that they'd agreed to meet again the next morning.

"Jeez, that's a bit heavy, isn't it?" Josh asked, and immediately regretted it when he saw the look on Tommy's face. Clearly his friend didn't see this as a one-night stand.

Halfway across the city, an almost identical conversation was taking place on the phone. Carey had ignored half a dozen text messages from Rachael while Tommy had been in her apartment, and when she finally called her friend, Rachael sighed with mock relief.

"I kind of assumed he'd killed you and cut your body up into little pieces. Wouldn't be out of the ordinary for Ingleby, really," she teased, before Carey filled her in on everything that had happened since she'd bundled Rachael into a cab the night before.

"Tomorrow? Are you sure you wanna do that?" Rachael asked. "Aaron hasn't even been gone a fortnight. Sounds like a rebou—"

"Don't say it, Rach," Carey interrupted. "It's not like that. Aaron and I were finished long ago. He was…I don't know, like a flatmate. A shit one. I really like Tommy. He's…he's nice." It was the same reason Tommy had fallen for her at the Dairy.

"Well, don't expect me to come all the way out to Ingleby if he does start to chop you up. He'd be finished by the time I got there."

Tommy and Carey proved their friends wrong. They met up the following day, and the night after that, and they both found that when they weren't together, the other barely left their thoughts. This wasn't anything new to Tommy, who'd spent an inordinate amount of time over the years thinking about Carey, about what she was doing and whether he'd ever see her again. In some of the quieter moments they shared, Tommy wondered whether Carey sensed anything unusual—whether as they lay in bed together, or ate breakfast, or even just laughed at each other's stupid jokes, she felt a connection that ran deeper and longer than the night they met at The Hole, something that went back to their days together at the Dairy. But if she did feel it, she never mentioned it to Tommy.

Truly, she wasn't hiding anything at all—in all their time together, Carey would never have one of those Hollywood moments when the spell breaks and the memories come flooding back. Any recollections of Tommy as a child in Upper Reach had long ago been wiped by the Reset, and even if Tommy *had* understood the mystery behind it, there was no way to retrieve what was already gone. But Tommy knew what he'd felt at his dad's house, at that happy, comfortable place that smelled like a home. He didn't have an instruction manual to tell him what to do, but the feeling that day had been almost overwhelming: a feeling that he could create a place like that too, somewhere he might be safe from the Reset. He couldn't get back what was already lost, but deep inside he harbored a little hope for the future.

It left Tommy with a dilemma. Should he reveal that he'd met Carey before, that they'd been friends, that he'd saved her life, and that he'd loved her ever since? It gnawed at his conscience. To keep it from her seemed dishonest, but he didn't know how to explain it without Carey either feeling like she'd been manipulated, or wanting to have him committed while she changed the locks and her phone number.

After weeks of late-night and weekend dates, both Tommy and Carey grew tired of the travel. But instead of separating, they decided to move in together, a move that worried both Josh and Rachael, but didn't really surprise them. Tommy jokingly suggested that Carey move into his dorm at Sunrise Backpackers. Instead, she handed him a key.

Tommy looked around the dorm one last time as he packed his clothes. He'd picked a fine day to move out; the rain was pelting down, hammering against the little window he'd fixed years ago. At least when the rain stopped, the next occupant of his bunk would be able to open the window again. He gazed at the bed and wondered who it might be. A lonely traveler, maybe; homesick, or unwell, or perhaps both, with a fever making them hot and miserable and wishing they'd never come on this stupid trip. He pictured them waking up in the morning, the fever having broken overnight, and the regret and loneliness swept away by the fresh, clean-smelling breeze that drifted in. He smiled. That window was the closest thing he had to scratching *Tommy was here* under the bunks. Some of the other residents had done that.

He preferred his window.

Bridget, the woman who'd checked Tommy in on the first day he arrived in the city, was on duty as always. The nose ring was gone, but the jangling bracelets on her wrist remained, and along with the constant hum of the overworked ceiling fan in his dorm, they had become part of the soundtrack for this period of Tommy's life.

"I'm checking out, Bridget," Tommy announced, and she pulled out the old folder with the details of her guests. In other circumstances, there might have been more fanfare for the departure of one who'd stayed for years on end, but as far as Bridget knew, Tommy had checked in on January 5 for three months and was now clearing out a week before he was due to depart.

"No refunds, sorry," she said.

The hostel's longest resident didn't appear to mind as he waved goodbye to Bridget and walked out the door with all his possessions in a borrowed suitcase. He caught the bus to Ingleby—it seemed to take forever, but maybe he was just impatient—and for the first time let himself into the apartment with the key Carey had given him, kissed her hello, then put his suitcase down in the bedroom that they now shared.

19

Tommy didn't see much point in signing up for social media accounts. He'd only have to rejoin each year. Besides, they often seemed to lead to trouble.

"Check out this one," Josh had said one afternoon, when he was sifting through job applications. He'd searched the applicant's name on Facebook and was scrolling through old photos with a grin.

"Is that his…?" Tommy asked.

"Yep, and he posted a photo of it…uh, seven years ago," replied Josh. "Jesus. Bet he never expected that to come back to bite him."

The application had gone in the bin. Tommy had felt a little sorry for the guy, who may not have even realized the photo was still haunting him online. He probably wished he could just hit delete and wipe out his past. Tommy would have gladly traded places with him.

So Tommy didn't bother signing up; it just didn't seem worth the hassle. Carey, on the other hand, had been worn down after years of pressure from Rachael. She scrolled through updates on her phone, happily telling Tommy the latest on people he didn't know and might never meet. She skipped over pictures of Aaron, smiling in photos posted by mutual friends. Tommy had heard enough to know that he'd hurt Carey, and the thought filled him with a fury he'd never felt before. But Carey scrolled past the blond hair and green eyes and the hands that had bruised her, determined to put it all behind her.

"Hey, have you met my friend Sophie? Look what she's posted."

Tommy didn't know Sophie and wasn't really that keen on the photo of her puppy. But he didn't mind; he just liked being with Carey and listening to her voice. She could have been reading the phone book to him and he'd have been happy.

It was remarkable how quickly Tommy Llewellyn and Carey Price eased into a comfortable routine together. To some it would have appeared boring, but to them it was perfect. Any free time they had was spent together in their apartment, talking, watching movies, or reading (Tommy had commandeered an entire two shelves on Carey's bookcase). Carey was trying to teach Tommy to cook on one of those quiet, cozy nights in late April (Tommy's day off) when her social media feed brought her bad news, delivered in the cold, impersonal way that only technology could manage.

"Oh," she said simply, and put her hand to her mouth. The color drained from her face.

"What's happened?" Tommy asked, putting down the knife he was using to dice vegetables. An onion rolled off the bench and onto the floor. He made no attempt to catch it.

Carey scanned the message she'd received, hand still covering her mouth in shock. Finally, she put down her phone and looked at Tommy. Her eyes were wet with tears.

"A friend of mine died," she said in a voice just louder than a whisper.

Tommy put an arm around her and squeezed her tight.

"She was...well, a social worker, I suppose. She ran that place I lived in for a bit when I was a kid," she said. "But she was more than that. She was like everybody's mum." A tear ran down her cheek.

The realization hit Tommy in the guts like a punch.

"What was her name?" he asked, though he already knew the answer.

Carey swallowed. "We called her Miss Michelle."

Over the next few hours Carey gathered more information from the other alumni of the Dairy. Miss Michelle had died that morning in the hospital at Mortlake. Just two weeks earlier, she'd taken herself off to the doctor for a check-up. She'd suspected she was stressed from running a facility for children twenty-four hours a day, seven days a week, with only a short break each year to see her sister. The doctor hadn't agreed with her self-diagnosis and ordered some tests. The results were conclusive—Michelle Chaplin had acute leukemia, and would likely die within weeks. Bizarrely, incredibly, she had continued to work, and explained her symptoms to the residents and staff at Milkwood House as just a side effect of getting old. The younger children had bought it, but the older ones and her colleagues had not; Miss Michelle—the soft-spoken, longest-serving staffer of the Dairy—had always seemed more fit and healthy than people half her age. The charade only lasted days, and when she collapsed at breakfast in the dining room downstairs, an ambulance had been called and the truth came out. Miss Michelle had begged her colleagues and the children not to broadcast the news; she didn't want her final days to be a flurry of grief-stricken goodbyes. Reluctantly they'd agreed, and Miss Michelle's death had been as quiet and unassuming as her life.

Carey cried openly when she found out, and then with each update she cried a little more. But even through her own grief she noticed Tommy's strange reaction; for somebody who had never met Miss Michelle, had never known how patient and kind and beautiful she was, he was taking her death quite personally.

Inside, Tommy was stuck in a terrible place. He couldn't explain it to Carey, but it was as though she'd just told him his own mother had died. Miss Michelle had raised him—she taught him to talk and walk and feed himself; she'd read to him and played with him and taken him in again and again when the universe spat him out like a newborn every year. She'd picked him up from the hospital when she didn't even know him, and brought him back to the only place he'd ever called home. Tommy Llewellyn was caught in a maelstrom of shock, grief, and secrecy, and he didn't know what to do.

The funeral was to be held at Upper Reach early the following week.

"I'll take you," Tommy offered immediately.

"You don't have to do that," replied Carey. "You didn't know her; you don't have to go to her funeral."

Yes I did, and yes I do, thought Tommy. So, insisting that he wanted to support her, he accompanied Carey back to Upper Reach.

On the morning of the funeral, Tommy and Carey were at the train station early, and anxiously watched the clock as the minutes counted down to the arrival of their train. Separately, they both thought it surreal to be returning to Upper Reach, particularly under such tragic circumstances. As the train rocked and swayed its way out of the city and into the hills beyond, Tommy put his hand on Carey's.

"You okay?" he asked, and she nodded. She started to say something, then stopped herself.

"Go on," Tommy encouraged her.

"I wish... I wish I could have said goodbye to her. Miss Michelle helped me in ways you wouldn't expect her to, you know?"

Tommy did know.

"And now she's gone, I can't say thank you, or goodbye, or anything. It just...it just doesn't seem fair," she murmured, and stared out the window. Outside, trees flickered past in a mottled green blur that turned a sudden inky black as the train charged into a tunnel. Carey found herself looking at her own reflection.

"I've never told you this," she said quietly, "but when I was living with her I was in a pretty bad place. It seems so silly now, but I was a kid and everything just seemed so much bigger. So much worse." She stopped for a moment, gathering her thoughts. "I moved to Upper Reach around the time I turned seventeen. I'll tell you something, Tommy—that is *not* a good age to start at a new school. I think I told you how we called the place where we lived the Dairy? Well, the kids at school did too. But I was the new girl, and I don't know why, but everyone there hated me. All the girls, I mean. And some of them started to moo at me."

She laughed. Tommy just sat with his hand on hers.

"It sounds so dumb when I say it now," she went on. "But I already had a few…issues. Mum had just died, and then my stepdad did too." Carey sighed. "And the last thing a girl needs when she's feeling…you know, self-conscious, is somebody mooing at her. They probably don't even remember doing it."

They probably didn't, and Tommy hated them for it.

"I stopped eating—you should have seen me, it was scary." Carey smiled tightly. "And then I had my exams, and I just couldn't concentrate, and…anyway. There was another kid—Richie—and he came and found me. Stopped me doing something stupid." Tommy grimaced. That wasn't how it happened. "I thought I was in love with him after that, but I forgot about him the moment I left Upper Reach. And then there was Miss Michelle. Without her I definitely wouldn't have got a job, or met the Hendersons, or studied law. I…I used to send her a birthday card every year, but I even stopped doing that." She shook her head. "I wish I'd gone back to see her, just to say thank you."

Me too, thought Tommy, *but Miss Michelle wouldn't have known why I was thanking her.*

The pair sat hand in hand in silence, and the train burst out of the tunnel into the bright early morning light.

They caught one of the only two taxis in Upper Reach to the Catholic church. Michelle Chaplin hadn't been a practicing Catholic for most of her life, but when she was told she could count her remaining weeks on just one hand, she'd rekindled her faith.

Tommy and Carey joined the mourners filing into the church and found space on a pew toward the back. From there they could both see the coffin at the altar, flowers laid on top. Next to it was a photograph on an easel, and the sight of Miss Michelle smiling happily hit Tommy hard. The photo looked like it had been taken around the time he left, and Miss Michelle was exactly as he remembered her. Tommy felt a lump form in his throat.

Carey nudged him. "I think that's Declan Driscoll, the guy who owns the Dairy," she said.

An old man was shuffling down the aisle with the aid of a stick, his once-perfect posture now bent and twisted by age. The elderly gentleman took a seat near the front, behind a trio of women; Tommy presumed they were Miss Michelle's sister and nieces, the only family he'd ever heard her mention.

Tommy looked around for familiar faces. He spotted Maxy, and Maisie, and then with delight he saw Sean, his foul-mouthed mate who'd stolen Miss Michelle's car to go to the pool before Tommy was bowled over on the road. He was looking a lot leaner these days.

Carey had also spotted him. "See that guy?" She pointed. "That's Sean. One of the funniest people you'll ever meet. It'll be nice to talk to him again."

At an unseen signal from the priest, the organist started to play, gentle notes drifting across the gathered crowd as the last few to arrive took their seats. One of them sat alone, two rows behind Tommy and Carey, his dark, tailored suit a statement of success to the town he grew up in.

Richie Sharpe looked at the photo on the easel and wondered again why he'd even bothered coming.

After the service, the hearse carried Miss Michelle away, and her family members followed to the cemetery on the outskirts of Upper Reach. The rest of the mourners drove in the opposite direction, a line of cars snaking its way to the wake at Milkwood House, where Michelle had spent so many years.

Tommy and Carey rode with Sean and his wife. Carey had introduced Tommy and Sean outside the church (an introduction only one of them needed), and Tommy was reminded of why they'd been friends each year during their time together at the Dairy. Sean spent the first part of the ride filling Carey in on his life since they'd last seen each other; he'd bought into the car dealership he was working at and was about to start another. His affable, easygoing nature had translated into success. But he was modest about it, and as the procession of cars left town and the speed increased, Sean steered the conversation toward his preferred topic: gossip about the residents of his alma mater.

"Guess who I saw in the church, Carey?" he asked, raising an eyebrow at her in the rearview mirror. He immediately answered his own question. "That slimy shit Richie Sharpe, sitting near the back."

"He's not a shit!" Carey retorted. (Secretly, Tommy was siding with Sean.) "He was good to me. A bit strange, but there's nothing nasty about him."

Sean snorted. "Let's review, yeah? He's a smug, arrogant little tosser who wouldn't come out of his room, wouldn't talk to anyone, and then just left without saying goodbye." He looked up from the road, and his eyes found Tommy's in the mirror. "Just wait 'til you meet him, Tommy. If he even deigns to acknowledge any of us, that is. Richie and your girlfriend had a bit of a thing once!"

Carey slapped Sean playfully on the shoulder, and he pretended to swerve off the road.

"It wasn't a thing!" Carey insisted. "Okay, maybe it was something. But it all got a bit weird."

"Yeah—like Richie," replied Sean.

They all laughed, but Tommy's mind was elsewhere. He was thinking about meeting Richie, and suddenly he was a kid again, part of an awkward semicircle outside the Dairy as Carey said goodbye. He could see her hugging Richie tight, kissing him on the cheek as the surly boy with the dark curly hair stood stiffly, seeming to repel her touch. The quiet loner, dropped into Tommy's place in Carey's life by the Reset.

When they turned up the driveway of Milkwood House, Tommy craned his neck for a look at the old building. He took in the garden beds—slightly weedy but still full of the greenery he'd planted—and the paint on the walls that, while a tad dusty, was yet to peel like the old layers he'd stripped off. Tommy Llewellyn felt a sense of pride as he surveyed his handiwork, a legacy he could lay claim to even if he couldn't share it with anybody.

He took Carey's hand as they climbed out of Sean's car and

made their way up the front steps. Tommy had never expected to come back here, and his thoughts were voiced by Carey.

"Didn't think I'd ever come back," she whispered. "Especially not without Miss Michelle."

Tommy squeezed her hand and they followed the other guests toward the dining room, which had been cleared of all the tables to make room for the gathering. Tommy was overcome by a surge of familiarity, as though it was the morning after the Reset and he'd just walked out of that room with a *3* on the door. It wasn't just being back at the Dairy; it was being reintroduced to the people he'd grown up with, like when he was a child. The only difference this time was that Carey was presenting him as her boyfriend.

In a quiet moment, Tommy turned to Carey. "How are you holding up?" he asked gently.

"Better than I thought I would," she replied. "It's actually lovely to see everyone again. I just wish I'd come back while Miss Michelle was here." Then her gaze moved over his shoulder and she said, "Oh. Hi." Carey sounded uncomfortable, and Tommy knew at once who she was greeting. He turned around. More than a decade had passed since he'd last seen him, but there was no mistaking Richie Sharpe.

"Richie, this is my boyfriend, Tommy Llewellyn," Carey said. "Tommy, this is Richie Sharpe."

Tommy held out his hand, and Richie shook it. His grip was cool and firm, and his deep blue eyes seemed to bore straight through Tommy. Richie's hair was shorter, and there was something about the hairstyle, along with the cut of his suit and the glimpse of an elegant watch under his sleeve, that suggested money, certainly more than they'd all grown up with. Tommy and Carey both felt it: Richie Sharpe had an air of arrogance about him. It was like he was there to prove that he'd outgrown Upper Reach, Milkwood House, and the people who'd been his family. Outgrown Miss Michelle.

"Good to meet you, Richie," Tommy said, reverting to his usual script.

Richie stared at him, and Tommy longed to know what he was thinking. After all, Carey had thrown herself at him before she left the Dairy, then moved on. Now she was here with someone else. But Richie had never cared about Carey anyway. He and Carey may have believed it, but it wasn't really him who'd saved her in the shed.

"Likewise. How have you been, Carey? Still doing insurance admin?" he asked, turning his attention away from Tommy.

"No, not for a long time," Carey said, and Tommy could see she was unsettled. "I'm a lawyer now. At Kirk & Singh."

If Richie was impressed, he hid it well. "Environmental law, huh? Never picked you for a greenie," he said.

Carey blushed. "I'm not really. But it's interesting work. What about you? What are you doing?"

"Finance," he said with a smirk, then stopped, clearly waiting to be asked for further details.

Carey took the bait. "Real descriptive, Richie. Care to be more specific?"

"Private equity. Mostly we buy and sell businesses. Buy them in distress, turn them around, and sell for more than we paid." He rattled off some names, companies that both Tommy and Carey had heard of.

"Wow," Carey said. "Tommy's in business too, you know."

"Oh really?" replied Richie, and Tommy wished Carey hadn't said anything. He loved her for trying to boast about him—but this was a competition he was happy to let Richie win.

"It's nothing. A friend and I run a bar in the city," he said.

"The Hole is really successful," Carey added loyally. "There's a line to get in every night."

"Is that so? Good for you, Tommy," Richie said, loading every word with his customary blend of sarcasm and disdain. For whatever reason, he was aiming to wound.

Tommy felt himself growing angry. Carey must have sensed it, because she said hastily, "It was good to see you again, Richie. Might bump into you in the city sometime."

Richie nodded, and in those cold blue eyes Tommy thought he saw a glint of something cruel. It was as if the chip he'd had on his shoulder as a kid had sharpened into something nastier.

If the universe—or whatever was responsible for the Reset— was capable of making noise, Tommy may well have heard it at that moment, clanking and grinding.

Moving its pieces into place.

Carey took Tommy by the arm and led him down the steps to the old tree that still stood tall in front of the house.

"Are you okay?" she asked. "Don't let Richie bother you. Like I said in the car, he's just a bit weird. He's always been like that."

Tommy didn't respond. He was seething; his long-buried dislike of Richie, an antipathy he'd felt from a time before he could remember, was still threatening to burst out. And if it did, other things would come out too, all the things he kept hidden away. He wanted to tell Carey how he'd known her for years, and had hated Richie for even longer. He wanted her to know that he too had been a resident of the house behind them. He wanted to point to the garden bed and shout, *I planted that!* He wanted them all to hear it. He wanted someone to remember him. He opened his mouth, but the words caught in his throat; if he started to speak, he wouldn't stop.

Carey was looking at him, waiting. When he didn't say anything, she murmured, "Let's go home, Tommy. I've had enough."

A taxi pulled up bearing the members of Michelle's family who'd come from the cemetery, and it left carrying Tommy Llewellyn and Carey Price. As they reached the end of the gravel driveway, Tommy turned. It was the last time he would see Milkwood House.

20

For the rest of that week and into the next, a feeling nagged at Tommy. It wasn't specifically what Richie had said, or the way he'd said it. It wasn't that he'd had to be introduced to all his old friends by Carey, or even how he was forced to hide his grief for the woman who'd raised him. He was, in some ways, used to that and had gone through a form of it every year since birth.

No, the sensation that sat in the pit of his stomach was different, a greasy feeling that made him uneasy, as though somebody was watching. And maybe that was it—a feeling that he was being toyed with, that his strange situation was all for the benefit of somebody else's amusement, as they watched him stumble blindly through life, the slate wiped clean each year, ready for another episode of *The Tommy Llewellyn Show*.

But Tommy was intelligent enough to realize he might have created that feeling himself to justify what he wanted to do. He wanted to tell Carey. He wanted an ally. But more than anything, he wanted to keep her by his side, to build that safe place that might offer him shelter. And that meant he either had to tell her his bizarre but true story and risk scaring her off, or he had to find a way to carry her through the Reset without her knowing, now only six months away.

As he wrestled with this, life charged on. Carey continued to work at Kirk & Singh, Tommy continued to work at The Hole, and they each continued to mourn (separately) the death of Miss Michelle, neither aware that another death was imminent. An older fellow by the name of Leslie Pritchard passed in his sleep from a heart attack. Those who knew Les were not surprised; the only surprise was that he'd lasted as long as he had. Les Pritchard had a love for cigarettes, certain illicit substances, and alcohol. So strong was this last love that he'd bought a bar with two friends and called it The Hole.

When Josh Saunders heard that one of the three owners had died, he knew immediately which one it must be. He also knew it meant an opportunity, and he sent Tommy Llewellyn a text message.

Can you come in early? Lunch on me. We need to talk.

"They're selling The Hole," Josh said within moments of Tommy's arrival. They were at the same café they'd dined at years earlier, where they'd shaken on their first deal to become partners one day. They'd made a similar agreement every year since, and each time Josh wondered at his good fortune in stumbling across someone whose ambitions for the business so closely mirrored his own.

"Right," said Tommy, his mind racing. He'd met the three owners many times now; there was only one reason they'd be selling. "Who died?"

"Les—no surprise there," Josh replied. He paused for a moment, as if to pay his respects, then got down to business. "We're going to buy it," he declared. "The boys always said they'd only keep the bar as long as all three of them were part of it. So now's our chance, Tommy. Problem is, it'll be at a premium. Only got myself to blame, I suppose."

Tommy smiled. That wasn't entirely true—Tommy was due a certain amount of credit, though he couldn't really claim it.

"What do you reckon they'll want?" he asked.

Tommy had thought he knew the bar's value, but when Josh gave him an estimate, his mouth fell open.

"That much? Christ." They might be out of the running before they could even make an offer.

"Yeah, I reckon that's in the ballpark. How much cash you got in the bank?" Josh asked bluntly. Anyone else might have played coy, but Tommy told him exactly, to the cent.

Josh's eyebrows shot up. "We paying you too much?" he asked with a grin. "All right—here's what I reckon we do." Josh pulled a notepad out of his rucksack and began writing, showing Tommy the figures and amending them as Tommy suggested changes. An hour later, Josh left to make some calls, determined to move quickly before someone else sniffed the opportunity.

Tommy still had a couple of hours to kill before his shift, and he strolled the streets, deep in thought. A promise to work together was one thing; a proper business partnership with large sums invested, where one partner happened to vanish each year, was a little more complicated. He walked without a destination in mind, and when at last he looked up, he realized he'd been following an old route. A sign above him showed a bright yellow sunrise appearing over the ocean. He had no desire to end up back here, alone, sharing a room with half a dozen unwashed, unencumbered travelers.

It was time to ask for help.

Once Tommy had decided to tell Carey his secrets, he felt lighter. But as one burden lifted, it was replaced by another— how to actually tell her. It was like a marriage proposal, he thought. The timing had to be perfect in order to elicit the right response. But what on earth was the perfect timing for a secret like this? Maybe it wasn't like a marriage proposal after all; more like a confession, a cheating husband owning up to his wife. It was likely to end badly, and the only thing to do was soften the blow and hope for the best.

The opportunity didn't come that night. When he arrived home from The Hole in the early hours of the morning, Carey was asleep, the bedside lamp still burning and a hardcover book facedown on the page she'd been reading the moment she nodded off. Tommy climbed into bed and stared at the ceiling, wondering if this would be the last night he'd spend beside Carey Price.

As the first rays of sun finally pierced the dark, Tommy was still awake, having spent hours mapping out a conversation that was now just minutes away. He climbed out of bed and dressed.

Carey stirred. "What's up, honey?" she asked sleepily. "You were so restless."

"Sorry," Tommy replied. "I know it's early. But can we talk?"

He realized how ominous the words sounded. The concern in Carey's eyes showed she did too.

"Are you leaving me?" she asked, now wide awake.

"No!" Tommy exclaimed. "Of course not. Never."

Carey sat up, her hair tousled from sleep, her eyes wide and wary. Beautiful, sweet, and scared. Overwhelmed by the fear he'd lose her, Tommy wished he could take back his words. If he said nothing, at least they'd have another six months together.

"What's wrong?" she asked, and Tommy sat back down on the bed. All the lines he'd rehearsed while she slept had vanished from his mind, and when he tried to speak, nothing came out.

Finally he sighed. "Carey, I love you," he said softly. It was the first time he'd ever said it, to anybody. The fear left her eyes, and she started to smile.

"Is that what this is about? I love you too," she said and leaned forward to kiss him.

He kissed her back, and then pulled away.

"But there's something else," he said and the smile disappeared. "I don't...I don't even know how to start." He felt like he was on a diving board, high above the water—so high he couldn't tell if there even *was* water below. Once he jumped, there was no going back. "I haven't spoken about this before. I mean, ever."

"Just tell me," Carey demanded, her suspicions aroused again. Clearly *something* was wrong. Seriously wrong.

"Okay," he said. He took a deep breath: he was diving in, headfirst. "We've met before."

Carey's forehead creased in confusion. "Really?" she asked. "When? Why didn't you tell me?"

"This is going to sound…well, it's going to sound ridiculous. But we met at Upper Reach, at the Dairy," he said, eyes fixed on hers, anticipating her reaction. "I lived there too—at the same time as you."

"No you didn't," Carey replied. "I knew all the other kids. I'd remember if you'd been there too. Unless…were you there for a weekend or something? A visit? Is that what you mean? How long did you stay?"

"Seventeen years," said Tommy.

Carey shook her head. "No you didn't," she repeated flatly. "We're not that far apart in age—we would have overlapped." Her eyes narrowed. "What's this about, Tommy? Is it a joke or something? Because I don't think I get it."

Tommy started to answer, but she cut him off, her voice getting louder.

"And if it's not a joke, then there's something wrong with you, or…or you're trying to make me think there's something wrong with *me*. And I *know* it's not me."

"It's not you," Tommy assured her. "You're right: there *is* something wrong with me. But it's different. It's…hard to explain."

"Try," Carey said, and the chill in her tone was like a slap in the face.

"People forget me. I mean, not just some people—*everyone* forgets me. Every year, on the same day. It's like I don't exist and I have to start over again. One day I'm there, and I could be best friends with someone. The next day, I'm still there, and they're still there, but they've got no idea who I am. I'm a stranger."

"Tommy?" said Carey. Her anger had worn off as quickly as it had arrived, and a genuine worry had taken its place.

"Did something happen last night at work? Did you…I don't know—did you take something? Are you okay?"

"I know how it sounds." Tommy held his hands out to Carey. "But it's true, every word of it."

"Prove it," Carey said.

"What?"

"Prove it to me."

"How?"

"I don't know, Tommy. This is your game; you come up with something. Tell me something you'd only know if we've met before. Something I haven't told you."

Tommy fell silent. There was only one thing he could think of that might prove it, but he had no desire to relive it, or to make Carey relive it.

"Please, Carey, can you just trust me on this? I was there when you arrived at the Dairy, and I was there when you left—and I saw everything that happened in between. You just don't remember me."

"No, I don't," she replied sadly, "because you weren't there. Tommy, I can't stay with someone who plays games. Not again." She threw back the covers and swung her legs out of bed. "I'm going to have a shower," she said. "I don't think you should be here when I get out."

"But I'm not playing—"

"Tommy, please! Just leave." Carey crossed the room quickly and opened the door to the bathroom.

"You were going to drink the rest of it," Tommy said quietly.

Carey froze.

"That afternoon in the shed. The weed killer. You tried to drink the rest."

Carey turned slowly, her face pale.

"What?" she asked in a voice barely more than a whisper.

"I'm so sorry, Carey. I really am. But I was there. It wasn't Richie. I was the one who found you. I saw your bag at the door. It was blue, a really bright blue. I was the one who stopped you. And the smell. I can still remember the smell. It makes me sick."

Carey heard a rushing noise in her ears and gripped the door as she swayed on the spot.

Tommy ran to her side, but she shrugged him off. A minute passed as she breathed deeply, mind reeling. She had intended to die that day. She *was* going to drink it.

But there was something else about what Tommy had said, something about it that rang true. In the years since it happened, it always seemed strange to Carey that Richie, the boy who'd hated everyone, had come to her aid. That the boy without compassion had been the one to save her.

What if it hadn't been him at all?

"Why are you telling me this?" she asked Tommy plainly.

"Because I need your help. I love you, and I want you to remember me after the fifth of January."

"I'm pretty sure I'll remember you, Tommy," Carey said.

"You didn't last time."

The sun was almost overhead by the time Tommy and Carey left their bedroom. Tommy had talked for hours, giving Carey the unabridged story of his life, the premiere performance of a tale nobody had ever heard before. For the most part Carey just listened, occasionally asking questions but otherwise letting Tommy talk. And as he did, he changed. There was an almost visible release of tension, the accumulated stress of decades of secrecy and isolation rising off him in waves. More than anything, more than the details he knew or the descriptions he gave, it was the physical change in him that convinced Carey that his story—which seemed so unlikely, so completely impossible—was actually true.

At last, Tommy reached the present day, and summarized his conversation with Josh about buying The Hole.

"And that's the problem—one of many, I guess," he concluded. "I just don't know how I'm going to do it. Each time so far I've been able to talk my way back into a job. I can't talk my way back into a half-share of the business."

Carey chewed thoughtfully on a slice of peanut butter toast, staring blankly through the kitchen window to the building opposite. She'd been asked to believe a lot over the last few hours. She'd tried to maintain a critical distance, and had even attempted to catch Tommy out, but he had an answer for everything. She kept coming back to one thing—he had no reason to make it up.

"I wonder," she said, half to herself, "if there might be a way around it. Just for the business stuff, right?" She looked at Tommy. "You said that whatever causes this—the universe, or whatever—goes through everything you've done, and either erases your involvement entirely, changes the record of what happened, or replaces you with someone else if it's just too big?"

"Yeah, that's pretty much it," agreed Tommy.

"But some things—the stuff around the edges, the stuff a bit removed from you—can avoid it."

"I think so. Well, yeah." He'd told her about the story he'd written that had lived on in the English department at Mortlake High. Maybe it had escaped the purge because he'd left his name off it, there was no handwriting to link it back to him, and he'd forgotten all about it after he handed it in. Plus it wasn't even the original, just a faded copy—one he didn't even know existed until his teacher handed it out in class. The only person who could identify it as belonging to Tommy Llewellyn was, well, Tommy.

"Why?" Carey asked.

Tommy shrugged. "I dunno. Whatever it is—let's agree it's the universe—seems to focus directly on me: the memories and the physical evidence. The stuff tied to me. But some of the little things I've done right out on the edges can kinda slip through. I've always thought of it as a loophole. A small one."

"Well that's got to be it then," Carey said firmly. "That's how to get around it."

"Sorry?"

"I'm assuming if you just took a document to bed with you saying that Josh owned half of The Hole and you owned the other half, it wouldn't work—even though you'd have the document—because Josh would have forgotten he even *had* a partner. Your name would be wiped from *his* copy of the contract, he'd think he's the sole owner, and if you tried to claim it, you'd be done for fraud."

"I think that's right. When he forgets me, he'll forget we had a fifty-fifty split. And with my name on Josh's copy of the contract, you can guarantee the universe is going to zero in on it. Josh gets my half, I get a worthless piece of paper." Tommy sighed.

"Well, what if you did it yourself, instead?" asked Carey.

"Huh?"

"Write yourself out of the partnership. Make your ownership of the bar so remote, so obscure, that the universe won't recognize the connection—or just won't care." Carey had put down her toast, her face lit by a mischievous smile as she outlined her idea. "You put your half of The Hole in a company without your name on it. That business is owned by another company, which is owned by another company, then another one and another one. With every new layer the link to you gets weaker and less defined, but when you go to sleep on the fourth of January, you take proof of ownership for that last company with you. It's got no meaning, no tangible link to anything you've done, or to anyone you've met, so it's just a piece of paper. But you wake up after the Reset, and we follow the paper trail right back to your stake in the business. People use it to dodge tax all the time; I don't see why it wouldn't work to dodge this too."

Tommy didn't say anything; instead, he leaned over and kissed her.

"Hey, I don't know if it'll work," Carey said. "There's not exactly a precedent for trying to cheat the universe, or whatever it is. But I reckon we should give it a go."

Tommy liked how she'd said *we*.

○

That afternoon, Josh Saunders made an unsolicited, unexpected offer to the two surviving owners of The Hole. They countered (a move Josh had anticipated), and Josh upped his bid, quickly and decisively. Two days later, on the afternoon before Leslie Pritchard was lowered into the ground, Josh, Tommy, and two grizzled men shook on a deal that would see The Hole change hands for the first time ever. They celebrated with a series of toasts—one to Les, one to the bar, and one to the new owners, who'd managed to secure one of the hottest properties in town without anyone even knowing it was on the market.

When the sale was made public a fortnight later, it appeared in the newspaper not once but twice. It was first noted in the social pages, with the reporter eagerly speculating about what changes the new owners would make to a bar that was already so successful. ("Wait and see," Josh had told the journalist. He and Tommy had plenty of things in store but were keeping their cards close to their chests.) The second mention was in the business section of the paper.

It was unusual that such a relatively small transaction would be considered newsworthy in a part of the newspaper devoted to companies worth billions, but a curious aspect of the sale had generated a frisson of excitement within the business community. One-half of the partnership behind the purchase was known to be the bar's manager, Josh Saunders, while the other half was represented by the head bartender, Tommy Llewellyn. But a title search on the company backing Tommy had returned a tangled web of connections in an elaborate corporate structure. It sparked gossip that one of the biggest hoteliers in the country had bought into The Hole. That man denied the reports, which only served to stoke the fires, and so the story (with a photo of Josh and Tommy standing proudly behind the counter) was reported widely.

"I still don't exactly get why you've done it like that," Josh said to Tommy a few days after the story was printed, "but man, I'm glad you did. We couldn't get this kind of publicity if we paid for it."

Tommy smiled and thought yet again how lucky he was to have Carey on his side. Carey had found a new purpose for her love of contracts, plowing through the endless reams of paperwork involved in registering a convoluted family tree of businesses: a corporate babushka doll with a little Tommy Llewellyn hidden at the center. She was busy, and happy. So was Tommy, who between long hours at The Hole and short hours spent with Carey, couldn't recall a time when his life had been better.

But still that guillotine blade dangled, ready to sever Tommy from Carey, and Tommy from his success. They didn't talk about it much. Both of them knew it was coming, and aside from the work that Carey had done to hide Tommy's involvement in the business, there was little more they could do until the time actually arrived. Tommy had tried to explain to Carey about the feeling he'd had at his dad's home. But he'd faltered, struggling to describe the sense of a sanctuary. It didn't seem like something he could manufacture in their little apartment with just a fresh coat of paint, a shelf of books, and a sign on the door that said *Tommy & Carey's Place*. That would hardly keep the Reset from sweeping through.

Instead, they focused on the simple pleasures of being a couple, of watching a movie together on the couch on Tommy's nights off, of reading books side by side while they ate at the kitchen bench, of stealing away for a few days at a bed and breakfast in the countryside (in the opposite direction of Upper Reach).

And suddenly, with all the solemnity and finality of a death row inmate's execution date, it arrived.

That January 4 was like no other for Tommy. For the first time since moving to the city, he didn't quit his job at The Hole. If their plan worked, he didn't need to fake a job vacancy sign to get back in the door. He even skipped his rostered shift, telling Josh he wasn't well. Josh knew a sickie when he saw one, but he didn't care—Tommy had earned the right to a night off. Josh was only surprised he didn't take more of them; he knew *he* would, if he had Carey waiting for him at home.

Tommy and Carey walked hand in hand to pick up takeout for their dinner, strolling slowly home as the sun sank over the ramshackle buildings of their neighborhood.

"If it doesn't work, what'll happen in the morning?" Carey asked, a question she'd been sitting on all day.

"It'll work," said Tommy.

"But what if it doesn't?" she insisted, stopping at the entrance to their building and turning to face Tommy.

"I don't know really," Tommy admitted. "I've never been with someone when it happens. But I guess you'll just wake up and find a stranger next to you. You'll either scream and hit me, or wonder how much you had to drink. I hope it's the latter."

Carey punched him playfully.

"But it'll work—I know it will," Tommy said. He sounded much more confident than he felt.

After their final dinner together (both of them trying hard to stay optimistic), they went to bed. In the last minutes before sleep, Tommy put on a pair of pants and slipped a few things into his pockets—his identification, his phone, and an envelope containing proof of ownership for the company at the center of the web Carey had woven. Another envelope held a small wad of cash—what little he had left after buying The Hole and transferring most of the balance of his bank account to Carey for safekeeping.

As he pulled on a shirt, then a second, he grinned at Carey. "Old habits," he said, but she didn't return the smile.

"So if we maintain contact all night, the connection will stay?" she asked for the third time that evening.

"It works for everything else," replied Tommy, also for the third time. "I hope it works for you too." He hoped it more than anything.

Tommy climbed back into bed, kissed Carey again, and wrapped his arms around her.

Sleep came faster than he expected, and within minutes he was out.

21

Tommy didn't dream on the night of the Reset; he never had. It was probably a good thing. The subconscious knowledge that the universe was working to erase his existence would likely not result in peaceful dreams. It meant that Tommy slept like the dead and didn't rouse at all until the early morning sun peered through the curtains in the bedroom.

When he woke, it was with a start, and instinctively his hands went to his pockets, picking out the familiar shape of his phone and ID, and also the envelopes he'd folded in half. But really, he didn't care about those things so much. What mattered was the person lying next to him.

Carey was facing the wall, and Tommy watched as she slept, wondering whether she'd wake to a stranger in her bed with a simple backstory conceived in her mind overnight. He begged the universe to let him have this one. Just once.

At last Carey stirred. Her breathing, so quiet and rhythmic, changed slightly, and then she rolled over. Her eyes blinked open and he smiled at her, hopeful and terrified.

She smiled back.

"Morning," Tommy said softly, his heart thudding almost loud enough to hear. He thought the anticipation might just kill him.

"Morning," she replied.

"Did it work?" he asked.

Carey gazed at him. Tommy was sure she was trying to place him, casting around in her mind to remember where they'd met the previous night.

Just as he'd convinced himself it was over, Carey smiled again, and nodded.

"It worked," she said, and Tommy could have burst from sheer joy alone.

Carey remembered him. He wanted to shout it out, to race outside and tell the world that they'd succeeded.

It worked.

But he didn't burst or shout. He just kissed her instead.

Carey had spent much of the night awake and motionless in Tommy's arms, holding his hand in a vice-like grip, dreading what might happen if she let go. The grip was so tight their hands had stayed locked together even after she finally nodded off.

When they'd gone to bed, there'd been a photograph of Tommy and Carey on the dresser: a selfie they'd taken on their weekend at the bed and breakfast, smiling happily as they shared a bottle of wine in front of a wide, green valley. The frame was still there, but Tommy wasn't. He'd been replaced by Carey's friend Rachael. The wardrobe had been stripped of his clothes and shoes.

But he didn't care.

A couple of hours later, Carey departed to buy Tommy some new clothes. As she left, Tommy pulled out his phone and dialed a familiar number.

"Josh? My name's Tommy Llewellyn. I know this is out of the blue, but are you free to meet with me later today? I've got something to show you…Yeah, it's kind of important."

Customers at The Hole that afternoon wouldn't have known what to make of the conversation in the darkest corner of the bar. One party looked hopeful and buzzed with nervous energy, the other was openly frosty as he stared at the stranger laying claim to half his business.

But as Tommy took Josh through the paperwork prepared so carefully by Carey, the company structure that showed Tommy at its core, Josh's opposition started to weaken.

"I've gotta admit, it makes sense," he conceded at last. "When your lawyer came to me last year and said she represented an investment fund, I figured it was someone keen to get their hands on this place for themselves. I was gonna turn her down. But if I didn't take the money, I would've missed out altogether—and every day since I've expected someone to tap me on the shoulder, try to push me out. Silent partners don't stay silent forever, you know?"

Tommy shook his head in wonder. It was so simple, some unseen force neatly writing him out of the story, and ever so briefly he asked himself what he'd done to someone in another life to deserve this. But the thought was fleeting, and instead he committed to memory everything he'd just said to Josh. It was the first draft of a script he intended to use many times over. If it worked once, it'd work again.

"Well, I've got no interest in forcing you out," Tommy said. "I just want to work."

Josh's grin was almost wider than his face. He left the table, and returned a minute later carrying two shot glasses.

"I'm not much of a drinker, but this calls for a toast." Josh had a good feeling about this guy. "To the start of a long partnership."

Well, not quite the start, thought Tommy.

"So, what are you like behind the bar?" Josh asked.

It was Tommy's turn to grin.

In May that year, Tommy Llewellyn and Josh Saunders made their second big play in business together. After much deliberation, they marched into the bank (as fate would have it, the same branch in which Tommy had opened his first account), and boldly asked for half a million dollars. As Josh slid the title deed for The Hole across the desk as collateral (so quick and simple for an act of such gravity), Tommy jammed his hands in his pockets so that nobody would see them trembling. But there was no visible hesitation from Josh. He radiated a confidence so unshakable it was almost contagious.

"Fuck me," Josh exclaimed afterward, on the steps outside. "Sky's the limit now, Tommy."

Twelve weeks later, The Pit opened on the other side of the city. Tommy suggested the name—the sister venue to The Hole, and another little mark he could claim as his own. Tommy and Josh did everything they could think of to build the hype for the new venue, but in the end, it sold itself—two young, good-looking guys opening their second bar after the raging success of their first was a story that again graced the social pages of the paper. And while it didn't rate a mention in the business section this time, the story was still noticed in an office staffed mostly by arrogant men in expensive-looking suits, not far from Sunrise Backpackers. The fact that the newspaper happened to open on the page showing Tommy and Josh's success was just a coincidence, albeit one accompanied by the silent clanking of the universe moving its pieces around.

The grand opening was a big deal, and Josh made sure everyone who was anyone received an invitation. They were both amazed by the turnout. A coterie of photographers hovered outside, keen to snap the arrivals, which included both the city's mayor and a government minister (who kicked his staffer out of the taxi a block away; his wife didn't need to see them together in the newspaper the next day), three radio presenters from rival stations, and a bevy of reality television stars. (The event was such a hot ticket, Josh had even fielded calls from publicists seeking an invite for their clients.) Then there was the rest—Josh's mates, Carey's friends (and a colleague or two, particularly the ones who helped make decisions about promotions for associates) and a bunch of people from the restaurant and hotel trade, happy for a chance to examine the competition up close. In fact, the only person on the guest list who didn't show up was

Josh's dad, Dave. The former manager of The Hole was nursing a chronic case of professional envy, and the condition appeared to be worsening with age. But his absence certainly wasn't felt (it was barely noticed by Josh), and the general consensus was that it was a hell of a party. The media coverage in the following days was better than they could have hoped for.

But when the party was over, it was Tommy who stayed on, tweaking and adjusting, determined to parlay the launch into something that would go the distance. It wasn't until an evening long after the opening that Tommy finally felt he could relax. He looked around the crowded bar, much brighter than The Hole, and marveled at the noise. There was a constant rumble of conversation, but the dominant sound was laughter from the small groups, twos and threes and fours and fives, and one gathering of fourteen celebrating the engagement of Scott and Emily, whoever they were. Tommy let out the breath he'd been holding since he and Josh had walked into the bank in May.

"You're a good team," Carey said to him late that night. "Josh is brilliant, no doubt about that. But together, you just get things *done.*" She paused. "I'm really proud of you, you know. To go through what you have, and to be where you are now, it's… well, it's pretty special."

Tommy put his head on the pillow and looked at Carey. He still had moments when the sight of her made it hard to think of anything else; her hair still damp from a shower, and her skin so soft and flawless. But it was the way she looked back at him that silenced everything else; there was nothing in her wide brown eyes other than trust and adoration.

"Let's get married," he said, and now those wide brown eyes registered surprise. Tommy swallowed and sat up as he realized what he'd said. "Carey, I've loved you since I was a kid. My life has changed around me every year, but you...well, you're the only thing that's stayed the same. Well, not you, exactly—but the way I feel about you, you know? I don't have a ring, but I can get one. You can help choose it if you want. And we don't have to wait; we could do it straight away. The wedding, I mean, not the ring." He was talking quickly, the words tumbling out of him as he noticed that Carey hadn't responded.

"Well?" he prompted.

Carey smiled sadly, and Tommy's heart sank.

"W-why not?" he stammered.

Carey took his hand. "I love you, Tommy. You know that," she said. "But—I don't know. Doesn't this all just feel kind of... temporary to you?"

"Temporary?" Tommy repeated. He dropped her hand. "Everything's been *temporary* for me since I was born. Can't you see what I'm trying to do, Carey? I'm trying to make something that lasts. I just—"

"Tommy," Carey interrupted, but he plowed on.

"—want what everyone else gets, what they get without even knowing it. I've tried to make a difference. Little things I've left behind. Things that get overlooked. The garden at the Dairy. Changes at work. Things I didn't even know I'd left, like that stupid story I wrote at school. But it's not enough—not anymore." Tommy could feel tears building. He blinked hard. "We already know we can get through the Reset together, you and me. It's not perfect, but it works. With you, I feel like...I feel like maybe I can finally create a life that's a bit more permanent. And I think this will help us do it. Marry me. Please."

Carey looked away, staring at the wall for what felt like an eternity. Finally, her eyes met Tommy's again.

"You know I love you too," she said to Tommy, "and of course I want to marry you. But, Tommy, this idea that you can make a safe place, some kind of cocoon, or whatever it is—you're basing it all on a *feeling*. Tommy, I can't put my whole life into that. You're asking too much of me."

"It's not just a—" Tommy started, but Carey wasn't finished.

"What if it doesn't work? What if something happens at the next Reset? Say you let go of me during the night, and we wake up strangers in a bed. What happens then? How do I explain the ring on my finger? When the gaps where you were are filled in overnight, does it turn out I'm married to someone else and cheating on them with you, a guy I just met? Or, I don't know, was I married before, and my husband died in some horrible accident, and I'm still wearing the ring? Stuck with the pain of losing someone I never even knew, pain shoved into me by the universe to explain a ring that was really from *you*? When you go through the Reset, it's not just you who loses, Tommy. But the rest of us who do…well, we just don't realize it at the time."

Tommy didn't know what to say. Carey's reply had torn him apart, and the spark of optimism that he'd always felt around her, the sense that things would turn out okay, started to dim.

"But…" Carey continued, and the spark sputtered back to life, "I *do* want to marry you. And you're right, we got through the Reset together once. But I need to know that we didn't just get lucky. So I'll make a deal with you. Ask me again. Not now, I mean, another time—when it feels right, you know? When it feels permanent. Like we're meant to be together. If you ask me again then, and if I still know who you are, I'll say yes. Then you're stuck with me."

Tommy looked at her, eyes glistening.

"Promise?" he asked. He sounded like a frightened child, but at that instant he didn't care. He only cared about how she'd respond.

"On my life," Carey replied. "Until then, we hold hands during the Reset. And if you let go, well—look out. I'll be coming for you."

Tommy Llewellyn was good with numbers—a gift from Dad—and pretty handy with words, too—thanks to Mum. But he'd also been blessed with a third gift, as though to make up for the monstrous disadvantage he'd been handed in life: Tommy had a pretty good memory. It was nothing extraordinary—certainly not photographic—but it'd helped him out as a kid when he'd had to reintroduce himself to everyone the morning after his Reset. He'd memorized the lines he used with Miss Michelle, the lines that would send her off chasing public servants and social workers and would ultimately lead to him being accepted as a permanent resident of the Dairy.

Now he found himself relying on it again as he woke after one, two, three, then four Resets. Each time, he watched Carey's eyes open and greet him with the smile of recognition that told him the night had been a success. Then, at nine o'clock exactly, he called Josh and asked to meet with him, the words coming to Tommy again every year like an aging actor reprising an old role. And each time Josh agreed to meet.

The first three times they met in The Hole, surrounded by day drinkers who ignored their hushed conversation. Tommy stuck to the script, and soon the pair were shaking on a partnership that had been formed and forgotten many times over.

Then, on the fourth occasion, Josh suggested they meet at a café down the street—the same one where they'd had lunch years before, where Josh had talked and talked and talked about his plans for their future as his burger grew cold. The same one where Josh announced they were going to buy The Hole. Perhaps that should have been a warning to Tommy: this was a place where big things happened.

Clank, clank, clank. The universe had finally got its pieces in order.

Unlike those previous meetings at the café, this time it was Tommy doing the talking, attempting to convince Josh that he was a partner in the business they'd built together. Sticking to the script.

"And then it's just me—I own the one at the top. Complicated, yeah. But my lawyer told me I had to because of some kinda sticky family stuff. Just know something though, Josh—I'm not trying to force you out or anything. I just want us to work together. Fifty-fifty, all the way."

Tommy smiled reassuringly at Josh, waiting for him to process an argument he'd now heard multiple times. And once he'd processed it, Josh would smile back.

But this time, he didn't.

This time, Josh went off-script.

22

"Slow down, Tommy. Take me through it," Carey said. She was supposed to be in a meeting with her boss, but she'd rushed home after a frantic call from Tommy to find him pacing back and forth in their living room. It was a tiny apartment. She reckoned he must have done a good couple of thousand laps before she got there.

"It was Richie."

"I don't understand," Carey replied.

"Well, that makes two of us then," Tommy said and turned for another lap.

Carey leaned on the arm of the couch. Tommy was usually so calm, so steady; it worried her to see him like this.

"I called Josh at nine this morning, like I do every time. He wanted to meet me at Carlo's, up the road from The Hole. Yeah, fine by me. But now I reckon he just wanted to keep me away from customers. But still with witnesses, you know?"

Another lap.

Carey shook her head. "Why would Josh need witnesses?"

Tommy turned. "He thinks I'm trying to rob him."

Carey's eyes opened wide. "*What?*"

Tommy completed another lap. "Richie's taken it, Carey."

"Taken what?" Carey asked, though her heart sank, anticipating his answer.

"My half. I don't know how, but Josh was convinced. Jesus Christ, even *I* was convinced! Carey, I saw Josh's copy of the contract—it had Richie's name all over it. His company. And…"

He shook his head. Did another lap.

"And the date on it," he continued. "The date was four years ago, Carey. Back when we set everything up, back when there were stories in the paper about us. You should've heard it, the way Josh talked about him. About Richie. Like they've been partners that whole time. Like it's the only thing Josh has ever known."

"I'm so sorry, Tommy. This is my fault. I must have missed something."

"No, I think it's the opposite. I think you did such a good job that it's taken the universe four years to figure out how to do it, to figure out the link. I don't know, Carey. It feels like I should've seen this coming, right from when we saw Richie at the funeral. It's like…it's like he came back into our lives, back into our orbit. It was only a matter of time before he was going to be used again, as soon as the Reset worked out how."

He turned for another lap, and then Carey was there in front of him. She took him in her arms and held him.

Carey didn't go back to work that day; she figured Tommy needed her at home.

And she was right. Tommy sat on the sofa in silence, staring into space. He couldn't get Josh's final words to him out of his mind.

"I don't wanna call the cops," he'd said. "So I won't. Just don't come near me again."

Then Josh had stood and walked away, and Tommy had watched as everything he'd worked for, everything they'd built together, went with him. The hours, the days, the years he'd put into their business. All wiped clean.

Josh had been angry. It wasn't like the red-hot betrayal that Tommy had seen on the nights he'd quit, only to be rehired the next day. This was a colder, calmer fury: Josh Saunders, businessman, protecting his success from a stranger trying to claim it.

Watching his best mate walk away had hurt, but as the initial sting faded, Tommy knew he could rekindle the friendship in a year. The next Reset would erase Josh's memory of the morning's events, and Tommy hoped the gold nugget could be dug up and polished once more. But from now on they could only be friends, the kind who meet up at the pub for a drink. Their partnership was gone for good. The Reset had replaced Tommy with a new business partner, one who wouldn't be forgotten on January 5.

And Richie doesn't even deserve it, Tommy thought bitterly. *He's just...* He cast around for the right word. *He's just the universe's stooge.*

At this realization, his anger—his deep, pure hatred of Richie—eased ever so slightly, almost against his will. Tommy didn't want it to ease, didn't want to excuse Richie. He wanted to keep hating him—this was *his* fault.

But he's a stooge.

Tommy sat for a long time, not saying anything. Turning it over and over in his mind.

"I don't know…" he said at last, answering a question he'd asked himself. "I don't think he's really responsible for what he's doing, even if he's benefiting from it. He's just the one who gets dropped into the space I leave behind." Tommy paused. "Christ, what does that say about him?"

"Tommy, are you feeling *sorry* for Richie?" Carey asked incredulously.

"Maybe. Probably not. Yeah, maybe." He sighed. "Think of it this way—the last four years of my life have been rewritten. Forgotten. But not by me and not by you, right? So *we* know what I've done. But Richie—he thinks he's spent all that time as the part owner of a bar. He hasn't lived that life. He just thinks he has—and it's replaced the stuff he actually *has* done. Carey, *it's all made up*. What a sad way to live—and the worst part is, he'll never know."

"So what do we do now?" Carey asked. "Is it worth trying to talk to Josh again?"

Tommy shook his head. "Next year. I'll figure out some way of making friends with him again. He's not getting rid of me. Not permanently, at least."

Carey smiled. "Okay. So what now then?"

"Tonight? Nothing. Tomorrow, I'm gonna get a job." He saw the look on Carey's face. "No, not in a bar; it's a bit soon for that. I don't know what yet. But I'll work it out."

◖

Tommy slept late the next morning, and when he finally rose, Carey's side of the bed was cool and empty. She was already at her desk in the city, though her mind certainly wasn't on the ream of papers in front of her. Tommy Llewellyn, she decided, was an anomaly—in more ways than just the obvious. Anyone else would've been destroyed by what had happened to him—losing everything he'd worked so hard for. If it had happened to her...she shook her head. Where Tommy drew his resilience from, she didn't know; he just seemed to have some internal well of optimism that kept refilling, no matter how much was drained.

Carey was, quite simply, in awe of him.

She wasn't to know that Tommy was parked on the couch: unshowered, unshaven, and a little uninspired. He had nowhere in particular to be—Richie and the Reset had seen to that. Tommy smiled grimly. *Richie and the Reset.* It sounded like a band from the fifties, all slicked-back hair and matching blazers.

His phone buzzed next to him, jolting him out of his daze.

"How's the job hunt going?" Carey was speaking in the hushed tone she reserved for conversations at her desk, ones that could be easily overheard by colleagues pretending not to listen.

"Good," fibbed Tommy. "I've...uh..."

"You're on the couch, aren't you?" she said, and laughed.

"Yeah," he admitted. "But I'm about to start looking."

"You know, Tommy, you could take a couple of days, just to get your head together. You've been through a lot. Watch some TV. Read some books without interruptions."

He glanced at the bookshelf. "Yeah. Maybe."

"Good. Just don't get *too* used to slacking off."

Tommy could tell Carey was smiling as she hung up.

◐

About two blocks from their apartment was a small strip of shops lining both sides of the road—Ingleby's version of a commercial hub—and it was there that Tommy went, looking for somewhere that sold books. (He'd already read everything on the shelves of their apartment. He'd found a Law Society journal on Carey's bedside table, but had only lasted two pages.) There was a greengrocer, dark and shadowy inside but with mounds of oranges, apples and melons piled in wooden bins near the door. Next to it was a tobacconist, then a laundromat, a hairdresser, and another greengrocer (which Tommy thought was odd, but the competition kept the prices down). A barber, a kebab shop, and a real estate agent.

Without pausing, Tommy passed the pharmacy where, more than thirty years earlier, Leo Palmer had bought medicine for his infant son on his way home from work. Then, at the next shop, he drew to a halt. In the window was a handwritten sign: *VOLUNTEERS NEEDED. COME ON IN!*

So he did.

◑

Tommy started work at the thrift shop the next morning. Tucked away at the back of the store, he'd discovered a treasure trove: shelf after shelf of books with dog-eared pages. Elsewhere there were tubs of shoes and belts, benches stacked high with plates and mugs and glasses (very few of them actually forming a set), racks of clothes—many of which should have been thrown out rather than donated—and a counter with a cash register that only worked some of the time.

Behind the counter stood a short woman in her early sixties, with patches of scalp faintly visible through her thinning brown hair, and friendly smile-creases that were now permanent wrinkles. Di wore soft shoes on the threadbare carpet, and barely made a sound as she moved around her store, helping the customers who shopped there out of necessity rather than desire.

It might have been musty, but there was something about the quiet simplicity of the place that Tommy found comforting. Maybe it was the repetition of sorting donations and cleaning shelves, or the conversations with shoppers as they rummaged through the clothes, or perhaps it was just that Di's gentle nature reminded him so much of Miss Michelle he almost forgot where he was sometimes. Whatever the reason, by the end of his first week he found himself thinking less about The Hole and even less about Richie. By the end of his first month, they barely entered his thoughts at all. He still missed Josh, but he knew that wouldn't be forever.

It also helped that he was surrounded by books, dozens of which found their way home with him, to be returned to the store's shelves when he'd finished. It gave him an idea, and one morning he let himself in early with the key Di had given him. By the time she arrived, he'd moved the mannequins in dowdy dresses out of the front window. In their place sat a new display:

a table of books stacked high, titles on show to the passing traffic.

"*This* is what people want around here, Di," he told her, and he was right. That day, the store had more customers than ever before, drawn in by the colorful covers, many of them walking out with books they hadn't seen since they were kids. Di shook her head in wonder. Tommy had only been there for six weeks, and he'd already left his mark on her modest little shop.

And on her, too. Shortly after Tommy started volunteering, Di had considered introducing him to her daughter. Claudia, she thought, was a perfect match for the clever, kind young man who'd come in off the street to work for nothing. But then he'd begun talking about Carey. He spoke about her the way a devotee worships a deity. It was such pure love and admiration that Di decided that this Carey was a lucky girl indeed. Then Tommy showed her a photo of Carey, and Di decided that Tommy was lucky too—although Carey was far more than just a pretty face.

"Guess what, Di?" Tommy said, excitement rolling off him in waves. It was mid-March; by now Tommy was opening the shop nearly every morning, and on this occasion had been waiting impatiently for Di to arrive.

"What, Tommy?" Di grinned in anticipation. The mood was a little contagious.

"Carey got promoted! She's not an associate anymore. God, she's worked hard to get there. I'm…well, I'm pretty proud of her."

"That's wonderful, Tommy," Di replied, and she meant it, although she didn't really understand the difference between an associate and whatever Carey was now. "You've got a good one there. Don't you let her get away."

"I won't," promised Tommy. He was still smiling widely as he began to sift through a box of donated goods. And as he sorted trash from treasure (heavily weighted toward the trash), he came to a realization.

It was time.

Despite Carey's lessons, Tommy couldn't cook to save his life. But what he lacked in ability he tried to make up for in effort (an equation that sounded good in theory, but still resulted in barely edible food). Every night since his Reset he'd made sure dinner was ready when Carey walked through the door; a small contribution to their household, considering his work with Di added precisely zero dollars to the ledger. Carey had tried to coax him toward the kitchen drawer full of takeout menus, but though a smart man, he hadn't taken the hint and continued to wage war with the oven each night.

So when Carey arrived home that evening to find three bags of Chinese food on the dining table, she knew something was going on. And she'd barely put her bag down before she found out what.

"I realized something today, Carey," Tommy told her.

"Hi," she said, kissing him.

"Oh. Hi," he replied, embarrassed.

"What did you realize?" Carey asked.

Tommy took a deep breath. "I didn't lose you."

Carey looked puzzled. "What do you mean? Of course you didn't lose me."

"I mean, when I lost everything else. When Richie took the business and I lost Josh as a friend, I didn't lose you."

"I know, Tommy. But you weren't going to lose me—you tied our hands together with a scarf!" Carey laughed.

"That's not really what I mean. Well, it is, I suppose, but it never felt like you were going anywhere. It never felt like you were at risk. I lost everything else, but I kept you."

Carey was silent.

"Forget all the other stuff. The Hole. Richie, all of that," Tommy continued, "and just think about us. It feels like we've got this thing figured out now. Like it's all gotten easier. You said you'd marry me when it felt permanent. Well, we might never get permanent—but *easy* comes pretty close, right?"

Carey stared at him, replaying the conversation they'd had a number of years earlier. The one where she promised that when things felt different, she'd say yes.

And it did feel different. Easier, like Tommy said. Maybe easy *was* the best they could hope for.

So she said it.

"Yes."

◑

Planning commenced in earnest the next morning. It would be small, just a couple of witnesses, and maybe a honeymoon on an island somewhere. It was an exotic thought for two people who'd never even been abroad.

But beneath the excitement, Carey felt a tiny pinprick of wariness—an acknowledgment that, despite how they both felt, the shadow of impermanence hung over them. She *wanted* to marry Tommy. She wanted to believe in his dream of building a life together, something entirely their own—a little bubble that might resist the Reset. But Tommy had no proof it could work. It was just an idea, an untested hunch.

Carey didn't doubt that if her hand slipped out of Tommy's on the night of the Reset, they'd wake up strangers. So yes, while they were getting through it all a bit *easier* now, that sense was still lurking—a feeling that it was all temporary. For so long it had been a filter through which she made decisions and plans.

At no point had a baby ever featured in those plans. But some accidents are just meant to happen.

As are the consequences.

23

Carey flinched as the cold gel was squeezed onto her stomach, and the technician smiled in apology.

"Sorry," she said. "I always forget to warn people."

But Carey wasn't listening; she was staring in wonder at their baby on the ultrasound screen. She stole a glance at Tommy, half expecting to see panic written across his face. Instead, he wore a goofy grin, as though he'd never seen anything more exciting in his life (which, to be honest, he hadn't).

"And do you want to know if it's a boy or a girl?" the technician asked, and the soon-to-be parents shook their heads.

"We want it to be a surprise," Tommy said, still grinning.

The woman nodded. "Well, everything else is looking good. Your due date is…" She did a quick calculation. "Ha—how about that. A New Year's baby. Well, almost."

Of course it is, Tommy thought, and the worry that had been nagging at him since Carey told him the news crystallized once more. Their baby would arrive just before the Reset. How on earth were they going to navigate it with a newborn in tow? As though their thoughts were linked, Carey glanced at him and Tommy squeezed her hand tight. But not even the Reset could wipe the smile from his face. He was going to be a dad. And with Carey Price, the girl he'd been in love with since he was fourteen.

If Di in the thrift shop thought Tommy had been excited about Carey's promotion, she hadn't seen anything yet. Carey gave him the all-clear after the scan, and he burst through the shop door, sandy hair flying, the news already out of his mouth before he'd even caught his breath.

Di gasped and wrapped Tommy in a monstrous hug that only came up to his shoulders. She was almost as thrilled by the news as he was.

From that moment forward, she started collecting baby things—donations that never made it onto the shop floor. A pram with brass fittings that would polish up beautifully, pre-loved toys, and bags and bags of baby clothes—blue *and* pink, so she was covered either way. She stashed them all in the store-room at the back, in a hiding spot Tommy noticed within about five minutes. Of course, he pretended not to see, although he knew that if she didn't gift the goodies before the baby was born, there was a reasonable chance they'd still be there when the Reset hit. Di would walk in the next morning and wonder why they weren't on the shop floor, and they'd be set out with an orange price tag sticker before lunchtime. They wouldn't go in the window, though; that space would still be reserved for the book display Tommy had set up. It had been such a smart move that Di had almost forgotten a time when the front window *wasn't* lined with books. After the Reset, she'd probably just assume it always had been.

Still, Tommy thanked whatever it was that had made him walk into the little shop the day after he'd lost his bar and his best friend. In what seemed now like a distant, parallel universe, that same best friend was preparing to open a third venue with his business partner. (The relationship was strictly professional; Richie Sharpe didn't make many friends, and in the five or so years he thought they'd worked together, Josh had never tried to push it. Richie was great with money, but he was just a little *weird*.) Tommy knew the growing empire should have been his, too, but it didn't sting the way it used to. It was more of a dull ache, one he could push aside with relative ease—especially now that his attention was being pulled in another direction. So significant was this distraction that even the wedding had been forgotten for now.

"We need to talk about what we do on the fifth," Carey said to him one night, shifting uncomfortably on the couch as her belly tested the thin cotton of her pajamas. Tommy looked up from the book in his lap and grimaced in sympathy. Carey looked like she could burst at any moment.

"No need," he said. "I've got a plan."

"Of course you do." Carey smiled. "Well, at least let me in on it."

"All right. Due date is the thirtieth of December, yes? We'll be home from the hospital by the third of January at the latest. On the night of the Reset, we sleep in shifts—you sleep, I hold you and the baby. When I sleep, you hold the baby and me. And just as long as we're all still touching, everything'll be okay. *You* don't need to be asleep for it to happen, only me."

Carey thought about it. "Do you really reckon it'll work?"

"Yeah, I do. We're following all the rules, not taking any chances."

Carey relaxed slightly.

"But," Tommy said, squeezing past Carey to get to the kitchen, "just in case, I'll take everything with us to the hospital. ID, money, the usual. In case we're still there on the fifth. And then we do the same in a hospital bed. Same end result. And if we—"

He swore sharply as he stubbed his toe on a cot standing against the living room wall.

"You won't be able to do that when the baby comes," Carey admonished him playfully.

"What, break my toe?" he replied through gritted teeth. "I'll do my best."

"You know what I mean. We'll both have to watch our language."

"It'll be easier once this is in a bedroom, don't you think? Couple of extra rooms, maybe a bit of grass too, somewhere for the kids to play," he said.

"Kids? As in more than one?"

"It's happened once, it could happen again. I just want to be ready, that's all."

And just like that, Tommy Llewellyn had made his own version of The Plan. His father would have been delighted.

Nothing in life had ever been particularly easy for Tommy—or Carey, for that matter. So it stood to reason that the birth of their baby was going to be difficult too. A day after fireworks had echoed throughout the city to mark the New Year, the pair still waited at home, Tommy's heart skipping every time Carey moved or spoke or grunted in discomfort. But at last it was time to go and the bags that Tommy had packed and stationed by the door almost six weeks earlier (just in case) were thrown in the back of an idling cab.

As they drew closer to the hospital, Tommy gazed up at the little squares of light marking the many wards and rooms within the dull concrete walls. It was in one of those rooms that he'd first kept his name through the Reset, recovering from surgery as a lanky teenage boy. It was in one of those rooms that he'd first met Josh, the friend he'd remade so many times since. And it would be in one of those rooms—somewhere inside that unremarkable building—that he would meet his child.

They called her Florence.

Or, more accurately, Carey called her Florence. Tommy was too busy staring at this tiny creature with damp pink skin and the most delicate fingers imaginable.

"Lovely," said the midwife. "Is it a family name?"

"Kind of. A middle name, at least."

"Lovely," she repeated. Then her expression shifted. "You

need to get some rest. That was a long labor, and you lost quite a bit of blood."

"Mmmm," Carey murmured. Right now, all she wanted to do was hold her baby.

"Dad can hold her," the midwife said, gesturing toward Tommy. "You need to sleep."

Reluctantly, Carey handed Florence to Tommy, and the midwife left.

"Just close your eyes," Tommy said quietly. "We'll be here when you wake up, I promise."

Carey nodded sleepily.

"Hey, I didn't know there was a Florence in your family. Who was it? On your mum's side?"

Carey frowned at him. "You're joking, right?"

He shook his head.

"Florence was Miss Michelle's middle name. Surely you knew that."

Tommy smiled. He didn't know. But it didn't matter. The name seemed pretty much perfect to him.

Carey was asleep in moments, and Tommy sat in a plastic chair by her bed, holding their daughter in his arms.

Florence slept too, as babies do, and Tommy watched in disbelief as those tiny fingers curled around his thumb. It was such a soft, weak grip, but she stayed like that for an hour, then two, then finally woke up crying, hungry, and Tommy passed her over to Carey. He'd fallen in love all over again.

●

In the back of his mind, Tommy was aware that he was approaching the Reset. He had a plan, though, and as long as he followed it exactly, they could get through it together. But his little family had more immediate problems. Carey was still unwell, exhausted; Tommy hadn't seen such dark circles under her eyes since those unsettled days at the Dairy, days that nearly ended in a dusty shed that reeked of weed killer and vomit. This time was different, he reassured himself. Now, she just needed to rest.

One of the nurses collected Florence, wheeling her down the corridor to a night nursery, then brought her back minutes later when her wailing woke the other babies sleeping there. Little Florence, it seemed, would only sleep in somebody's arms—and she'd chosen Tommy.

And so they fell into a routine of sorts: Carey sleeping, then waking to feed their baby. As soon as Florence was full, Carey passed her back to Tommy, sitting in the molded plastic chair intended only for short-term visitors. His back ached, his feet were numb, and he was tired—so tired—but the moment those dainty fingers wrapped around his thumb and Florence closed her eyes, all discomfort seemed to fade away.

"I'm just gonna take her out into the corridor," Tommy whispered to Carey.

Carey didn't hear him; her chest was already rising and falling in the depths of sleep. Florence snuffled softly in Tommy's arms, full of milk but not yet ready to settle. Tommy wandered up and down the length of the corridor, mumbling quietly to his daughter, saying nothing in particular. A nurse passed and smiled to herself.

At the end of the tenth lap, Tommy turned back and found

his way blocked by a cleaning trolley. Not wanting to break his rhythm, he ducked through a door leading out of the maternity ward. It was busier here, but he kept chatting to Florence as he walked.

"Hey, Flossie," he murmured, "I think I know where we are."

Ahead of him, Tommy saw a door leading outside. He pushed it open with his shoulder and stepped into a courtyard, surrounded on all four sides by the soaring concrete walls of the hospital. Overhead, a shade sail, gray with lichen and age, kept the late afternoon sun off them, and Tommy smiled.

"Come and look at this," he said quietly, and stopped at the planter boxes along one wall. They were full of shiny green leaves and small white flowers, big patches of pink and purple and orange spilling over the sides. Then, in the corner, he saw it.

A cactus, short and dull, but still there. Stubborn.

"Daddy planted that one, Flossie," he whispered. "With your uncle Josh."

Florence was asleep, tiny hand wrapped around his thumb. Tommy sighed happily.

He stood in the courtyard for half an hour, swaying gently from side to side as his daughter slept. Gazing at the garden bed, he could see himself—a younger version, bruised but healing—bending gingerly to help a smaller child press the dirt around a plant. He could see Josh standing next to him, the two of them giggling at a joke none of the little kids understood, and he could see a nurse—was it Amy, the pretty girl with an Irish accent?—watching from the shadows with an almost maternal pride.

What he couldn't see were the other people who'd stood

exactly where he was now in the years between Tommy Llewellyn's visits. The mums and dads, doing their crying alone in the courtyard so the kids wouldn't see them. The nurses who did it too. For a long time Amy had been a regular visitor to the garden, where she sat and stared at the bright orange impatiens, and the cheery little daisies. She ignored the stubby cactus in the corner; there was nothing soothing about its dry skin and short, cruel spikes. She dimly remembered a group of kids gathered around the empty garden bed, some sicker than others, taking it in turns to dig holes and plant the seedlings. But for the life of her, she couldn't remember who'd planted the cactus. *Somebody must've, because there it is.*

Amy had gone back to the courtyard at her lowest ebb, when all she could see each time she blinked was her patient: a pale little boy with shallow breaths and a sunken chest. She made it to the garden before the tears came, but the daisies and impatiens did nothing to slow them.

Until she spotted the cactus.

The flower was a faded pink with a brilliant yellow heart, and it looked so perfect that for a moment she thought somebody must have just pinned it to one of the spikes. But there was another bud next to it, and another. The next day Amy had wheeled her young patient out to see the flowers, and for the first time in weeks, they both smiled.

As Tommy rocked his baby daughter in his arms, he remembered Amy's voice, and wondered if she still worked at the hospital.

She did, but not on the children's ward anymore. She was rostered elsewhere in the building, looking after adults; they made her cry less. But she often thought about the kids she'd cared for.

Amy never thought about Tommy because she didn't remember him.

But she did think about that cactus.

"It's gonna be a bit tight," Carey said, wriggling to one side of the hospital bed as she fed Florence. The color had begun to return to her face, and the doctor had said she would be released from the hospital at the end of the week. It wasn't where Tommy had wanted to spend the Reset, but they still knew what to do.

"We can manage," Tommy told her. "We don't need to be comfortable, remember—it's one of us sleeping at a time." Taking in her still-wan complexion and disheveled hair, Tommy was struck again (as he was almost every day) by how incredibly beautiful she was. Then he yawned.

"Tommy, you're dead on your feet. You've been holding this little chicken round the clock. Go and get some fresh air."

Tommy started to protest.

"No, seriously. You need to be ready for tonight. Get a coffee or something. We'll be fine." She nudged him with her foot. "And bring one back for me."

"Are you sure?" They'd already had a lecture about caffeine and breast milk.

"Don't judge me," Carey ordered. "Just do it."

They laughed, and then, with a lingering look at the pair of them, Tommy did as he was told.

He fought the urge to close his eyes as he stood in the queue at the hospital café.

"You look like you could do with a coffee," said a voice behind him. It was a young man dressed in nursing scrubs.

Tommy nodded. "That's what I'm here for."

"Then give this place a miss—the coffee tastes like dirt." The nurse pulled a face. "There's a great café a couple of streets away. It's a bit of a walk, but it's worth it."

If Tommy had been a little more alert, he might have remembered the directions more clearly. But he turned right when he should have gone left, and then he missed another turn entirely, and strolled the streets for almost an hour before he finally found the café. The nurse was right—the coffee was good. Certainly better than dirt. He turned back toward the hospital, wondering how he'd get Carey's takeaway cup into her room without a midwife seeing it.

Perhaps if he *had* been more alert, he might have had a sense of what was about to happen. But he was tired, and he was thinking about coffee cups, and about midwives, and about the Reset. Tommy was running through the plan for that night, so he could keep his little family together while the Reset did its thing.

At no point on his walk back did he realize he was about to disturb the pieces as they moved into position.

Tommy followed an older lady along the footpath outside the hospital, the air thick with exhaust fumes as the afternoon traffic roared past. She was clearly on her way to visit some-one—a son maybe, or even a grandson—and had in her arms a care package: blue cellophane wrapped around a magazine, a block of chocolate, and a Tupperware container of homemade biscuits. Tommy was trying to read the cover of the magazine upside down when he caught a glimpse of someone walking on the other side of the road. He dismissed it, but deep inside an alarm bell went off, urgent and loud.

The alarm made a strange noise in Tommy's head.

Clank, clank, clank.

He stopped.

There was a crowd gathered on the other side of the street, waiting for the traffic lights to stop the steady stream of cars and buses so they could cross. At first, Tommy couldn't see who or what had made him look up. A dozen people stood impatiently—nurses, a doctor, a mum with a toddler, an older couple with matching walking sticks, a group of women staring at their phones without speaking. Then, there: tucked in behind the group was a tall, broad man, maybe a few years older than Tommy, watching the traffic glide by. He was well-dressed, with an open-necked shirt and a security pass on a lanyard.

Tommy had seen him before, fleetingly.

He recognized the short blond hair and green eyes. Carey had flicked past the pictures quickly, but Tommy had still registered those eyes, the hair, the jaw. The face of the man who'd hurt her.

The coffee cup Tommy was carrying for Carey dropped to the ground, and the contents splashed on his feet.

A woman next to him jumped back. "Hey!" she said angrily, but Tommy didn't notice.

Aaron Gallagher was here.

Aaron, Carey's ex-husband, was at the same hospital as Carey. At the same hospital as their baby.

This is not a coincidence, he realized with absolute certainty. *He's been brought back in to replace me. Tonight.*

Tommy felt the anger billow up inside him.

Just like Richie—it's Aaron's turn to be used.

Pulled back into Carey's orbit. Ready to slip into the gap.

Ready to be Flossie's dad.

The traffic stopped and the crowd surged across the street. Standing at the entrance to the hospital, Tommy watched him come. He had no plan, just instinct. And rage.

Tommy's fist collided with Aaron's mouth and blood exploded from his lip. Behind them, somebody screamed, and someone else yelled for security. Tommy didn't hear either of them.

"What the fuck?" Aaron put his hand to his mouth, then looked at the blood dribbling across his fingers. He stared at Tommy, and those green eyes flashed. In that split second, Tommy wondered if that's what Carey had seen before Aaron hit her. Then the bigger man grabbed Tommy's shirt and punched him once, twice; both direct hits on Tommy's already-crooked nose. Blood spurted out and Tommy's mouth filled with a coppery, bitter taste.

Then he was on the ground, and Aaron was on top of him, knees on his chest.

"Somebody call the cops, quick," Aaron called to the bystanders. "This guy just attacked me."

Tommy lay on the concrete, reeling. He'd never hurt another person before. But he wanted to get up and keep punching and punching and punching until Aaron's face was broken and twisted and Carey and Florence were safe.

"Get off me," he grunted.

"Police are on their way," a woman yelled from a safe distance.

Tommy strained under the weight of the other man.

Aaron stared at him, then leaned closer. "Who the fuck are you?" His voice was deep and gravelly.

Tommy ignored the question. "Why did you come here?" he gasped. His face hurt, but his chest hurt even more where Aaron had him pinned to the ground.

"What?" Aaron asked, confused.

"Why are you here?" Tommy managed. He moved his head slightly, gesturing toward the hospital.

"Jesus Christ!" Aaron exclaimed. "I'm working!"

Tommy's eyes flicked down to the lanyard that hung round Aaron's neck. It had his photograph with the word *CONTRACTOR* printed underneath, now smeared with fresh red blood.

"Why'd you hit me, you piece of shit?"

"How did you know she was here?" Tommy persisted.

"What the fuck? Who's *she*?" Aaron was shaking his head.

"Carey," Tommy replied. His chest burned with the effort of speaking. "Carey Price."

Aaron's eyes widened. "Carey?" He looked surprised. "She's here?" He glanced up at the hospital.

A siren echoed up the street, bouncing off buildings, getting louder every second. The police were approaching.

In that instant Tommy saw it all laid out in front of him. Aaron had been guided into a job at the hospital, the universe making sure its latest stooge would be nearby tonight. And now Tommy was at risk of being carted away by the police. Away from the hospital, away from Carey, away from their daughter. And if he wasn't there for the Reset…he'd have nothing left.

And Carey would be with Aaron: charming, cruel, and violent.

Tommy had to get away.

With a grunt he rolled slightly to one side, and Aaron swayed, thrown off balance by the sudden movement. Tommy rolled back to the other side and pushed up against the more powerful man. Then he was on his feet, and Aaron was scrambling up too.

"Grab him!" the woman nearby yelled, and Aaron lunged for Tommy.

But Tommy was possessed by a terrified urgency, and as a hand landed on his shoulder he shrugged hard and twisted away. Aaron staggered backward, nearly tumbling onto the road. But then he stopped, and steadied himself on the curb.

Just like Richie Sharpe, Aaron's unwitting role in the Reset depended on him being in the right place at the right time. It was all he had to do to slide into the gap left behind when Tommy's story was rewritten. But on this occasion—possibly the most crucial occasion of all—he was in the wrong place. Only slightly, by an inch or two at the most, but an inch was all it took.

Aaron's skull shattered as the side mirror of the bus clipped the back of his head, a soft thud too quiet to hear over the roar of the engine. The bus thundered on, the driver unaware; he was three minutes late on his run. One of the passengers noticed the impact, and the last thing Aaron saw as he crumpled to the ground was a young girl in a school uniform staring at him from the bus window, mouth open wide in a silent, horrified *O*.

Those green eyes flashed once more, and closed.

Then chaos.

"I need to get back to the hospital," Tommy pleaded.

The sergeant at the arrivals desk of the police station shook his head.

"Not happening. Not yet, at least. Maybe later, mate."

He was a different officer from the one who'd grabbed Tommy as he waited for the elevator to go back to the maternity ward. In hindsight, Tommy realized he should have run. Should have hidden somewhere safe, then returned to the hospital later. But his only thought had been to get back to Carey and Florence and their happy little bubble.

He only hoped it wasn't the worst mistake he'd ever made.

Tommy wasn't responsible for Aaron's death. Sure, they'd had a fight, but Tommy didn't kill him—it was just a terminal case of bad luck. But the woman who'd called the cops had pointed in the direction of the hospital foyer, telling the officers that the man who'd hit the poor guy now lying on the footpath had bolted inside.

As Tommy was marched out the front of the hospital, Aaron was being wheeled in. Tommy thought he looked dead. He was. Now the police were trying to decide whether Tommy should be charged with anything. The sergeant, who looked far too young to be a sergeant and almost too weedy to be a cop, stood behind a counter filling out paperwork. He took down Tommy's details and asked him to hand over the contents of his pockets.

His mobile phone, his wallet, a small wad of cash, and a new addition—the folded forms he'd completed after Florence's birth—were all placed in a see-through bag, and Tommy was handed a receipt. A receipt for everything he needed to get through the Reset.

"You can collect them when you're released, unless they're seized as evidence," the sergeant told Tommy.

Tommy knew the scrawny cop was reading from a script, but it sounded mighty ominous to him. He'd been allowed to make a phone call, dialing with a shaking hand as shock set in.

"Carey, I've been arrested," he said as soon as she answered.

"*What?*"

"It's a long story." Tommy paused. "It was Aaron."

"Aaron?" Carey asked. "As in my ex? What did he do? Where was—"

"It doesn't matter," Tommy interrupted. "I'm pretty sure he's dead."

Carey was silent.

"We had a fight." The sergeant's ears pricked up. "I was trying to get away from him, and he…Carey, he got hit by a bus." Tommy let out a big, rattly sigh. "I'm going to get out of here as soon as I can. I'm sure they'll let me out tonight."

"They should. If it was a bus that killed him, then you didn't do anything wrong," Carey said.

"I guess. But just in case…you know, in case they keep me here, I'm going to stay awake. All night. So it doesn't happen."

"Jesus, Tommy, the Reset. If you don't make it…"

"I will, I promise."

Tommy was never going to be released from custody that night, and he and Carey both knew it. That part wasn't the universe conspiring against them; it was the simple fact that a man was dead, and Tommy had been involved. He was going to be interviewed the next morning. He took the news with a sort of sad inevitability.

He thought of Carey and Florence. It was well and truly the longest time he'd spent away from his daughter, and he wondered whether she would be able to sleep without him there. Without his thumb to hold with her soft little fingers. He hoped so, for Carey's sake as much as the baby's.

His own exhaustion settled over him as he looked at his home for the night, a small holding cell about half the size of the room at the hospital. Along one wall ran a bed—a metal platform with no sharp edges and a mattress about three inches thick on top. It was right next to a toilet, also made of a dull metal with rounded corners and no visible joins. And that was it. Outside his cell, on the other side of the room, sat a tub containing his shoes. He'd been required to take them off (presumably so he didn't string himself up with his shoelaces; he had been wearing boots without laces, but rules were rules) and was also told to turn his pockets out. The receipt for his belongings had fluttered to the floor and was tossed into the tub next to his boots.

He needed to stay awake until he could get back to Carey and Florence. He wanted to be back there so badly that it hurt. The last three nights he'd only napped for an hour or two here

and there, and the shadows under his eyes were already a pur-
plish black, but he needed to stay awake.

The Reset wasn't necessarily bound to the clock; he knew
that from his experiment as a kid and his shifts at The Hole.
No, if he was awake at midnight, then the universe simply
waited until he was unconscious—fewer moving parts, fewer
problems. So all he had to do was stay awake, stay upright, stay
moving until he was interviewed in the morning and allowed
to go. Once he was back with Carey and Florence, the universe
could wipe everything it bloody well wanted, he thought. But
not before. Please, not before.

Stay awake, he told himself.

The mantra ran through his head dozens of times before
midnight; this was the easier part, as the adrenaline from the
day gradually dissolved from his system. Tommy was more
worried about the small hours of the morning, when everything
would be quiet, everything would be still, and most people—
including him—were normally asleep.

Stay awake.

If he flattened his face against the door to his cell—there
were no bars, just a reinforced acrylic screen so the cops could
keep an eye on him—he could just spy a clock on the wall further down the corridor. It was 1:15 a.m. The fatigue was crashing over him in waves. It was too quiet. Too still. But he couldn't
fall asleep. For Carey, for Florence.

Stay awake.

Tommy was alone in the holding cells. He had nobody to
speak to and no way to pass the time. No books, no TV, no
magazines. Prisoners usually slept.

Stay awake.

As the clock ticked toward 3:00 a.m., he repeated it again and again, both silently and out loud. *Stay awake stay awake stay awake.* He recited his times tables, chanting them like he'd done at school, then listed every country he could name. He did it again in alphabetical order, then worked backward through cities that hosted the Olympics, petering out when he got stuck on '52. He sang every song he could think of, his voice echoing tunelessly around the empty remand center as he paced the floor of his cell.

Stay awake.

He had to, for Carey. For Florence.

By 4:05 a.m.—a mere fifteen minutes since he'd last checked—Tommy wanted to weep from exhaustion. His legs ached. He just needed to sit and rest for a moment. He wouldn't fall asleep. His eyes felt like they had grit in them; rubbing them was like grinding sand into an open wound. Oh, what he wouldn't give for the chance to close them, just for a moment.

He sat briefly on the edge of his mattress then jumped straight up again, slapping his own cheeks with great resounding thwacks, forcing adrenaline into his body. But in minutes it was gone, and he found himself leaning against the wall, head resting lightly on the exposed concrete. He stood up straight, paced the cell twice, then without thinking sat down again on the stiff plastic mattress.

He fell sideways slowly, like a toppled tree.

And closed his eyes.

"What are you doing in there?" an unfamiliar voice asked, and Tommy jerked upright. He blinked, startled by the sudden noise in the otherwise silent room. A female police officer stood outside his cell, peering at him. She looked confused.

Tommy didn't say anything, but took two steps forward and pressed his face against the transparent wall. It was 4:15 a.m. A cold dread spread slowly through him. He'd closed his eyes for a few minutes at most; surely he hadn't fallen asleep.

"Who are you?" the cop wanted to know.

"Uh, Tommy Llewellyn," he said, hoping desperately that the officer's confusion was just because of a shift change.

The police officer—Sergeant Bennett, according to her name badge—looked up at a board on her side of the cell and shook her head.

"I'll be back in a minute," she said. "Don't go anywhere."

She smiled at her own joke, but Tommy didn't smile back. His panic was growing, a gaping black hole that threatened to consume him. She should have known who he was; he was the only prisoner in a cell.

The sergeant returned. "Had a bit to drink, did you?"

"Sorry?" Tommy asked.

"You're not on the system, so I'm guessing you're here to sober up, yeah?" Then, more to herself than Tommy: "It's supposed to be recorded."

"Uh, yeah," said Tommy, but he was no longer listening. The black hole was sucking him in.

It had happened. The Reset.

Not long after, Tommy stood alone on the street outside. Sergeant Bennett had deemed him sober enough to go home and duly released him. As she unlocked the cell, Tommy asked about the belongings he'd been forced to surrender. Of course, she wanted to see his receipt—which, like his shoes, had been sitting in a tub across the room. The tub was empty, the Reset having snatched the contents away.

Tommy looked so defeated that the sergeant took pity on him and went into the storeroom to look anyway. She came back with nothing. His phone, cash, even the paperwork for his baby daughter: it was all gone.

As he stood in the predawn shadows, away from the glare of the lights at the front of the station, Tommy Llewellyn looked and felt like a beaten man. Then, the pavement hard against his bare feet, he started to walk.

He was heading for the hospital. He still had to try.

There was no blood on the footpath. Tommy didn't know what he expected to see; he figured the spot where Aaron had died would be marked in some way, but it wasn't. It'd been cleaned so thoroughly that it was as though Aaron had never been there.

Kind of like Tommy.

The rising sun streamed through a gap between buildings, and Tommy cast a long shadow on the front doors of the hospital. He paused for a moment. What would he say to Carey? How would he explain who he was? The warmth of the early morning light on his back gave him a little bit of hope. For what, he didn't know. That something would be different, perhaps. That maybe this time, there would be a glimmer of recognition in Carey's eyes.

A doctor passing through the foyer looked Tommy up and down; his bare feet were black with grime from the city footpaths, there were flecks of dried blood on his face, and he looked like he hadn't slept in days. But the doctor was busy and kept walking, and so did Tommy. He hit the elevator button once, twice, then again, desperate to get up to the maternity ward.

It dinged gently and then Tommy was rising to the seventh floor. He could feel his palms sweating, and his heart racing with equal parts longing and terror, picking up pace as the elevator rose higher.

Then he was there.

A woman behind the reception desk looked up and frowned as the doors opened. It was the midwife who'd delivered Florence. "Can I help you?"

She didn't recognize him. The sliver of hope he was clinging to became even smaller.

I'm here to see my baby, he wanted to say. But he didn't.

"Uh...I'm here to see Carey. Carey Price?"

The midwife looked at him suspiciously.

"And you are?" she asked. The man was a mess, and it was well before visiting hours.

"I'm her..." Tommy searched for the right thing to say. Partner? Fiancé? Suddenly he was back at Upper Reach, back at the Dairy, standing outside his bedroom door, talking to Miss Michelle. Looking for the words he needed to slot back into a life he'd been erased from. Anything to get him through.

"I'm her brother."

The midwife's expression cleared. "Good," she said. "I'm sure she'll be happy to see you. Just take it easy on her, okay? The baby's not sleeping too well."

Tommy nodded mutely.

He stood at the door of Carey's room for what seemed like hours. He felt like he was standing across the street from Leo Palmer's house again, watching that neat little home as he tried to summon the courage to knock on the door and talk to his father. He'd loitered for so long, terrified to cross the road. Why had he been so afraid back then? It seemed almost trivial now. After all, he'd been entering the house of a stranger, someone who'd forgotten him long ago.

The fear that gripped him in the doorway to Carey's room—his family's room—was entirely different, and so much greater.

Tommy's legs felt heavy as he stepped across the threshold into the only place in the universe that mattered to him.

The blinds were drawn, and it took a moment for his eyes to adjust to the half-light of the room. He could hear a gentle whimpering noise—was that Florence?—and he saw Carey in the bed, passed out from fatigue.

A soft, milky scent hung in the air, mixed with—Tommy sniffed—perhaps baby powder. And there was something else that he couldn't quite identify. A clean, comforting smell. A safe smell. The freshly washed clothes they'd brought from their home; the old, dry pages of the books he'd packed to help Carey pass the time. The pieces of their lives that he'd brought to the place where they'd become a family.

It was like standing in the front room of Leo Palmer's house. Similar, but different. This wasn't Leo's life. This was his.

He gazed at Carey: her hair looped down over one cheek, framing the face he'd adored since he was a child. He loved her completely, and though he wanted her to sleep, part of him longed for her to wake up and see him.

So he'd know for sure.

He heard the whimpering again. It was coming from the other side of the room, and Tommy tiptoed around Carey's bed. The dead weight of his own exhaustion and the fear that had paralyzed him in the doorway were melting away. The corridor outside, and the rest of the hospital, and the rest of the city: they all felt miles away, hours away, in a different place altogether.

This was his cocoon.

Florence lay in a bassinet, making a snuffling sound as her arms flailed in jerky little movements, eyes squeezed tightly shut. Tommy stared down at his baby, at her velvety skin and the fine fair hair that covered her head. He stroked her cheek gently, and a tear ran down his own.

Her eyes opened and she squinted, unfocused, at the shadowy blur above her. For a moment, Tommy thought she was about to cry, a high-pitched wail that would wake Carey, bring a nurse running, and pop the bubble that seemed to have wrapped itself around the three of them.

But she didn't cry.

Instead, as Tommy picked her up and cradled her, Florence wrapped her fingers around his thumb and fell asleep.

Tommy Llewellyn swayed as his daughter slept peacefully in his arms.

Behind him, Carey opened her eyes.

And smiled.

EPILOGUE

"Nervous?"

"Nope," Tommy replied, and Carey squeezed his clammy hand.

"Liar," she said.

Tommy grinned. "I don't know why I am. I did this all the time when I was a kid."

"It's different now, though," Carey replied as they walked through the gates. "More riding on it."

A small crowd was already gathered on the grass, standing in groups of three or four as they made small talk, drinks in hand. Someone had strung a strand of fairy lights along the outside of the classroom, looping and twisting down through the garden beds that lined the edges of the lawn. *Nice touch*, thought Tommy.

"Dad! Hurry *up!*"

"You go ahead," Carey said softly. "We'll catch you up."

Tommy nodded, mouth set firmly.

"Hey, Tommy?" Carey added. "Relax. She knows what to do."

He nodded again, and jogged forward to where Florence stood, hands on hips in a way that ten-year-old girls seemed to master almost instinctively.

"Sorry, Floss," Tommy said. "I'm ready."

She led him onto the grass, weaving between groups of adults and a smattering of kids. Looking for someone.

"Ugh. Your hand's sweaty," she whispered as she scanned the faces. Then she smiled. "There! Come on, follow me."

Tommy wanted to remind her that she had a tight grip on him, and he had no choice but to follow her, but Florence was already off.

"Hi, Mrs. Harding," the girl said, and her teacher smiled at her.

"Florence! How was your Christmas?" The woman shifted her focus from the child to the adult. "And who's this?"

"Mrs. Harding, this is my dad."

"Tommy Llewellyn," Tommy said.

"He works overseas," Florence continued. "He's been there for ages but he's back now."

Word-perfect, Tommy thought, and felt a little swell of pride. *Almost there, Flossie. Just the last bit, then we're done.*

Florence's eyes flicked up to her dad's with an almost imperceptible glint of mischief. "He studies penguins. In Antarctica."

Mrs. Harding's eyes widened, and Tommy laughed despite himself. He shook his head at Florence. "Close. I was an accountant for a mining company in South America. But penguins would be *much* cooler."

Mrs. Harding laughed. "Well, it's great you were able to make it tonight. Nice to put a face to the name," she said, though she was quite sure Florence had never mentioned her father before. "It's a good chance to meet some of the other parents before the new school year starts." Another woman waved at her from across the crowd. "Like Tracey over there. She'll be ready to sign you up for the Garden Committee. She's always on the lookout for parents who can help. It's been a long process, turning Ingleby around."

"I'd be happy to lend a hand," Tommy replied. *Who do you think planted these garden beds?*

"Penguins, Floss?" he asked as Mrs. Harding disappeared into another conversation. "What happened to the script?"

"Sorry, Dad," his daughter said with a grin. "It was so *boring* last year. I thought we could at least give you a cool job this time."

"Yeah, but what if they ask me about penguins? I don't know anything about them! At least if they ask me about being an accountant I can fudge it a little."

Florence rolled her eyes. "Fine," she said, then squealed. "Ivy!"

A girl about the same age as Florence barreled into her and they hugged. Half a dozen steps behind were Ivy's parents.

"Hi," Tommy said. "I'm Tommy, Florence's dad."

"He's been overseas for ages," Florence said. "He had a really boring job. But he's back now."

"Hi, Tommy," Ivy's dad replied. "I'm Paul."

I know, thought Tommy. *You came to our house for dinner six weeks ago. We had a barbecue and drank wine, and the kids watched a movie and fell asleep on the couch.*

"Good to meet you, Paul."

"So you've been working overseas?" Paul asked.

"Yeah. But I'm back for good now. Career change, I suppose. I've just bought a shop—about three blocks that way." He pointed.

It was a half-truth. Carey had bought it in her name—"Let's keep it simple," she'd said—and it had actually happened when Florence was still small, just after they'd married. Di couldn't believe her luck. The lovely young man with the beautiful wife and the sweet little girl—Flossie was such a cute name—had only just started volunteering at the shop. One minute Di mentioned she was thinking of moving to the country to be nearer to her daughter Claudia, and the next they were handing her a check for about five grand more than she was asking. It was the books in the window, she'd explained to Claudia. This gorgeous couple loved the idea of opening a bookshop in Ingleby, and the young man had even said he wanted to keep selling secondhand books too. Something about him seemed almost *at home* there among the lost and donated and abandoned things. *Funny the way these things worked,* Di thought. She couldn't remember when she'd decided to move the books to the front of the store, but she was glad she had.

"Well, I reckon we'll be seeing a bit of each other this year, Tommy," Paul said. "The girls are kinda inseparable. I'll give you my number."

Tommy already had it, but he pretended to add it to his phone anyway.

As Paul walked away, Tommy exhaled. *I don't know why I get so nervous. Everything's fine.*

"Come on, Floss. Is there anyone else you want me to meet?"

She took his hand again, and in an instant he was back at her first birthday. He'd held her hand so tightly all night, and Carey had held the other. Neither of them had slept, both just staring at each other, pale-faced and terrified that whatever was in Tommy, whatever had made his parents forget him when he turned one, would be in Florence too. But the elderly couple from the apartment downstairs had knocked on their door as Tommy was making breakfast, and they were holding a stuffed unicorn with a glittering rainbow mane. A gift for a little girl who'd turned one. A little girl whose birthday they'd written on their calendar, and remembered.

As Tommy scanned the gathering, looking for familiar faces, he wondered whether that kind elderly couple were still living below Carey's old apartment. It was only a couple of streets away from their new house, and he thought maybe after the mixer was over they could drive past and see if the building had been done up. Everything else seemed to have had a coat of paint. Even his shop had new neighbors—a pair of cafés, a restaurant, a nail salon where Carey took Florence every year for her birthday. Ingleby was changing.

Small fingers tugged on the leg of his trousers. He looked down.

"Pick me up, Daddy," Hamish demanded, and Tommy did as he was told.

"You'll be coming here in a couple of years, mate," Tommy said. "Would you like that?"

Hamish nodded. His cheeks were starting to lose the plump toddler look, Tommy noted. He was becoming a little boy.

"All good?" Carey asked quietly from behind them.

"Yeah," he replied. "You were right. Nothing to worry about."

Tommy held Hamish in one arm, as Florence pulled him through the crowd, Carey tagging along.

Despite the warmth of the evening, he felt a shiver ripple

through him, struck again by what might have been. He thought about it often, the way a driver might replay over and over the instant a truck had swerved into their lane, and only a twist of fate—perhaps steering that pulls slightly to the left—saved them from losing everything. For Tommy, that moment had been in the hospital when Florence was just a few days old; the twist of fate had been a hungry baby who refused to settle. Carey had been holding Flossie for hours that night, but only a fraction of that time really mattered. She'd been holding her the second Tommy fell asleep in the police cell. The second the Reset swept through.

Little Florence was, it seemed, Tommy's proxy in the hospital that night. But he didn't like to think of her that way. She had his DNA, but it was more than that: she was just part of him. So was Hamish. They remembered him, and *they* were his sanctuary, sharing the burden of carrying on through the Reset simply by being *his*. Any one of the three of them could be in contact with Carey during the Reset, and she'd remember Tommy.

"Dad, look! It's Gem!" Florence squealed again, as though it had been years since she last saw her friends, not just a few weeks over Christmas. "Come on!" She dragged Tommy across the grass toward Gem and her mum, just as Carey was cornered by Tracey from the Garden Committee.

"I'm Fiona. Call me Fi, though," Gem's mother said.

Tommy had been calling her Fi for five years already, but he nodded and smiled.

Florence went through the script: Dad works overseas, back now, bought a shop.

"Oh, you should meet my partner," Fi exclaimed to Tommy. "He's…well, he's pretty new on the scene too. Maybe you two could have a beer together or, I dunno, whatever you guys do when you're not at work."

She grabbed the arm of a man facing away from her, making polite conversation with another couple, and spun him around.

"Josh, this is…I'm so sorry, I've already forgotten your name."

"Tommy. Tommy Llewellyn."

"Hi, Tommy. Josh Saunders. Good to meet you. And this big guy!"

As Josh had a one-sided conversation with Hamish, Tommy sought Carey's eyes across the crowd.

"Did you know?" he mouthed silently.

She shook her head.

Tommy shrugged. Looked like the gold nugget was getting a little help this year.

By the end of the evening, Tommy had met dozens of people. Parents he'd stood on the sidelines with while Florence played soccer with their kids. Mums and dads he'd volunteered with in the school canteen. Teachers who'd been into his shop, and had all known him as Tommy Llewellyn, father of Florence and Hamish, and husband of Carey.

As they left the school, Tommy sighed.

"Are you okay?" Carey asked.

"Yeah," he replied. "It just gets tiring, you know? I like it when it's just us, at home. Just us and the kids, and I don't have to pretend."

Carey put an arm around him. "Me too. But you're not doing it by yourself. We're in it together, remember?"

Tommy smiled.

Yes, he remembered.

READING GROUP GUIDE

1. Tommy's parents wake to find a little boy in their home. Unaware he's their son, they call the police. How did you feel when they didn't even know how to hold their own child? What did this tell you about how comprehensively Tommy had been wiped from the minds of his parents?

2. In some ways, the foster system works for Tommy and his strange circumstances. Why is that? What does this say about the system he is forced to grow up in?

3. When he's fourteen, Tommy falls in love with Carey Price, who's also in foster care at the Dairy. How does the love he has for Carey in his youth change the way he feels about the Reset? How does that change impact the way Tommy acts as a teenager?

4. Though Tommy is exceptional at staying positive and optimistic, there are still times when he asks, "Why me?" Reflect on moments in the novel when Tommy let his situation impact him emotionally, especially when he is a teenager living at the Dairy. Would you react in the same ways? Why?

5. When Tommy is in the hospital after his accident, he meets Josh, his future best friend and business partner. As Tommy prepares to go back to the Dairy, Josh tells him to "come and find me." Why do those words stick with Tommy? How do they change his outlook on life when he returns to foster care?

6. If there is one person in his life that Tommy looks to as a parental figure, it's Miss Michelle. Describe their relationship over the years, the impact it has on Tommy to always be forgotten by her, and the significance of Tommy's surname to Miss Michelle. How did this make you feel when reading the story?

7. Tommy's run-in with his birth father is a pivotal moment in the story, as Tommy is forced to consider what his life could have been like. Think about the idea of "what could have been." What do you think Tommy yearns for when he sees his father's life without him? How did this encounter impact you while you were reading?

8. Tommy has never forgotten Carey Price, and when they are finally thrown together one night, they form an instant connection. Do you think fate, or the universe, has anything to do with their relationship? Why or why not?

9. Carey tells Tommy that it's not just his life that is affected by the Reset, but in fact, many people's lives are changed forever when the universe wipes him. When looking at it this way, whose lives have been changed because of Tommy's? Does this shift in perspective change the way you think about the Reset and its consequences?

10. Tommy ends up feeling sympathy for Richie Sharpe because he's been used by the Reset. Do you think this sympathy is deserved?

11. Discuss the themes of remembrance and legacy within the novel. Then, reflect on and discuss the ways that *you* want to be remembered, as well as the legacies you hope to build.

12. Discuss the end of the novel. Do you think Tommy got what he most hoped for in life?

13. If you only had a few items, including people and pets, to bring through with you during a Reset, what would they be and why?

A CONVERSATION WITH THE AUTHOR

The idea of a universal Reset is so unique. What was the inspiration behind this?

It started with social media and our digital lives—this idea that everybody has a digital footprint that will stay with you, even if you'd rather be forgotten. Somehow, that made me think about the opposite scenario: What if you wanted to be remembered and something—some huge, unknowable force— was preventing it? It was a bit of a leap between the two, but I knew immediately that it had the makings of a good story.

The Reset is complicated, and it impacts every aspect of Tommy's life. How did you keep up with all the consequences the Reset would or could have on Tommy while writing?

I just kept thinking about it, turning it over and over. I know that sounds boring, but I just kept examining the story in my head, looking for the consequences of the Reset, as well as the

loopholes and the opportunities within it. Most of this thinking took place in the shower. We ran out of hot water on many
occasions.

How to Be Remembered **has many emotional touchstones, and
Tommy's situation is sure to make readers feel both sadness
and joy. Were there any challenges that came with writing such
an emotional novel?**

I have two young children, so the scenes early in the book
were the toughest—when Tommy is only small and doesn't
understand why his parents aren't there anymore. I think the
biggest challenge though was ensuring that Tommy's situation
wasn't too miserable, too horrific: he was already suffering from
the unique circumstances of the Reset, so the unending kindness
of Miss Michelle, the friendship of Josh, and the ongoing hope
of finding love with Carey were important counterpoints.

**What is your writing process like? Are there any ways you like
to get creative inspiration?**

When I'm working on something new, it feels like there's an
urgency to get it down. I prefer to write in the morning, but it
also has to fit in around our kids and business and a bunch of
other things—so this might be at 5 a.m., or it could be at midday.
Creative inspiration usually arrives in the shower, though I also
had a few good breakthroughs while riding the streets of our
suburb on a bike with a child seat mounted on the back.

What do you hope readers take away from this story?

Mostly hope, really. It's a story about resilience, about strength, about kindness, and about the idea that we can all impact other people without even realizing it—so we should do everything we can to make sure it's a positive impact.

If you were to bring anything with you through a Reset, what or who would it be?

It would be my wife and kids. As for physical belongings, I'd probably be okay with the Reset wiping most things—it might be a convenient way of decluttering the house.

What are you reading these days?

My secret shame is that I'm actually a relatively slow and distracted reader, and am eternally envious of people who can race through a book in a day or two. That said, I'm a fan of Liane Moriarty, Matt Haig, Jane Harper, Sally Hepworth, Stephen King, and plenty of others—it just takes me a while to get through them!

ACKNOWLEDGMENTS

A large chunk of writing a novel seems to take place on your own, with the door closed and, in my case at least, in complete silence. But that chunk is only part of it, and it's what happens *outside* the door that allows an overly long, slightly waffly Word document to become a real book.

To my incredible agent, Catherine Drayton, and her colleagues at InkWell Management: thank you for seeing something in my work and for taking a chance on me. Without your guidance at every turn, none of this would have happened.

To the team at Sourcebooks: a huge thank you to Deb Werksman for knowing Tommy's potential right from the start and to MJ Johnston for the insight, the passion, and the patience to help me draw it out. Sourcebooks has an extraordinary group of people doing amazing work.

To the team at Allen & Unwin: Annette Barlow, who asked all the right questions and made this a better book; Tom Bailey-Smith, who kept it all together; and Ali Lavau, whose editing prowess and ability to spot repetition of words some forty pages apart should be registered as a superpower.

To my mum and dad (Sue and Chris) and my siblings (Sarah and Andy): thank you for not only being so supportive and excited but for maintaining those levels of support and excitement over a very, very long time. Likewise, thank you to Maj and to Tim, who was also on call for my medical questions. Any medical inaccuracies are my own!

To my first readers—my mum and my wife, Sian. Your encouragement meant everything. Thank you for being honest about the parts that needed work, for being enthusiastic about the parts you liked, and for understanding that when I said there's no rush, it actually meant I needed immediate, detailed feedback.

And to Sian in particular: thank you for putting up with me disappearing to write, for looking after the kids, for supporting me through every twist, for listening to me ramble on and on about it, and for only on one occasion declaring that this book better sell. Without you, and without Henry and Maeve, I couldn't have written it. Thank you.

ABOUT THE AUTHOR

© Sally Flegg Photography

Michael Thompson has been a successful journalist, producer, and media executive for the last fifteen years. He now co-owns a podcast production company and is the cohost of one of the highest-ranked podcasts in Australia. He lives in Sydney with his wife and two young children. *How to Be Remembered* is his first novel.